Michael Jecks began to write the Templar series because of his love of Dartmoor and his fascination with medieval English history. His stories are based upon real court cases and coroners' rolls as well as ancient Dartmoor legends.

All his novels featuring Sir Baldwin Furnshill and Bailiff Simon Puttock are available from Headline.

Michael and his family live in Northern Dartmoor.

Acclaim for Michael Jecks' previous mysteries:

'If you care for a well-researched visit to medieval England, don't pass this series' *Historical Novels Review*

'Michael Jecks has a way of dipping into the past and giving it the immediacy of a present-day newspaper article . . . He writes . . . with such convincing charm that you expect to walk round a corner in Tavistock and meet some of the characters' *Oxford Times*

'Brisk medieval whodunnit' *Literary Review*

'A torturous and exciting plot . . . The construction of the story and the sense of period are excellent' *Shots*

'Jecks' knowledge of medieval history is impressive and is used here to great effect' *Crime Time*

'A gem of historical storytelling' *Northern Echo*

THE TOLLS OF DEATH

Michael Jecks

headline

First published in Great Britain in 2004
by HEADLINE BOOK PUBLISHING

First published in paperback in 2004
by HEADLINE BOOK PUBLISHING

10 9 8 7 6 5 4 3 2 1

Cataloguing in Publication Data is available from the British Library

ISBN 0 7553 0175·7

Typeset in Times by Avon DataSet Ltd,
Bidford-on-Avon, Warwickshire

Printed and bound in Great Britain by
Clays Ltd, St Ives plc

Headline's policy is to use papers that are natural, renewable and
recyclable products and made from wood grown in sustainable forests.
The logging and manufacturing processes are expected to conform
to the environmental regulations of the country of origin.

HEADLINE BOOK PUBLISHING
A division of Hodder Headline
338 Euston Road
London NW1 3BH

www.headline.co.uk
www.hodderheadline.com

This book is for
Mark, Sarah, Laura and Emilia
with thanks for all the music.

Acknowledgements

First and foremost, I have to thank my wife Jane and my daughter, for tolerating my hibernation during the writing of this story, while all about me the house fell apart. Luckily my wife is an angel who is capable of controlling builders.

My thanks also to the champion chippie, Kieran, the amazing disappearing plumber, Martin, the specialist sparkies, Andy, Laurence and Tony, and the perfect plasterers, Andy and Peter for all of them working so efficiently that I was able to work all the time they ripped my house apart around me.

Finally I must thank Amy Philip for her help and support in the production of this book during the *interregnum*.

Cast of Characters

learns there is a murderer in their midst.

Alexander

The Constable of the Peace for the vill of Cardinham, Alexander is determined to improve his own and his family's wealth. He can never forget how devastated his father was when his mother died, and how the family lived in desperate poverty ever afterwards. Fond of children, his own marriage is sadly barren.

Lady Anne

Although her husband is not a knight or squire, Anne is called 'Lady' by all who know her, as though she was genuinely the lady of the castle. She arrived at Cardinham one day while on her way to Exeter, and as soon as Nicholas saw her, he set his heart on winning her hand.

Aumery

The older of Serlo and Muriel's children, Aumery is nearly four years old.

Gervase

The steward at the castle, Gervase is responsible for the farming in the manor, as well as the courts and rents.

Hamelin

The younger of Serlo and Muriel's children, Ham is eight months old.

Iwan

The old blacksmith, who has seen and heard much during his long lifetime.

John

Priest at the little church up at Temple, John owes his position to the help of Sir Henry of Cardinham, but he is a reluctant recipient of Sir Henry's support.

Julia

A young widow, Julia cooks and cleans for the other priest, Father Adam. Although there is nothing in his or her behaviour to merit censure, she is looked down upon by some who assume she provides additional services.

Letitia

Alexander's wife is of better birth than him, but his astuteness with business attracted her. Her only disagreements with him involve his brother the miller, Serlo, whom she considers a fool and a wastrel.

Muriel

Serlo's wife, Muriel is a generous, calm woman who is devoted to her children. She is careful with her husband, because he can too easily flare up in anger, especially when he has been drinking, but she wouldn't dream of leaving him.

Nicholas

While Sir Henry of Cardinham is absent, which he has been for many years, having other more profitable manors nearer the centre of power, Nicholas the castellan has responsibility for the defence of the castle and manor.

Richer

Born in Cardinham, Richer left in

1316 when his family all died in a fire. Now he has returned to work as a man-at-arms in the castle.

Serlo

Serlo was spoiled when young by his older brother Alexander: there was nothing he desired that Alex wouldn't procure for him. Now he is a moderately successful miller, and is pleased with his two sons.

Susan

The alewife at the tavern in the vill, Sue is attracted to Richer and Warin, but keeps her feelings in check. She's always nervous of falling in love with another wastrel like her husband – now, fortunately, gone. He ran away with a serving wench three years ago and she hopes he's dead.

Squire Warin

Arriving with a letter of introduction from Sir Henry of Cardinham, Warin is viewed askance by other members of the castle's team because he remains aloof from them, preferring the company of Richer. A quiet, observant fellow, he carries some authority but appears happier to listen than comment.

Author's Note

I had great fun thinking of the possible routes by which Simon and Baldwin might have returned from the Scillies to their homes* in Devon, but the main thing for me was the idea that they might become embroiled in the turbulent politics of their times. Not the greater politics which are so often portrayed – the disputes between the King and his most senior advisers – but the lower level of politics i.e. how Edward II's arguments affected his realm, and how people even hundreds of miles away from his court in London could get caught up in national affairs.

These were fraught times. The famine was still a recent event, and all could remember the horror of it; everyone had friends or family who had died. In the aftermath, there was what we would now probably call stagflation, with economic failure. Many people fled from their old homes seeking new lives in towns and cities, although poor Richer in my story had a more pressing reason to leave his vill.

For a more in-depth look at the period, I can heartily recommend Michael Prestwich's excellent *The Three Edwards: War and State in England 1272–1377* – a well-researched book which helped me no end, and Ian Mortimer's superb *The Greatest Traitor*, which starts with one of the key events in my novel, the escape of Roger Mortimer from the Tower of London.

For many centuries Mortimer's life has been glossed over, with his period of control mentioned in one brief sentence between the death of Edward II and the accession of Edward III.

* See *The Outlaws of Ennor*.

Since Edward III had a much more interesting reign even than his own father – since it encompassed the plague, the beginning of the Hundred Years War, and his fabulous military victories – it's possibly no surprise that Mortimer has been left as a footnote to history.

But he was not merely some treacherous bandit who sought to overthrow his King and take power. Mortimer's was a much more convoluted fall and rise. His ancestors had always been loyal servants of the Crown. It was his grandfather who, in 1265, found Hugh Despenser, a loyal supporter of de Montfort, King Henry III's enemy, on the field of Evesham and killed him.

In years to come, the Mortimers remained devoted supporters of their Kings, and were always included amongst the royal companions – a situation which came to an end during the dismal reign of Edward II.

Early on, Mortimer had been a close associate of the King. His position was weakened when Edward grew infatuated with Piers Gaveston, but even during that period, Mortimer remained loyal, and was gradually given more power and authority. When the people of Bristol revolted during the Tallage of 1316, it was he who laid siege to the city and recaptured it. He was also shown to be a competent commander, both when he captured Llywelyn and halted the Welsh revolts, and during his Irish campaigns as well.

While Mortimer flourished as Lieutenant of Ireland, the power of his worst enemy, another Hugh Despenser, was growing apace in England. By 1321 Despenser's authority was pivotal to the whole realm. Any man who wished to speak to the King and petition him had first to win Despenser's support. And that meant money. He was an atrocious man, utterly without mercy when seeking his own advantage.

Mortimer, the monarch's most loyal servant and warrior, was imprisoned in the Tower for raising his flag against Despenser along with the Marcher Lords. However, Despenser was not stupid enough to believe that he ever would be safe while his most bitter enemy lived. He persuaded the King that Mortimer must be executed. When Mortimer heard that he was due to die in August 1323, he broke free on the first day of that month.

That famous escape led to a series of panicky messages, sent to all Sheriffs and other keepers of the law throughout the realm, to apprehend and hold Mortimer, whether dead or alive. On hearing of the man's flight, the King had gone into a rage. Mortimer was one of his best generals – exactly the sort of man who could raise an army in rebellion and seek to wrest the kingdom from him. For Mortimer the spoils would be vast.

This was the land to which Simon and Baldwin returned from their pilgrimage to Compostela in 1323. Their country was rent by divisions: the King and his friends seemed all-powerful and undefeatable, while they ravaged the nation. Despenser was rapacious, grabbing lands, castles and treasure. He would capture anyone, even widows, in order to extort what he wanted. He set himself up as the ruler of most of Wales, controlling vast swathes of land, and with his mastery of the King, he not only took plenty of money in bribes, but also prevented any news which reflected badly on him from reaching Edward's ears. In an environment similar to the Soviet state, all were suspicious of each other. Few would dare to state their opposition to the King because to oppose him was to invite death and destruction. King Edward II had already slaughtered his own cousin, Earl Thomas of Lancaster, and hundreds of others after the short-lived campaign leading to Boroughbridge.

Yet in a place like Cornwall, so far removed from the politics of the court, the peasants wouldn't have worried themselves quite so much. They had their own battles to fight, making sure that the harvest was safely brought in, keeping weasels and stoats from their chickens, protecting their piglets from foxes and their lambs from magpies and crows, praying, always praying, that God would not send another famine to devastate the land and kill off all their children.

This was a time of total insecurity. The King was weak, his nation under attack from the Scottish, from his own people, and from the elements. He gave his support to one group of thieves for whom the law meant nothing, at the expense of another. Because, make no mistake, Mortimer was little better than Despenser, just as Despenser himself was no better than his own predecessor, Piers Gaveston. When Roger Mortimer later grabbed the reins of power, sadly he was just as greedy and vengeful as Despenser had been.

However, at least he had the honour to have tried to live by his oaths to the King, until Edward himself turned his face to another. Who can tell what sort of a man Mortimer might have been if the King hadn't first been disloyal to *him*?

Cardinham is, thank heavens, by-passed by the A30. The village is a pretty little place in green and rolling countryside with views to the moors of Bodmin beyond. From the moors east of Temple, the real isolation of the place can be imagined. During the winter, this area would be more or less cut off from all the rest of Cornwall, and even in summer, the roads and lanes must have been atrocious. Only carts or packhorses would have been available for transport; nothing in the way of decent wagons could have coped with the hills and the mud.

The church deserves a visit, and it's pleasing to note that it lists the vicars and priests who have served the community there, going back to 12 September 1271 and Odo de Prydies. I have taken the liberty of inventing Father John because I have a deeply ingrained dislike of ascribing thoughts and feelings to real men and women who are long dead and unable to answer for themselves or threaten legal retaliation! To my mind, using real people in books is a form of post-mortem slander and I always prefer to create new characters.

South of the main village, the castle's remains stand on private land, but the raised mound of the motte can be seen quite clearly. My own description of it is based on guesswork because I've seen no detailed archaeological reports into how the buildings stood there, but I think there is some evidence for the layout I've suggested. It wasn't a large place, but as a small fortress, I think it would have been pleasing.

North and east stand the church and buildings of Temple. This place was surely another of the small manors owned by The Temple, or the Knights Templar, and would have been a place of some solace to Baldwin. However, the priest living in so lonely an outpost would have been desperate for any form of companionship.

The search for more accurate information about English law and how the various Constables, Keepers, Coroners, Sheriffs and others managed to administer justice at the courts over the counties of the south-west, is ongoing, but I have to thank the scholarly works of Anthony Musson. His books *The Evolution of English Justice* and *Medieval Law in Context* are regularly pulled off my shelves.

All the persons described are figments of my imagination, but I have based these events on things which did happen in these areas. At a time of mounting dissatisfaction with the King, in the run-up to a civil war, all parts of the realm grew more lawless; even a small community in Cornwall would have become less manageable as Edward II's power waned.

Naturally any errors in location and in facts are entirely my own.

Michael Jecks
Northern Dartmoor
August 2003

Prologue

There were two happy men that day in Cardinham in the summer of 1323, and one who was fearful.

Serlo the miller had every right to be concerned. Although he feared ruin, he was about to be murdered, for reasons he could not begin to comprehend, and at the hands of one whom he would never have suspected.

Nicholas of Cardinham sat on his palfrey, eyeing the villeins at work in the castle's fields with a profound sense of satisfaction.

From here, high on the edge of the moors leading up towards Bodmin in the Earldom of Cornwall, he could see for many miles in the bright sunshine. The golden, drooping heads of the oats in the fields bobbed in the wind like ladies moving to an unheard tune. Wonderful! It was a sight to make a man give thanks to God, and Nicholas, a religious man, did so gladly.

Although the calls of the sweating peasants were loud, he could still hear the larks trilling high overhead. With every breeze the leaves of gorse rattled dryly, their yellow flowers dancing. To this was added the mechanical hiss of the reapers. With every sweep of their scythes, dust was thrown upwards in clouds of fine mist. The music of men rehoning their blades with long stones sang in the air. Others were collecting the sheaves of oats, two to every man, stacking them in stooks while their womenfolk and children plucked gleanings from the ground and placed them in their aprons or cloths tied about their waists with thongs. They were welcome to their meagre harvest; Nicholas had already seen to his lord's profit, God be praised!

Although not tall, Nicholas had the ability to fill a space with his broad shoulders, immense right arm and neck of corded muscles. All men-at-arms had powerful bodies, but Nicholas carried his with a calm authority that went with his humility. Unlike so many of his friends and companions, he had not risen to the highest orders, hadn't even made it to become a squire but now, at forty-six years old, he was content. He was respected enough to have been given this command, the Castle of Cardinham in the Earldom of Cornwall, in charge of twelve men-at-arms, some of them squires in their own right.

His hazel eyes rose to survey the landscape. Set in his leathery, sunburned face, they shone with intelligence and confidence. He was a man who had been tested, and who knew his own measure – and, more importantly, Nicholas was content with the result. At his age, after so many wars and battles, he would be a sad man indeed if he hadn't been happy with himself.

The last years had been tough. The famines of 1315 and 1316 had been much worse in other parts of the country than down here, but people had still starved. Men found that their teeth became loose in their jaws, children grew peevish and irritable, many dying long before they should, and some folk had left the land altogether and sought their fortune in towns and cities. A few had returned at last; but only a few. Nicholas was short of manpower even now, but the men who had come back were not the sort he could count upon. They were more likely to cause trouble. And trouble *was* brewing – he could feel it in the way that the villeins watched each other and him. The King was close to war with the barons again. All knew it.

No matter. For now the most important thing was to get the harvest in. Oats might be viewed with less favour than other grains, but it was the only crop which thrived here in the windswept, rainswept western part of the realm. Others merely drowned or were blown to pieces. Wealthier men from other parts of the country looked down upon this land; they chose to laugh at people whose staple diet was the same as their beasts', but Nicholas didn't care. Not today of all days.

So long as the food was safe for the winter, the peasants would be biddable. When the long cold nights and tedium of winter made them fractious, however, that was the time to worry. For that was when they started bickering and squabbling.

There was an unsettled atmosphere about the place at the moment. Had been ever since the King crushed the rebellion of his cousin, Thomas of Lancaster. Peasants rightly feared another war. If there was one, their most able-bodied men would be taken away, their food stores raided by the King's purveyors, and those who remained would have more work to do. All suffered when war threatened.

He gave a curt nod to the castle's steward, Gervase, who stood at the edge of the communal fields, staff of office gripped tightly in one hand as he surveyed the folk working, occasionally bellowing at a shirker. Then Nicholas pulled his mount's head round with a sigh. It would have been good to remain here, but he needs must go home.

He had always enjoyed watching his men reaping the harvest, would even join in with their celebrations later as they drank their fill of the best ale and cider, and ate the meat from the ram which was already spitted and turning slowly over the fire. As usual it was watched by the ancient figure of old Iwan the smith, who scolded and threatened young Gregory, his six-year-old grandson, while the boy sweated, turning the great spit's handle to keep the meat rotating. Gregory's father was a farmer who worked down towards the Holy Well, a man called Angot who was even now honing his scythe, Nicholas saw. Angot wasn't one of the manor's tenants, so was likely here to earn some extra cash. His own harvest hadn't been very good, apparently: some of his seed had turned sour over the winter. Still, it meant that the grain here would be gathered in that bit sooner, which was all to the good.

Now Nicholas must get home to his darling wife, though. And with that thought, he clapped spurs to his mount and trotted down the lane.

Aye, his wife: my Lady Anne. Anne of the dark hair, the slender body, the almost boylike figure, the small, high breasts, the perfectly oval features, the warm, soft lips . . . Anne, his own lady, his love. She was enough to make an old man like him want to give up fighting. He might be a grizzled old warrior of six and forty years, while she was only two-and-twenty, but she swore that he pleased her more than any lad her own age, and by God's heart, how she had proved it! He was exhausted by her when she had taken too much wine.

He was still smiling to himself when he saw Athelina walking ahead of him on the road. *Beautiful* Athelina, as the men had always known her . . . now past her prime. Even Gervase wouldn't look at her, these days. He now had a new strumpet, so village gossip said.

Athelina lived out on the road towards Susan's tavern. She stopped at the sound of his horse. A tall woman, she was still striking, in a shabby way. At her side were her two sons. One, the twelve year old, held on to her hand, while the other, a couple of years younger, clutched at her skirts as he stared at Nicholas.

Poor Athelina had been widowed some while before. Her husband Hob had contracted a wasting disease that killed him within a fortnight. Now she had nothing: only a rented, tumble-down cottage, insufficient food for herself and the boys, not even the solace of a man. It was very sad. She depended utterly on the generosity of others.

Yes, Nicholas had cause to be proud. His own wife would never be a beggar – he'd see to that. Anne would never want for anything while he lived.

Nor yet, he hoped, when he died.

To the west of the vill, Serlo the miller scratched first at his beard, then at his groin. The last of the flour was trickling into his sacks while the rumbling of the great wooden water-wheel continued behind him. He glanced at the deeply engrained bloodstains on it, then at the bright white oak of the four new teeth.

Milling was not the easiest of jobs when the harvests were poor, and Serlo had much to do to make up the losses of last year. Damn all apprentices! The idiots! They were none of them worth their upkeep. Danny, the last one, had never worked as hard as he should, and then, last year, the miserable churl had slipped as he passed by the machine.

Serlo kept reliving it in his nightmares. For months afterwards he had a sickly fear of going to his bed. When Danny had stumbled, his left hand was holding a full sack at his shoulder. As he toppled, Serlo could read the thought in his startled, fearful eyes: If I drop this, he'll thrash me to death!

Serlo was furious when he kept dropping the sacks. Dan had wasted so much good flour, it would have been cheaper to tip away a twelfth of all his millings than to keep the apprentice on. The next time Dan let a sack slip, Serlo warned him, he'd thrash him until there was no flesh left on his back. And so poor Danny had kept a good hold as he went over, and this was his undoing. His right hand grasped the first thing that came to him – the moving, toothed wheel – and before he knew what was happening, his arm was caught by the great teeth and crushed between the upper and lower wheels.

Serlo had tried to prise the lad free, to slow the wheels and save his life . . . but he was fighting against the power of the mill and the river. He could do nothing, and Danny was chewed inexorably into the machine, his face contorted in a final scream of terror. Then a great gush of blood spewed upwards, covering the miller, his apprentice and the wheels which had destroyed him.

At least his body hadn't ruined the mill. Four teeth had to be replaced, which cost some money, but the seven-year-old bones weren't hard enough to do much damage to the machinery.

The real expense came from that interfering old git, Sir Simon of Launceston, the Coroner. He'd hurried there at the first sniff of money, and fined Serlo instantly for removing the body from the machine, then fined him again for not calling the Coroner personally. Finally, and punishingly, he had fined him the *deodand*. Whatever the material or animal that had caused a death, it was always *deodand*, its worth forfeit for the crime of murder. If a man killed with a knife, if a maid was crushed by a bull, if a mill killed a boy, the knife, the bull or the mill were assessed so that their value could be taken. The mill had crushed the boy: the mill-wheel, the water-wheel, the two great cogs – all had led to Danny's death, so all must be *deodand*.

That was the Coroner's argument, and it took all of Serlo's eloquence to persuade him that it was only the wheel which was at fault. You couldn't blame the water-wheel or the shaft or the building, it was just the cogged wheel. The Coroner countered that it was both cogged wheels at least, for the lad was crushed between the two, and although Serlo tried to point out that one had captured Dan and dragged him in, so only one was guilty, the Coroner would have none of it. If Serlo wanted to argue further, he said, Serlo could do so in the King's court.

Not that it was all down to Sir Simon. At each argument the knight conferred with his clerk, a greasy little toe-rag called Roger who stared at Serlo like a man studying a dog's turd on his boot.

And now Serlo had a thundering debt on his hands. He had been forced to borrow heavily just to be able to pay the *deodand*. Eighteen whole pennies, for one wheel alone! Christ's cods, that was a huge amount for one cretinous apprentice who couldn't even walk straight. Then there were the extra charges – the one for the grave, the cost of the services held in the brat's memory, the fee for the mourners . . . as the apprentice's master, Serlo had to foot the whole sodding bill.

Danny had cost Serlo dearly, and yet the miller couldn't help but miss the little devil. His cheery smile, his prattling . . . Not that he'd let people realise that. He didn't want them thinking he was some weak, sentimental fool. No, if he did that, they'd all assume that they could get away with fleecing him. He knew that many of the locals considered him a fool, a few sticks short of a bundle. They respected his brother, but only because Alexander was ruthless, so Serlo copied him as best he could. At the Coroner's inquest he'd pretended to be unaffected by Danny's death. Maybe he ought to have shown his sorrow, but then people would have sniggered at him.

Life, he sighed to himself, was a shit.

Hearing a shout, he glanced up. Someone was trying to cross the bridge. Serlo grunted and made his way up the stairs to the bridge, where he had erected a gate. 'Who's there?' he demanded suspiciously, his hand straying to his cudgel.

'Travellers, miller. What's this thing here?'

'Can't you see the board?' Serlo asked sarcastically. 'It's a toll. You want to cross the bridge, you have to pay. It's two pennies.'

'Why should we pay?'

'It's no business of mine, master. If you won't, you won't, but then you'll have to ride back to the other road, a good two miles west, and approach the vill again. That'll take you a good couple of hours.'

'There never used to be a toll here.'

This voice was lower, more malevolent. Peering at them shortsightedly, Serlo felt a sudden twinge of fear. Both men were on horseback; their mounts were large beasts – good, expensive-looking horseflesh. One of them was so dark it was almost black, the other was deep chestnut, but it wasn't the horses that caught his attention so much as the riders. Both, now he studied them, had the aura of wealth, like servants in a rich man's household. The bigger of the two was wearing a green tunic and hosen, while his companion was clad in a red tunic; there was a richness to its colour where the sun caught it, like a fine silk. Here, some distance west of Cardinham, Serlo was more than a little exposed. If these two were of a mind, they could vault the gate and chase after him on their mounts. He'd not be able to escape them.

'Lordings,' he said with more respect, 'it's not my choice to charge honest men to cross the river, but my lord's. We built this bridge with our own strength, and still owe money for the work. What else can we do? My lord said that we must ask travellers to pay for our efforts, because the thing's not here for our benefit. It's for yours.'

'Scant benefit to me,' shrugged the rider wearing the green tunic. He was the larger of the two, and as he ambled his mount forward, Serlo saw that he had a massive frame, with a right shoulder that held muscles like knots in an oaken board. The tendons of his neck were as thick as ropes.

'Miller, open that gate!' the man commanded.

'Look, give me a penny if you like and I won't tell my master that I—'

'Silence! We could push the thing over if we wished,' the first man said. 'If you have any complaints about us not paying, let me know later when I'm in a mood to listen.'

'It sounded as though this miller was asking us to pay him instead of his master,' said the second pensively.

'Is that what you wanted, man? You'd embezzle money due to your master?'

'No, of course not. That would be treason! But my master will want me to settle any missing debts. I'll have to tell him that you both passed by without paying the toll levied here.'

'Your master? What's his name?'

The man-at-arms made an irritable gesture.

Reluctantly, Serlo moved forward and slid the bar from its rests, swinging the gate wide. 'Sir Henry of Cardinham, lord of this manor. Not that he's here right now; he lives in his own big palace near the King, so I hear. He's part of the King's household, so you shouldn't cross him. Nicholas is his castellan. He's there in the castle now, I expect, and he has a foul temper – so I shouldn't try to plead ignorance about the tolls and evading them.'

'Oh aye? Then we'll be careful, won't we, Richer?' the larger man said. 'If our new master is so brutal, we'll have to watch ourselves!'

Serlo heard his laughter, and felt the shock of the words like a wave that broke over him. He peered at the second man, and recognition kicked in his bowels. It was mutual.

'So, *little* miller, it's you! You weren't a miller when I was last here.'

'Some of us have bettered ourselves in the last years, I suppose,' Serlo said defensively.

'Aye, that's true enough,' the man called Richer said softly.

As the two meandered away, up the lane eastwards towards the castle, Serlo could only wonder what Richer atte Brooke was doing back here in Cardinham.

After all, it was fifteen years since he'd fled the vill, when all his family had died in a fire.

Gervase, steward of Cardinham Castle, watched Nicholas leave with a sense of relief. It was hard enough keeping the men working *without* having the master of the castle hanging around, watching everything with that stupid grin plastered all over his face. It made Gervase feel queasy. Nick had once been his best friend, but now . . . Well! It was better that the fool should go and leave his steward to do his work without interruption.

He sighed, leaning on his staff. Before Nicholas had married the pair of them had grown into an easy, comfortable relationship; they had become close. As castellan, Nicholas was responsible for the law all about the manor, while Gervase was in charge of the maintenance of the estates. Under them, the manor had flourished. And then, six years ago, *she* had arrived, the Lady Anne, and Gervase had lost his companion.

Cardinham Castle had, until then, been a quiet place. Sir Henry had won favour with the King, and was today a member of Edward's household, surviving the many twists and turns of politics. He had been given an estate in Kent, once the possession of a man who had been proved to be a traitor, and lived with the King. He had not been to Cardinham for at least twenty years, so the place was more or less under the permanent control of Nicholas and Gervase his steward.

Anne had been a forlorn traveller, only sixteen years old, orphaned by the Scottish wars and half-starved by the famine. Nicholas had seen her, this sad little chit, and apparently been immediately smitten. His heart was hers. It was a strange sight, the grizzled old warrior so besotted. It was more than simple lust. If it had been only that, he could have taken her and been satisfied, but there was something else about her that attracted a man. Gervase had felt it too. She was fresh and fragrant – *lovely*; bewitching to any man with red blood in his veins. Even her melancholia was entrancing. It made a man want to slay dragons to lay at her dainty feet. She was adorable.

When the two made their oaths at the church door, Nicholas holding her hands with reverence, as though he was holding the hands of an angel, Gervase had felt his heart swell with pride, a sense that the manor was honoured. He had looked at his friend's smiling face, glad to see him so happy. Nicholas had lost the frivolity of bachelorhood and gained the stern duty of responsible manhood. He now had a woman to serve and protect, a duty and honour he would relish, Gervase knew.

At the time, Gervase had not realised that he had lost his companion for ever.

Stumping into the vill later that day, Serlo frowned at all about him. He was in no mood for a chat. He had a task to perform – not a pleasant one, either.

Serlo had tried figuring out all the ways he could of earning a little more money. There were the tolls, of course. He'd done what he could with them, but the fact was that the threatening clouds of war were putting travellers off. Even the merchants who normally came this way had stopped. Serlo had borrowed heavily to buy 'the farm of tolls' – the right to charge – and it was all wasted. It was so bad, he'd gone to speak to Gervase, but the steward had only grinned smarmily at him, saying that once he'd bought the right to charge tolls there was no mechanism to reduce it or give him a refund.

The only way to make money from the tolls was to conceal a proportion of them from his brother. Alex had helped to buy the farm for a share of the profits, and it wasn't Serlo's fault that there were none. Anyway, Serlo could bump up the share to Alex when things looked a bit better. He didn't want to steal from his own brother. No, but he had to show that he was competent.

That was the problem. Serlo, the younger, always felt that his brother was patronising him, even when he knew perfectly well that Alex had no intention of doing so. He was just as good as his brother, Serlo told himself: he'd not had quite the same luck. Alex always managed to make money, but when Serlo tried to do so, it never quite worked out. It wasn't his fault; these things just happened. Alex could stick his hand into a midden and come up grasping rose petals; Serlo would find nothing but turds.

For now, the main thing was to get hold of some extra money. He'd decided to start by increasing Athelina's rent. She had a lover – let *him* pay. He could afford it, God knew. He was one of the richest men about here.

He had reached her home – a large building with a door in the middle of the whitewashed wall that faced the road. Walking down the path between her vegetable beds, he saw how her plants were thriving. She could easily afford to pay a little more, he thought. He needed the money more than she did.

At her door, he braced himself, then rapped sharply on the timbers.

It was a week or more before Athelina approached her lover, and then her nerve almost failed her. She could do nothing until she had spoken to her protector – but he was unavailable again. For a long time Athelina had been used to being received with some honour at the gate, courteously escorted to the room where she could be enjoyed by her man in peace, but now, that was no more. The nearest she got was the lewd suggestion from the gate-keeper that he should service her in the place of her man.

That was proof enough. If the doorman dared try his luck, all in the castle must know that her man had deserted her. It was no surprise, after all. She'd guessed as much when she saw the strumpet in the vill. It was clear that he'd found a new woman, and had no more interest in her.

Still, all was not lost. It was not easy for her to play the whore, because she'd always made love *for* love's sake, not for money, but now she must earn her keep. Whatever happened, they must not lose their home. She could not make her children suffer like that. No, she would entertain any man who could afford her. So she combed her hair, standing in front of her plate of polished copper. Studying herself, her tunic untied, she could see much still to admire. Her breasts were large and firm still, not flaccid like drained sacks; her belly was flat, her hair luxurious. In a darkened room, it was possible a man might notice her large eyes and ignore the lines of age and care. Or so she hoped.

When the knock came, she felt her heart thud painfully, but then she took a deep breath and strode to the door, pulling it wide. Giving a smile, she welcomed her visitor, stepping back into the room.

Before he could speak, she pushed the door shut, then bravely put her lips to his as her hand fell to his groin.

Chapter One

It was two days later that Richer rode back alone from a hunt with his squire and Nicholas the castellan. Richer's rounsey had thrown a shoe, and Richer knew perfectly well that a man-at-arms looked to his horse before his own pleasure. Some day his life might depend on it. Pleasure could be sought at any time.

The vill was quiet as he clattered slowly along the stony path. He felt surprisingly relaxed. After fleeing from here in such a hurry all those years ago, he had anticipated an overwhelming sadness when he finally returned. And fear, too: this was the first time he had passed through the vill on his own, without the protection of Warin or one of the other men-at-arms.

From here the road curled up towards the church and soon, through the trees, he could see the little belltower ahead. It was only a short way from there to the place where he had been born and raised. The long low thatched cottage had had a large log-pile at one side and a barn behind, where the family pig and some hens were housed. His father had been a serf – a peasant who owed his labour to the lord of the manor – but Richer had gained his freedom by running away and not being caught. He wondered what his parents would make of him now. Probably they'd be unhappy at his chosen career, a henchman for a lord, but there was little else he felt he could do. At least he wasn't a mercenary. He earned his robes and food from his loyalty to his squire, and if he was employed indirectly by Sir Henry of Cardinham now, it was on a more equitable basis than being a mere serf like his father.

At least he had travelled and seen a little of the country. That was more than most could say, especially fellows like Serlo. Cheeky bastard, trying to thieve money from people passing by his mill. Richer had asked about this at the castle, but apparently it was legitimate: the miller had bought the farm of the tolls. Which was weird, because if he owned the farm, there was no reason why he should let people through at a reduced rate, unless he was desperate. Perhaps that was it. Serlo's family had always been money mad, ever since his father's failure. Some men could be driven like that. As far as Richer was concerned, it was a curious craving. He preferred the security of belonging in a household. Especially since losing his family.

It was odd coming back here. Glancing about him again, he saw how little changed the place was. He would have expected the vill to show the scars of loss, some memory of the disaster which had taken his parents from him, but there was nothing. It was almost as if their deaths hadn't happened. The houses were the same, the green unchanged – even most of the people were immediately recognisable when he saw then. A part of him expected to see his home; maybe he would meet his father again as he turned a corner. But he couldn't. They were all dead: it was why he had run away in the first place. All were gone.

There was one welcoming face he longed to see, but after fifteen years, she must surely have been married. Yet he hadn't seen her since his return. She wasn't dead; he'd asked about her generally, and received some grunts from servants in the castle, as though mention of her was somehow bad luck, but he didn't get the impression that she was in the graveyard. Christ's bones, but he hoped not. He had loved her so much . . . so, so much.

And then, as though she had heard his wishes, he saw her on the way ahead. A tall woman, bent with hardship, but still strikingly attractive.

'Athelina!' he called in a choked voice.

She turned, and for a split second, her face registered astonishment. Then her face tightened, and resumed its expression of anguish. In her eyes was no pleasure, only a grim horror, as though she feared any man she met.

Even him.

It was almost a whole month later that two men stood high on a hill at the coast, one disconsolately throwing pebbles at an ant scurrying about a rock. He looked up again, a dark man with a dark face, and said emphatically, 'No!'

The tall knight with him turned and gave his companion a stare. 'Are you sure of that, Simon?'

'Quite sure, thank you, Baldwin. I want no more of your damned boats,' rasped his friend. 'First I nearly die of sickness on the journey to Galicia, then I nearly die on the return, then we are blown from our course to hit those benighted islands, *then* we both nearly died under attack on those islands! And now we have struck our homeland again, thanks to that drunken oaf of a shipmaster, and you ask me to take another sour-bellied whore of a ship? God's thigh! Be damned to you, man! I'll take *no more vessels*. For me, it's dry land from now on.' He shuddered. 'Christ save me! I could be seasick just walking over a puddle! No, leave me to ponder your fate while you go on alone!'

The two men stood staring down at the little vessel which had brought them this far and which had now failed them. One, a tall, rangy knight with the strong arms and shoulders of a man who had trained for his vocation since a lad, the other a thickset fellow with the ruddy complexion of one who had spent much of his life in the open, his hair bleached by the hot sun of Galicia.

'It would be a great deal faster,' the knight said mildly. 'All I wish is to return home to Furnshill as soon as possible and see my wife and child.'

His friend sighed. 'Baldwin, I want to get home too, home to Meg and Edith and Peter – but I don't want to die in the process. Every attempt to travel since we first left home has left us close to death. For me, the land is so much more secure; I'll take no other route.'

'Yet the land itself holds dangers, Simon,' said Sir Baldwin de Furnshill, his attention travelling inland. He had penetrating black eyes, which some said could see through a man's skin to the sins beneath, but that was the merest nonsense and he was intensely irritated to hear such chatter. He simply had the skill of listening, and usually heard when a man spoke untruthfully.

'Yes, all right,' Simon Puttock agreed. 'But at least the risks you take on land are the sort which a knight like you and a man like me can protect ourselves against.'

Baldwin nodded. His companion, the Bailiff of Lydford Castle in Devonshire, was more than capable of defending himself, and the pair of them had been involved in many fights both together and apart. It was the strength of Simon's courage in battle that Baldwin found so confusing: a man prepared to brave a sword or arrow shouldn't fear the sea so much – not in Baldwin's opinion, anyway.

'If we were to sail, it would be a great deal faster,' he attempted.

'I will not sail.'

'It should be more comfortable, too,' Baldwin pointed out. 'No lurching nag, but a gently rolling deck . . .'

Simon flinched. He had been so badly seasick during the last voyage that he had prayed for death. 'Give me a lurching brute. I *prefer* a lurching brute.'

Ignoring him, Baldwin blithely continued, 'And wine available from a smiling fellow sent to serve the guests . . .'

Simon held up his hand. 'All right, all right – you want to travel by ship? Very well.'

Baldwin tried not to gape. 'So we can continue by ship when she is mended?'

Simon glanced over his shoulder. The sun was low in the sky, and the western horizon, away over the land, was gleaming pink and gold. Leaves were licked with fire, and even Baldwin's face shone with an unearthly glow that lit up the thin scar on his cheek. It was a knife-mark, Simon knew, nothing like so damaging as the other wounds, the scars of swords and axes that marked his torso, but in this light it showed up livid and vicious. It made him look curiously threatening, a harkening back to the great civil wars of the past century. Even his beard was an anachronism. No one wore smart, trimmed beards nowadays, but Baldwin was proud of his. Once he had been a Templar knight, and in that Order it had been illegal to shave.

'Simon, this beard is a mark of respect to those of my Order who lost their lives when the French King betrayed us,' he had explained to his old friend. 'If I allow it to grow wild, it would be a mark of *dis*respect. I will not allow that.'

To Simon's disgust, he had even purchased a pair of small scissors from a cutler passing through the vill this morning. It was a well-made tool, Simon could acknowledge, like a small pair of sheep shears, with two sharp blades connected by a horseshoe-shaped spring that held them apart until the fingers squeezed the cutting edges together, but simply unnecessary. He could as easily have bought a pair in Crediton when he got there, but no, he needs must have his beard kept trim.

The sea was now a chill grey mass, occasional waves sparkling gold, while the ship lay, a black shell in the shadow of the hill in whose lee she sheltered. Simon winced at the sight of her and shivered in recollection of the night before.

Roaring drunk, the shipmaster had deserted his post at the tiller and fallen in a stupor after finding a bottle of burned wine. This powerful drink, apparently made by monks boiling wine and cooling its steam somehow – a process Simon neither understood nor cared about – had completely ruined the man after only a pint, and yet Simon had seen him consuming a quart of wine the day before! Without a helmsman, the ship had struck a sand bar, breaking her mast, and for the second time this year, Simon had thought that he was about to drown.

The memory was enough to stiffen his resolve. '*You* sail if you must, Baldwin, but my journey continues on foot.'

The knight made a great show of puffing out his cheeks and shrugging. 'If you feel so certain . . .'

'I do.'

'Then it is fortunate indeed that I hired the best of the inn's horses. Otherwise another might have secured them!' Baldwin said, and laughed at Simon's expression.

On the Sunday following this conversation, Serlo the miller left his house to walk the short distance to church, leaving his wife Muriel to prepare their tiny sons Ham and Aumery for the Mass. Serlo needed to speak to his brother Alexander, the Constable of the Peace, about some business, and the church was the usual place for men to discuss their trades.

He shrugged himself deeper into his thin tunic. The summer was nearly over now and autumn held the land in its fist. Last night there had been a slight frost, and the chilly atmosphere suited his temper. Since the arrival of Richer and his squire, Serlo had noticed people in the vill watching him. He didn't need their fingers pointing to know that he was the object of all the gossip in the place. Damn them all! Too many remembered how Richer ran away as soon as his family was discovered dead, and many recalled the rumours at the time, that Serlo had been there at the house before it burned down. Rubbish, of course, but throw shit against a wall and some would stick.

He glanced into the fields nearer the vill and then at the

lowering clouds. If it were to rain, the stooks could be ruined. The grain would get damp, and if it wasn't properly dried it would not last the winter, which would mean disaster for everyone. Some men were already recalling the last war, when the stocks for half the winter were stolen by the King's Purveyors. Christ's bones, the weather here was as inconsistent as a woman's moods.

His wife Muriel was always whining, demanding money as though all a man need do was wave a hand and coins would come sprinkling from the heavens. She swore that she and the children were always hungry, that they had nothing to live on since the failed harvest last year, as though it was Serlo's fault. Stupid cow! Why couldn't she comprehend that he was doing his best for her? Like any other man, he relied on his skills and cunning to wrest as much as he could from the mill, but there was little enough he could do when things were as bad as they were at present. All must be patient. Perhaps now the harvest was in, provided there was no rain for a little while, there would be more money. A harvest meant grain to be milled, and he would take his tenth from each sack – occasionally more, if the owner wasn't watching too carefully as Serlo weighed his portion.

He could do with the cash himself, since apart from all his debts, he badly needed a new surcoat. This old thing was too threadbare to keep him warm. It had been fine the winter before last when he bought it, but now it wouldn't keep out the chill of an autumnal morning. And the evenings were already creeping in. Soon it would be winter. The years flew past so quickly. His father had once told him that: as a man grew older, the days passed by more swiftly – and he was definitely not getting any younger, he acknowledged sourly.

He had to get hold of some coin! That was why he was trying to do deals with travellers instead of taking the tolls to which the manor was entitled.

Athelina hadn't paid him any rent for months now, not since Easter-time. He'd been patient because her man had sometimes been a little slow to cough up for her, but now she said that his generosity had dried up and she had nothing. Well, Serlo's patience had run out along with her money. Jesus's heart, he had hated that confrontation. Athelina had looked at him silently, the tears springing into those magnificent eyes as he told her to go and whore at the tavern. That was what a woman did when she was desperate and her family needed money. Mind, a woman as skinny and ravaged as her, Serlo thought morosely, would scarcely bring in enough to buy him a kerchief, let alone a new surcoat.

One of her whelps had rushed to her, snivelling brat, as though to defend her honour against Serlo. Shame the cur hadn't protected her from her last lover. Maybe she'd still have some self-respect and honour if he had!

Deep in his thoughts, he was aware of nothing but the path itself. Serlo cursed as his thin boots slithered over stones, almost making him fall.

'Ho, now! So it's our favourite miller, Master Serlo!'

'I'm not in the mood, Richer,' Serlo growled on hearing the familiar, taunting voice. 'Leave me to go to church.'

'Why, don't you wish to chat?'

Peering ahead shortsightedly, Serlo could just make out two shadowy figures. In the swirls of freezing grey fog they appeared larger than men, much taller than Serlo himself, and for an instant he felt crushed. Then a breeze cleared the mist, and in that instant Serlo saw the church standing tall and serene behind his enemies. 'May God forgive you both,' he grated. 'You're holding me from the church.'

'We aren't stopping you, Serlo. Feel free to continue on your way.'

Serlo steeled himself and strode on, chin high, but when he was level, he hissed, 'You'll push a man too hard one day, Richer.

Not everyone's scared of you just because you carry a sword for the castle.'

'Perhaps it will be you who is pushed too far, eh, Serlo? Go on, you corrupt bladder of wind! Go to church. You need the solace of God's forgiveness more than most, I expect.'

Serlo walked on as though he hadn't heard those words, but when he was gone a short way further up the track, he heard Richer's voice again.

'By the way, miller, I recall you asked me and my friend for a penny to pay no toll at the bridge. That was only a short while after you'd asked the steward for a refund of your investment in the farm of the tolls, is that right?'

'What's it to you?' Serlo snapped, attempting to hide his fear.

'Nothing . . . except that my master would be very interested to learn that you were pocketing gifts. Why, that would be defrauding him of his legitimate income. Theft, Master Miller.'

'It's a lie!'

'Is it? I should ask Nicholas then, should I? Think on it, miller.'

Serlo said not a word. He walked on as though there had been no interruption, but even as he stepped into the security of the church, he felt the shiver of fear coursing along his spine as if Richer atte Brooke was again threatening him.

'God's bones, you bastard son of a Saracen harlot, I'll have my revenge on you for your insults,' he swore quietly. 'If you've reported my tolls it'll make repaying my debts that much harder. By Christ's wounds, I'll avenge any grief you bring on me: aye, an hundredfold. You'll regret coming up against me and mine, just as your father did!'

Chapter Two

On that same day Simon and Baldwin rose early and celebrated Mass in a tiny, all but empty chapel before leaving the coast to set off inland for home.

Later in the morning, reaching a small stand of trees at the top of a hill, they paused a while, staring north and east, then dismounted and took a drink from their skins. Sitting with his back to a young oak, Simon closed his eyes and sighed. 'It was almost worthwhile climbing this far just for the pleasure of halting and resting!'

There came a grunt from his side. Bob, the young boy whom the ostler had sent with them to bring back the three mounts when they reached the next town, was feeling distinctly put out, and Simon grinned to himself. A gangling lad of some eleven or twelve summers, Bob had declared himself more than happy to ride with them as far as they wanted, but that was two days ago, and now he was tired and irritable, glowering at Simon or Baldwin whenever either spoke. He obviously felt he was being taken too far and too fast for the penny he had been promised, and his expression as he gazed about him showed that he was nervous in these foreign parts. Simon wondered how far from home he had travelled before. Surely not so far as this, he thought.

'A little exercise is always good,' Baldwin remarked. He was standing still, staring out to the east. 'You should try it more often, lad.'

Simon heard a snort, but as was his wont, Bob said nothing. Instead, Simon sat up and rested on his elbow. The ground was damp and chilly, but he was overheated. 'Do you know any of this country?'

Baldwin shook his head. 'Sometimes a man from Cornwall would come and present a matter at Exeter, and I have met knights at the court of our lord, Hugh de Courtenay, but I have never travelled this way myself before.'

'A great shame,' Simon grunted as he rose to his feet. 'Christ's pain. If I sit there any longer, I swear I shall fall asleep.' He stretched, then gasped. 'Ow! I am too old for all this toil and meandering about the countryside. Once we arrive home, I'm going to rest for at least a month.'

'What? The new master of Dartmouth will rest on his laurels when there is all that work to be done?' Baldwin asked with malicious pleasure.

Simon's face fell. 'You evil . . . I'd forgotten that for a moment!'

'Yes. Your move to Dartmouth.'

'Must you remind me that the first thing I have to do on returning is pack up and move to the coast, to live with hordes of sailors and shipmen. My God! And my daughter . . . I wonder what has become of Edith in my absence.'

Seeing his crestfallen expression, Baldwin regretted his brief attempt at humour. Their relationship was too important for him to want to upset the other man. 'Simon,' he said, going to stand at his friend's side, 'when you reach the coast I am sure that it will be a delight to you. There can be little better than a home near the sea. The atmosphere is cleaner, fresher and more invigorating there.'

'And it will no doubt remind me at every opportunity of the pleasures of this pilgrimage,' Simon rasped sarcastically.

Baldwin sniffed, but couldn't restrain his grin. 'Perhaps.'

'Well, let's get on with it, then. If I'm to be reminded of my pains and sores, I might as well reflect on them from the warmth of my own fire as soon as possible.'

'Masters, I have to return soon with these mounts,' the boy piped up.

Baldwin eyed him with dissatisfaction. 'We have paid for them and for you.'

'That was money to travel to the next town, but you have forced me to come twice that distance. Do you expect me to go all the way to . . . to Exeter?' Bob demanded, picking the most distant city he knew of.

'Not quite, no,' Baldwin said unsympathetically. Then Simon touched his arm, and Baldwin gave him a sharp look, which slowly transformed into comprehension.

Simon had lost a son only a few short years ago, and a matter of days ago he had been responsible, in part, for another young man's death. That death was a sore regret to him, as Baldwin knew. It was a matter he could all too easily understand, because the reason for both of them launching themselves upon their recent pilgrimage was another death, one for which Baldwin was himself responsible.

Baldwin nodded, and it was good to see Simon give him a short grin in return. There was no need for words. Baldwin understood his feelings: Simon had no desire to see this boy taken too far from his home and put in danger. Any long trip in these uncertain times was hazardous. Horse thieves could easily murder a youth like Bob to get their hands on the mounts. Better that he should be released from their service as soon as possible and sent homewards.

'Young Bob, you have to return to your home. Do you know how far it is to the next town? If we can find an ostler prepared to hire us more horses and a boy to ride with us, we shall release you. Will that suffice?'

'Yes. I suppose.'

'Where is the next town, then?' Baldwin asked.

Bob scowled. 'I think it's Bodmin. After that, all is rough moorland.'

'At least you'll feel at home there, Simon,' Baldwin said lightly.

'Yes,' Simon said aloud, but inwardly he felt a little clutch, like a small hand pulling at his heart's strings. It could be one of the last times he rode over stannary lands. Soon he would be installed in Dartmouth, and then he'd have little to do with miners or moors.

With a pang of loss, poignant and terrible, he realised how much he would miss both.

Richer atte Brooke chuckled quietly to himself as he trailed after Serlo on the track to the church.

'You are pleased with your threats?' Warin asked stiffly. 'For my part, I see no advantage in them, and the potential for a lot of disorder in the vill.'

'But did you see the fat arse's face?' Richer asked with delight.

Warin's voice was colder as he said, 'Friend Richer, I do not wish for the peasants to be roused to anger over your insults against one of their own.'

'There will be no disorder, Squire,' Richer said more seriously. 'The fat fool is pushing too hard. He seeks ever more money from people, and this shows him I have a hold over him. If he misbehaves, I can crush him. The news that I am aware of his appeal to have some of his payment for the farm refunded will keep him sensible, and then I can speak to him of other matters.'

Warin eyed him speculatively. 'Do not endanger the vill's peace. I would be very unhappy, were you to do that.'

'I won't,' Richer said easily. And he wouldn't – not unless Serlo gave him no choice. Not that it was Serlo with whom he must concern himself – the dangerous brother of the two was Alex. If the Constable thought that someone was giving his kid brother a hard time, he'd wade in to protect him.

Yes, he should be more cautious with Alexander.

* * *

In the church, Father Adam watched over his flock with a feeling of distaste.

Look at these foul peasants! Standing in small groups, haggling over their bits of business – didn't they realise that they were in God's House? Tatty churls, breath reeking of garlic, unwashed armpits adding to the stench, their hosen soaked and foul with mud or worse, their faces grimy and hands all blackened and callused – they were hardly the sort of men Adam wanted in his church.

He saw Serlo arrive, and watched him cross the floor to join his brother Alexander. What a pair they were! Alex was at least intelligent, which was more than you could say about Serlo. The latter was revered only for the strength in those great biceps. Men were naturally cautious about upsetting someone who could pick them up with one hand and toss them into the next field, but they should worry more about his brother, the suave, collected Constable of the Peace who appeared to own more than half of the vill. As usual, Alex greeted Serlo with a broad smile and clasp of his forearm, slapping him on the back. Then he introduced him to the group around him. No doubt discussing the hire of his oxen, Father Adam thought. The beasts would be in demand to haul the heavy carts laden with the crop, and Alexander possessed a near monopoly of them.

Still, Alexander was the least of Adam's problems. If the people of the vill were owned by him, Adam was owned by another man. And he was terrified.

At two and thirty years, he was old enough to know the dangers and escape them, but his life had ever been a series of errors and misjudgements, and now he had made the worst mistake of his life . . . if it felt natural and *right*, that was surely only a proof of the depth of his fall. Once he had been a good, right-thinking man, devoted to the cure of the souls in his little parish, and never, not even once, had he been tempted by the pretty women of the vill. Now, though, he had lapsed. He was in love, and had even declared his love. *Oh, Christ in Heaven, save me,* he prayed.

Love . . . yes, that is what he felt – and yet it was unreciprocated! That filled him with a yearning so intense, he would prefer death to this dreadful half-existence. What is more, the rural dean must soon hear of the affair. Oh, Christ in chains! That evil-minded old pig would be sure to come and haul Adam off to his court, and the priest would be lucky to escape a severe punishment.

That in itself was not the worst of it, though. Punishment was one thing: it lasted a short period, and then life should return to normal. However, the rural dean might well ensure that he was taken away permanently, perhaps installed in a convent and left there to wither until he was a terrible old man, like the ancients he had seen during his time at Buckfast Abbey. The thought of ending up like them was petrifying. Holy Mother, the idea was enough to make his eyes prickle with tears.

Damn them! Damn them all! He'd *not* be taken away again. Adam had been installed in that accursed monastery when he was little better than a child, and when he'd tried to escape, he'd been declared *apostate* and hunted down like a dog. Excommunicate, he had lived in perpetual terror, knowing that he might be found and returned some day.

And then they'd caught him and back he'd gone. There he'd been forced to endure the snide remarks of all the other monks, their bitter jibes and the corporal punishment, the humiliation of lying prostrate before the altar, the grim effort of speaking the psalters, the fasting . . . so many punishments, and all wrong; *all wrong*!

The Bishop had saved him. It was when he had visited the convent and the new Prior, God bless him, had spoken to him of the crimes committed by Adam and – so Adam shrewdly guessed – hinted that there was something not entirely right about his position here in the monastery. Later the Bishop had asked to meet Adam.

He had been exhausted at the time after yet another fast day spent on his knees in the Lady Chapel, but then he told his tale, how he had come here as a novice, but after his year's probation, he had been taken through to the church and persuaded to make it his profession. And this when he was not yet fourteen years old! It was illegal for him to have been bullied into professing so young. It was wrong in any case for his novitiate to have begun before he was thirteen, and he was not old enough to make the vows. The whole matter was organised by his stepfather (his real father had died some while before), who wanted a potentially rebellious and expensive brat permanently removed from the family home.

The Bishop, Walter of Exeter, was enraged by this injustice. Seldom had Adam seen a man of God in full flow of righteous anger. The monks were bawled out for breaking the law, especially when one confessed that the motivation behind their actions was the promise of money for the priory.

So he had escaped the place. With the Bishop's help, he had been trained as a rector, and now he had the cottage behind the church here. It was a spacious place, so that he might offer hospitality to those who needed it, even if it was far too large for him as a single man. Still, that meant he was able to look after poor Julia and her child, which was good. Protecting her was saving her, and her parish was saved embarrassment too. Mind, the extra money she brought was welcome. He was saving it against the day when he might have to leave this place and run again.

The day when he must again wear the wolf's head.

Richer entered the church with Warin and stood surveying the congregation. He could see Serlo standing with his brother, and as the door slammed shut behind him, Richer smiled broadly to see how both men's heads snapped around, as though they were expecting him to launch some sort of attack on them even here in the church. Serlo in particular had the look of one who was about to suffer a ferocious headache. Richer had suffered from them himself over the years and he knew what it was to have a migraine.

He sauntered towards the pillar on the right-hand side of the church with his companion, leaning against it negligently and avoiding the stares of the two brothers. He had many years of antipathy stored up against them, and his deep dislike for Serlo had been exacerbated on hearing of Athelina's terror at the possibility of being thrown from her house. Serlo and Alex obviously thought they could run this vill as if it were their own private fiefdom, even to the extent of evicting poor Athelina and her children from their home. Well, it was time that their tyranny was ended, and today was as good a day as any to begin the process.

If Richer could, he would have given Athelina all the money he possessed, but he had none. God, but Serlo was a pathetic churl! If only he hadn't depended all the time on his brother's protection, perhaps he would have grown into a stronger fellow, a man in his own right. As it was, he was little more than Alex's henchman.

Look at him! Peering back over his shoulder like some fishwife who suspected that the stall next-door had spoken of rotting herring in her barrels. Alexander was no better; his face was twisted with hatred, like a man who'd bitten into a lemon thinking it was a sweetmeat. Pathetic, the pair of them!

Serlo was a shortish man, florid-faced from too much strong ale, and with a belly to match his consumption. He and his brother, who was nearly as short, had strange, heavily jowled faces that were somehow broader than long, and both had the same pale shade of hair: not red, but not brown, as though their Celtic ancestry had been washed from them just as their blood had been watered by mixing with too many foreigners. The two brothers were very similar – until a man came close to them.

Yes, it was when you drew nearer that you saw the differences, Richer reckoned. Serlo was born some three years after Alexander, and he had been stamped from a seal which was already worn from over-use. Alexander was sharp, clear and bright. His eyes shone with intelligence, his face was calm, his language precise, like a man who measured every word he heard or spoke. He had the brains, and balls to go with them.

Not so Serlo. Hazy of intellect, all he understood was bullying, if what Richer had heard in the castle and vill was true. Serlo was harsh but cowardly, the sort who might beat his wife or children. He enjoyed power, and threatened anyone weaker than himself. He had little enough actual courage, yet stronger men would look to their safety, for Serlo would bottle up his bitterness and let it rush out in a torrent of rage when his enemy was least expecting it. He'd employ a chance ambush, taking a defenceless man by surprise and beating him – or worse. Oh yes, a weak man could often be the most dangerous, as Richer knew.

The brothers' only saving grace was their loyalty to each other. Alexander had always taken immense pride in his younger sibling, and although Serlo was an evil brat, he could never see any wrong in him. All throughout their boyhood, Alex would forgive Serlo's peevishness, his avariciousness and cruelty. Whenever another lad sought to put Serlo right, Alexander would protect him; even when Serlo had stolen from another child, Alexander denied his guilt. It had started when the two boys had lost their mother – not that her death was an excuse. They were bad, both of them. What they wanted, they would take.

He could remember the pair of them from when he was young, and the stories about them and their father – and the death of their mother.

Their father, Almeric, had crowed over his firstborn, apparently, and had been prompted by the rector to name him after some King of ancient times; then, after many miscarriages, Serlo had been born too, their mother dying during childbirth and leaving their father broken-hearted. At once Alexander had taken responsibility for his sibling. A friend of Richer's mother had given birth not long before and was still in pap, so she wetnursed the new baby. When Serlo cried for milk, Alexander fetched her; Alexander changed his soiled clouts and washed them. It was Alexander who fed the child when he was weaned, and Alexander who taught him to walk, to play, and later to use a sling to bring down pigeons for the pot.

It was a lot for a youngster to cope with, but Almeric had been useless. Devastated by the death of his wife, he became jealous and resentful, as though he blamed everyone else in the world for her going. He grew into a tight-fisted, grasping soul who saw any money as his own, and only relinquished it with difficulty, as though handing it over was more painful than drawing a tooth. It was no surprise that afterwards his sons should have become so money-minded.

In a small vill like Cardinham, a man's behaviour towards his children was noticed and commented upon, and men often had to warn Almeric to stop chastising the boys. Richer could remember his own father going over there to restrain Almeric when he was drunk. The trouble was, Richer heard his father confide to the old blacksmith Iwan over a pot of cider, he had never forgiven Serlo for causing his wife's death, and could scarcely look at the boy without cursing him. When Alexander defended him, Almeric took his strap to Alexander too, reinforcing the unity of the pair, until they became as one, like two pieces of steel forge-welded by a smith, crushed together by the blows of fate until no man could have separated them.

The two lads had grown like that, bullied by their father, who relied on other men's wives to see to his children and growing ever more bitter. No matter how diligent he was in the search for more wealth, he remained poor. His general ineffectualness with his sheep and single ox meant that he was never in a position to improve his lot. Alexander had been loyal, though. He had defended his incompetent father before all the rest of the vill, resorting to fists from an early age. Once he had thumped Richer when he laughed at Almeric's foolish rage after one of his sheep had escaped from his fold and wandered onto the lord's lands. It ate the lord's corn, and was thus forfeit at a time when Almeric could least afford it. Alexander battered Richer unmercifully for that, but he wouldn't try that again in a hurry. Not now. Richer was stronger than both of them and had the protection of the lord of the manor.

Alexander was staring back at him now, with those curious, pale eyes of his. He had a way of staring that was unsettling; like a man who was so taken with concentrating on a single thought that normal human instincts were forgotten.

If it weren't for having met Athelina again, Richer could regret ever coming back to Cardinham. There was nothing for him here; the brothers ruled everything. Or had done. Perhaps now Squire Warin would make a difference.

Glancing about him, Richer tried to spot Athelina, but there were too many people in the church as the priest stood intoning the strange words of the language which only priests and religious understood. Richer often wondered if the words actually meant something. Monks and canons said that they did, but if a man couldn't understand words, didn't that prove they were meaningless?

No, there was no sign of her through the press of bodies in the nave. It was a shame. Athelina alone made his return worthwhile. She was older, a little worn, beset by a thousand fears and regrets, but within she was still the same loving woman he had known before. Her smile could outshine the sun, and seeing him again, she had lost that hunted look. She was, for a few moments at least, his lover from fifteen years ago. He could love her again. Perhaps he could marry her . . . she might accept him, even after all this time.

As Richer mused, he saw Serlo nudge his older brother again. They were scared; both of them. So they should be! If Richer could, he would put the wind up them infinitely more before many hours were past.

There were times when Alex could cheerfully have put his hands about his brother's neck and throttled him. The damned fool was so keen on antagonising other people.

However, it was hard to see what Serlo could have done this time. Richer had only recently reappeared, and he seemed to have taken up where they had all left off so many years ago, hating Serlo and Alex just as much as before. He couldn't blame them for the accident, surely. Then he saw Richer gaze about him expectantly. Perhaps that was it – Athelina! Yes, he'd loved her before he left, and maybe he hoped to pick up with her again, all these years later.

Whatever his gripe. Alexander wouldn't demean himself by exchanging nasty stares in the middle of the Mass. Instead he faced the altar again and relaxed. He was in God's House.

If only he could have taught poor Serlo to be more self-possessed. The trouble was, whenever he tried to correct him, his brother got upset – wore a confused, hurt expression as if to say, 'Can't I be praised even this once?' For Serlo, there could never be enough praise.

Perhaps it was all because he was so spoiled when he was younger. He didn't have to work as a child – not so much as Alexander – and didn't appreciate the efforts needed to protect himself and his family now that he was grown up.

Still, no matter what, Alexander would continue to protect him.

Alexander knew how to, and knew he must. There were always ways. And if Richer atte Brooke thought he could march back to his old vill and start throwing his weight about, he had another think coming.

As Father Adam lifted the cup of wine high over his head and muttered his incantation, Alex promised himself that he would personally draw Richer's guts if the man posed any threat to Serlo. He'd kill any man who threatened his little brother.

As Father Adam broke the bread, in the cottage nearby, beyond the broad green, there was a creaking. A rat scuttled under the door and squatted, sniffing, his nose twitching at the rich odours. Soon he lowered himself again and pattered silently along the edge of the floor until he reached the palliasse. There he stopped and sniffed again, and his tongue shot out to lick at the mess on the edge of the rough mattress.

When a gust of wind blew, the door rattled and the rat hesitated, but it wasn't that which made him pause and then scurry from the place: it was the slow and mechanical squeak from the rafter overhead.

The slow squeak of the hempen rope bound tightly about the woman's neck.

Chapter Three

The view here, so high on the moors, was splendid, and John never tired of it. His little Mass complete, he stood in the small churchyard at Temple and gazed about him as the tiny congregation departed homewards.

Here, staring out over the peaceful countryside, John was filled with a sense of ease, of all being well in his world. Strange to think that even a short time ago this had been such a sad place. On the orders of the Pope himself, the King had confiscated the manor and forcibly evicted those living here, for this had been the site of a flourishing little manor owned by the Knights Templar, the Order to which it still owed its name.

John was some eight and thirty years old now, so when the Knights were all arrested in France, he would have been twenty-one; that was back in 1307. The Knights were tortured to confess to their sins. Terrible they were, too – so foul, so heinous, as to deserve the censure of the whole world.

This little manor, like so many others, had been run by the Temple's lay Brothers. A wounded Knight might arrive every so often, to be rested and refreshed ready for another battlefield, but not many came here. Most remained nearer London, that great cesspit where all the world's malcontents eventually drifted. There the Templars had their great Temple. That was where the King had expected to find them when he was instructed by the Pope to arrest them all. However, Edward was a friend of the Knights. They'd helped him when he was younger, and he repaid them now, raising objections and dissenting from the French King's view that the Templars should be eradicated. Instead he gave them time to escape, and when he finally agreed to arrest those whom he could catch and was instructed to torture them all, he replied that England had no need of torture, and therefore, unlike the French, England had no trained torturers. It was illegal in the King's realm. He refused the Pope's offer of experts in such fields.

So for years King Edward II had procrastinated, against the wishes of God's own Vicar on Earth until, in the end, he submitted and confiscated the Templars' lands. Many had gone into exile. Some, it was believed, had gone to Scotland and repaid King Edward's support by joining his foes at Bannockburn. It was rumoured that the *Beauséant*, their white and black flag, had been seen there, although John was not the only man to disbelieve that. He had known many Templars, and yes, the bastards were as prickly and arrogant as only the truly rich and wellborn could be, but that didn't make them disloyal.

The Pope demanded that their lands should all go to the Hospitallers, but Edward had again demurred, and many, like this manor, had been held by him and parcelled out to his friends and members of his household. This one had gone to a friend of the Despensers, and because of Sir Henry of Cardinham's loyalty during the recent wars, he had carried some authority when there was a debate about who should be installed as the priest. Luckily for John, Sir Henry had carried the day, and John won the post. That was nearly ten years ago, when he was eight and twenty, already quite an old man for his first parish, but that didn't take away from the pride and delight he felt in possessing it.

And to Sir Henry's credit, he had never asked anything in return. Perhaps, John thought with a grin as he made his way out of the churchyard, the fellow was softening in his old age!

He was determined to keep himself hidden down here in Temple. As one opposed to the King, it was wise to maintain a low profile. That was partly why he had grown so angry when that silly chit Julia had admitted her pregnancy. It drew attention to the parish, would gain it a bad reputation. He could have imposed the *leyrwite*, of course – the fine imposed for women who were less chaste than they should be – but thank God, it proved unnecessary as Adam had been willing to take her. After all, imposing the *leyrwite* was no way to thank his master for this living. No, better that the silly girl took herself off to the parish where the father lived.

Mind, that was before John had realised his error with Adam. The other priest had turned out to be an equal embarrassment and threat to John's own safety. He could deal with it by reporting Adam to the rural dean, and yet that seemed too cruel. No, John would keep that threat up his sleeve for now.

For this magnanimity, John must live with the awareness of his danger at all times, for rumours could attach themselves even to the innocent.

Especially at a time when war was brewing.

The inhabitants of Cardinham left their church with their spirits uplifted by the priest's assurances of the wonderful life to come, during which all men and their women would be safe from hunger or cold, from fear or from sadness. The poorest today would be rich in Heaven, while the rich and powerful would be barred from Heaven's gates. They could wail and gnash their teeth as they were herded away, down to Hell.

Bolstered by this cheerful prospect, the peasants of the parish mingled at the church's yard before setting off homewards. Some, like those from Colvannick, had a walk of more than a mile back to their homes, and they were reluctant to set off immediately. Sunday was one of the few days when people could talk and enjoy themselves without fear of the lord's men noting their laziness and reporting them.

Serlo took a look about him and started off on his way.

'Something wrong, miller?' Richer called.

'Nothing.'

'Yet you seem in a hurry. Where are you going? Home to your lovely wife?'

'Leave her out of it!' Serlo answered. People, he saw, were listening. Many would like to see him pulled down a peg or two, he knew, and he curled his lip at old Iwan the smith and Gregory, his grandson, who were taking it all in. He felt hurt that they should listen so insolently – it reminded him of when he was young, and some of the older boys picked on him, taunting him about his father's drunkenness. In those days he was swift to burst into tears, and he was aware of a tingling at his eyes even now.

'What are you staring at?' he snapped peevishly. 'An old fool, and a young one, both listening to things that're none of their business. Go and join the women gossiping if you're hard up for news!'

'Anyone can listen to me,' Richer said mildly. 'I don't mind. You've been charging people for your own benefit instead of asking for the proper tolls, haven't you, Serlo? I think you ought to account for that missing money. We wouldn't want a thief to profit from his stealing, would we? The castellan wants to know what you've been up to.'

'Don't tell me that Gervase and Nicholas are bothered! This is nothing to do with them! I *own* the farm of the tolls. I bought it. No, this is all because of *you*! And there's only one reason a murderous hireling would be interested in my affairs.'

'A . . .' Richer felt his throat tighten with rage. 'And what would that be?'

'The same as any other *mercenary*. You're just looking to line your own pocket!'

The slur hurt, and Richer was about to punch the arrogance from his face, but better counsel prevailed. If he was to punish the slob, better that he should do so later, when there were fewer witnesses. 'Miller, I am no "hireling", as you put it, but I am loyal to my master, unlike you.'

'And you want to sit there to toll all travellers yourself, I suppose? It's no wonder you left no friends behind here when you fled the vill, Richer! You've none still, have you? Where's your big companion now? He take a dislike to you, same as all others with a brain?'

Alexander's wife Letitia was chatting to another woman when she overheard her brother-in-law's rising tone and sighed inwardly. It was only with an effort that she prevented herself from rolling her eyes in despair. Serlo, she was quite sure, would be the end of her husband. The fool could make an enemy of a saint.

She sought her husband, and seeing him in deep conversation with Adam, decided to save Serlo herself from making an even greater fool of himself than usual. Crossing the yard she smiled sweetly at Serlo. 'Brother, how are you this fine morning?'

The miller scarcely acknowledged her. 'You never married, did you, Richer?' he ranted on. 'Never had the money, I suppose. It's hard if you can't give a woman a stable life.'

Richer's smile returned, although it was a little glassy. 'You think I should be sorrowful? I am happy enough. What, should I be like an old gossip who sits at the gate to a vill and charges money for others to enter? I think not! And then to defraud his master . . .'

'I have defrauded no one!'

'Only a thief would steal from travellers,' Richer said, studying his fingers nonchalantly. 'Or from his own master.'

'You're a liar!' Serlo bellowed. 'I'll have your head, you black-hearted son of a lunatic and a—'

'You are in a churchyard!' Letitia hissed, staring frantically towards her husband. Something in her eyes must have caught his attention, for he immediately started moving towards them.

'It is well enough!' Richer said. 'Let all hear who wish to! I accuse this miller of taking gifts from people instead of the lord's tolls.'

'Still your mouth, you heap of dung!' Alexander hissed as he drew near. 'This language will have you fined in our lord's court, I swear. You leave our vill and return filled with new ideas and expect us to listen? I say I piss on your words, and I piss on you too! If you keep up this kind of malicious villeiny-saying, you'll find yourself in more trouble than you could imagine.'

'You think *I* am causing trouble?' Richer said mildly. 'I do nothing compared with your brother! He acts as thief, this miller, and you do not seek to stop him.'

'I am Constable here,' Alexander said. His eyes were glittering coldly, and he glanced about him as though to measure the support he might gain from others. 'I'll see to this.'

But he was too late.

'I'm no thief, you liar!' Serlo screamed, and to Letitia's disgust, she saw the spittle fly from his lips. He lurched forward, his fingers curling as though already feeling the gristle of Richer's neck in them.

Richer stepped aside, but his hand was at his dagger's hilt. 'Call off your pet, Constable, unless you want him to feel the sting of my blade. Call him off, I say!'

As Serlo tried to leap on him, old Iwan grabbed one arm and held it in a vice-like grip; the other arm was gripped by Iwan's son Angot. They held Serlo firmly while he roared at Richer: 'You threaten *me*? You accuse *me*? Iwan, let me *go*, you old bastard! Richer, I'll have your ballocks in my purse for this!'

'Oh you will, will you?' Richer said coolly. 'Friend Serlo, if you try to harm me, I swear that within the hour, I'll see you in Hell. You go back to threatening children and your wife, *little* man – leave real men alone. We deserve more capable fighters than cowards like you!'

He stepped forward, letting his hand fall away from his knife, and as he passed Alexander, he held the man's gaze, speaking low.

'Keep that piece of shit away from Athelina in future, understand? Otherwise all this will come straight to the attention of the lord of the manor. I swear it. Leave her alone, and leave her safe, or I'll ruin you.'

Letitia heard his words, but did not know what he meant by them. Athelina had little to do with her or Alex, apart from living in one of the houses which Alex and Serlo owned. In any event, Alex wouldn't have harmed her. Since losing his own mother, he had taken great care to protect other mothers so far as was possible.

Then she saw Richer's expression as he stared at her husband. That was when she understood. Richer didn't care about *Serlo*. His words may have been aimed at Serlo, but their import was intended for Alex. This man Richer had returned here after many years abroad; now it appeared that he and Alex hated each other. Why, she had no idea, but she was sure that Richer was threatening her man. It should have worried her. Richer was one of the men-at-arms at the castle, after all, but she couldn't be anxious about Alex. He was too sensible and self-assured. No matter how dangerous Richer might be, she was convinced that Alex and she could meet the threat head-on. He was the Constable of the vill, when all was said and done, and Letitia was more than capable of helping him.

But, she acknowledged with a sigh, her brother-in-law was a different matter. Serlo was forever causing problems for them, starting brawls in the tavern, insulting men and women as though he was safe from prosecution, and now he had even threatened one of the castle's men in full view of the vill.

It was clear that he detested Richer with a loathing that went much more than skin deep. And, as usual, it would be the protection of Alex's brother which would cause the friction between herself and her husband, she saw with a swift intuition. So be it.

'Yes, Serlo, you leave me alone before you get hurt,' Richer said more loudly again, with a chuckle in his voice. 'And in the meantime, I look forward to the next court in our lord's hall, if you persist in taking gifts. You're reducing the amount he can expect from his tolls, by reducing the charge, and he won't like that.'

He tapped his dagger's hilt meaningfully and then stepped back a few paces, his eyes still on Alexander and Serlo, before he span on his heel and left.

Alexander put his hand through his wife's crooked arm. 'Come, my dear, we should get back to our home,' he said. 'Serlo, you should join us. Would you care for some wine and meats?'

'No. No, I'm going to get on home,' Serlo said, shrugging off the hands of those who had held him fast. 'Next time you try to hold me, I'll punch some sense into your heads, you . . .'

Iwan smiled at him, his wrinkled old face unperturbed. 'Oh yes? You'll punch sense into me, will 'ee, Serlo Almeric's son? You try it, fellow. And when you've come round, you can remember to be polite to your elders. Just think on: you're in *our* tithing. If you break the King's Peace, it's goin' to be me and Angot here who knock some sort of sense into *your* thick head, because we won't pay fines for your stupidity.'

Alexander broke in quickly. 'Don't threaten him in my presence, Iwan. I won't have it. If a man misbehaves in this vill, I'll tell him, and I'll bring it to the attention of Gervase at the castle, too.'

'Oh, I weren't threatenin' him,' Iwan remarked happily. 'I were just tellin' 'im 'ow it were to be.'

Serlo spat at the ground at Iwan's feet, then barged the old man from his path. Alexander saw Iwan's fist clench, and snarled, 'Iwan, leave it!'

'Weren't doin' nothin',' came the reply, Iwan's blue eyes opened wide in innocence, and as Serlo disappeared from view, Alexander turned from the church and made his way homewards, his arm still linked with that of his wife.

As the two made their stately progress home from the church, Gervase, the steward at the castle, finished his discussion with the cook about the meals for that day and strolled downstairs, just in time to see Lady Anne and her maids leaving the chapel.

She was still small, neat and perfect, he thought. This was the woman who had come between him and his only real friend, Nicholas the castellan, first by taking Nick from him, then by stopping him from indulging in those lengthy debates which both had enjoyed so much. They had invariably been drunken affairs, meandering on late into the night; during which they had spoken of manor business and then, as the wine flowed more freely, the politics of the nation. Nick was of a mind with their lord, that the Despensers must be curbed before they took over the whole kingdom, while Gervase held the pragmatic view that it was better to have the Despensers as tyrants ruling all, including the King, because that meant the kingdom was quiet and secure. Any move to restrain them could only lead to war again, and that was to be avoided at all costs. Their disagreements never led to anger on either side. Both could lay down their opinions without offending the other.

But Lady Anne had not enjoyed having her husband arrive drunk in her bed each night, and she had sweetly suggested that they should use different rooms, if he wished to carouse the night away with his old companion. So, as Nick said, 'just for a little while' they'd best drop the custom.

This was only the first of the signs that Gervase had lost his friend. Nick started to take breakfast in his bedchamber with his wife rather than in the hall where the two men had been wont to discuss their plans for the day. Now commands came down from Nick, often an embarrassed Nick, which indicated to Gervase that it was his wife who had demanded changes to the steward's list of chores.

At first Gervase had accepted all this in good heart, knowing that it was only right and fair that Nick should be allowed to enjoy his wife. No one should come between a man and his woman. Gervase knew that well enough.

'Master steward! Good morning. It is a fine one, isn't it?'

He fixed a smile to his face and nodded briefly. 'My lady, yes. And you look magnificent.'

'You flatter me,' she said shyly. As so often before, he felt his heart lurch as her gaze darted away from him as though she was ashamed, or fearful, of seeing too much. It was said that the eyes were the windows to a man's soul; well, she was ever scared of seeing love in another's face.

It was no surprise, he reflected. She was temptation made flesh. Perfect in all ways, from her flawless skin to the slim, lithe body beneath her tunic, she was enough to make any man forget his oaths.

'No man could flatter you, Lady Anne. Flattery supposes that the comments are not merited, and in your case they are.'

She returned her gaze to him then, a smile on her lips. 'I thank you.'

He watched as she moved away, still captivated by the thought of that lovely body . . . before he was wrenched back by the memory of the pain he had suffered, the loss of his best friend, and the betrayal.

It hurt so much, he could weep.

Chapter Four

Walking quickly, Richer left the churchyard and made his way along the path towards the castle. He had not gone above a hundred paces when at the bend in the road where the trees obscured the view, his companion Warin appeared suddenly at his side.

'Christ's tears, I wish you wouldn't *do* that!' Richer declared. 'The way you appear, it's enough to make a man have a fit!'

His friend glanced at him. 'Why? You think I'm more likely to give a man a fit than you? It wasn't me who tweaked the tail of that little monkey.'

'It wasn't only *his* tail I was tweaking,' Richer said smugly. 'It was his brother's.'

'Don't forget,' his friend said unsmilingly, 'that this is not an affair which concerns only you.'

'I am aware of that.'

'Good. If you upset the Constable and his brother, it may have unfortunate consequences for the tithing and the manor, and I cannot allow that.' Warin's voice was sharper this time.

Richer had rarely heard his tone so cool. The man was a squire, yes, and of course he had a legitimate interest in the workings of the manor and in the loyalties of the peasants because of his position with the castle, but Richer felt as though he had been deserted by his oldest companion. Their relationship had been one of mutual trust, rather that of friends or brothers than squire with his man-at-arms. To hear Warin speak so was enough to make Richer feel as he did when he prepared to ride into a battle: an awareness of danger to come.

'This business of the tolls should interest the castle,' he said. 'I don't understand why the steward does nothing about it.'

Warin frowned. 'Don't change the subject. We're talking about *you*. This matter goes much deeper than the foolishness of a tollkeeper. It is an ancient feud.'

'I never liked him,' Richer answered simply. 'And now, seeing how he's treated my woman, I dislike him all the more.'

'*Your* woman? You left her fifteen years ago, you tell me she has two brats from her dead husband, and still you call her yours?'

'She may be mine again,' Richer said seriously, but then he looked up at his squire and grinned. 'Don't worry about Serlo – he's no real danger to us. Alex is the one with the brain. He'll understand that all I want is to see Athelina safe, remaining in her house. They'll work out for themselves that it's better to do what I want, rather than have me making trouble for them. If they leave her alone, I'll leave them alone.'

'The two brothers together could be a risk. They are upsetting the folk about here with their depredations. They are like those other thieving devils, Despenser and his father,' Warin growled. 'If you keep up this affair of trying to settle an old score, Serlo might decide to harm you. Perhaps even waylay and kill you.'

'Not while we are at the castle. Even they wouldn't do anything while we live under Nicholas's protection. He's the representative of Sir Henry. No one would dare to gainsay him in the lord's own manor.'

'Perhaps.' Warin's eyes were a curious light hazel colour with green flecks. When those eyes were fired with rage, they glittered like gold shot through with emerald. Although he was large and strongly built, he was no dullard, like some of the blockheads who regularly fought in the lists, but an intelligent and educated man. Now he turned on Richer a look which seemed to shear through his words like a sword through butter.

Richer's laugh was less certain under that scrutiny. ' "Perhaps" – nothing! And while I'm here, I won't have the pair of them robbing everyone including their master!'

'Very well, but I don't wish the area to be unsettled. This used to be a stable, secure place. I want it to remain so.'

'Yes, Squire, and I shall see to it.'

'Good,' Warin said. 'With Despenser running the land there are already too many problems in the realm without us seeking to create more here in the manor.'

'The problems aren't of my making,' Richer protested. 'I didn't tell the miller to ask us for a gift.'

'Yet you are happy enough to continue the argument, aren't you? And you'd like to smack Serlo's fat face, wouldn't you, friend Richer?'

Those unsettling eyes were on him again, and Richer had to shrug in agreement.

He had always disliked Almeric's family. Then, when he had suffered his own personal disaster and lost everyone belonging to him, it seemed cruel and unjust that they should have remained in Cardinham and prospered while he was absent. It served to make his dislike more intense.

Alexander and Serlo had been nasty pieces of work from as early as Richer could remember. Never the sort to leave the vill and make their own way in the world, they preferred to remain in the backwater where they had been sired and whelped, making themselves kings of this little territory. But like kings of many another small land, their rule was permanently at risk. Alexander liked to believe that he was master of the vill because he was the Constable; Serlo liked to believe that he was a prince among his peers because his brother ran things.

The brothers had managed to acquire much power and influence here, by judicious use of gossip, spreading malicious tales about others in order to enhance their own positions. When all else failed, they resorted to threats of violence, but from what Richer had seen, that was a rare occurrence. Most people in the vill didn't bother to argue.

If they demanded a piece of land to graze their animals, the farmer would give way. It was easier than preventing them. And in that way, they encroached on other men's lands and increased their flocks. Small parcels were borrowed, and then after some months or a year the neighbour might see that they had put up a fence to prevent their sheep escaping, and soon that fence became a wall and hedge, and then Alexander would claim that since he'd been using the land for so long, it was easier to include it on his lands, and how much would the farmer want for it? All too often the farmer would agree to let him make use of the land because, as Alexander said, it was better for the manor that his profits were kept high, since they formed such a large part of the manor's total profit.

Aye, Richer thought, the two had come a long way from the young lads who had been so fearful of their father, a man so drunken and stupid, he couldn't even keep his sheep in their fold.

Warin appeared to think he had made his point and was silent for the rest of their march, but Richer was not persuaded that he was happy. Warin did not like the mess that was this little manor. There was too much corruption, and too many intense rivalries.

And they still had business with Nicholas, of course. Perhaps that was what occupied the squire's thoughts: how to make him bow to Warin's will.

On the Monday following these events, Simon and Baldwin bade farewell to the morose young ostler; they sent him on his way with two pennies instead of the one they had agreed on as a fee. When he received the money, he stared at the coins as though in disbelief at their niggardliness, before shaking his head in disgust and mounting his horse, leading the others away with him.

Soon Simon and Baldwin were on their way again, this time with a fellow who was as different from their last stony-faced companion as he could be; this one appeared unable to keep his mouth shut.

Ivo was an engaging youth, perhaps fifteen years old. He wore a pair of hosen that were far too large for him and which rumpled about his knees alarmingly. They were tied to his belt underneath his tunic, a bright blue-coloured wool garment which looked warm and comfortable. On his head he wore a coif with a hood, which he was constantly pulling up over his forehead, and then shaking it free, as though he was practising the best method of removing it whenever he had an opportunity.

When the hood was down, Simon saw that the lad had an unruly shock of tallow-coloured hair over his long, thin face. It was the sort of face Simon would have expected to see on a clerk: pale, with hooded eyes, high cheeks and a long nose, small mouth, and a chin which was all but non-existent – but for all that Ivo was enormously cheering company. He plainly enjoyed telling and hearing stories, the more bawdy the better. Already Simon had heard two tales of an alewife and her lovers, together with a couple of crude verses based upon a miller who tried to rob a pair of northern clerics of their grain, but who was bested by them when they slept with the miller's wife and daughter before the daughter took pity on them and showed them where their grain had been hidden.

Simon's amusement was only enhanced by the often repeated expression of shock on Baldwin's face. It was rare that a villein on Baldwin's land would have dared utter such talk in his presence, Simon realised, and although the knight was used to hearing such language from convicted felons, he was entirely unprepared to hear it from a boy who was his servant.

They had slept well at Bodmin, and found that their route out of the town took them up a hill and over a pleasantly sheltered way, with spreading oaks and beech trees high overhead, and strong turf hedges at either side. Soon, however, these started to disappear, and the path, although well-trodden, became noticeably less well-maintained. This far from the town, the farmsteads and vills were more widely separated, and Simon couldn't help but wonder how safe it was. His eyes were drawn to tree-trunks and bushes, looking for ambushes.

'The Keeper of the King's Peace down here doesn't seem to pay much attention to the law on keeping the verges clear,' Simon noted.

Baldwin, who was himself the Keeper for the Crediton area, smiled. 'Perhaps he feels it is far enough from danger down here?'

'More fool him, then. A felon can attack here as easily as in Buckinghamshire. Vigilance isn't a matter of relying on good fortune,' Simon grunted. 'Pirates could land at the shore and attack; a peasant can turn outlaw here as easily as a man from Exeter.'

'True enough,' Baldwin nodded.

'Did you ever hear the story about the apple-selling girl who accused the vintner of taking her virginity?' the ostler asked eagerly.

Simon was taken off-balance. 'What was that?'

'See, she's teased by him into his bed, right?' Ivo continued happily. 'She wouldn't have gone with him, but he promises her five pounds in gold, he wants her so much. So afterwards, next morning, she says, "Right, you've had your fun, where's my money?" but he says, "Last night was so good, I'll have you again tonight. Stay here, pretty maid, and let us play again." She says, "I can't stay, and I won't stay! Pay me like you promised," but he isn't having any of that. He says, "If you won't stay, I'm not paying." So she goes to the court, says this vintner he promised her five pounds in "cellarage" for a night, and she wants her money.

'Well, the Justice sends for the vintner, and he responds quick, like, to explain why he hasn't paid up. The vintner says, "I would have paid on possession, but didn't use it. I never put anything into her cellar, other than one poor pipe of wine." Right? Get it? To this she says, quick as a flash, "You had two full butts with you which you left at the door – why ever didn't you bring *them* in?" See? He'd two butts outside – you get it?'

Simon and Baldwin exchanged a look.

While Ivo roared his delight at the joke, Baldwin muttered, 'This fellow is more degenerate than many a man twice his age.'

Serlo hadn't been away from the mill all day. There were no travellers so far, and his wife Muriel was alarmed to see his mood. There were days when he could be a devil, and if this was one of them, she'd give him as good as he gave. She'd had enough of being trampled on like a slave.

In the late morning she called him for his lunch. He came stomping into the house, standing at their fire and staring down at the flames. The mill was warm enough for him, because running about and lifting the heavy sacks made his blood course faster, but when Muriel herself went in, she felt the cold eat into her bones. The air was always icy that close to the water, and even on a hot summer's day, the sun couldn't warm the mill.

Once, she had asked her husband why he didn't light a fire, and he had sneered at her foolishness. The fine powder would explode, he told her. If he had a fire in the mill, just the merest spark could set the whole place ablaze.

It was a terrible thought. Muriel had stared about the place with alarm, suddenly struck with a fear that her sons could come in here and be hurt. Of course Aumery was only four years old, and Hamelin a matter of eight months, so they wouldn't be likely to play with fire yet, but young boys were always trouble, and they might, in the future, be silly enough to do something stupid. This was just one more thing for her to worry about.

'Do you want some drink, Husband?' she said at length. Hamelin was settled against her, nuzzling at her breast. Without thinking, she opened her tunic and let him suckle, smiling down at him, feeling the warmth of her love for her child.

'Yes. Ale,' Serlo responded, busy with a jammed block and tackle.

Still feeding her child she filled a jug one-handed and took it back to Serlo, setting it down on the table near him. There was a loud rumbling and the constant sound of water from the mill nearby, but they were reassuring sounds. While she could hear them, she knew that there was food for them, that there would be a store through the winter, and that they should survive through to the spring. Hunger was a terrible affliction, and Muriel could all too easily remember the horrors of the famine.

Yes, sitting here, she could be content. As the trees swayed gently outside in the soft breezes, occasional gleams of sunlight darted in at the window, making the dusty interior glow with a godly light, as though He was indicating His own pleasure. Meanwhile her child supped at her, instilling that feeling of maternal wonder and pride that always made her so happy.

Serlo ignored her, glowering at the block as he tried to release it. He said nothing as Muriel sniffed at Hamelin's backside, which smelled again. She settled him on a mat near the fire and pulled his legs apart, untying the clout and throwing it from his reach before wiping him clean and binding a fresh shred of cloth about him. The old clout she put in a bucket out by the door ready to be washed later, and then she filled a pot with ale for herself and sank down to stir the pottage.

She spent much of her time these days feeling tired. The effort of looking after the two boys was draining, especially while she was still breastfeeding. And their father was so sullen. He was more uncommunicative than ever since little Danny had died. As though that wasn't bad enough, she had the clenching ache in her womb that spoke of her monthly time coming. She would have to wash all the clouts today to make sure that there were enough for her as well as for Ham. She longed for the baby to be clean. Some were clean at two years, she knew; her Aumery had been one of them.

If only her husband were prepared to help – even a little. Just to take the two boys off with him for a morning or so, so that Muriel could get on with her washing. But he wouldn't, and to be fair, Muriel knew full well that she'd never trust him with her children . . . *their* children. He was too forgetful.

In the past he had been different. A kind, considerate lover to her when he wooed her, he had grown more distant since their wedding. Over the last year since Dan's death he'd been really morose. Now there was seldom a chance for them to spend time alone together, apart from when he wanted her. Then he could be charming for a while. But only for a while. After that, when he was done, he'd roll over and start to snore, sated. A good meal, a pleasing congress, and he was content.

'We need some—' she began, but he cut through her speech like a saw through wood.

'You always want more money, woman! When will you get it into your thick skull that we don't have enough?'

'We do quite well!' She retorted, hurt. 'We'll have more when folk start bringing us their new grain.'

'That isn't going to be enough – not if you keep asking for more all the time! And those brats want feeding and clothing, damn them both!' he shouted, his face red with frustration. 'Christ's balls, there must be a way to get more.'

His voice trailed off and Muriel watched him silently. Better to wait than incur his wrath.

'I could try it,' he muttered thoughtfully, his low brow creased with the effort.

'What, dear?'

'Ask Lady Anne to cough up – to pay me for my silence. She's no better than any other, but she wouldn't want her name spoiled by me.'

'What do you mean?' she asked again. There was something in his cunning expression that alarmed her.

'Don't you worry, maid. She'll pay – otherwise the castellan might learn what I know of his wife.'

'The castellan . . . Husband, be careful! Nicholas would have you in his court as soon as look at you, and then where would we be?'

'Don't be a fool, woman! The castellan's wife will do anything to make sure others don't hear of her adultery. What, would she allow her husband to find out he's got a cuckoo in the nest? If he learned that another man knew his wife, he'd kill her.'

Aumery was listening, and he repeated slowly, 'Another man knew his . . .' before Serlo slapped him around the head.

He picked up his son and stared into his eyes. 'Don't ever say that again. Not while I'm alive, boy. You repeat that to anyone while I'm living, and I'll break your head!'

Muriel took her son from him, now shivering with tiny sobs of terror and gentled him. 'Daddy didn't mean it, Aumie. He just didn't want you to tell anyone what you heard. It's secret.'

'I meant it,' Serlo grated. 'While I live, I'll kill anyone who talks about it.'

Simon and Baldwin had ridden alongside a river and continued up the trail. It was, like most of the roadways in Devonshire, a poor track. Grasses grew thickly all about it apart from the edge where horses' hooves had cut into the turf. The soil was thick and dusty, even close to the stream, while every so often swirling flies attacked their exposed flesh. At one point they passed a large byre, and here the buzzing of flies was deafening. Swarms rose into the air from the dung as they passed, and Baldwin put his arm about his nose and mouth. Flies were to him repellent; although he was immune to Simon's dread of corpses, Baldwin had seen flies too often about the faces and bodies of dead men to want them to touch him. War had scarred him: the raking knife-cut on his face was the least of his wounds, but sometimes he thought that the scars were mostly in his mind.

Now, having passed through an area of thicker woodland, they found signs of coppicing. Although the road narrowed a little, they had better views afforded them by the thinning trees, and up ahead there was the unmistakable sight of smoke. This could only mean a village. There was too much smoke for it to have come from one homestead. Baldwin, like Simon, stared ahead keenly.

Villages should be places of safety, but all too often a stranger was viewed as a threat, even on a road which was, theoretically at least, as busy as this. This way was the most important route from Bodmin and the whole of the far western side of Cornwall to Devonshire, so it was supposed to be busy – not that Simon and Baldwin had seen much evidence of other travellers. If the folk hereabouts weren't very used to seeing people, they might be less than welcoming.

'What do you know of this place, Ivo?' Baldwin asked their guide.

'Cardinham? The normal haunt of churls and fools,' Ivo said with the contempt of a town-dweller for a peasant community. 'They are harmless, though.'

'Good,' Baldwin said. 'Let's go and see what sort of reception we merit, eh, Simon?'

Chapter Five

Having few duties that morning, Richer walked with his companion to the house which had a bush of furze tied to a post above its door. 'Ale!' he shouted.

'If you want ale, you can ask for it like a man of manners, and not bellow like a lovesick ox,' the alewife Susan called out firmly.

'Woman, you have two men dying of thirst out here,' Richer said.

'I doubt it. Oh, so it's you, Richer'. A small, mousy-haired woman appeared, with a gap between her front teeth and a few too many wrinkles, but attractive nonetheless. 'Who's your friend?' she asked.

'This is my master, Squire Warin.'

'It is, is it?' said the woman, peering at the man. 'I've heard much of you, Squire.'

Richer knew that there was good reason for her to stare, just as there was good reason for Serlo to be fearful at the sight of the man beside him. Squire Warin was a sight to behold, the stuff of some women's dreams. Tall, with the broad shoulders and thickened neck of one used to charging with the lance, he had thighs as thick as a woman's waist, and a chest like a barrel. His features were craggy and square, the jaw heavy, as though he could bite through stone. When he was angered, Richer had seen the great muscles at the side of his head knotting until his entire head looked like a clenched fist.

Now he was not angry, and feeling safe enough from the scrutiny of a woman like this, Squire Warin was content to treat her to a wide grin. 'Lady, do you object to serving men of common fame like me?'

'No,' she said, although doubtfully. 'I suppose not. Although I'm surprised you've not been in here before. You've been living in Cardinham more than a month.'

'The ale at the castle is good,' Warin smiled, 'but if I had known that your tavern held such an obvious attraction, I should have come here much sooner.'

Sue winked at Richer. 'You taught him well, Rich. He can flatter as well as you! What's it to be? A quart of ale each?'

'That would be good,' Richer said easily.

She went off, and was soon back carrying a great jug and two mazers. 'Try some of this. It's good, I'll wager. It was made for the harvesting, and it's near perfect.'

Squire Warin took a long swallow. 'It is good,' he said, his approval echoed by Richer. 'It is your own brew?'

'Who else would make it?'

'Your husband? I had heard you were married?'

'To a wastrel, yes. He lived here for a while,' she said, her face setting rigidly for a moment. Then, like a cloud passing from the sun's face, the mood left her and she chuckled slightly. 'Then I booted him out. He drank all the ale he could, spent money on buying drinks for others, took my purse when he had little left himself, and near lost me this house. It was my parents' place, you see. Well, he's gone now. I won't have him back.'

'I see.'

'I doubt it. So, that's my story . . . why are *you* here?'

Richer coughed into his ale. 'Woman, don't think to question a nobleman!' he spluttered.

'Why? What's so wrong about asking that?' she asked with a sly glance.

'I think you know already,' Squire Warin said. 'My lord

died, and I was without a master for a while, but then I was sent here, and Nicholas at the castle has taken me on as a guard.'

'You are lordless?' she asked, eyeing his rich clothing. 'And yet you seek to make trouble.'

'Me?' Warin rumbled.

'Richer does, and you'd support him, wouldn't you?' she countered.

Richer smiled at her. 'We seek no trouble at all.'

'Really? Yet you want to pick a fight, don't you?'

'You mean Serlo? He has been robbing the vill for too long. If he steals from your lord, the lord will fine everyone here. But he takes money from strangers as gifts so that they don't have to pay tolls; when he is discovered, everyone else will be forced to pay. Is that fair?'

'As fair as life usually is,' she countered. 'Ah, but I don't know. I can't care. I don't know how many summers I've seen in my time, but I don't suppose I'll see many more. What is it to me if you pick a fight with him?'

'I don't want to fight him, just expose him,' Richer said. In truth he didn't want either. All he wanted was for Athelina to be safe in her home, secure from Serlo's threats and unreasonable demands for money. It was Serlo who'd suggested that she should whore for the money. Richer could remember the rising fury when she had told him that. It had made him want to go and slaughter the miller on the spot.

He hadn't seen her for some days now. He'd been busy, of course, with his duties as a man-at-arms, but when he had gone to the house, it had been empty. Only last night he'd banged on the door, but before he could push it open, he'd seen old Iwan watching him, and the awareness that entering a woman's home uninvited was improper and could give rise to rumours of her incontinence, made him stop and walk away.

Susan was watching him carefully. 'If you upset those two, it'll end in a fight, mark my words. And even you might find it hard to defend yourself against both together.'

As Sue spoke, had she but known it, three travellers were approaching the tollgate over the miller's bridge.

Serlo heard them from his little cottage and cocked his head. Aumery, his older son, was whining about something or other, but a flick from Serlo's hand to the boy's head and, 'If you don't shut up, I'll give you something to cry about!' soon made him silent. Muriel hurried to the snot-nosed brat and soothed him, watching Serlo with wide, bitter eyes.

Yes, it *was* horses. Hopefully, Serlo rose and hurried out through the door and over to the gate. Once there, he leaned on it and gazed westwards down the lane. The road bent immediately after the bridge, and although there were few trees there lining the stream's banks, they stood rank behind rank, obliterating any view of the roadway.

Surely this must be merchants, or a pair of fellows hurrying to a market? Serlo's face was wreathed in smiles at the prospect of making a little money. And Christ's tears, he could do with it! Muriel was always on at him, as if he needed that sort of nagging when he was already worried about Richer. She should learn to keep her trap shut.

There was a flash of colour through the trees. Yes, it was two – no, *three* men on horseback! Serlo felt his mood slip a little, because so many might be able to dispute his right to charge anything, just as Richer had. Then he shrugged. If they did, there was little he could do to change that. They shouldn't, anyway. Most didn't.

The leading rider was a bluff-looking fellow, big in the saddle, wearing a green tunic with pale red hosen. Behind him was another man, one with a thin line of dark beard following his jaw, wearing a blue tunic, red hosen and a floppy-brimmed green hat. The last rider was clearly a servant, clad in tatty ochre-coloured tunic and hosen. No other men, no one on foot. Yes, Serlo reckoned, this was an easy mark.

'Masters!' he roared as the men approached. 'Godspeed!'

'Godspeed,' replied the leading man, his eyes all about the place as though suspecting an ambush. 'What is this, friend?'

'My master built this bridge from his own funds, and he collects tolls to help pay for it.'

'Does he have permission?' asked the second man. He spurred his horse on, and studied Serlo. His eyes seemed black and intense, and Serlo felt nervous of meeting that flat, determined stare.

'Permission, master? I suppose so. This is his manor, after all.'

'I should like to speak to him about this, then, and see the authority which permits him to charge travellers at will.'

Serlo smiled and ducked his head. 'If you don't want to pay, masters, maybe I could help? Give me a halfpenny, instead of the penny toll each, and I'll forget you passed this way.'

'So you would halve our fee?' the bearded man asked quietly. Suddenly his horse jerked his head, and Serlo found that the man had approached the gate with an angry set to his face. 'Do you mean to say that you would betray your master's trust, churl? Would you forget his tolls in order to make your own profit?'

'I am trying to help you, that's all,' Serlo said. He regretted not bringing his cudgel with him now. 'If you don't want my help, go back the way you came, and find another route. It's nothing to me!'

'My name is Sir Baldwin of Furnshill. I command you to open that gate now, fool, before I ride both it and you down! Be silent! Open the gate at once in the name of the King! I am a Keeper of the King's Peace, and I swear this to you now: when I see your master I shall enquire as to the legality of this tollgate, and if I learn that it is not legal, I shall return to question you.'

He was leaning low over his horse's neck now, his eyes fixed upon Serlo like a snake's upon a rabbit, and Serlo was petrified. The movement of the rider's hand towards his sword-hilt decided him. There was nothing he could do to defend himself against a knight trained in battle. With a bad grace, he lifted the bar once more and hauled the gate wide, keeping behind it. 'I'll tell my master of this,' he muttered sulkily. 'He won't be happy.'

'When I have told him you are stealing from him, I should doubt that he will be,' Baldwin said coldly. 'And I have little doubt that his mood will match mine perfectly.'

It had all happened – her marriage, security, and then the child – as though by accident: that was how Anne thought of it, when she did at all. She considered her past life only rarely. Some superstitious instinct warned her that such things might again become reality, were she to consider them too deeply, and she had no desire to relive her life. For her, now was all. She asked no more than this.

The manor where she had been born was by the coast, a windswept place of moors and woods, wonderful to play in. Anne had many friends, and now, recalling those times, she could see Sal, Emmie and Chris, always smiling. Each summer was filled with laughter beneath the bright heavens.

But then the King attacked the Scottish. Her father went to join the King's host, as had so many, but he never came back. He died without even seeing the battlefield, for a man told Anne's mother that he had fallen prey to a disease, and was buried in a church in Exeter.

Disaster was striking all, not only Anne's family. The rains, which had been expected during the winter, never stopped through the following summer. The men went to work the fields, and returned encased in mud. Their faces, hands and bodies were smothered in it. Boots rotted, hosen became loose, flapping things, and even the men's legs became whitened and wrinkled like hands left too long in a stream. There were few men to labour, for many had died in Scotland, so the women must help, and the children. Anne and her mother spent their days in the fields.

First to die was Chris. It was a surprise when one of their party disappeared; it was hard to believe. They all knew what death meant, of course, they saw it all about them, but it happened to the very young or ancient, not to a girl of nearly marriageable age like Chris. Her thin frame worked hard to help bring in the harvest, but as the crop rotted black on the stems, she lost all hope. One day she simply didn't waken.

Next was Sal. She died early the following year as the rain continued unabated. There had been little grain to keep back for planting the following year, but the vill had, by starving themselves and rationing, saved sufficient. The lord of the manor had to buy in grain; his farms wouldn't support him, and if there wasn't enough for him, there was less to share amongst his peasants. At least he could *afford* to buy food; Anne's mother couldn't. She died one day while working. Anne saw her crouch and cough, a hand over her mouth. Then she settled herself at a tree and closed her eyes. When Anne went to wake her later, she saw the eyes wide in the skull-like face, the mouth slack, the hands like claws resting in her lap. There just hadn't been enough energy for her to continue living.

That was when hopelessness overwhelmed her. She believed she would die too, and when she was told that the vill couldn't afford to feed her – the food was needed to keep the men working – she accepted the decision without complaint. Taking her mother's shawl and a knife, she walked into the rain. She was sure that she was walking to her death, and hoped that she would soon see her mother and father again in Heaven.

Her luck was about to change. A man met her on the road and offered her shelter at his inn if she agreed to service his clients.

For a while at least she had food, if no rest or peace, but then the innkeeper evicted her – she ate too much, he said – and she was left to wander again. She sat mournfully at the roadside outside his inn, wondering what to do, once more anticipating, and almost welcoming, death.

But the idea took hold that she might at least see her father's grave before she died. She set off eastwards, and soon was overtaken by a band of strangers. There were pedlars, pilgrims on their way to Canterbury, a brace of men-at-arms, and a friar, all seeking to escape starvation. Gladly she joined them, and the warriors shared a loaf with her, but later the friar tried to rape her. Fleeing, she ran into one of the men-at-arms, who protected her, but told her that she wasn't safe. 'The man's desperate to have you, wench. You'd best be gone, 'cos by Christ's passion, if you stay in the same group as him, he'll take you, and you won't be able to accuse him. No one wins by accusing a goddamned friar.'

His words made her want to seek safety away from the group, but she didn't know how. Shortly afterwards, they happened to pass the castle at Cardinham.

It was mere good fortune. The rain started again as they left Bodmin, and Cardinham was the first place they reached. Although the Constable – this was before Alexander's time – had said that they could sleep in the Church House, one of the pedlars had known of the castle and asked that the castellan be told of their plight. He hoped that not only would they be granted a warmer room to sleep in, but that they might also be given food and drink.

As soon as she saw this place, Anne had felt safe. It exuded stolid reliability in a way that she hadn't known since her father's death. She felt its all-encompassing sense of sanctuary like a warm blanket. Surely there must be a place for her here.

An old-fashioned strongpoint, Cardinham Castle was a simple tower on its own great mound of earth and rock, enclosed within a broad courtyard surrounded by a strong wooden palisade. The gateway gave out onto a long corridor that followed the line of the outer palisade to a barbican, which had its own doors at the farther end. Any man intending to break into the castle would have to force those doors, run the gauntlet of the corridor while weapons rained upon him, and then try to break down the second doors into the bailey. Not an easy task. This place had the appearance of a stronghold that was impregnable without a large force and heavy artillery, but on that day as she approached it for the first time, Anne saw only a place of serenity.

There was no one on the walls in this weather, with the rain tipping down, but at the southern entrance of the arched gateway there burned two torches, cheerily illuminating the gate. It made her feel glad just to see them, even though the rain drummed ever more loudly and the trickle of damp running down her back became a small torrent.

Inside was a gatehouse with a smiling, sympathetic keeper. He sent a boy for the castellan, and the man who was to be her husband came to meet them.

To Anne, Nicholas was a bearlike fellow, strong, hearty, sure-footed and calm. He looked a lot like her father, with the same bold features and quick eye, but was more cultured and more gentle. Anne noticed that he avoided her after a brief intro-duction. He glanced at her when they first arrived, he looked at her again when she was dried and when they sat down to eat, but for the rest of the time he spoke to only the men from her party. Even the pedlars were treated respectfully, which appeared to surprise some and scare others, but Anne was ignored, probably because she was nothing more than a bedraggled peasant. It wasn't hurtful. Any great man would ignore the lowliest wench unless he wanted her to warm his bed. It was a relief in some ways, after her experiences at the brothel, and on the road with the monk.

Gervase, the steward at the castle, was different. She saw him on the first afternoon, when he arrived to offer the travellers dry clothing. There was a laundress with him, who took their old stuff to be dried on lines in the stables. As soon as Gervase saw her, he smiled broadly and began to make fun of her. Before long he had her laughing with him. It made her happy simply to be there, but being the target of such an accomplished flirt was delightful. For a while he made her forget her hideous existence in the brothel.

She could feel only gratitude that she was free of the friar's insistent overtures. He tried to fondle her, but Gervase happened by, and the friar withdrew. Then he attempted to rape her once more just before the party left – and she stayed.

It was the day after the friar's first attempt on her at the castle that she had met Nicholas walking in the yard. That had been a wonderful day, and a perfect night, and as they talked, the sky had darkened and then assumed an astonishing pink and golden hue that made her catch her breath. It was incredibly beautiful, and for love of it, she began to sob, reminded of evenings before she had been thrown from her home – evenings when her father and mother were both alive.

Even before her tears he had been quiet, after shyly mumbling his thankfulness for her arrival because it allowed him to show her his hospitality, which pleased him. Once more he avoided her eye, although she caught sight of his sidelong glances that flitted towards her and then away. She had wondered at it, thinking perhaps he knew of her past and was wondering whether to offer her money to lie with him. If he had, she would – she had no coins in her purse – but he made no such suggestion. And later, when they parted, she was aware of a sadness in her heart, as though she was reminded of her solitude and loneliness.

Later she had heard him marching slowly up and about the yard and walls. Even late into the night she could hear his steps, a steady, unhurried pace. They continued even as she dropped off and sank into a deep sleep. It was comforting, like a heartbeat.

Gervase was Anne's closest friend during those first days. He brought her sweetmeats made by the cook, gave her access to the bath with the water already heated, and passed her a tunic that was hardly faded, let alone frayed or torn. She would never forget that tunic: it was a dull shade of red, and set off her features to perfection. So much nicer than the scraps she had owned before. Somehow Gervase procured a bone comb too, and she was at last able to care for her hair. Although she lacked the basic trappings of a lady, at least she could dress and present herself as one.

That first night with her new tunic, she sat up late simply looking at it, occasionally reaching out and touching it, stroking the material, tracing the line of the throat and the shoulders, even sniffing at it and burying her face in the softness of the bunched cloth. It was so lovely she could have wept for sheer joy.

By the next morning, she had realised what she wanted to do. She acquired some thread and a needle from a maidservant, and set to work. By lunchtime she had embroidered the hems and the breast with a small pattern of leaves picked out in white thread, and then set off to find Gervase.

'My dear, you look like an angel,' Nicholas had breathed, his voice choked, when he saw her enter his hall.

Only then did she appreciate his feelings. Suddenly she understood that his sadness was mere proof of his knowledge of the futility of his unrequited adoration, and she left his hall filled with confusion. He was kind to her, he was protecting her here in his castle, and yet she felt sure that she couldn't return his love. She had never experienced a grown man's *love* before. Only lust.

Father Adam finished working on his little glebe and was about to go home for a late lunch when he saw the three large rounseys appear. His guilt was always at the forefront of his mind, and seeing them, he instantly wondered whether the rural dean had already heard of his sins and had sent these fellows for him, but he soon dismissed the idea. No, the rural dean couldn't call on a belted knight and his men to help him. These must be travellers. That was what they looked like: a knight, his man-at-arms and a forester or bowman to guard them.

Of course, some mercenaries would kill as soon as look at a man, especially one with a price on his head. It was such an alarming thought, he almost dropped his basket of beans and Good King Henry, all freshly picked for his pottage. Adam slipped back into the protection of the doorway. He would hide there and let the men pass by. Better to treat all strangers with caution. Since the war, after which the Despensers had returned to the realm, there were all manner of tales of knights becoming outlaws, and whole shires being ravaged by trail bastons and murderers. Even priests were treated no better than peasants.

To his horror, he saw that one of them, a tall, rugged-looking man with a bright blue tunic and red hosen, was looking straight at him. He pointed at Adam, and all three headed towards him.

'Father, I am Sir Baldwin of Furnshill and this is my friend Simon, Bailiff of Lydford. We are riding to Devonshire. Is this the right road?'

'I am told so,' Adam responded. He glanced over the three, and although he saw that the two were armed and capable-looking men, he had a feeling that they were not dangerous. 'I . . . ah . . . I live over there. If you would desire a break in your journey, I would be happy to give you some lunch.'

'That is most kind, but we have a long way to go,' Baldwin said. 'Perhaps we could take a little ale or wine though, if you have some to spare, Father? Something to slake our thirst would be gratefully received.'

Adam grinned with relief that these were no wandering outlaws.

'In a place like this, we rarely see decent wine, Sir Knight, but I can promise you the best ale in the vill.'

'Then we should be delighted.'

'Please follow me.'

His house was timber-built, a small place but comfortable, at the northern tip of the churchyard. At the westernmost end lay the buttery and pantry, with a small chamber over them for guests, while the eastern bay held another chamber over a small byre in which the vicar's animals would live. At present there was nothing there.

Seeing Baldwin's interested glance, Adam said, 'The oxen are out with my villeins. There's always more work to be done.'

'Yes, of course,' Baldwin said. 'Tell me, what is the lord of this manor like?'

'Sir Henry has been absent for many years,' Adam said. 'He is a member of the King's household, so he rarely comes this way.'

'Who looks after the manor in his absence?'

'There is the steward, Gervase, and the castellan, Nicholas. Both hold responsibility for the estates.'

'Are they honourable?'

'Why yes, I believe so,' Adam said with genuine surprise.

As Baldwin nodded, a young woman in her early twenties entered, a baby at her breast. She took a long look at the men in the room, and then walked to Adam, a hand resting on his forearm while she talked. Soon he was nodding, and she left him there, hurrying from the room to fetch drinks.

Baldwin shot a look at Simon, who met his gaze unblinkingly. Both were sure that the woman was Adam's 'priest's mare', his concubine. Simon was not bothered by this, but Baldwin found it repellent that a man should swear chastity to God and then sink into the arms of a woman. When he had been a Knight Templar, he had taken the vows of poverty, obedience and chastity like other monks, and he never knowingly broke them until his Order was betrayed. Only many years afterwards had he been persuaded that his oath was redundant, and even then it had taken some while before he could face the thought of marriage. It felt like treason. Not that he could regret marrying Jeanne – he adored her.

But it was different for a priest who yet remained in Holy Orders. He wondered that the priest should be so blatant with his bastard. It was shocking.

Looking at Adam, it was surprising too. Baldwin wouldn't have thought he had it in him. But there, the man was probably attractive to women with his slender features and pale complexion. The large eyes could be thought pleasant, he supposed, and the man's gentle manner might appeal. To Baldwin's eye, he looked rather effeminate.

'Lordings, please be seated,' Adam said hesitantly. He was aware of a sudden tension in the room, and he nervously ignored it, busying himself fetching stools. Soon there was a rattling sound, and he hurried to the buttery door. 'Come in, Julia. Let me help you . . . Ah, that smells good.'

He took the heavy pitcher from her, grabbed the wobbling cups from her tray, and poured ale for them all. 'Julia is looking after me. I am afraid I cannot cook to save my life, and it's pleasant to have someone to talk to. Sir Baldwin? Here is your ale.'

Baldwin nodded ungraciously, and sat so that he couldn't see the girl any more. He wanted to be out of here as soon as possible.

'Where have you been?' Adam asked innocently, and Baldwin groaned to himself. Sure enough, Simon instantly leaped into an explanation of their adventures, starting with the crazed monk of Gidleigh, and then leading on to the tale of their pilgrimage.

It was a whole four months or so since they had left their homes, he realised. Terrible to think that he had not seen his darling wife in such a long while.

'Father! *Father!*'

Father Adam looked as though he was never an entirely calm man, to Simon's mind. He had the thin, almost gaunt features of one who carried a community's sins on his shoulders, and Simon saw that his nails were all bitten to the quick. Hearing the cry, he shot up, scattering drops of ale like seeds from the sower's hand. 'Gregory? What is it, in God's name?'

The boy ran in, slipped on the rushes, and fell headlong. Before anyone could reach him, he sprang up again and gasped, 'It's Athelina! Oh, good God in Heaven, please come, Father!'

Chapter Six

Of course the odd thing was, as soon as he'd realised that Nicholas had snared the girl, Gervase had seen that she wasn't the spotless virgin that Nicholas took her for. Nick, bless him, always wanted to see the best in people. It would lead him into trouble one of these days. Well, it already had, hadn't it?

Thing was, Gervase was more worldly wise than his castellan. He had always enjoyed the company of women, had had plenty of dealings with them and knew their ways. Nothing wrong with that. Any man would bed all the women in the world if he had a chance, and Gervase had simply more chances than most. He knew how to compliment females, and he was genuinely interested in their thoughts and moods. It wasn't all just so that he could pull up their skirts and get in there.

However, his experience with women had led him to see through their wiles. That was the problem with people like Nick. The silly devil believed in love at first sight, even at his age, and thought that Anne adored him too. There was no fool like an old, besotted one.

Baldwin and Simon left Ivo at the priest's house. He appeared content to chat with Julia and waved them off like a lord indulgently granting permission to a child. It made Baldwin want to thrash the youth, but only fleetingly. Gregory's face stilled any annoyance. Baldwin left Adam's house feeling only a grim expectation.

The cottage was a short way from the church and Adam's home, a poor dwelling north of the main vill. Although the front garden was well cultivated, its walls were all but tumbledown, the rude cob failing where the thatch overhead had been twisted and pulled away by birds and rats. Green was the prevailing colour: the green of ivy and creepers tugging at what limewash remained; green mosses clinging to the thatch and all the cracks in the walls; green, foul water lying in the small pond in front of the place. The thatch had utterly failed some years before. It must have leaked and poured water in upon the miserable inhabitants whenever it rained. Baldwin felt compassion for whoever had existed in this miserable place.

Seeing his expression, Adam said apologetically, 'There are always some poorer than others, even in a good vill like this.'

'She was a poor woman? Not married?' Baldwin asked. In a well-run manor like his own, all the peasants were made to help widows and the poor. It was also the duty of a churchman – of Father Adam here, for example – to assist those who were unable to look after themselves.

'She was once, yes. Widow Broun, she was called.'

'What happened to her man?'

Adam shrugged sadly. 'The usual thing. He was ambling homewards from the harvest a year or two back along, and slipped and hit his head. Thought nothing of it, but then he caught a wasting disease, and in two weeks he was dead.' He tapped his tonsure with an open palm. 'It's so sad when a father dies like that. Young family, of course, and . . .'

'What of the family?' Baldwin asked sharply.

Adam paled.

Gregory tugged at Adam's sleeve. 'Father, please! Athelina's inside . . .'

Dispassionately Baldwin studied the priest. Now that they were here, Adam appeared fearful and reluctant to go inside. It added up to a weak figure for a man of God, Baldwin thought. Priests were usually stronger in the belly than this. Adam should be there to welcome new members of his congregation, and would invariably have to minister to those about to depart from it. It was all a part of his job, just as seeking killers was the duty of Simon and Baldwin.

Baldwin and Simon walked to the door, leaving Adam standing in the roadway alone, his face cracked and desolate, like a man who was suddenly ancient.

The door consisted of four rough planks pegged together. To prevent as many draughts as possible, an old piece of material had been stretched between them, like a new cloth on tenterhooks, set there to dry after milling so that it wouldn't wrinkle or warp. Except this was no new material; it was a revolting piece of thick fustian, sodden and stinking of horses. Baldwin assumed it had been a horse blanket, saved when it was no longer good enough for the beasts but adequate for a poor widow. That thought made him set his jaw.

He pulled the door wide. It grated on the dirt threshold, the leather hinges groaning quietly. To Baldwin, there was a sad tone to the sound, like an old woman moaning about pain in her limbs, knowing the pain would always be there, that there was nothing she could do to avoid it. Grief and pain were woman's birthright ever since Eve's betrayal.

The interior had a fusty odour, but over it Baldwin could detect the harsh, metallic tang to which he was grown so accustomed – *blood*.

'Sweet mother of God,' Simon breathed.

Baldwin nodded. Then the two entered, Baldwin leading the way.

Inside, it was cool, with a strange atmosphere. Even Baldwin felt claustrophobic in the quietness, and both men found their eyes straining in the darkness after the bright daylight outside. Stepping forward, Baldwin struck a rafter with his forehead, and then was more cautious. Gradually their eyes grew accustomed to the gloom, but before they could discern the interior, the boy Gregory had poked his head around the door and called to them.

'She's there, sir, *there*!'

At last Baldwin could see her.

'Poor soul!' he heard Simon mutter, and Baldwin nodded to himself.

She was a tall figure in a cheap woollen dress. Her head was thrust forward, the knot of the hemp at the back of her neck suspending her so that her feet dangled a foot or so from the ground; she swayed a little in the still air. Thick hair fell about her shoulders, uncombed and lank. Simon and Baldwin went to her without hurry, for it was clear that any attempt to save her would be in vain. She had been dead for some little while. There was no breath in her, no twitch of muscle clinging to life.

While Baldwin steadied her, his arms about her waist, Simon drew his sword and hacked at the rope bound to the rafter above her. It soon parted with a crack like a whip, and Baldwin had her full weight. He took a step backwards and almost tripped over the stool which lay near her.

Simon saw. 'She stood on that, then stepped off . . .'

Baldwin was about to nod when his foot knocked something else. 'What's that, Simon?'

As Baldwin half carried, half dragged the body out into the bright sunshine, Simon reached down and picked up a dagger. He took it with him as he followed Baldwin, and once outside he had to close his eyes in the glare. Gradually he could open them again, and then he gave a short grunt of revulsion.

'What is it?' Baldwin asked, settling the woman down on the ground.

'Is she bleeding much? Christ Jesus, why'd she stab herself as well?'

Baldwin stared down at her. 'She's got blood on her hands, but there's none elsewhere,' he said, lifting her hands and studying her wrists.

'Then whose blood was this?' Simon demanded, showing him the dagger, its blade all besmeared.

It was Adam who answered in a hushed tone. 'Where are her children?'

Baldwin and Simon re-entered. That was when Simon saw the blackened river of congealed blood that seeped from beneath the palliasse.

Lady Anne heard the noise as she left her chamber. It sounded as though all the men in the castle's yard were shouting at once, and she stood near the opened window in her solar to listen, a hand resting softly on her rounding belly.

It was rare indeed for such a commotion to be raised in the castle. Generally things were calm and ordered. It was the way that her husband, God bless him, liked to run his life, and the idea that someone should be here causing such mayhem was more than a little disturbing. There were only twelve men-at-arms here, when all was said and done, and that was hardly enough to cope with a real attack, even with the help of their servants.

Then she forced herself to be rational. There was no clash of arms, only the roaring of commands and the answering shouts of men.

Soon she heard feet pounding up the wooden staircase, and her husband hurried in. Nicholas was dressed in his normal tunic of rough red wool, and the shade matched the colour in his face.

'Dear heart,' she murmured, and swiftly she went to him, bending her head to rest it upon his breast. Once more she felt secure, protected in his warmth, just as a child might. That was the effect of his love on her, the sense that she was entirely safe with him. As soon as his arms went about her, all memories were gone. She could sigh with comfort, forgetting that she had been a *whore*.

'I have to go, my dear.'

'Where?' she asked, looking up at him. 'Is it all that shouting?'

'The priest sent a man – a woman's dead. I have to go and see that it's not murder, send a man for the Coroner, arrange the guards about the body – all that sort of thing.' She shivered suddenly, and he bent over her with compassion. 'My love, don't worry! This is just a poor woman who seems to have killed herself from despair.'

'Killed herself?'

'Don't worry yourself.' There was already that subtle distance in his tone, as there occasionally was when he spoke of matters which he felt could upset her. It was as though he was protecting her from the trials of his job here in the castle. He had taken it upon himself to guard her from those who could cause her grief; but today she wanted to know what was happening outside in the world.

'Who was it?' she asked, a faint frown at her brow. It was horrible to think of someone dying when she'd been sitting here enjoying herself.

'The madwoman – you know her, Athelina. She's apparently killed herself and her children. Hard to conceive how—'

'My precious, don't,' she said quickly, putting two fingers over his lips. There was a cold worm in her bowels. Nicholas felt the lack of an heir so keenly, she knew. It was terrible for a man to have reached his age and still not have the certainty of his name going forward. Forty-six years old, and he had no one to whom to leave his treasure. She would give him an heir soon, she swore to herself. 'Anyone could see that she was a lunatic.'

He nodded. 'Perhaps.'

His tone was enough to make her lift an eyebrow in query. 'It is the full moon, isn't it? I suppose her humours were unsettled.

Anyway, she's been teetering on the brink of destruction for a long time, hasn't she? This was probably the last straw, when the moon affected her.'

'To kill her children, though. Such a terrible crime . . . and then herself, too.'

She shuddered, a hand going to the child in her swollen womb. 'You should be gone. Don't worry about me, just see to her and return as soon as you may. Perhaps I should come too?'

'No, my love. You stay here.'

Nick tried to smile at her, but there was a terrible absence in his eyes where usually she would have seen his love shining.

'You stay and forget all about this. Just concentrate on our son.'

He attempted another smile, but Lady Anne could see on his face only the awareness of man's potential for hideous cruelty.

Alexander's wife Letitia heard the rumours spreading about the town. She was in the middle of cheese-making, using a spare gallon of milk, the remnant of last night's milking, mixed with fresh milk from this morning. It was curious that cheese always tasted best when it was made from two milkings; she sometimes wondered about it, and why that should be, but it was God's way of doing it, and that was enough for her.

The pot on its trivet had been warmed to blood heat, the curdled milk from a calf's stomach added, and she had stirred the pot carefully away from the heat to let the curds form. The other pot, her cooking one, was over the fire now, the fine muslin boiling. She'd use that to strain the curds from the whey before wrapping the cheese in it and binding it. There was a nail in the beam near the wall where she could hang it to cure and drip itself dry.

Curious at the noise, she left the pot and went to the door. There, she saw old Iwan and his son Angot talking. They looked serious and more than a little alarmed, standing in the track and staring back towards the church.

She was hot from her cooking on this warm day, and intrigued to learn what they were discussing, because although the good God knew she was no gossip, there was sometimes something to be learned from the sort of talk that flowed about the vill; especially if it had any bearing upon her husband. That was, of course, a perfectly valid reason for her listening to the chatter of others.

Quickly, she busied herself. The pot with the forming curds could be safely left now. She wrapped straw about it to keep it warm, holding it in place with an old tunic of Alexander's, and wiped her hands on her apron before giving detailed instructions to Jan, the foolish child who served her as maid. She was so stupid that even the simplest of tasks would challenge her, and Letitia went through the small jobs that needed doing, all the while watching Jan's face to see that she understood. With a grimace, Letitia finally waved her away. The girl Jan would somehow mess it up: she always did. That was the trouble with peasants like her – they had no sense!

Still, as she left her house and felt the sun's warmth on her face, she could allow a small smile to pass over her features. This was a good vill, her man the Constable of the Peace was important and growing wealthy, and they had a pleasant life. Only one thing marred the tenor of their lives – the lack of children – but, as she reminded herself, there were many with the same problem, and perhaps God would soon favour them.

'Godspeed, Iwan, Angot. It is a fine day,' she said to the two men.

'Aye, for some,' Iwan said.

She smiled at him. He was a funny old devil, but she rather liked him. He was rumoured to have been a ferocious soldier in the old King's armies when they marched through Wales to quell the rebellious churls over there, with their fraudulent usurper, but now all she could ever see was the twinkle in his eye as he spoke to her or one of the other wives in the vill. Iwan may have been a fine fighter, but she was sure that he had been keener on other forms of fencing. She'd seen him often enough, whenever the vill had a celebration and the ale had flowed freely, making up to any woman within reach. None would really want him for a lover – he was ridiculously old – but he had a roguish grin and was always ready with a compliment. For some women, that was enough to let a man lie with them.

'Is there something troubling you?' she asked. 'You look upset.'

'It's poor Athelina,' Angot burst out. 'She's killed herself and her children.'

'Oh, the evil woman!'

Letitia felt Iwan's glance flare at her like red-hot cinders. 'Her in't evil, mistress, only sad. Her's dead because of money. 'Twere that made her do it.'

'That's true. When Serlo asked for more rent for the cottage, she couldn't find it,' Angot said sombrely. 'He put her rent up, and she couldn't scrape anything together. So that's why she's dead now: her and her children.'

Letitia gasped with some annoyance. 'It's ridiculous! There's no need for someone to commit self-murder, nor to murder their own children. There's a church here, and plenty of alms can be given. Why, she's made use of the church's money before now. And she's had our scrapings and some bread, too. There's no excuse, none whatever, for this horrible crime.'

'That's what some might say,' Angot pulled a face, 'but 'tis hard for a woman to live without a man to guard her and her little 'uns. She walked the rope for so long, and today she slipped.'

'I scarcely think her life was one long tightrope,' Letitia scoffed. 'But has anyone told my husband? He should be there.'

'You'll see him at her house, mistress,' Angot said.

She left them there, Iwan looking as grimly forbidding as a man-at-arms should, and less like a friendly old smith, and Angot merely looking confused and upset. He'd grown up with Athelina, Letitia reminded herself. He had probably been quite fond of her, as men and women could be in a small, close-knit vill like Cardinham.

The way to Athelina's house took her down the lane towards the church, then left and across a muddy field. Already, from the front of the church, she could see the people gathering, and she had to stop her feet from hurrying. Too much haste would appear indelicate and ghoulish . . . yet she *was* fascinated!

As soon as Susan heard the cry, she went to the door of the inn, a cup of cider in hand. There she saw a couple of women running past, their skirts gripped in their hands as they pelted up towards the church.

'What's the matter?' she called out, but either they didn't hear her, or they were in too much of a hurry even to respond. Shrugging, Susan drained her cup and wiped her mouth with the back of her hand. Probably a fight between men in the fields. Some of the lads working the scythes there came from the next vill, and natural rivalry often flared into actual violence. It was only three years ago that two men stacking the sheaves had suddenly set upon one another, and one fellow had died, stabbed in the heart. That had cost the vill dear.

She put the cup into the barrel of water to rinse it, and then sat on her stool in a patch of warm sunlight with needle and thread to mend a shirt which had torn.

This was a good vill. She had grown up here, initially as the daughter of the inn, and then, when she married and her father died, drowned in the vast quantity of ale he had consumed over the years, she and her husband had taken the place over. Wonderful. She would have been happy to live as her father had, taking part in all the vill's events and making a fair sum from the sale of ales, but not Tom. He was a dreamer. That was the problem

with some men, she knew. They had dreams which they constructed endlessly in their minds, but when it came to putting
them into practice, they couldn't do it. They just weren't as
practical as women.

It was the same all over. She'd been told that by her mum.
'Don't think that because a man's supposed to be master in his
home that you can't guide him,' she'd said once. It was half in jest,
but then she had become serious. 'It's a foolish woman who won't
make sure she gets what she wants. You look at your father. He
always knows what he wants and what he wants to do, but he
doesn't often end up getting his way when it's important. I never
tell him he can or can't do something, I just ask him about it; keep
questioning him until he thinks it's not such a good idea. If you
ask a man the right way, he'll realise what he's said is stupid. Or
you make out that it's going to be better for you than for him. Men
can't bear to think that their toys will be used by their wives
instead of them. Don't ever try to stop them by pointing out you
can't afford something, though. That'd make them buy it out of
bravado!'

They had laughed at that, their amusement curtailed only by
Susan's father walking in to ask what was so funny. His bemuse-
ment was increased by their response, still more giggling. It wasn't
as though he was a hard master; he was a kind, generous soul. The
trouble was, like all men, his mind ran on one road: what pleased
him. Anything else was of no interest whatever. He adored Susan
and went out of his way to make her happy, and would spend
money they could ill-afford to buy her a trifle.

It was the same with her mother. Many was the time she sent
Susan's father to market to get an essential item, only to have him
return without it, but with a pretty bolt of material or ribbons.
Or he came home hangdog, having found a game of dice and
blown all his money on ale and gambling. The two curses of an
innkeeper's life.

Men weren't *safe* with money. It was what appealed to her as an alewife. If a man came into her house, she could fill him with ale, feed him some bread and cheese, flirt and make him happy, reassure him that he was desirable, and send him away smiling, while she pocketed all his money. It was a silly game, life, but she played it for all she was worth. She enjoyed it again, now that her fool of a husband was gone. Never again! She had no need of a man!

No, all she needed were punters walking through her door, that was all. But just now there was no one to serve. Usually by this time, she'd have had at least a few of the locals in, demanding ale or cider to soothe parched throats.

As though on cue, a shadow fell over her threshold, and looking up she saw Serlo. 'Ah, an ale?'

He glanced at her as though hardly seeing her. Then he nodded, thoughtfully wandering to the stool near the window.

'Quiet today,' she said as she passed him a large jug.

'Reckon there's something happening folks want to see,' he grunted.

'What's that, then?'

'Athelina. Heard she's been found dead,' he said, his face still and unemotional. 'Silly bitch! She was useless in life, and now she's killed herself.'

Chapter Seven

Muriel watched the proceedings, fascinated by the sight of the strangers. Many of the women were scared, she saw, but she concentrated on the two men in quality clothes talking to the priest.

She had been to see the smith for Serlo. His old shovel had finally given up the ghost, the steel rusting away completely, and Serlo had grumpily accepted that he needed a new one. Once she'd put in her order, she returned past the cottage, and saw the people gathering. Since it was her husband's cottage, she wanted to know what all the fuss was about, and stopped to gawp and listen.

Poor Athelina! She must have been so desperate to have done a dreadful thing like that. Muriel hoped that the recent rent increase hadn't tipped her over the edge. No, it couldn't be Serlo's fault. Athelina had always been a nervous type, a scrawny wench, too much like a game chicken, Serlo used to say, with her thin thighs. Well, she spent so much time hungry, it wasn't surprising. But to kill her boys, that was terrible . . . Muriel couldn't have done that, not in a hundred years.

'Who are they?' she asked a neighbour. It was young Gregory, and he was staring with his mouth agape at the sight of these strange men talking to Adam.

'Foreigners,' came the gruff whisper. 'I think they only got here this morning, an' soon as they came here, they found her. Do you think they murdered her? Might have. Can't tell with foreigners. They talk funny, too,' he added as an afterthought.

Muriel was about to comment when Nicholas came marching up with two men-at-arms. The three men stopped at the sight of the trio in front of the cottage, then made their way to join them.

From where Muriel stood, she thought that Nicholas looked wary, like a man who feared sudden attack. He stood slightly distant from the two strangers, his hand near his belt.

'Lordings, Godspeed. I am the castellan, Nicholas of Bodmin. What is this about Athelina?'

Adam began talking quickly and in a high-pitched voice like a man who was close to tears but daren't shed them, the words falling over one another. 'She's in there, Nicholas; she hanged herself and slit the throats of her boys! It's awful in there. It's a slaughterhouse! How *could* she?'

Muriel shook her head. It was appalling! Those poor boys! Unknowingly, she pushed her way through the crowds until she was at the front and could hear more clearly.

One of the strangers was taller and, although his hair was showing silver at the temples and he wore a beard that just followed the line of his jaw, he looked quite young. His movements were as precise and assured as a man in his early twenties, but somehow Muriel knew that he was a great deal older than that. He spoke now, waving a hand at the open cottage door.

'Sir, my friend and I were with the good priest here when he was called to see this woman. My name is Sir Baldwin de Furnshill, and this is my good friend Bailiff Simon Puttock from the Stannary of Lydford. He is appointed Bailiff by Abbot Robert of Tavistock, and has helped the Devonshire Coroners in many murders. I myself am Keeper of the King's Peace in Crediton. We have both some experience of murders, so we came as soon as we heard of this sad case, and we cut the woman's body down.'

His companion had flesh that looked as though it had been bronzed by the sun, but now he was pale, his features stretched and haggard. It was an expression of anguish and horror, Muriel could see. When Aumery suffered from a nightmare, he often woke with that same look set upon his face, his eyes wild like this man's. It made her realise just how hideous the scene must be in the cottage.

Sir Baldwin continued, 'If you would care to follow me, I can show you the bodies. The woman is here, but her sons are still inside, covered by their palliasse. They should be left where they are for now, so that the Coroner can see them *in situ*, but that is no reason why you shouldn't satisfy yourself about their situation.'

'I have no need to see her or them.'

'She must have been truly evil,' one of Nicholas's men commented, staring at the cottage with a curled lip.

At his side, Muriel saw her husband's terrible enemy, Richer. He was pale and fretful. 'She was a saint, you *fucking* cretin!'

Nicholas glanced behind him at the men of his party. 'Silence, both of you! Richer: be still!'

'She was a woman who had lost all hope,' Sir Baldwin said with cold deliberation. 'A woman who kills her children is one who has learned true despair. She saw no life for them. That was why she slaughtered them before hanging herself. You should pity her, not scorn her.'

Muriel looked at him sharply. She almost expected to see him draw steel, his voice was so harsh. It made her heart go to him, this odd knight, because he obviously felt compassion for poor Athelina. It was rare enough for anyone to feel something for a beggar like her, other than distaste.

'Sir Knight, I am sure he didn't mean anything by his words,' Nicholas said, meanwhile giving his man a look of chilling contempt, 'although a man may believe that a woman who murders her child must be particularly foul.'

'I have seen too many real murders to believe that. If a woman has done this, it is because of desperation or lunacy, not innate evil,' Baldwin said. He stared at the man-at-arms.

'Do you think that this woman was lunatic?' Nicholas asked.

'It is possible. There are some diseases which can affect a person's mind,' Baldwin said. 'You need only think of the *rage* which affects men after they have been bitten by a dog. It makes a man crave water, but when it is provided, he is driven insane. Perhaps this poor woman had a disease which made her lose her mind.'

'Some sicknesses are terrible,' Nicholas agreed thoughtfully. 'Sir, I have sent a man to fetch the Coroner. Is there anything you observed in there which could be useful?'

'She has grown stiff already, as have her children, so I should think that she was dead yesterday, or even before that. Perhaps Saturday – perhaps Friday. Only God knows. The smell is repellent, so it is possible that the blood has been upon the walls and floor for some days. Do you know when she was last seen?'

'No. We can ask, though,' Nicholas said, glancing at the silent, listening crowd. 'Has anyone seen Alexander? Where is that Constable?'

The men had all gone, and Gervase saw Lady Anne at the door to the hall. She turned away as soon as she saw his eyes on her, the bitch!

He could have loved her – that was part of his problem. She was adorable. If unattached at that time, he would have tried his luck. Jesus! He would have considered marrying her, if he hadn't realised that she was stale. That much was obvious as soon as he had seen her reactions to poor Nick. She'd been experienced beyond her years, and Gervase, with a punter's knowledge of whores, had been able to see it, whereas poor Nick was so infatuated that he couldn't see it. And it wouldn't serve to save him. No, he was bound to be made miserable by her.

Christ Jesus – wasn't Gervase the man to prove it?

* * *

When a boy had been sent to fetch the Constable, Nicholas spoke quietly. 'We'd best set a guard about these bodies until the Coroner arrives. Who actually found them?'

'Me, sir.'

Muriel saw young Hob step forward. He was a close friend of Ben, Athelina's oldest son.

'What were you doing here?' Sir Baldwin asked in friendly fashion. He appeared to lose the aura of authority which Muriel had detected before, and in its place was a curious youthfulness, as though he was actually nearer to Hob's own age than his advanced years.

'Sir, I was trying to get Ben to come with me. I had to go and scare the birds from the gleanings, and I thought he'd like to come too. I didn't expect . . .' The boy faltered. Tears shone in his eyes.

'No, of course not,' Sir Baldwin said kindly. 'Was the door open?'

'I . . . yes, I think so. A little. It never closed well.'

'And you walked straight in?'

'Well, I called out first. Then I went in.'

'And saw them?'

'I only saw her. Didn't see them.' He shuddered violently.

'When did you last see Ben?'

'Saturday.'

'Two days ago. That would make sense,' Baldwin said.

Nicholas was frowning, as was Muriel herself. What did the knight mean by that?

'Why do you say that?' Nicholas asked.

'Because of the way that the bodies are lying. The two boys were killed on their palliasse in the corner. As I said, they died some little while ago. It was dark in there because the shutter is pulled across the window, so I think it could be that this woman killed them at night. That would explain why the two boys died together. She slit their throats when they were asleep. Then she covered them with blankets, horrified with what she had done, and hanged herself, dropping her knife as she died. Both lads were asleep, so neither could give the alarm to the other. She must have planned this. Poor woman.'

'Poor children, more to the point,' Nicholas said, and Muriel had to agree with him. She could feel little empathy with a woman who could slaughter her own children like lambs for the pot.

The scene was terrible, and although she would have liked to see the bodies removed, because all men and women must be intrigued by death, yet she was suddenly taken with a feeling of guilt, as though she was intruding. Athelina must have been dreadfully depressed to have committed this grievous crime, and listening to these men speculating on her last moments felt almost blasphemous.

At the mill, when she returned, she told Serlo about the woman's death.

He was quiet for a few moments as he absorbed her words, but then, when he turned to her, his face twisted petulantly. 'Bugger! It'll take an age to clean all the blood away. How are we going to get money in from the place if it stinks like a charnelhouse?'

She was left with the impression, as he walked off, that he had already known of the matter, and she wondered why he hadn't admitted it. Serlo was not the type to bottle up such things. If he thought that he knew more than another, he would gladly boast about it. Most unlike him, she reckoned, but then she heard Aumie cry, and her maternal instincts took over for a while. It was only later that she returned to the theme. 'It was terrible, Serlo!,' she told him. 'Those two poor boys, dead like that! I don't know what to say!'

'Then shut up,' he said unsympathetically. 'I don't give a toss for that beggarwoman or her brood. Now what's for supper?'

She couldn't ignore his mood. All too often in the past when he had been in this frame of mind, he had beaten her. Rather than risk that, she offered him a thickened pottage with some lamb meat, and left him to his solitary contemplation of the fire, walking out to watch over her children as they played in the yard. She was still there a while later when he came out.

'I'm going to see my brother,' he said, and strode off up the road towards the vill and his precious Alexander.

He was a hard devil to please sometimes, that husband of hers.

Lady Anne heard the men return from the vill and, rather than wait for her husband, she walked carefully down the stairs to greet him and learn what had been happening.

He was still in the yard when she reached the top of the staircase outside the hall. Like so many newer castles, this one was built with a view to defence, so the hall was up a flight of stone steps; beneath was a large undercroft for storing foods. From her vantage point, she could see that Nicholas was visibly upset. He had the expression that he usually wore when a dog misbehaved and sprang the game too early, or when a peasant didn't turn up for his traditional labour days. He carried his head lower, like a bull preparing to charge, and his brows came together above his nose, giving him, so Anne thought, a deliciously aggressive aspect.

Others would quail in his presence when he wore that expression, but not Lady Anne. She knew her man better than that. For her, there was no danger from him. Although he could be as terrifying as an ogre to the men-at-arms about the castle, towards her he was ever a polite and kindly gentleman. Even now, she saw the two new men-at-arms, Richer and Warin, receiving a blunt reproach from Nicholas. Richer, she noted, looked close to answering back. For a moment Anne actually thought he would, but then Warin took his shoulder, and he calmed down. Fortunately, Nicholas hadn't noticed; he was shouting at a groom for being lazy.

'It was Athelina? She is dead?' she asked Nicholas, running down the stairs to his side.

'Yes,' he responded. His eyes met hers for a moment, and then he roared at a servant to fetch him wine. 'She killed her boys, too. No one's seen them for a couple of days, not since Saturday evening, so we think she did it then. Christ Jesus, but I have no idea why! What can she have been thinking? Oh, my love, I am sorry!'

Anne had winced on hearing his words, a hand instinctively rising to her belly as though to shield her child's ears. She could feel herself blench even as her husband rested his hands upon her shoulders, his eyes full of compassion. 'My dear, I wasn't thinking.'

'It was a terrible thing to kill the boys,' she said.

'Dreadful! The pair of them lying there, their throats . . .' He looked drawn. Anne put her hand up to cover his on her shoulder as he continued. 'I've seen enough of rapine and murder in war – you *expect* it. Every man's heart hides a wild brute, and it's only in time of war that the beast is released to act as it wishes . . . but this? It's abnormal *wicked* to see children murdered by their own mother – the woman who's supposed to seek only their safety and protection.'

'It is the way sometimes, though,' she said. He was haunted by these deaths, she saw, and she wanted to comfort him, but wasn't sure how. She'd never seen him so affected. Yet it was natural, surely, for an honourable man to feel this way? Especially when his wife was expecting her own first child, she told herself with a faint sinking sensation in her heart.

She loved him. She adored him. How *could* God have deceived her so and made her betray him?

'Who's that?' Letitia muttered as she heard the footsteps, but she needn't have wondered. There was only one man who would walk to Alexander's door at this time of night without hesitating.

'Where is he?' Serlo demanded, seeing her at the hearth.

'If you mean your brother, I expect he's still at Athelina's. Someone has to keep an eye on the place until the Coroner arrives, and goodness knows when that will be.'

'I want to see him,' Serlo said.

Letitia saw how he grimaced as he said it. There was something on his mind that he knew was going to annoy her husband, and she stood up, wincing slightly as a knee clicked. She knew that she was intimidating to Serlo; it had something to do with her height, for she was at least two inches taller than him, but it was also her manner.

She had been born into the family of a merchant in Bodmin, a wealthy enough man, and when she agreed to marry Alex, it was a move designed mostly by her father. Alex was even then a forward-thinking man, and his fame was travelling farther than merely Bodmin.

She deliberately used her 'older sister' tone. It was the same tone she had used to intimidate her younger brother when they were children, and she had always found that it suited her perfectly in dealings with Serlo. Standing taller than him, she inclined her head until she was looking down her nose at him. 'What have you done now?'

'I ain't done anything!' he snapped. 'Least, nothing much.'

'Have you been demanding money from travellers again? You've been warned already by that fool Richer only yesterday. Alexander was very upset to hear that. You were stealing from us – from him. If he learns that—'

'I'm not scared of that scrote Richer. He can go and—'

'Save your great oaths for your customers, Serlo. I have no use for them,' Letitia said, holding up her hand. 'All I want to know is, what's upset you this time?'

'It's nothing. I'll find him myself. He'll be at Athelina's place, you say?'

'I imagine so. You should try there first,' she said, with a distant expression. If the fool didn't wish to confide in her, that was fine, she thought, but as he slammed the door behind him, she could have kicked the hearth in annoyance. The ridiculous fellow! Walking in here as though he owned the place! He'd probably been caught with his fingers in someone's sack of grain again. The idiot was so incompetent, he couldn't even rob his customers without being found out.

He was looking very sad, though. Letitia began to wonder whether there wasn't something more important at the heart of his strange behaviour. But for the life of her, she couldn't think what it could be.

Chapter Eight

It was almost dark when Letitia heard her husband returning down the lane. He was declaiming loudly, as he sometimes would when he was particularly incensed by some petty or foolish action.

'The fellow should be set in the stocks for all to throw their waste at. Fancy thinking he could get away with it!' he was saying as Letitia opened the door for him. She gave him a perfunctory kiss on his cheek and took his jack from him, hanging it from a hook on the back of the door. Serlo she left to his own devices.

'Alex, come to your chair, dear.'

'In a moment, wife. My brother has much to tell me, apparently,' Alex said, in that bluff, hearty way of his that Letitia liked so much. It was at once open and friendly, but simultaneously powerful – so masculine. 'Serlo, sit and take some ale with me. You fetch it, while I kiss my wife. You know where it is.'

Serlo grunted, and Letitia thought, he *ought* to know – he's guzzled enough of our best ales over the years. Just as he has eaten our best food. Always appearing whenever we're sitting down to eat or drink, the foul, scrophulous chancre. Then he sits and dribbles, glopping his drink like a ploughman in an alehouse. It's enough to make you want to throw up.

Alex knew her feelings only too clearly. He went to her and patted her hand, but in a way that showed he wasn't best pleased with her.

'Letty, he's my brother.'

That was just what she needed to hear! 'I think, husband dear, that I knew that already,' she said with poisonous sweetness. 'But I was hoping to be able to talk to you myself tonight. I didn't realise that we were once more to be joint advisers to your brother.'

His smile was a little warmer than his pat. 'Come on, now. He won't be here for long. You know what he's like. He gets a bee in his shirt and has to shake it loose. I'm the only man he can trust. It's always been that way. Remember, he's never known a mother. That sort of thing marks a man.'

'Marks him enough to steal from you?' she asked pointedly.

'If he's been making a little on the side – well, you can't blame him,' Alex said, but less forcefully.

'He's robbing you after all you've done for him!' Letty hissed. 'You heard what Richer said at the church just as I did.'

'Richer's always been an enemy to us.'

'Maybe, but was he lying?' Alex was so unlike his brother, Letitia thought gratefully. He had seen his father's decline into poverty and ruin, and it was that which had spurred his own ambition. Alex had started with a cottage and a few chickens, but in four years he had developed his assets and now he had this house, a large share of the mill, three sheepfolds, and numerous other investments. He was the most important man for ten miles in any direction outside of Bodmin.

Serlo followed in his father's footsteps. What he had, he risked in gambling; what he didn't have, he tried to win by threats and cajoling. Sometimes he succeeded, because many people here had a nervous conviction that what Serlo wanted, Alex would get for him.

Letitia watched as her brother-in-law sat down on the bench in front of her husband's chair. Alex sat easily, relaxed. This hall was a recent acquisition, but he wanted a home that suited his new status. The size of the place went to prove how important he was; the dimensions dwarfed the people inside. It was even larger than the hall in the castle. The buttery and pantry always contained food and drink for friends.

'I'm sorry, Alex. I . . .'

Alex waved a hand. 'Come on, Serl. What's the matter this time? Is it that arse Richer again?' he asked, leaning forward keenly. 'If it is, I'll deal with him.'

'No. It's just that bitch Athelina. I wish she'd killed herself out on the road and saved us all this trouble!'

Alex allowed a short frown to cross his face. Letitia knew he hated to hear women slighted.

'You ought to show her a little more compassion, brother. She's dead, isn't she?'

'Oh, stuff that. She was asking for it. Useless baggage. Never did a decent day's work after her husband died, did she? No. As for those squalling brats . . . I'm not surprised she topped them first. I'd have done it for her if I'd had a chance.'

Alex sucked on his teeth. 'What is the problem?'

'You know how behind she was with her rent. I told her to get out if she couldn't pay. Said she must find the money somehow or I'd break one of the boys' legs.'

'And? Is that all you said?'

'She didn't pay.' Serlo shrugged.

Letitia watched him with a feeling of intense, sickening rage. She daren't open her mouth in case she screamed abuse at him for using those words, those cruel, horrible, unrepeatable words. In that moment, she learned what true hatred was.

'I'd have done it if she had the cash and was holding out on me, but since she hadn't, what was the point?' Serlo continued, 'There wasn't any way she could get that money together. She had nothing. I'd asked for it so we could empty the place and put someone in for more money, but now! Well, how in God's name can we find new tenants when it's crawling with guards and the castle's men? And even then, it'll take a load of money to get the stench of death from it. Who's going to want to live in a place that smells of filth?'

'Blood isn't filth,' Alex remonstrated quietly. Letitia thought he should have bellowed. When she looked at his still, inexpressive features, she saw that in his heart he had.

'The blood of two bastards and their bitch of a mother is. She must have rutted like a stoat before her husband died. Probably wore him out – that's why he had that fall.'

Letitia felt as though the air itself was starting to throttle her as Serlo continued his vile tirade. Her face was reddened in shame and self-disgust, she could feel it. It was almost as though her head could explode from the pressure of her humiliation.

Serlo must have known that she and Alex had been trying for a child all their married life, while he himself, who had been married only half as long, had already managed to produce two boys.

All those nights when she had sweatily and hopefully rutted with Alex, all those happy days when she thought her monthly time was going to be missed, and the despair when she had suddenly felt the menstrual ache grip her abdomen.

They had agreed now that they couldn't continue like that. There was no point in worrying about children, not when every other aspect of their lives was so good. Their marriage was strong, much more so than those of many others, and Alex was growing ever more successful in his work, so there was no need to torture themselves any more. Better by far to enjoy the lives they had and hope that some day God would reward their patience. The barrenness could be caused by any number of problems and Alex, bless him, was as aware as Letitia herself that the culprit could be either of them. There were as many dogs who couldn't father a litter, or bulls a calf, as there were barren bitches and cows.

Their lives had taken on a relaxed, even tenor since their

agreement. They made love whenever they wanted now, rather than when Letitia thought it was most conducive. There was less straining, more loving. Alex was a kind lover, and Letitia had never doubted that he adored her. He often told her so.

And now here was his moronic brother throwing their failure in their faces like sand.

Serlo had no idea he was doing it. He couldn't ever get beyond his own petty desires and fears. Those of other people were irrelevant to him. Letitia felt her anger rise, peak, and then begin to subside. It was as Alex had always said: his brother was spoiled, and Alex was largely at fault for that. When Serlo had made a mistake, he rarely had to own up. It was Alex who shouldered all the responsibility.

She looked at her brother-in-law. Now he was going on about the folk up at the castle. He'd had enough of Alex's strong ale to make him more calm, more expansive, and he sat back on his bench like a toad after eating a dragonfly, a broad grin on his face, his belly protruding. Letitia thought him never so repellent as when he sprawled back like this.

'That little filly Nicholas caught is showing now. Have you seen her?'

Alex sighed. 'Yes, but what of it? I heard she might be with child a long while ago.'

'Ah, but who's the father? That's what I'd like to know.'

Alex shot a look at Letitia, but she was calm enough now. She shrugged slightly, then gave him a half-smile. Before long she'd go out and make sure that her chickens were all locked up, and then she'd leave them to it. The pair of them could talk for hours when the mood took them.

Alex returned her smile, but she could see that he was annoyed. 'This sounds like more tavern gossip.'

'Why don't you speak your mind, Serlo?' Letitia said, perhaps more sharply than she truly intended. 'What do you mean to imply?

Don't just repeat rumours!' Alex gave her a quick look, but Letty didn't care. She was staring angrily at Serlo. 'Well?'

'There've always been rumours about her, haven't there? 'Twas said Gervase had his eye on her. I reckon he's been forking hay in the wrong barn!'

'Oh, don't be so stupid!' Letitia said scornfully, but then Alex held up his hand.

'Why do you think that, Serlo?'

'I saw them,' the miller said smugly. 'I saw them together, when they didn't realise there was anyone about. Athelina too – she was there. It was four or five months ago, just before that last cold spell when the rain started a couple of days after. You remember? Well, I saw them down by the river, walking along the bank. They'd been over to the fields, I think, but then they stopped and sat by the river for a while. He put his arm about her, and—'

'This is sheer malicious nonsense!' Letitia burst out. 'I don't believe a word of it.'

'If this is true,' Alex said, 'why didn't you mention it before?'

Serlo gave a half-shrug. 'What was the point? It wouldn't do any good, would it?'

'So why mention it now?' Alex demanded astutely. 'There's a reason, isn't there?'

'You heard what Richer accused me of doing,' Serlo muttered with embarrassment. 'Taking gifts instead of tolls. I'm sorry about that.'

'You admit it?' Alex asked.

'I did ask for cash from a couple of people, but nothing more than that.'

Alex had stood, and now he towered over Serlo with an expression of such hurt in his eyes that Letty found it hard to watch him.

'So you lied to me, and then stole from me, Serl? All you had to do was ask, and I'd have helped you. Instead you cheated me.'

'It wasn't really like that.'

'One third of the tolls were for me, but you didn't take the tolls. That means you stole from me,' Alex said quietly, and passed a hand over his face, sitting again as though exhausted. 'Anyway, what is this about? Why mention Lady Anne now?'

'I thought I could ask her to ensure that Gervase doesn't press the matter. She wouldn't want her affair in the open, would she? And I could even charge a higher toll, maybe? If the steward was squared, we could ask what we wanted!'

'You've kept it quiet all this time so you could fleece the travellers?' Letitia said scathingly. 'How good.'

'Which makes me wonder why this has occurred to you now,' Alex said.

Serlo's face lengthened. 'That bastard Richer's determined to see me suffer, and the men I stopped today, they'll try to make sure he's supported in the castle's court. One of them's a Keeper, and the other one's a Bailiff. I don't stand much hope against them, unless Gervase squashes it.'

'You could pay Gervase to leave the matter off the court's rolls. Perhaps it'll get forgotten. The Keeper and his friend can't be here for long,' Alex said ruminatively. His tone was quiet, but Letitia could see his inner tension by the way that his right hand picked at the arm of his chair, while his left cupped his chin. It was a posture she recognised only too clearly.

'Aye, maybe I'll try that,' Serlo said, brightening.

'But in the meantime,' Alex said, fixing his brother with a glittering eye, 'you'll stop charging people these "gifts". And you'll stop making sour comments about Athelina. At least in front of us.'

And the note of suppressed anger in his voice was enough to calm Letitia again. She detested her brother-in-law, but Alex's words had shown her why she was so happily married to her husband. They were so much in agreement.

She did love him.

* * *

Richer put his hands to his face again and pressed hard. His brain felt as though it was about to force its way through his skull, the pressure was so great. Rarely had he suffered from so much pain. He could scarcely comprehend that he had lost his love after dreaming of her for so many years.

The worst loss he had experienced was when his entire family was killed. Yet even that had not hurt him as much as this did. Somehow, losing Athelina was worse because God had given him the renewal of hope, then removed the object of his adoration. It was a terrible, cruel thing to have happened.

She was the same woman he had left fifteen years ago, with the same smile, the same kindly eyes, the same strong, taut figure, if a little bent from work, and if her face bore witness to the trials she had suffered, did that not apply to them all? No, she was his lovely Athelina, the same woman he had left when he learned of his family's death. And now she was taken from him too. If only he had insisted on helping – rescued her from poverty and that damned miller's clutches. She and her boys would be alive now.

It was this damned vill. Cardinham was an unwholesome, ungodly place. There was something evil here, that affected him, no one else. If there was any justice, the man suffering like this would be Serlo, or Alexander. Why should he, Richer, be forced to feel this? He'd done nothing to anyone and yet he was given the burden of grief.

Poor Athelina. She'd done nothing either, nor had her boys. Yet they were dead, rotting, ruined.

'Aw, Christ Jesus, why?' he howled to the sky.

'Richer, come,' Warin said gently. 'We should go and fetch some food. You need to eat.'

'Do you really think I'm hungry?' Richer said, but without anger. He didn't expect anyone else to comprehend his loss. Least of all someone like Warin, who had so much. 'Food would make me puke.'

'You should try to eat, nonetheless, and if you won't, you should attend on me, because I am ravenous,' Warin told him. 'The best cure for such an anguish is wine, and I should be happy to fetch you a pint of the best.'

Reluctantly Richer allowed himself to be drawn towards the hall. All the way, in front of him, he was sure he could see the shade of Athelina drawing him onwards.

It was a relief to Nicholas that Gervase was nowhere to be seen when he ushered his guests into the hall of the castle. Sad, but there it was.

In his early years here, before he had found his wife, Gervase was his close comrade. Ever since Nicholas had come here, Gervase had been his sole friend and confidant, but since Anne had married him, things had changed and the steward seemed to have withdrawn into himself. Nicholas was forced to consider that he might be jealous of the relationship between himself and Anne. Possibly because Anne was so obviously in love with him.

Whatever the reason, Gervase had become an embarrassment and irritation. He seemed to exude the hurt of a man who had once been a close associate, but who was now spurned . . . it certainly made Nicholas feel uneasy when he sensed Gervase's reproachful eyes upon him. Whenever the steward entered the room these days, Nicholas felt uncomfortable. If only the man would leave and find himself a new position with a different lord! All he had done was to marry and be happy, for God's sake!

He loved Anne. It was so strong, the link between them both, that he felt almost sick with longing when he was away from her. The only time, thank God, he'd had to leave her was when the King had been involved in his spat with the Lords Marcher. Then Nick had left his comfortable existence here and travelled up to

Wales, helping protect the border with a small force against the might of the men who would seek to remove the King from his throne.

Well, nothing much wrong with that, in Nicholas's view. He'd be perfectly happy to see the King gone, and those appalling thieves the Despensers, so long as the replacement was stronger and safer. Trouble was, the next man was usually worse than the first.

The main thing was, as soon as he returned, his wife proved her adoration for him, and now, as a result, he was confident of a child, a boy who would take his name and reputation onwards.

Christ, but he was proud of his darling wife. Thank God Gervase wasn't here with his long face and cow-like eyes, spoiling everything.

He almost made Nicholas feel guilty. And what angered him was he had no idea why he should feel that way.

Chapter Nine

When she was introduced to the two strangers, Lady Anne was struck first by Sir Baldwin's quick, searching observation of her, and then by his smile. It lit up his whole face.

It was in the hall, early in the evening, while servants set out the table on the dais for them. This was not to be a great banquet, for the household had already taken their food at their accustomed time, a little before noon, but in the presence of such guests Anne had seen to it that there was a good selection of dishes prepared. It was only a shame that they had been so long in coming.

The hall itself was an excellent place to entertain. With the high ceiling of smoke-blackened rafters and thick thatch, it was Anne's favourite room in the castle. Large enough to squeeze all the vill's men inside for winter's celebrations, yet cosy enough with a good fire for a more intimate gathering.

She had set stools and benches about the fire, which was glowing and crackling nicely, throwing light against the walls. A pair of cressets at the wall flickered warmly, and candles of good quality lit the table on the dais. There was a pair of heavy chairs for Nicholas and herself, and opposite them a bench for their guests. They could eat at the table, then relax before the fire. More than adequate, she thought.

'My lady, I am honoured to meet you.'

'This is Sir Baldwin de Furnshill,' Nicholas said. 'And his companion, Bailiff Simon Puttock.'

She saw the dark-haired knight smile. 'Hardly my "companion" – Simon is not my servant, he is my oldest friend. We have been on pilgrimage together to Santiago de Compostela, and are on our way home. It was the merest chance that we happened to be passing here.'

'But your presence was welcome, especially since you could confirm my suspicions about Athelina's death.'

'So far as we could,' Sir Baldwin sighed.

'And her poor children,' said the Bailiff. Simon Puttock looked to Anne as though he had a less firm stomach than the knight. His face was decidedly pale, and she gave him an understanding smile.

'It must have been a horrible sight. My husband told me a little about it.'

The servants entered, trays laden. This might not be the greatest castle in the land, but the men knew how to present themselves. Each carried the platters high, while all had a large towel draped over their shoulders. Anne began to usher her guests to their places at the table. As she took her own seat, she cast an eye over the dishes, but confessed herself content. Ralph, the cook, had exceeded her expectations.

Sir Baldwin sat and surveyed the dishes with a sober expression, like a man who was interested but not devoted to food; for his part the Bailiff appeared to lose his yellowness, and instead his face took on a ruddy hue. Probably the normal colour for a man who spent much of his time in the saddle, Anne thought. He was a pleasing-looking man, with his regular features, dark hair and pale-grey eyes. When he caught her glance, he grinned. 'This makes me feel more at home! Real English food.'

'You missed it on your travels?'

Seeing Nicholas begin to eat, Simon speared a slab of meat with his knife and almost thrust it into his mouth, only hesitating when he realised he should answer. 'I did. Foreign food is peculiar. It isn't so hearty as ours. Doesn't mix well in an English stomach. Down in Galicia, I was ill for weeks. It must have been the food that did it.'

'You must stay here as long as you like and rebuild your strength, then,' she said warmly.

'I am sure that there must be an inn?' Baldwin said politely, but there was little enthusiasm in his face.

'Yes,' Nicholas said, 'but it is not attractive. My wife is quite right. You must remain here with us. I am sure that there is no urgency in your journey homewards?'

'Only the urgency of a man who misses his wife and family,' Sir Baldwin remonstrated gently.

Lady Anne grinned broadly. 'I wish my own husband had been so devoted, when he was on his travels!'

'He travels much?'

'No, but during the wars with Mortimer and the Lords Marcher, he had to go. This is the result of his homecoming,' she smiled, patting her belly.

Sir Baldwin inclined his head graciously. 'Any man would find it impossible to leave so beautiful a companion, let alone stay away from her.'

A compliment that was meant honestly was always a delight, but coming from a man who was so senior in rank, that made her almost light-headed with pleasure. It was kind of him, very kind.

Her husband was talking again.

'The Coroner should be here before too long, I hope. He lives just outside Bodmin, so he could be here before noon tomorrow, if he is nearby. I only hope he hasn't been sent away on another murder.'

Baldwin said, 'We could wait until he arrives. It would be pleasant to speak to him, and he may have questions for us. We weren't the First Finders, but we were early witnesses of the bodies.'

'So long as it's a quick inquest,' Simon growled through a chicken bone. 'I want to get home.'

Baldwin laughed and leaned towards Anne. 'He is not only keen to see his wife, he has a new job.'

'Aye, well, I'd like to get there before the end of the year,' Simon said.

Nicholas glanced from one to the other. 'What is that? What new job are you to take?'

'I've been asked to go to Dartmouth as the Keeper of the Port for Abbot Champeaux. He has bought the farm of the port, and wants me to manage it for him,' Simon said.

'That is fascinating,' Anne said. 'You must be very pleased.'

Simon nodded, but he was keen to avoid further discussion of the matter. He kept his head down.

Anne was surprised, because from being a mere bailiff on the moors to becoming responsible for the Abbot's Farm of the Port must represent a marvellous improvement in position. It was more than she could hope for, she thought with a pang.

Nicholas was no youngster. He was certainly valued by Sir Henry, but it was unlikely that he would ever rise beyond this little castle. He had achieved his highest position, and although he professed himself content, and Anne would never suggest that she felt otherwise, both, she knew, had a sneaking jealousy for men like this Baldwin. She would have liked to be wedded to a man who had the possibility of receiving golden spurs and a knight's belt.

Born to rule, this Baldwin had the grace and courtesy which she associated with the best-born men in the realm. If he was ill-at-ease, he hid it. He was also clearly a man with brawn. His arms were as thick as her own husband's, and his neck muscles were enormous: he was obviously used to wearing armour and riding a destrier.

Here, in the hall, with the different candles and torches throwing their light haphazardly, she saw a long history in his face. It was a face that had seen a lot, perhaps witnessed too much cruelty and horror. He had suffered.

They were there in Nicholas's face too, the hard edges of a warrior's suffering. He, like this knight, had deep gouges carved in his cheeks and forehead, the channels of pain without which no fighter could advance. If a man wished to make his living by war, he must gain such wounds, unless he won the other, less honourable signs of dissipation and excess. Such men were not to be entertained in Lady Anne's hall, though.

'How many men do you have here?' Sir Baldwin was asking.

'Including myself, twelve at present. We are a small garrison, but then our lord lives away, and his main household is with him.'

'Excuse me, but you are not knighted?' Baldwin asked.

'I am afraid not, Sir Baldwin. I never earned that accolade.'

'My friend, I am sure that you deserve it more than many a gilded parrot in the King's court,' Baldwin said easily. 'You are a man who has been to war, I see, and from your look you've not always been on the winning side.'

'What does that mean?'

'Nothing, Nicholas,' Baldwin said with raised brows. 'I meant no insult, my friend, but it would be rare indeed for a man who fought in several wars not to have been on the side which did not win occasionally. It is no reflection upon your martial prowess, I assure you.'

'Yes, well, a man who has been in the service of the King must have known defeats,' Nicholas said.

'Of course. I too have known defeats, my friend,' Baldwin said softly, but Anne was sure that she could see sadness in his eyes as he spoke.

Anne took a little more meat from the pile in the dish. She and Nick had never discussed his past in any great detail. There was not a lot to tell, he always said, but for how wet the Welsh borders were, and how miserable the climate for a young soldier. Of the fighting he had said nothing, and Anne had not pressed him. It would have given her no pleasure to hear that he had been a brutal, violent killer. So the two avoided that subject – although now she could be tempted to find out a little. It was so strange to hear him flash out in near anger.

'I apologise, Sir Knight. It's just been a painful day, with that poor woman being found.'

'Especially with her dead children,' Anne said pensively, her hand back on her bump. She felt, rather than saw, the eyes of the three men turn to her.

The door opened, and the new squire called Warin entered. He glanced at them, crossing to a table and gesturing to a servant. Soon Richer also walked in and joined Warin.

There was something about those two which she found unsettling. Warin seemed to hold little respect for her or her husband, and she had mentioned his insolence to Nicholas already, but Nicholas had been quite short, saying only that Warin came with a letter of recommendation from their master – and if Sir Henry of Cardinham felt that this arrogant fellow was a suitable guard for his castle, who was he to disagree?

This was the age-old problem. Nicholas had more experience in his little finger than this Warin possessed in his entire soul, yet Warin was presumably well-born. He would one day be knighted, while Nicholas would remain here, mouldering slowly until he expired.

Looking up, she saw that Warin was watching Richer. The fellow seemed withdrawn, like one who was close to collapse. She wondered at that, but then she saw that Warin had turned and now studied Sir Baldwin and his friend. Nicholas noticed his interest, and called Warin and Richer over. The two were introduced to the guests, and Anne was secretly pleased to see how Sir Baldwin cast a negligent eye over them both, although he glanced at Nicholas as he was introduced to Richer. Anne herself noticed that Nicholas was as fulsome introducing Richer as he was Squire Warin. It was strange: he was respectful towards Warin, a man so much his junior, and almost affectionate towards Richer, who was a mere man-at-arms and rated no respect.

'You are a squire?' Sir Baldwin asked Warin.

'Yes. I hope to be knighted before long, Sir Baldwin,' Warin replied.

'But until then you are here to protect the castle under the castellan here,' Baldwin said pointedly. 'In whose service were you before you came here?'

'That of Sir Henry,' Warin said.

'You have been long in his service? That is good. Perhaps you knew the castellan before coming to serve him, then?'

'I fear not,' Nicholas said. 'Sir Henry has rarely been this way, and then only for short visits. We had never met before Warin arrived here some few weeks ago. I am sure that he shall be a credit to the castle, though.'

Baldwin turned to Richer, saying, 'You knew that woman Athelina? You seemed protective when another man belittled her.'

Richer looked at him with eyes that had dulled with loss. 'I used to live here, but I left many years ago. When I left, I loved her. I still do.'

'You left her?'

Richer was pale, unsettled. His eyes were slightly narrowed, and he raised a hand to his brow like a man with a headache. 'My family died in a fire at our cottage while I was at the harvest celebrations. When I saw that they were all dead, I just wanted to get away.'

Nicholas, ever the generous-minded master, Anne thought, bless him, said, 'Are you well, Richer? Would you like to rest?'

'I am well, master. Just a . . . a slight headache, that is all.'

'Where did you go?' Baldwin continued.

'I joined Sir Henry's men, and I've been with him ever since. And with Squire Warin.'

Baldwin gave a sharp frown, but then Anne saw him shrug slightly as though it was of no matter. 'Tell me, did you see her on your return? Was she so apparently crazed that she might murder in desperation?'

'If I had seen that, I'd have saved her!' Richer exclaimed, and then his hand returned to his head, and he gulped wine from the cup in his other. 'No. I don't believe that she could have murdered anyone. She was too gentle, too kind and loving.'

'There can be little doubt,' Nicholas said softly. 'Who else would wish to harm her or her children?'

'No one!' Warin said. 'My friend here wondered whether it could be some madman who had tried to rob her, but a felon would scarcely go to the effort of making it appear that she had hanged herself after cutting the throats of the two boys. No, she was clearly mad.'

Baldwin nodded. 'You knew her?'

'Not at all, no.'

'Yet you pass judgement,' Baldwin said, his eyes upon the miserable features of Richer.

'Under the circumstances I am happy to do so. Can there be any doubt of her guilt?' Warin asked, and Anne was sure that she saw his gaze flash briefly to *her* as though he was making a comment on her propriety! She flushed to the roots of her hair with shame and vexation. The man had no right to look at her like that! Could he know of her treachery? Did *others* know? she suddenly wondered with a keen fear.

That last time with her lover, walking by the river, there had been someone there, she knew. Later she had seen Athelina walking nearby with one of her whelps, smiling at her as though butter wouldn't melt, but there had been something in her eyes . . . It had turned Anne's belly to ice at the time, but then she had forgotten it. After all, she had been so lonely.

Baldwin, she was sure, had seen Warin's look as well as her

own response. Now the knight glanced again at Warin, but then looked at Anne with a smile, plainly dismissing the squire, and Anne was left with a thrilling in her heart, certain that this knight had chosen to insult the squire because of his cavalier attitude towards her husband and herself.

'My lady, I am deeply sorry to have brought any news of death with me into this charming home,' Baldwin said, and Anne was sure he was sincere. His serious, dark eyes bored into hers for a moment, and then he smiled, looking down at her swelling belly. 'It is good to see that new life is coming.'

'Yes,' Anne returned happily, and glanced over at her husband. For some reason he was staring down at his plate with an expression of pain and bitterness on his face. Anne almost touched his arm, but then she withdrew her hand and began to chat with her guests.

Her husband was quite certainly out of sorts, she said to herself. She only hoped he was not sickening for something.

Muriel heard the hooves quite late on the following Tuesday morning, and went to the door to ensure that her sons were nowhere near the roadway. If there was a danger, they'd be likely to find and embrace it wholeheartedly.

There was more than one horse, she realised as she stepped outside into the cool of the cloudy morning. She could hear this, rather than see it, as the view from their cottage was restricted. First there was a bend in the roadway, so they couldn't see along it until they'd walked to the edge of the logpile, but there were also the enclosing trees. From here, down in the valley, she could see their trunks rising in ranks up the hills.

People thought it a dreadfully lonely place, but that was how she liked it. Some folk enjoyed the bustle and speed of the vill, but not Muriel. Here she was safe, she felt. The place was sufficiently far from the vill for them to be secluded, yet near enough should they need urgent help. Not that there *was* much help in the vill. If there was a broken bone or torn muscle, Iwan the old smith could sometimes help, but there was no one else with any knowledge of leech-craft. A few older women claimed to have some understanding of plants, but Muriel would prefer to ask the priest for a little prayer to be said for an injury. Somehow the idea of mashing plants together and using them as a poultice never appealed to her, and in any case, if the Good Lord had decided to take her, she was content with His decision. So long as her children were safe, that was all that mattered. And her husband, of course, she added loyally.

She stared along the roadway and saw her sons approaching. Hamelin was sitting in the small cart and Aumery was pulling it; both lads were gurgling with delight. The scene made her laugh aloud, for their enjoyment was very infectious.

The little cart had been made by a wheelwright some years before for his own children, and when they had grown too old for it, his wife had offered it to Muriel. A simple two-wheeled vehicle with six-spoked wheels, the man had made it for fun on his pole-lathe largely to prove to himself that he could do something so delicate. For a child as young as Aumery, a two-wheeled cart would have been too easily tipped up, so the man had set a peg in the base of the cart, so that it could be pushed about the yard easily. Now there were lines in the dirt all about the cottage.

'Here, Aumie,' she called, and the boy turned.

She smiled at him, crouching with arms open wide, and chuckling with laughter, he pushed the cart about until it was facing her, then started to run to her.

Then the noise of hooves suddenly grew louder. In her delight at the sight of her two sons, Muriel had forgotten the riders and now she realised with horror that Aumery was only partly across the track. The horses were coming closer, faster – *too* fast! They must arrive here any moment! They would run down her children!

With a cry of fear, she sprang up and ran across the path. The horses had come around the bend in the road and were almost upon her. With a last desperate cry, she snatched her sons, enfolding them in a close embrace to protect them from those terrible hooves.

She'd often heard that horseshoes could grow as sharp as a razor by cobbles and paving slabs, but it wasn't until three years ago that she'd seen how evil a weapon a horseshoe could be. A girl had been struck a glancing blow by a stallion. Instantly her face was a mass of blood. Nobody was concerned at first, because they knew a head wound would bleed appallingly. Then someone wiped away the blood and saw the the bone, sheared through as though by an axe, and the grey mass beneath. Muriel had stared for an instant, then her stomach heaved.

Now she waited with dread. It could only be a matter of seconds. She gripped Aumery's head and pulled it to her breast, tugging Hamelin to her lap and safety as he started to wail. Aumery was already sobbing in fear, and there was a terrible rending inside her which, she suddenly understood, was her own sobbing.

There was a rush of noise, a slamming of hooves, and then a hideous blow on her head . . . and she toppled forward into the dull nothingness that opened to swallow her.

Chapter Ten

Letitia was the first person people thought of calling whenever something bad happened. They went to her not because she was the wife of the Constable, but because she was one person upon whom everyone could count. Letty always knew the best way of dealing with a problem. It was her steadiness in an emergency that had her summoned to the difficult birthings, or to the child with a scalded arm, or the man with a stab wound. All would go to her, and she would deal with each eventuality as she saw fit.

Susan the alewife it was who appeared at her door, her face drawn and anxious. 'Letty, there's been a terrible accident.'

'Who?'

She was already pulling on a shawl as she listened intently. There was no point in rushing off and then arriving without the necessary tools; better by far that she waited until she knew what was needed. There was satisfaction in being prepared; just a few moments of her time could make the difference between a person suffering and surviving.

'It's poor Muriel,' Susan said breathlessly. 'She's been run down – by the Coroner of all people!'

'Poor Muriel,' Letitia echoed, appalled. 'Is she dead?'

'She lives, but her head is cut open. She heard the horses and sheltered her sons. They were playing in the road.'

'She would.' Letitia nodded approvingly. 'We can only hope that she isn't too badly hurt. Head wounds can be so dangerous.'

'It's not too bad,' Susan guessed. 'The skull looks unharmed, but her flesh is cut away.'

Letitia nodded. She could wash out the wound with some oil, and then put on a poultice to draw out the evil humours. 'And there are the boys, of course?'

'Yes. You'll have to look after them. Serlo won't be capable on his own.'

'Huh! Not that arse!'

'Aha! What has your marvellous brother-in-law done this time?'

There was always a comfort in talking to Susan. She was a confident, sensible woman, independent and bright. Although she was a tavernkeeper, she could hold her tongue when asked. Not that there was anything secret in this. It was woman's talk. 'He came to our house last night. Told us that Athelina was little better than a slut because she had two children in as many years. Surely he knows Alexander and I have been trying . . .'

'It'll come for you surely, Letty,' Susan said, patting her hand consolingly. 'It's just some folks find it takes longer than others.'

'The way he spoke of her! You'd think he hated all women, especially those with children.'

'He's just a fool,' Susan said. 'I'll refuse to serve him in my alehouse if he's not more polite.'

'Do that and you'll lose all your profits,' Letty joked. 'I can't help thinking that he despises all women – perhaps because he never knew a mother when he was a child. All he knew was Alexander.'

Susan smiled but there was nothing to say.

Soon Letty sniffed, wiped her nose, and stood. 'Right!' she said briskly. 'Is Muriel at her home?'

'Yes. We didn't want to move her after the accident. But the boys . . .'

'They can come here, and so can she. I can look after them, although I don't know how we'll cope with Serlo as well. That would be too much.'

They were soon done. Letitia packed her bag, hesitated over the basket of eggs, and then selected the freshest she could find. Muriel deserved careful protection and egg-whites could help clean deeper cuts. Ready, she led the way at a fast trot to the mill.

Outside were a pair of dark brown mounts, one a large rounsey, the second a smaller pony with a splatter of light brown coat on his flank. Letitia scarcely gave them a glance, but instead shoved at the door and walked into Serlo and Muriel's house.

It was a small, rather noisome place, filled with the odours of a home: a baby's excrement, sour milk, vomit, and the smell of sheep from the small fold at the farther end of the long, narrow cottage. The fire sat in the middle of the earthen floor on a hard clay base, and it had been carefully tended, Letitia saw with an approving nod. A clerk squatted at its side, a doleful little man with a pasty face washed free of any semblance of cheer. He glanced up. There was a sombre look about him, as though he was waiting to be accused of murder, and Letitia assumed he was the rider who had struck Muriel.

Muriel's bed was a low wooden frame with a thin mattress stuffed with fragrant herbs and hay, and she lay on it with her head flung back like a corpse. Her eyes were closed and her face dreadfully pallid, so much so that Letitia wondered immediately whether she had dallied too long and was here to witness the death of her sister-in-law. Yet even as she turned to whisper to Susan, Muriel's eyes opened. For all that they were dull and had bruises beneath them, there was none of Athelina's despair or madness in them.

That at least was a relief. Letitia crossed the floor and squatted beside her. 'This is not going to hurt too much,' she said, and Muriel smiled faintly up at her, as though recognising the dishonesty of the statement. Then she closed them tightly as Letitia began to examine the wound.

Later, when she had cleaned it and rinsed it first with oil, then with a little egg-white, she wrapped a clean linen towel about her head. Only then did Letitia glance at Susan. 'Where are the boys?'

'They're out with their father,' said a deeper voice. A man in a faded grey tunic appeared from the darkness near the doorway. He was young, with olive skin, of slender build for a knight, but he wore the spurs and belt like a man born to the noble class. He stepped forward until he was close to Letitia. His eyes were dark as soot, set rather close together about a hawk-like nose. Now he looked unutterably sad. 'I ordered that the miller should come and collect them while their mother was seen to. Will she be all right?'

'She should live, unless she's unlucky,' Letitia said, holding Muriel's hand gently. 'You'll be all right, won't you? Godspeed, Muriel. Sleep well. I'll look after your sons.'

There was a subtle reciprocation of pressure on her fingers, and then she put Muriel's hand back down on the blanket.

'So your clerk managed to knock her down? He must have been riding very fast,' she said accusingly, staring at the whey-faced fellow by the hearth. 'I hope you will compensate this woman for her suffering.'

The man glanced at his clerk, then turned back to her with a little grimace. 'It wasn't him, I fear.'

'It was *you*. Always the same: it's the wealthy and careless who inflict pain on others,' she said uncompromisingly.

'In this case, it wasn't frivolous, madam. I was hurrying to another body. A woman who died in the vill here?'

She looked at him. 'You are the Coroner?'

He gave a wry smile. 'You think me too young?'

'I do not care about your age, sir, but I fear the inexperience of a man who might cause one death while investigating another.'

He winced, she was glad to see, and apologised. 'It was this summons, madam. I had to come and view the body, but I also

have two other suspicious deaths to investigate. I was in a great
hurry . . . and now, because of my haste, I could have killed a
young mother protecting her children. It is a miserable man you
see before you, madam.'

'That's all very well,' she said, glancing once more at Muriel.
'You may also have made a widower of her husband and taken
away the mother of two sons.' I have seen what that loss can do to
a man, she thought to herself, and was vaguely disquieted by
the reflection. There was nothing wrong with her man, nothing
wrong with Alex. The only one who had grown ill-favoured and
unpleasant was Serlo.

'My apologies. I only hope she recovers. In the meantime . . .'
The Coroner reached into his purse, pulled out a few coins and
studied them carefully, the coins close to his nose, his eyes
narrowed to slits. 'Here.' He handed her one.

She could feel by its weight that it was a valuable coin and
thought she should give it to Serlo, but then rejected the idea.
That would be madness indeed, giving that wastrel and spendthrift
money – she might as well pass it straight to Susan. No, she must
keep it safe, she thought.

'Thank you, sir,' she said. Then: 'Susan, I must see to the boys.
Can you remain here until I have fetched Jan from home?'

'God's blood! Of course I can wait to help poor Muriel. I've
got to get back before too long, though. There'll be the harvesters
arriving.'

'Good. Do you remain here then, and I shall send my maid to
take over shortly.'

'We should be continuing our journey, then,' the knight said.
'Come, Roger, we have to go and view this body.'

Julia, the young woman who acted as housekeeper for Father Adam,
had woken later than usual this morning. The death yesterday had
shocked her, but she knew that she must continue as though nothing

was altered; otherwise the priest might notice and wonder. When he returned after his services, she had to hurry to prepare his food; her thoughts had been so tangled, caught up with Athelina and her miserable end, that she hadn't noticed the passing time. Mind, she had time to consider the new fellow – Ivo, the lad with the winning grin, the smutty sense of humour and strong frame. If she were ever in danger, this fellow might rescue her.

'I'll have an egg today, Julia,' came the call from the little hall, and Julia leaped to her feet, startled, before setting her child on the floor and hurtling about the room. She readied a platter, cutting bread into rindless sheets, and set a pot of dripping beside it on a tray. Going out to the nesting place of the irascible white hen, who shot off angrily to the other side of the yard after pecking viciously at her hand, she rescued the egg and took her prize back into the house, only to see the baby crawling off through the doorway into the parlour. Hurrying, she gathered up the tray with the bread, a wooden board and knife, and carried them to the priest's main room.

It wasn't large, but at least it smelled wholesome in there. He didn't have a dog so his reeds weren't infested with bones and shit, and Julia was happy that her boy was safe in there, although when she had set the tray on the table by Adam, she heard his swift intake of breath, and spun round to see her son crawling towards the fire. She swept him up and set him back on her hip. 'You little bugger, you'll be the death of me,' she said with exasperation.

'You shouldn't swear at him,' Adam remonstrated, but she gave the priest a glare.

'What else can I do? He's into everything right now, and I can't do anything but smack him to warn him.'

'He'd be happier with a little gentle persuasion, I expect.'

'Father, you stick to what you know and I'll look after this one. He's a little animal, just like any other, and he needs training.' She chucked the fellow under the chin. 'In't that right, Ned? So keep off the fire, you little devil, or I'll tan your hide for you.'

She plonked him down again and fetched a griddle, sitting it straight on the embers. There would be enough heat to cook Father Adam's egg. She broke it onto the warm disk, and waited until it was whitened through, the yolk a pale yellow in its midst, and then picked the griddle from the fire and brought it to him, using a knife to prise the egg from the metal and slide it onto his platter. Then she sat on his bench and watched him eat.

He was an odd fellow, this young priest. When he'd asked her if she'd like to cook for him, she assumed he was after her body, thinking she was a typical desperate woman who would be prepared to turn harlot to satisfy his whims. Well, at the time she wasn't! She was a young mother, but her man was happy to support her, so he said, and the last thing she needed was a randy vicar trying to get into her skirts. No, thank *you*! But her man told her not to be daft, the priest was helping them, and she ought to go cook for him.

And so she did. But more recently, when she learned that her lover, the father of her child, had lost interest in her and their boy, she suddenly had no means of supporting herself, and then of course she was glad of her place here in the priest's house. It didn't matter if he'd wanted to bed her then – she'd have accepted him as she would accept any man who might protect her. He gave her food and shelter – who was she to refuse his advances if he needed something in return? No mother could turn her nose up at food and a warm bed for herself and her child.

But early on it became obvious that her lover had been right: Father Adam showed no interest in her. He knew of her lover, and was content to let her come and go as she wanted. Perfect. Yes, and her man could visit, too, out in her room, so they were all happy.

She'd never forget that first day. Adam had offered her a job in his home, but there was no unsubtle hint about his virility or her beauty such as she had anticipated. Instead, on her first night, he had directed her to the little haybarn beside his house.

'Bring hay from there and we'll make you a palliasse.'

As good as his word, when she brought in an armful of hay, he had already put a blanket on the floor. He spread her hay on it, then draped a second blanket on top. He himself was to sleep in his chamber, a tiny room constructed high in the roof.

Once, much later, when her lover had grown bored with her and moved to his next woman, she had watched Father Adam climb the ladder to his own bed, and then, from gratitude but also with some curiosity and in acknowledgement of her debt to him, she followed him. When she reached the top, she began to untie the thongs that held her thin dress about her, but he put a hand up and shook his head.

'There's no need,' he said softly. 'You may return to your own bed.'

And, vaguely confused, she had done so. She huddled in her cold bed with a strange sense of discomfort. No man had ever rejected her before, and the experience of first her lover and now this priest refusing her was not pleasant. She found herself touching her arms, feeling her waist, cupping her breasts, reassuring herself that there was nothing wrong with her. No, all seemed well. And if that lad yesterday was anything to go by, men could still fancy her. He, Ivo, had sat at the table and watched her as she went about her cleaning and tidying, at last offering to help when she had to fill the bucket from the well. As she filled it and he bent to pick it up, his hand touched her breast, then her thigh, and he grinned at her when she drew away, slapping at his hand. He had no shame, that much was certain. But he had a nice smile.

Her life at Father Adam's house had been smooth and easy, and it was only now, with the death of Athelina, that there was an undercurrent. Julia had felt it as she entered the room yesterday with those two strangers here, before she'd even heard of Athelina's death. The tall knight, he'd been suspicious. She'd seen it in his eyes as soon as he caught sight of her. Thought she was some mare with an itch in her tail for a priest. Well, he could think all he wanted, but as far as Julia was concerned, at last she'd found some peace and she wasn't going to give it up just because some stranger got the wrong idea. Although she wouldn't want him to think badly of Adam. That wouldn't be fair. No reason for the priest to suffer just because he'd been kind to her.

Poor Athelina. Adam was pained by her death, she saw. It wasn't right to kill her poor sons – she shouldn't have done that. Christ, the thought of killing her own little Ned . . . it was just unthinkable, a nightmare. No, she loved her little boy. Didn't matter that his father was a shit and bastard, who had refused to marry her. She'd lost her reputation already, sleeping with a man who wasn't yet her husband and then, when she began to show the pregnancy, she lost her home too. Father John, the priest at Temple where she used to live, had told her that there was no place in his flock for a fornicator, and said she should leave – go to the parish where her child's father lived. So here she'd come, and Adam had taken her in.

Athelina had asked for no help from him. She had her house already anyway, somewhere to put her head. But she was widowed, and her lover had abandoned her. Perhaps that was why she felt so bad. She'd got used to having a man in her life, and when he left, that was that so far as Athelina knew. There was nothing now but the steady, unrelenting demands of motherhood.

Julia could all too easily understand that desperation, that loneliness. She had to – it was she, after all, who had stolen Athelina's man from her; it was she who had enjoyed his money for that little while. Yet now, that too had dried up. It was fortunate that Adam seemed to like having her in his house to keep it clean and warm.

Yes, Julia would have liked to comfort poor Father Adam, but she knew, after that last time, that any approach by her would be misconstrued. Best to leave well alone.

Anyway, why bother the priest when there was a happy-go-lucky ostler at a loose end? Ivo was a good name, she decided, and she wondered idly what his surname was.

Letitia found the mill operating slowly; the wheel and the stones graunching together, making a steady, rhythmic din that she could only assume emanated straight from Hell. It took the fourth bellow of *'Serlo!'* to attract his attention, and at last he peered down at her from a trapdoor in the ceiling, his face smeared with flour, his hair prematurely grey from the fine dust that permeated the entire building.

'What?'

She coughed from the mist that seemed to clog her nostrils and throat. 'Come down here! I can't bellow at you all the time. Where are the boys? I've come to take them back to my house. You can't look after them here.'

He disappeared for a while, then reappeared and clambered heavily down the ladder. At her insistence, they left the mill to talk, and once outside he grunted, 'They're fine. I'll see to them.'

'Don't be a fool! You can't keep an eye on them here. You'll end up with them getting hurt as well.' At least here in the open the noise was dulled to a thumping and shaking that she was sure she could feel through the soles of her feet.

'My wife ought to be looking after them. That bladder of pus who knocked her down, he ought to pay,' Serlo blustered. 'He could have *killed* her! Fucking Coroners!'

'Yes, well, fine, but what about the boys? You can't keep them in there with you. Where are they?'

'I left them outside so they'd be safe. Didn't want them falling into the machine, like the silly fool of an apprentice I used to have.'

'*Where* outside?'

'Over near the logs.'

Letitia stared at him. 'You mean by the leat? What if one falls in?' In her mind she had a vision of the great paddles on the wheel beating Aumery's head into a froth of red bubbles at the water's surface. She fled to the leat and could only gasp in relief to see them both playing with old snail shells and nuts at the edge of the woods.

'See?' he said nastily. 'I told you they'd be fine.'

'You have no idea, do you? I'm taking them back to my house.'

'You can't. They're fine. I'll look after them.'

She peered down her nose at him once more, but it didn't seem to have any impact. 'I want my nephews put somewhere safe, Serlo. Let me take them to your brother's house.'

'I said *no*! You always look down on me, don't you? Well, I can take care of my own sons, Letty. Leave us alone.'

'At least let me take them to your house, then. My maid will be there to look after Muriel. They'll be safer there.'

'Oh yeah? That's where their mother was nearly killed this morning, woman! You think that's safer than here?'

Chapter Eleven

If he had wanted to make a worse entrance, Coroner Jules was not sure how he could have done so.

He'd never forget turning that corner and seeing the woman curled in a ball in the middle of the roadway. She'd tightened, like a hedgehog when a dog approaches, until she was like a small knot of muscles, and then his rounsey had tried to leap over her. Mostly, he succeeded, too. Sir Jules's horse was not trained in war, and would automatically avoid stepping on other creatures, and he shied, leaping, but as he did so, Roger's palfrey barged into them, and the rounsey must slip sideways, catching the poor woman a glancing blow.

At first he thought it might be worse than it actually was. He had thought that one of the children might have been hurt as well, but fortunately both were safe, as their lungs testified . . . astonishing how much noise a brat could make. It was their mother whom he hit, though, and the sight of all the blood probably made them anxious. The scene certainly made him anxious! It was hardly the duty of the Coroner to create more bodies to investigate.

Sir Jules had only been made Coroner a short while ago, when Sir Simon of Launceston died in an accident, falling from his horse. He couldn't wait to get back home again. Still, at least he wouldn't have to remain here for too long. He would go and make records of the other deaths, and then head for home again, and a chance to rest awhile.

Away, he thought, from this blasted clerk.

Roger swung down from his palfrey and glanced at Sir Jules. 'I think that this is the house.'

Julia opened the door to find a pair of men waiting.

'Is this the house of the priest? I am the Coroner, and this is my clerk. Where is the priest, in the church?'

'I am here, Coroner. Please come inside. You are here for poor Athelina?'

'If that's her name. I was called here last night and came as swiftly as I might,' the Coroner said. 'I am Sir Jules of Fowey. You are . . .?'

'Adam Tailyour at your service. It is a sad case, Coroner. A woman tormented by widowhood and poverty, and the despair got to her.'

'Didn't the vill help her?'

'The vill did all it could, yes. The castle and others gave her alms, and kept her clothed and fed. But sometimes a woman will become frenzied in her loneliness. This Athelina did so, and she killed her two boys before killing herself. A terrible tragedy.'

'I see. Well, we should go to the place as soon as you have gathered the jury and called the First Finder and other nearest people. Please send a message to the Constable to tell him I'm here and am eager to call the inquest as soon as possible.'

As he sat, Julia saw him lick his dry lips and glance about him nervously, and she thought to herself, Aha! You aren't eager at all, are you? You're nearly shitting yourself at the thought of the inquest, Coroner!

Baldwin and Simon were warned by Ivo that the Coroner had arrived, and the three made their way to the yard before the church.

'You can stay away if you like,' Baldwin told the youth

ungraciously. He had a dislike of ghoulish interest, and he was unpleasantly aware that there would be many watching the inquest just for a sight of the bodies.

'Don't mind if I do,' Ivo said cheerfully. 'Might get a chance to see the girl from the priest's house again. Anyway, there's nothing to do up at the castle except play at dice, and I've already won a fair amount from the guards there. Probably best I don't hang around alone.'

'You're after the priest's maid?' Simon asked in disbelief. 'I doubt whether she'd risk her position there. If he learns she's been playing with you, he'll have her out in an instant.'

'Why d'you reckon that? She's not his mare,' Ivo said confidently. 'He's more interested in men.'

'You mean he is a catamite?' Baldwin asked with surprise, and then he realised his error of the day before. The man was no womaniser.

Simon had a less understanding attitude to homosexuality and he scowled with revulsion. 'Are you sure? I thought the child was his.'

'No. She told me that she was made pregnant by a lover, and the priest gave her sanctuary. She cooks for him and keeps his home warm, but that's all.'

Baldwin looked about him as they reached the church. 'Is she here?'

Ivo swept the area with a sharp eye. 'Nope. Maybe I'll see if she's at home. I'll find you later.'

'Arrogant puppy,' Baldwin muttered.

'Look,' Simon said, all thoughts of the priest gone. 'There's Lady Anne. I wonder what she's doing here?'

'Hardly a maternal act, coming to view a pair of boys' corpses,' Baldwin said with disgust. She wasn't alone, however. The whole vill seemed to have turned out.

*   *   *

It was not the bodies of the two poor murdered boys which tempted Lady Anne to join her husband and go to view the inquest, it was the body of Athelina.

Anne was more shocked than she had allowed her husband to know by the death of the other woman. What's more, she thought she knew who was responsible: a lover who had discarded his mistress for a younger one.

She shivered. The weather was improving, and there were occasional gaps between the clouds, but it was still chilly, giving the place a curious atmosphere of doom. Not, Anne reflected, an unsuitable mood for an inquest of this type.

'Hear me! I am Sir Jules of Fowey, Coroner for this county, and I call on all who have any knowledge of the deaths of this woman and her children to come forward and answer my inquest.'

His voice was a surprise. When he shouted, the weaselly-looking man had a deep voice with a slight trace of a foreign tongue. Perhaps it was Burgundian. There were several men whom the Lady Anne had met who came to this part of the country from there. It was their interest in trade that first brought them to the ports, usually seeking markets for their strong red wines, and some travelled inland to see whether they could do business with the tin miners.

Sir Jules began in the normal manner, stripping the three bodies and declaring his findings, but once Anne was over the shock of the sight of the two boys' throats, with the gaping wounds where the knife had slashed, she found the whole matter tedious.

Athelina's body was more shocking, in some ways. She had throttled herself, the rope bruising her neck, but not breaking her spine. She must, so the Coroner said, have dangled there for days. The marks of nibbling at the feet and hands of the two boys showed that the three had been there long enough for the rats to grow interested. That image, of the dead woman, desolated after her husband's death and broken by a life of continuous hardship, hanging from a beam and swinging gently for days because no one knew nor cared enough to seek her out, burned itself into the other woman's imagination. She could all too easily understand Athelina's state of mind.

All women needed companionship, and Anne had lost her friends and family at the same time because of the awful starvation which had affected everybody in the kingdom, not merely in Cornwall alone. And then, as if by a miracle, she had come here to Cardinham, where the kindness of Nicholas had given her fresh hope. Now she lived in the present and tried to forget the crushing loneliness she had known when she had lost all those closest to her. She was unable to succeed entirely, of course. Losing them had felt like having her soul ripped from her living flesh.

That was why she had sunk to giving herself to another man.

It was fear that drove her to it. Nicholas had been gone such a long time, and she had convinced herself that he had died of a disease, like her father. Panic set in. If her man was dead, she must find another to protect her. So she sought one who could, for a few moments, make her forget this latest loss and who would, she hoped, take her in when she was declared widowed. She had craved the feeling of a man's arms about her once more. Once only – but it had been enough, as she knew, feeling her belly kick.

Serlo caught her eye, and to her surprise, slipped away from the jury and strode towards her. He was going to speak to her, she realised, and felt her face redden. Nicholas was frowning, wondering what on earth the miller could want with his wife.

'Lady Anne, I crave a favour,' Serlo said humbly. 'It's my tolls. I've—'

'You've been taking gifts instead of tolls, and that's a crime!' she snapped, astonished that he should approach her about it. 'You'll have to speak to my husband about that, not me.'

'Oh, but if I do that, I'll have to speak *openly*,' he said insinuatingly. 'If you get my meaning?'

'What are you talking about, miller? It's none of my affair.'

'Oh, isn't it though?' he winked. 'Athelina was there. She told me. You and him – rutting in the field.'

In that moment Anne thought her heart would stop. She could hear the walls of her secure life crumbling. If her husband should learn that her child was not his, he must grow to loathe her, as any man must detest the woman who hung the cuckold's horns upon his head.

She looked down at the lifeless, abused body of Athelina. You sold my secret for your security, Athelina? she asked her silently. She should have felt hatred, but she couldn't.

Only compassion mingled with her own terror at the thought of what this might do to her husband.

Letitia saw Serlo go to Anne, but she was more interested in the whereabouts of her two little nephews. She glanced about behind him for his children, but they weren't there. Even as Serlo took his place amongst the jury, she searched among the ranks of women to see who was absent, who might be back at the cottage, sitting with the children. Jan was briefly back home with her, leaving Muriel asleep, and Serlo in charge, so she had told her mistress.

Many of the mothers were there, she saw, but for every three or four, there was another who had not come. These were the women who had elected to stay behind to look after their own and perhaps another's children. Good. Serlo must have left his with one of them, she thought, and turned from him. If she could avoid the sight of him, so much the better.

The Coroner was showing the bodies in a calm, unhurried manner. He held up the bloody knife and displayed the blade to the jury, asking whether anyone recognised it as belonging to Athelina. No one remembered seeing it with her, of course, but then how often did a man take notice of a woman's little knife? It was just an accoutrement, like a spoon. A spoon was more noticeable, because few peasants could afford to own one, so any spoon was noteworthy, but a knife like this? No. Nobody recognised it.

There was shouting and some children went running past the scene, two pausing to gape at the bodies, before shrugging and haring off after their companions.

Letitia wished that death could be so easily shrugged off by an adult. She felt so sorry for the two, lying there so slack and sad. The boys' wounds were hideous; blackened and decayed. They demanded her attention all the time, no matter how she tried to look away.

It was preferable to look at Serlo. And there weren't many things, she told herself, that fell into *that* category.

Muriel woke with a jerk. She could feel that she was in her bed. She felt warm and cosy and knew that, were she to turn to her left, she'd see the fire. Smoke was rising, and she could hear bubbling, like soup in a pot. Then her nose began to twitch. There was a delicious smell on the air.

Her head hurt as though someone had inserted a bellows into her brain and was pumping it, the pain rising to a peak and then falling again. When at a crest, it was enough to make her weep, it was so intense; yet a moment later it was perfectly bearable.

What had happened? She could remember going to the door and seeing Aumery and Hamelin at their games, but then all grew hazy. She was sure she could remember cuddling the two of them . . . perhaps there was something else, though. There was a painful scrape and bruising at her inner thigh, and she couldn't think why until she had turned her head a little and saw the shattered remains of the cart lying just inside the door.

It all came back to her then! The mad rush into the road, snatching up Aumery and covering him with her body, the cart between her spread thighs as she kneeled, Hamelin keening in surprise, and then the slamming blow. A quick, sharp terror flew into her throat. Her boys! Her children! What had happened to them? Were they safe? *My Christ, please don't let them be dead. Holy Mother, what . . .*

Her fears were not allayed by the rattling crash. Looking around, head throbbing wildly, she saw Aumery with a long stick in his hand playing at stabbing his shadow on the wall. He was unharmed. Hearing the breath hissing in her throat, he turned, his face panicked, and then his features broke into a broad grin as he saw his mother.

Hurling the stick aside, he ran as quickly as he could on his bare feet towards her, and threw his arms about her neck: 'Mummy, Mummy!'

Although it was agony at first, she was so happy to feel his arms about her that she could only sob faintly and murmur, 'There, there. It's all right. Where's your brother?'

He looked over his shoulder and pointed with a chubby fist. When she looked, she saw Hamelin sitting near the fire and examining a used bone from the floor. He seemed happy enough. 'You must look after him,' she said as she slumped back on her bed, closing her eyes against the waves of pain.

A sudden thought made her ask, 'What made all that noise? Something woke me.'

'It was the pig, Mummy.'

She lifted her head, wincing, to stare about her. There, in the corner of the little room, was the family's sow. She had come in from her sty, and was rootling about the mess on the floor, among plates and bowls knocked from the table.

'No!' she cried, and even over the pain, she felt the urgency. Clapping her hands, she tried to scare the pig from the room.

Sensing that this was a new game, Aumery raised his own voice, shouting as loudly as he could and jumping in excitement. Even Hamelin seemed to want to join in. From the corner of her eye Muriel saw him gazing at her and his brother, then leaning forward to rest on his hands, he began to crawl towards her.

The pig was alarmed, and she retreated at first, until her tail and arse struck the wall. Squealing, in panic, she turned her snout to left and right, seeking an exit. Then she seemed to gather up her courage, and bolted.

Muriel felt some relief as the animal thundered out, but then she saw the movement farther in the room, and an animal shriek of horror emerged from her wide-open mouth.

Letitia suddenly heard something like a whistle piping far away. At first she dismissed it as children playing. Boys who played in the water meadows would sometimes pluck the massive bulrushes and cut them up to make their own whistles. The cleverer ones could cut small holes in the stem and play tunes.

She returned her attention to the Coroner, but there was something about that sound . . . something that made her flesh crawl. A ridge of goosebumps travelled up her arms, and the compulsion to go and find its source was too strong to ignore. It sounded as though it came from beyond her home, down towards . . . the mill!

Letty's face tensed, and then she was pelting away from the crowd, down the lane, past her home and on along the narrow, tree-darkened track, past the gates to the meadows, on towards the chuckling stream, tripping once and nearly falling over, then up on her feet and rushing at full tilt, on, on, the screams and sobbing coming ever more distinctly, until she was at the mill's house, and she could see Muriel, kneeling in the dirt, howling in anguish, while beside her Aumery bawled, hands to his eyes, not understanding, blaming himself for his mother's grief. And on Muriel's lap was the small still figure of her younger son, his eyes wide in death, his flesh a single huge, open sore where a whole pan of boiling soup had tipped over his tiny body.

Chapter Twelve

Coroner Jules concentrated on the faces before him, but it wasn't easy. My God, no! What a terrible state of affairs. The woman strangling herself from a beam while her children's bodies lay beneath her. And the smell in that little cottage! Everyone knew that bad air could kill even the strongest men, and Jules had put himself at risk, going in there to see the bodies *in situ*.

Still, at least the case was almost done.

Why ever had he taken on this revolting job? he asked himself. Roger was a nasty little man who treated him like a dog's turd on his sandal, and the men here in the vill hardly seemed to notice him. The Keeper, that tall, intense man, he seemed to constantly hang about nearby as though he was watching every error Jules might make. Well, damn him! Jules might not be the best Coroner in the land, but he was conscientious. He was doing his best in very difficult circumstances.

Sir Jules glowered at the jostling men and women before calling for silence again. These noisy brutes! They had no idea about the correct behaviour at a time and gathering of this sort. They were restless and keen to hurry off to the nearest alehouse, he guessed. Well, they could wait. He wasn't going to rush just because a bunch of yokels might miss their lunchtime cider!

Roger was waiting for him to continue, reed poised over his parchment, and Jules pointed to the next witness, fitting a stern expression to his face.

Sternness he could manage. It involved muscles which might otherwise display his anxiety and horror. Even here in the open

air the smell from the corpses was overpowering. He could feel
nausea threatening.

Next time, he would bring some fruit or sweet herbs to conceal
the stench, he swore, before taking a deep breath and posing his
next question.

Baldwin and Simon remained at the edge of the clearing
before the church after their evidence had been given to the
Coroner.

For Simon it was unpleasant listening to an inquest on such a
sad little incident, but the two had seen worse. In recent months
they had witnessed sudden death in all its hideous variety, and
Simon himself had almost been killed, first in Spain and then on
a ship attacked by pirates. Somehow, though, this was more
poignant.

He had left home months ago, and he missed his wife dreadfully
– and not only her. A proud father, he longed to see his son and
daughter too. There was some fear in him. He had adored his little
Edith from the day she was born, so perfect, so blonde and
beautiful; and now she was old enough to seek her own husband.
Soon she would be readying herself to become a mother and
preparing to make all the same mistakes that he and his wife had
made with their children.

There was some time left before she departed from his household, and he wanted to make the most of those months, to enjoy
her company – but also to learn how to live without her. It would
be a hard loss when she went.

Somehow this inquest made him feel maudlin. The sight of the
mother with her dead children made him appreciate his own family
that much more. Especially when he heard that the woman was a
widow. He realised just how grim his wife's life would be once he
had died. If he were to die here, for example, before he reached
home, dear Meg could be put under the same sort of pressure as

this poor maid. Perhaps she, too, would be threatened with eviction.

That news had brought a black scowl to his face. It was Iwan, an old smith, who had volunteered the fact that Serlo the miller owned Athelina's cottage and had told her to pay more rent or go. The miller didn't deny it, but blustered that he had no responsibility to the chit. It was her problem if she'd podded two children and couldn't feed them. If the Church wanted her saved, the Church should have donated enough to see her remain in her home, rather than accuse an honest man who tried only to make a living.

Simon wondered whether he was an honest man. To his mind, Serlo looked a brute; the dead bodies like so many chickens slaughtered in a yard by a fox. The vision of this man threatening the woman, clenching his fist and demanding more money, repelled him. How could a man cause so much suffering and death, yet show no remorse? If anything, he seemed intent on proving that he didn't care a fig for the dead.

'She and her children were useless mouths,' Serlo was blustering now. 'Can we afford to keep a house for her sort, when decent men and women are struggling to find a room of their own?'

'Her boys would have grown to be men,' Baldwin observed with a tone that could have frozen the pond.

'Perhaps. How long would we have had to feed them before they grew?'

'Is it your place to assess the value of another's life, miller?'

'Sir Baldwin,' Sir Jules said with a note of some petulance, 'I think you can leave the questioning to me. I *am* the Coroner.'

Baldwin subsided with a poor grace, turning his back on Serlo. Simon was disappointed. He would have liked to see Baldwin launch into a verbal attack on the miller.

Serlo appeared amused by Baldwin's discomfiture. He grinned

broadly until Sir Jules snapped, 'Don't smile in the presence of death, churl!'

Simon wondered how the man could smirk like that when his greed had led to these three deaths, but as he told himself, there were many unscrupulous people who were equally greedy. If Baldwin was right, the King's own advisers were among the most avaricious men yet born. The Despensers were capturing highborn women and holding them prisoner in gaol until they agreed to sign over their inheritances. It made Simon very glad to be living under the protection of the Abbot of Tavistock, Robert Champeaux. 'God Bless Abbot Robert,' he muttered quietly to himself.

'Bailiff?'

The quiet voice of Lady Anne brought him back from his reverie. 'My lady?'

'There is something I feel is odd – something about the woman. Surely, yes, she was desperate . . .'

'Go on.'

Anne's face was troubled. 'If she was utterly without hope, if she was convinced that she had no reason to live longer . . . I can comprehend her despair although I know self-murder is a sin. Yes, but to kill her sons? I met up with Athelina many times, and never saw her show anything other than love and affection to her children. She adored them both individually, and also as the last remaining vestige of her husband. I find it hard to believe that she could have killed them.'

Simon wanted to pat her hand, but restrained himself. It would be presumptuous. Instead he lowered his voice. He could all too easily remember his own wife, Meg, failing to understand human cruelty when she had been pregnant.

'Lady, it is often hard to understand how a woman's mind works when she is deranged. As we have been told, she was in a frenzy and that was why she killed the boys.'

'Who saw her in a frenzy, though? *I* did not, and I have not heard anyone else say they did. It sounds like an assumption: Athelina is dead, the children are dead, so she must have killed them. If she did, she must have been mad, so she was in a frenzy.'

'It makes some sense,' Simon said soothingly. Women weren't as rational as men. Well, apart from his Meg, of course, who was brighter than many men of his acquaintance. This wife of Nicholas's wasn't in Meg's league, though. She was a pretty thing, but clearly she was upset because she was close to giving birth herself.

'And another thing,' she said.

Simon turned a patronising smile upon her. 'Yes?'

'You must have seen many dead bodies – as a bailiff, I mean?'

'Yes, of course.'

'Is it normal for a hanged woman to have those marks on her throat? What would have made them?'

Simon's smile grew a little stiff as he wondered what she meant. But then he peered down at Athelina's neck once more and decided it would be rash to dismiss this woman's intuition. 'Baldwin. Look at this!'

The knight was still smarting from the Coroner's rebuff, but hearing Simon's urgent tone, he glanced down, but just then there came the sound of sobbing, and all present turned towards the gate. There, walking slowly, holding in her arms the sobbing figure of Aumery, came Letitia, followed by her distraught sister-in-law, cradling her second little son in her arms.

'I congratulate you, Serlo,' Letitia spat as she neared him. 'You looked after your sons so very carefully, so very well!'

Baldwin had nothing but sympathy for the miller. The man stared as though disbelieving, and then he put out a hand as though to touch his son's face, but his wife drew Hamelin away from him. She stood staring, eyes wild, a woman driven insane, and Baldwin was shocked to see how blood coursed down the side of her head from a raking cut.

Suddenly she screamed again, a high, wordless shrill sound that tore at the hearts of all who stood there.

'*He was your son! All you had to do was give him to another woman to protect him, but you left him playing in our home, with no one to look after him!* No one,' she sobbed, falling to her knees, still holding her scalded son. 'No one . . .'

She bent her head to his little body, and wept again for Hamelin.

Serlo said, 'But I don't understand . . . what happened? What's wrong with him? Letty, for God's sake tell me what happened.'

'I offered to take both the little mites off your hands, but you refused to let me! *You* killed your son! You left them alone with their mother when she was in her bed, unable to care for them. Look at her! She ought to be there now, but because of you she's here, bleeding, with a broken heart. All because of *you*.'

The Coroner stepped forward and glanced at Baldwin. The knight saw the indecision in his eyes, and quickly shook his head. While Serlo stood uncertainly, his eyes brimming and a single tear falling down one cheek, Baldwin moved to Sir Jules's side and whispered a few words into his ear.

'Wife, your child needs to rest in the church', the Coroner said compassionately to Muriel. 'Take him there, and pray for his soul.' He looked at Letitia. She gave him a stiff nod, ignoring her brother-in-law, who stared after them in deep shock. Baldwin was relieved to see Iwan, as well as Alex the Constable, go to Serlo's side and gradually draw him away.

'I think, Coroner,' Baldwin said quietly, 'that we'll have to leave this matter until later.'

'Perhaps so,' Sir Jules said, and he seemed glad of the fact. 'And I shall have to remain here a little longer in order to hold an inquest on the child, too.' He looked about him. 'Nicholas, it would be cruel to ask that poor woman what happened now. She is in no fit state to speak. Will you have the jury come here again tomorrow morning, and we shall review this matter and hear the cause of this latest tragedy, too?'

'Certainly.'

Simon, Baldwin saw, was staring at Athelina's body, and now he caught the knight's eye and beckoned. 'Look,' he said.

Baldwin followed his pointing finger. 'What? Her neck?'

'Scratches,' Simon said bluntly.

Baldwin peered closer. When they had cut her down, they had left the rope about her neck, and until now he had not been near enough to study her flesh too closely. The murder of her children and her own subsequent suicide had seemed so convincing, he hadn't deemed it necessary to look further. Now he cursed himself for a fool.

'Yes,' Simon said. 'She scratched at her neck in a fight to save her life. She never wanted to die. And if she didn't, she couldn't have killed her children. This woman was murdered.'

Julia watched the early part of the inquest, but she didn't stay long. It was all too depressing, and more than a little unpleasant, with those bodies there. Anyway, when she caught sight of Ivo, who had gone to find her and given up, she reckoned she could spend her time more fruitfully than by playing the ghoul.

Soon she heard his hurried footsteps, and a breathless, 'Hello, maid.'

She sniffed and didn't face him. 'Oh, so you don't mind talking to me now, then? I thought you were too busy up at the castle with your fine friends to bother seeing me again.'

'How could you think that?' he asked with mock hurt. 'When the most beautiful woman in the vill is down here?' Over her shoulder he saw Squire Warin riding off towards Temple, and he opened his mouth, but shut it again. Julia wouldn't like him to be distracted.

'Who's this beautiful woman, then?'

'Aw, I can't think right now,' he said playfully. 'It'll come to me. Everything does in the end, you know!'

'Cor, you're a cocky bugger, aren't you?' she said, turning to look at him at last. 'Think yourself special, do you?'

'I know I am, maid, and I think you reckon it too,' Ivo grinned.

She turned away again.

'Did you know her?' he tried after a moment.

'Athelina?' She shot him a look, then nodded. 'Yeah. She was all right.'

'Doing that to her boys, though. Terrible, that.'

'She was desperate.'

'Why?'

She shrugged. 'Her man paid the rent for that house of hers, and he'd lost interest in her, so she couldn't afford to stay. She didn't have any money or anything.'

'Still a terrible thing to do.'

Julia pulled a face. 'What else can a woman do when she's got nothing? Without money, she'll starve and so will her children. Maybe she reckoned it was better to save the boys a long starvation. As for her boyfriend, he's moved on now, the bastard.'

'That was said with feeling!'

'Yeah. He moved from her to me, and then he dropped me when he found another skirt to reach into.'

'You think she killed herself because he ditched her?'

'Maybe she loved him!' Julia snapped, but now when she faced Ivo, there were tears in her eyes.

In the church house, Nicholas the castellan frowned irritably. 'I don't understand the logic of what you are saying. She could have repented and decided to save herself at the last moment, surely?'

Baldwin motioned to Simon to explain. For his part, he was still so angry with himself that he could hardly speak. His incompetence was inexcusable: he had seen what others expected him to see. He had heard a little about the woman and instantly believed the scene placed before him; he hadn't thought to seek the truth below the cord that killed her, he hadn't enquired about the circumstances of her death and the fabrication that now seemed so obvious.

'It is clear,' Simon began, 'that she was killed there by the rope. It strangled her to death. We had thought that she was mad – the miller's threat to evict her could have sent her insane – and that she had killed her boys, then hanged herself. But that would mean she'd committed the worst crime there is: infanticide. Could she then regret her own death? If she was mad when she slaughtered them, it could only have made her still *more* mad. In God's name, no woman could have decided to save herself after destroying those she most loved. If anything, a sane woman who killed her children could become more mad afterwards, but never *sane*!'

'Perhaps she wanted vengeance? Having killed her sons, she decided to seek the man who forced her to do it, in order to make him pay?' Sir Jules suggested.

Baldwin waved a hand impatiently. 'Coroner, are you a father?' When the man nodded, Baldwin continued harshly, 'Then suppose you yourself murdered all your children. Would you give a damn about anyone else in the world? If despair so entrapped you that you were committed to destroying all that you adored, you would simply wish to end your life as swiftly as possible.'

'Perhaps the woman had time to repent her crimes and sought to live longer to find God's forgiveness,' Adam suggested.

'You seriously think a mother could do that?' Simon demanded. 'I know of no woman who could kill her children and then save her own life. Not if she loved them.'

'And she certainly seemed to,' Nicholas breathed.

Sir Jules looked from one to the other. 'I bow to your greater knowledge on this. I have never held an inquest on – uh – such a case.'

'You have only recently been given this task, Coroner?' Simon asked tentatively.

'I have been enquiring after sudden deaths for some days,' Sir Jules said haughtily, but then added more honestly, 'Nearly a week and a half. I believe I have much to learn.'

Baldwin reflected that he too had much still to learn. 'The woman had the rope around her neck, but she struggled with it, trying to insert her fingers behind it to pull it away, yet she failed. The killer managed to throttle her, and then staged her suicide.'

'Not easy, surely, with a dead body?' Nicholas said.

'No, but not impossible. She was no great weight. A man could set the rope about her neck, the other end over the beam, and pull.'

The men nodded.

'I think we should seek a murderer.' Simon looked at the Coroner. 'I was glad you didn't think to try to hold an inquest on the woman's child.'

He pulled a face. 'I couldn't! I was too appalled. The very woman I all but brained in the morning loses her child in the afternoon . . . I've never been so close to a recent death, and seeing her so . . . grief stricken – well, I couldn't face questioning her. That would have been unbelievably cruel.'

'Which means we shall have another inquest tomorrow as well as completing Athelina's,' Baldwin noted. 'And seeking her killer, of course.'

'Quite so,' said Sir Jules. His face was drawn and fearful with this new responsibility. 'Yes . . . quite so.'

Chapter Thirteen

Richer went straight from the inquest to the alehouse, and he stood in the doorway looking for Susan.

'Leave me *alone*!'

The enraged bellow came from Serlo, who stood in the far corner of the room with a quart pot in his hand. He took a long pull of his drink, then glared about him. 'I'm staying till I've drunk enough,' he said truculently, 'and no one's going to stop me. Sons of whores and bitches, the lot of you!'

Richer immediately knew he should leave. Staying could only provoke the man, and that wasn't fair, not when he'd just lost his son. Also, Richer's headache felt like it was about to develop into a migraine after seeing poor Athelina's body. He had no wish to pick a fight today.

Serlo continued, 'This place! Athelina's dead, and suddenly everyone's miserable. Why? She was only a whore with two bastards. Should have snuffed it long ago. Look at you all! Creeping around because she's dead, but my baby, my little *Ham* . . . no one cares about him, do they? All you want is me quiet, isn't it?' He wiped his eyes with the back of his hand. 'It wasn't my fault he died. He was my *son*,' he continued, more drunkenly introspective. 'My little boy. I didn't think he'd get hurt in my house, in God's name! In my own house . . . I'd even got the pottage on to cook. How can he be dead?'

Richer was almost at the door, when he heard Serlo give a hoarse oath.

'Hey, you! Come to gloat, have you? What, going already? You scared of me or something? I'm only a poor sod who's lost his son, you know. Nothing to be afeared of!'

'I wasn't here to gloat, Serlo. I am sorry your son died. I'll leave you to your grief; I've no desire to increase your pain.'

'Increase my pain? Huh! How *can* you? When I look at you, I see a man who lost his whole family.'

There was no point in staying any longer.

In this mood, Serlo would only attack him.

Richer was at the outer door when he heard the miller's next words. The shock made his hand stay on the door, and he knew that, were he to move, he must topple and crash to the floor.

'Well?' Serlo taunted. 'One of my boys died because of a fire, but your whole family went up in smoke. I wonder who was responsible for that, eh?'

Richer shook his head blindly, pulled the door open and stumbled out into the warm afternoon sun.

'So, Father Adam,' Baldwin said as he and Simon followed the priest out from the hall. 'What do you think of this news?'

Adam stopped and faced the two men. 'I think it's nonsense. How could anyone suggest such a thing! Athelina broke her heart after losing her man, and it led to those terrible events. That's all there is to it. It's sad, but of course she did it.'

'I should have expected you to defend the members of the vill,' Baldwin said.

'I just don't believe this fabrication you have put together.'

'Did she turn down your advances?' Simon demanded.

The priest's response was enough to confirm Ivo's allegation. Adam paled and his lips flattened like apples in a press. Then he hissed, 'How *dare* you suggest such a thing. I refuse to speak further.'

'The other woman: Julia. What's *she* doing in your household?' Simon said, ignoring his protests.

'She is my maid. She looks after me and that is all.' And at that Adam spun around to march home. He would say nothing more to the uncouth son of an Oxford tavern whore.

The Bailiff and the knight wouldn't understand anyway. Such men were too rooted in the here and now to be able to comprehend the sort of thing he attempted: to do good to others as Jesus would have wanted.

Except Jesus would have tried to look after Athelina as well, he reminded himself.

To Father Adam's annoyance, the two wouldn't leave him. They walked with him, one on either side, and Baldwin studied him as they went.

The priest was white with fury after Simon's bluntness, and although such a rage might have meant his decencies had been offended, Baldwin shrewdly guessed that there was more to the man's mood than pique. After all, a rural priest was as aware as any peasant of the realities of fornication, and many would make their own use of the women of a vill. He glanced at Simon and nodded. Ivo was right.

Baldwin spoke again in a more conciliatory tone. 'Father, we have to understand your position if we're to learn who killed this woman.'

'No one else was involved, I tell you! Scratches on her neck? It was probably the hemp that did it.'

'*Father!*' Baldwin called, and this time Adam stopped. There was a depth of tone that brooked no argument.

'What?' he snapped.

Baldwin walked slowly up to Adam, a frown on his face as he approached to within a pace. Adam recoiled, but he gripped his cross and held it tight in his fist. 'Don't hurt me, Knight!'

'I should hardly dare do so,' Baldwin said. 'You are a man of God and I trust you to do your best by the people here. My good friend Bishop Walter of Exeter would not be thankful to me for breaking the head of one of his priests, would he?'

'Then what do you want with me?'

'The truth! This maid is dead, and we believe that she was murdered. Imagine, Adam, a man throwing a cord about your neck. He's behind you as you walk into your house, and as you fumble for a spark from your steel, the rope is over your head and you're being throttled. Imagine being lifted by that intolerable bond, slowly dying as your breath rattles in a throat that is so constricted you can't fill your lungs, and imagine the sense leaving your body. The little spots bursting out on your flesh, your eyes bulging, your tongue filling your whole mouth, and all the while, perhaps, you can see your children lying before you, both murdered. All you can do is try to haul that cord from your neck, but although you tear your own flesh, there is no escape from encroaching death. And then you die. Imagine all that, Adam, and tell me – *dare* to tell me – that you won't help us.'

Adam held his stare without flinching. 'A nice story. One to scare the children perhaps, but not me. I'm a priest, damn you! You accuse me of molesting my own maid and then ask my help?'

Simon stepped over to Baldwin's side. 'Tell us about her, then. Whose child does she raise if not yours?'

'I will not talk to you!' Adam blurted out angrily. 'How could you suggest that I, a man of God, could do such a thing? I am sworn to celibacy.'

'Such things are not unknown,' Baldwin pointed out.

'They may not be unknown where you come from, but for me it is entirely unknown. In God's name, I swear I am innocent.'

'Then help us! Supposing we are right, who could have wished her harm?'

Adam held his gaze for some moments, but then he had to look away. There was a depth of intensity about this knight's stare that made him uncomfortable. It was as though the fellow was stripping

away all of the skins with which he had covered himself until only
the bare soul remained, and he was still too ashamed about that to
be able to talk about it. Looking down, he shook his head, but as
the silence grew intolerable, he spoke quietly.

'Sadly, some could have wished to harm her. The man who
owned her cottage, Serlo, wanted money. Since his apprentice
died last year, he's been in financial trouble. Then there were men
who desired her body, I have no doubt, and sometimes wives of
such men can do murder in jealousy and anger, protecting their
family by destroying the woman who threatens their stability.'

'Serlo?' Baldwin mused. 'Why should he wish to kill her if he
knew he could evict her?'

Adam grunted. 'Perhaps he thought he might persuade her to
give herself to him so that he might have an alternative rent from
her?'

Baldwin glanced at Simon. 'Perhaps. Yet why should he then
kill her?'

'Some men do not enjoy rejection.'

'More likely that he would rape her. For a woman to prove rape
is all but impossible normally,' Baldwin said.

'True enough – in fact, the Constable is Serlo's brother Alex,
so it would be still more difficult for a woman to win a case of
rape in this vill.'

'Could there be another man who loathed her for some reason?'

'I do not know.'

Baldwin eyed him. There was something Father Adam was
keeping back, he felt sure. 'Did you know this woman well
yourself?'

'Are you suggesting again that . . .'

'No. I am trying to understand her, and through her, her
murderer. Was she incontinent?'

'No. I believe she was honourable. I never heard that she was
the sort of woman to take many lovers.'

'So another man could have been jealous of her affection?'

'It's possible.'

'How did she afford that house?' Simon asked. 'If she had to rent it, did her husband leave her a lot of money?'

'No,' Adam said before thinking, and then scowled at the ground by his feet.

'So how did she pay?' Simon demanded.

'Her lover paid.'

At this moment, Sir Jules and Nicholas appeared in the doorway to the hall in the church house. Baldwin beckoned for them to join him. Sir Jules's face, Baldwin saw, had lost its greenish hue, and now he looked simply anxious. Nicholas did not join them, but set off towards the castle as Simon continued questioning Adam.

'Athelina was not made pregnant by her lover.' Adam said. 'She was a widow, and both boys had a legitimate father. Athelina was a good wife, and it was her misfortune that her husband died young.'

'What of your maid?'

'She was persuaded by a man that he would marry her, but then he left her some months after she came with child. I took her and the baby in to protect her from endless censure. At least as my maid, she would always have food and drink.'

'A kind thought,' Simon said flatly. He disliked this priest; he also disliked the reminder of his earlier thoughts at the beginning of the inquest: what would happen to his own wife, were *he* to die? 'Why didn't you do the same for the poor widow?'

'I can't take in every woman with no man,' Adam huffed.

'No,' Simon agreed. 'But Athelina had at least been married, and she had two boys to protect. You could have done more good perhaps by taking *her* into your home.'

'She had a home already. Julia came to me because she was thrown from her vill by the priest.'

'Hardly the most charitable behaviour from a man of God,' Baldwin commented.

'Father John is an exemplary priest,' Adam said hotly, 'but he saw no reason to support another parish's son. I took her in when I heard of her plight.' It wasn't the whole truth, but it was adequate for these two.

'Does that mean you thought that the father might be here in your parish?' Baldwin asked shrewdly.

'Whoever the father may be, I am sure he's confessed his sins to God,' Adam said.

Baldwin nodded thoughtfully. 'Thank you. I suppose we should ask Serlo about the woman. He may know more about her and her death than he has so far confessed.'

'You cannot!' Adam burst out. 'I expect he is in my church even now, praying for his dead son. I am going there myself, and I shall attempt to soothe his soul. I will not have you interrupting a man in his grief.'

'Father,' Baldwin said coolly, 'we have a triple murder to investigate. We may upset some folks, but I will not stop because of other men's feelings – including your own.'

Adam nodded stiffly, gave Simon a withering look, and then made his way across the green of the yard to the church itself.

Once within the safety of the nave, he kneeled and offered a quick prayer in thanks that the two had not learned the real reason for having Julia in his house; at least that secret was secure. If ever the truth came out, the rural dean would be here in no time, and on him like a ton of rock.

'Oh God,' he breathed, and suddenly he felt the weight of his personal guilt sitting upon his soul. 'I am sorry, so sorry . . .'

He should have taken in Athelina and protected her and her sons. Her death was incomprehensible, but the last thing Adam wanted was an investigation here. Tongues would wag, and the result must be his own ruin.

Maybe Athelina *had* been murdered. If so, perhaps it was a result of her badgering her lover, who might have killed her in anger. Her lover... who had thrown her over for Julia. At the time Athelina had told Adam of her desperation, but he had not believed her, had brushed it aside. Anyway, he thought it was better that she should leave the vill. Otherwise, she might see her old home rented out to Julia, and that would bring untold dissension to the vill. In all conscience, Adam couldn't allow that. So instead, he'd taken Julia in and left Athelina to her fate. And now she was dead. Her murder was his fault.

He must rise, he must rise and seek out Muriel, the distressed mother, and Serlo too, if he was there in the church with her. Standing, Adam stared ahead to where the body lay. He could see Letitia by the side of the church hearse, and then he saw the figure of Muriel, her head once more wrapped in linen to staunch the blood that had stained the shoulder of her thin tunic, but there was no sign of the miller.

Yes, he should go to her and offer her what consolation he could, but right now, all he wanted to do was fall on his face and beg forgiveness for his own sins. To beg forgiveness for the death of Athelina and her two lovely little boys.

'I should have thought that *I* was to be the man leading any investigation,' Sir Jules said with some force once the priest was out of earshot. It was hard enough to keep a grip on an inquest without these dabblers barging in.

'Of course,' Baldwin said easily. 'But Adam was there, and a few questions occurred to me.'

'They would have occurred to me as well, Sir Baldwin,' Jules said with hauteur.

'Of course they would. And you'd have asked them as quickly as us,' Simon said. 'Except we beat you to every one, didn't we? Very unsporting.'

Sir Jules looked at him contemptuously. 'Perhaps you can't understand, being a mere Bailiff; when you have my responsibilities, others getting under one's feet can be a hindrance.'

Baldwin set his jaw. 'Sir Jules, when you hold your inquest, all the facts I have learned can come out. Perhaps until then we should unite in order to seek this murderer.'

'If there is a murderer to find,' Sir Jules said. 'There is little enough evidence of that.'

'Perhaps when you've stopped looking at responsibilities and instead have real *experience*,' Simon said kindly, 'you'll realise the importance of marks like those on her neck.'

Sir Jules's nostrils flared with rage, but before he could say anything, Baldwin murmured in his most placatory tone, 'We need your expertise, if we are to make sense of the matter. And your perspicacity must surely lead to the identification of the murderer. Why don't we go to the alehouse to discuss the affair?'

And before Simon could speak again, Baldwin kicked out and felt his toe connect with the Bailiff's ankle.

Julia only just had time to smooth the blanket on her palliasse before the priest arrived back at the house, pale and angry still after his questioning. As soon as he slumped in his chair he shouted at her to bring him some ale.

'Father, what is it?' she asked.

'Those men are intolerable! Quite insufferable! I should complain to Nicholas – demand that he makes them treat me with respect. As though the woman could have been murdered!'

She passed him his cup and a jug of strong ale, and as he sat staring at the embers of his fire, he didn't see how she had been rocked by his news. 'Athelina – murdered?' she repeated faintly.

'It's nonsense,' he said dismissively. 'Complete rubbish. And they so disordered my thoughts that I was incapable of lending any form of solace to poor Muriel in the church.'

She left him there, and went through to her own room again, sitting on the bed. Ivo's warmth was still there, and she spread her fingers over it, feeling the little glow of satisfaction from his lovemaking gradually seep away from her, to be replaced by a sense of concern.

If Athelina had been murdered, Julia was sure that the only man who could have done so was her lover, Gervase. Everyone knew that Athelina was desperate about money, and that she kept pestering him for help. And Julia herself had been asking him for money too, recently.

She looked at her sleeping child, and suddenly hoped very strongly that she hadn't upset the steward of Cardinham Castle with her demands for cash.

Chapter Fourteen

Richer left the tavern and walked along the roadway until he reached a tree trunk lying by the road. Here he stopped and sat down, a hand at his head, eyes closed in pain.

Once he had been prone to these headaches, suffering at least one a month, but now he was unfortunate if he was so afflicted more than once in a year. Yet this, for all its suddenness, had attacked with more venom than any he had known in the last five years. His eyesight was affected: as he stared at the trees, their trunks at the bottom of his vision, to his left, were all moving oddly, as though he was watching them through water. Farther left, his vision ceased working altogether. He had to screw up his forehead against the pain that stretched across the back of his skull.

It was Serlo's words that had made it blow up like this. The bastard! He *had* to mention the fire.

Richer could recall it all only too clearly. The night sky lit up like a beacon, with the sparks flying into the air, madly whirling in the roaring heat. Richer had been out at the fields helping his father with the harvest all day, but when their work was done and when the lord's ale casks and cider barrels were opened, his father had made his way home, like other older men, leaving the field to their sons and daughters. The end of the harvest often led to a rash of births, and marriages in Maytime the next year; it was the way for natural desires to be slaked, and no one objected.

From an early age Richer had been enslaved by Athelina's beauty. A child's view of marriage was different to the reality of hot, sweating bodies moving to create a new life, but Richer had always been sure that he would have her. He knew that he loved her. And that night, he almost won her.

The evening had drawn in and the sky was purpling. As the swooping swallows and martins ceased their loud screechings and the bats began to dart as darkness deepened, Richer lay on his back on the bed of straw he had made for himself, and kissed Athelina. Their passion excited by hard work and copious quantities of cider, they were soon engaged in the pursuit of their pleasures, when they heard a scream and a cry for help.

'Ignore it,' Richer had said as distinctly as he could while his mouth was welded to Athelina's, but she pushed him away. Forced to pause, while the blood yet boiled in his veins, Richer heard the cries calling all to join in putting out the blaze. Over his protests that they could be little aid after all the drink they had consumed, Richer found that he and Athelina were soon joining the crowd heading back towards the vill. He could still remember the ferocious face of Serlo at the rear of the group, sneering at Athelina for disappearing with Richer. 'You should have come with me, wench. I'd have given you something to gag on!'

'Leave her alone,' Richer grated, but then his attention was drawn away as he saw the towering column of flames in front of him. It was very close to his parents' house, he thought with dread, and he wondered which of the nearby homes it could be. Through the trees it was hard to gauge, but as they drew ever nearer, he saw that it was . . .

In his mind there was a blankness, a stolid refusal to believe what his eyes told him. He preferred to think that it was the woods behind the house which were alight; his family should gather up all their belongings as soon as they could, and try to escape, he thought frantically; then he pretended that it was a fire in the small barn his father had built a few yards from the house, and that it would soon burn out; then the log store on the side. Someone should find a grapnel and tug the logs away so that their flames couldn't hurt the thatch . . .

Even now, after so many years, he could recall the horror he felt as the enormity of the disaster hit him. His father was in there, so was his mother, Avice, his brothers, his beloved sister . . . and the family home was an inferno. Flames thrust up through the thatch like daggers of gold and crimson; thick, greasy smoke coiled and spread high overhead like a cloud belched from Hell.

Richer stood back, appalled, and then cried once for his mother. He was about to dart forwards, when strong hands grabbed him. It was Iwan, the smith, who held him back, tears streaming from his eyes. 'You'd never make it, lad. No. You can't go.'

He had tried, he'd clenched a fist and swung it, but Iwan was faster, and caught the fist in his palm. He gripped his fingers tight, in a hand that used a three-pound hammer for hour after hour every day, and there was nothing Richer could do. He wept as he watched his home burn; he continued weeping as the roof caved in with an almighty gust of hot air like the Devil's exhalation; he wept as the walls fell in, as the sparks were flung higher, as the timbers glowed pale in the night air, and he continued weeping long after.

They found the bodies three days later. It took that long for the fires to cool sufficiently. His parents' skulls were easily discernible, although those of his brothers were difficult to find. His sister was reduced to two hipbones and her jaw. All other sign of her had been crushed or burned away. It was only a few days afterwards that the first of his migraines had begun.

'Master, we met last night at the castle.'

The strong voice brought him back to the present with a jerk. He squinted up. 'Who is that?'

'I am Sir Baldwin of Furnshill. This is the Coroner, Sir Jules of Fowey, and my companion Simon Puttock.'

'Sir Knight, I have a dreadful ache in my skull – it is hard to see anyone or anything today.'

'Friend, I know others who suffer from the same sick headaches. You have my sympathy. Tell me, do you know this area well? You said you were born here, but have been away many years.'

'I can recall it all tolerably well. I've been back a few weeks now.'

'You knew this Athelina?' Jules asked.

'She was my first love,' Richer said sadly. 'But I left this place fifteen years ago, and only returned this summer.'

'You were a free man?' Baldwin said.

'No. But I lived free in Exeter and then London, and I've returned a free man.'

Baldwin nodded. That was the law. If a peasant could run away and find himself a job for a year and a day, he was considered free from then on. 'You were a man-at-arms?'

'Yes. I have fought with the King's host.'

'Under whose banner?'

'My lord Sir Henry of Cardinham's. He took me on when I told him who I was.'

Simon frowned in surprise. 'It's not usual for a lord to take on his own runaway peasant as a man-at-arms, is it?'

'Perhaps not all lords would have done so, but Sir Henry is a fair man. He took me, and now I live in the castle.'

'This woman Athelina – do you know of anyone who had cause to wish her harm?' Baldwin asked.

'Why do you ask that?'

'We believe that her suicide may have been faked. It's possible that she was murdered, and her children too,' Baldwin explained.

Richer squeezed his eyes tight shut as another wave of pain forced its way through his head. 'That's impossible. No one could have held so much hatred for her!'

'Yet you have not known her for fifteen years,' Baldwin pointed out. 'A woman can change a great deal in that time. She gained children, she wedded and lost a husband. Perhaps she won an enemy.'

'I refuse to believe it.' Richer's voice was hoarse. 'She was a kind girl, generous-hearted and warm. No one could have wished to kill her. I still find it hard to believe that she is dead, let alone murdered. Dear God – who could do such a thing?'

'I am afraid there is no doubt,' Baldwin said gently. 'There were marks upon her neck which show that she was murdered.' He stopped because the man-at-arms before him suddenly dropped his head into both hands.

Richer pressed hard with his palms against his temples. Athelina *murdered*! It was impossible! She had done no harm to anyone in all her life . . . He had doubted from the first moment that she could have killed her children, though. It simply didn't ring true. A despair terrible enough to kill herself was possible, but not to kill those whom she adored the most. Never.

'I knew her well. I wanted to marry her, but there was a fire at my parents' home and my family was burned to death. I left soon after. When I returned here after many years of wandering, it was like becoming young again just to see her smile at me. She was my first love, and I don't think I ever lost my adoration for her.'

Baldwin smiled understandingly. 'It can be difficult to meet again with an old lover. Sometimes they can wish to renew a former relationship.'

'She didn't,' Richer said sadly, but then he stared up at the serious-faced knight. 'You mean, did I want to jump upon her at once and she refused me, so I killed her! If you believe that, you are a cretin, Sir Knight.'

'Not many men speak thus to a knight,' Sir Jules growled, his face hardening.

'I doubt whether you accuse many men of murder and rape in the same breath,' Richer replied equally harshly. 'If you don't wish to make enemies, you should pick your words more cautiously.'

'We are investigating a murder,' Baldwin said.

'Leave it to the Coroner. It's his job.'

'It is the job of all to seek justice,' Baldwin stated flatly, a hand touching the Coroner's arm. Gradually Sir Jules allowed his temper to cool.

'Then seek justice for *me*! I've lost my parents, my siblings, and now my love! You tell me you seek justice – who will seek justice for them, eh?'

'I am sorry about your loss,' Baldwin said more softly. 'But my priority has to be this woman and her children. She was a widow, I hear?'

'Yes. Her husband Hob was a good man. I used to know him.'

'Did he leave her much money?'

'What! Do you now accuse me . . .'

'I accuse you of nothing, but a thief could break in to steal from her and commit murder if she discovered him. Calm yourself, Richer.'

'I apologise. My head . . . Very well. She was left nothing, so far as I know. He died a good while ago, so she told me.'

'How long?'

'She'd been widowed more than nine years.'

'And since then?' Simon asked. 'It's a long time for a woman to be alone. How did she survive?'

'I don't know. Perhaps she had a lover – I didn't ask. You heard that Serlo demanded more money for rent, and I know that worried her. I offered to help, but she said another should pay. Maybe that's what she meant – a lover.'

'Did anyone try to stop him demanding more?'

'I was attempting to. You know of his behaviour with the tolls?

I told him to leave Athelina alone, or I'd bring the matter of the tolls to Nicholas's attention.'

'He tried to charge me for crossing his bridge,' Baldwin agreed. 'I persuaded him against the idea.'

'So did I. I think he was trying to get money together to pay for his fines. He owes a lot of money for his apprentice's death.' Richer was still a moment, and then he raised his head, his face white. 'My Christ in Heaven! Do you think that he would have dared to kill her to get back at me? He has always hated me.'

Baldwin studied the ravaged features before him, and slowly shook his head. 'No. I think that whoever the murderer was, he killed her for his own motives. If he was attempting to implicate you for some reason, he would have made your guilt obvious. This crime was concealed.'

'The bastard!' Richer sobbed.

'Friend Richer, please sit,' Baldwin said, putting a hand on his shoulder and persuading him to rest again. 'You have no evidence against Serlo, and if you go to him now, you will be guilty of murder yourself. Leave the affair to us. We can investigate the matter.'

'Yes, very well,' Richer said, but he was scarcely listening. Another thought had struck him, a memory from over the long years since the death of his parents. The voice which had first raised the alarm – it had been Serlo's surely, the voice of a man who was coming from the vill to the field, as though he had seen the fire and was rushing to fetch help to put it out.

Yet it could have been the voice of the man who had himself started the fire, he now realised.

Letitia left the body of Hamelin soon after Adam returned from his meal. He stood silently over Muriel, like a broody hen contemplating a warm pebble, the fool! The man always irritated her, but rarely so much as now, with his jargon and his fake sympathy.

Letty could dimly comprehend Muriel's devastation; she had always wanted children of her own, but she was barren. Whether it was her fault or her husband's, she didn't know, nor did she care particularly.

For now, she was only worried about one thing: her nephew Aumery. The poor fellow had seen his mother almost killed, and witnessed his brother's hideous death. She took his hand and pulled him away from Muriel. He started to wail, but she picked him up and he rammed his face into the corner of her shoulder, sobbing. She carried him out to the lane, and started down the road to her home. She was concerned for Muriel, her state of mind and her debility, but the woman needed to sit out the vigil.

Already the shadows were lengthening, the air growing cooler as the sun slipped behind the trees. Letitia shivered at the thought of the night to come. It was long past summer, and although the fruit and vegetables had been stored carefully, the beans and peas dried, the grain packed away, even so, she hated this time of year. It was the period of plenty, with the curse of hunger to come as winter gripped the land in a frozen embrace.

Come now, she told herself. There's no starvation in the vill now, and hasn't been for seven years since the disaster of the rains, and Alex has been successful. Even Serlo had achieved much, although Letitia felt no equivalent pride for him as she felt for her husband. Especially after today.

Why the fool hadn't agreed to let her look after his sons, she would never know nor comprehend. Jan had come back to Letty's when Serlo told her she could go, never dreaming that the man would clear off to the mill, leaving a sleeping wife, a pot simmering over the fire, two unsupervised children and a pig with her sty gate open. It was an accident waiting to happen! Just another example of the stupidity of the man. He was responsible for his younger son's death. Yet he'd probably convince himself that it was all Muriel's fault and, knowing her, the poor mouse, she'd agree. As usual. There was no man in the world so certain of the correctness of his own opinions than Serlo. Letitia always thought it was a sign of a defective mind, the inability to appreciate when it was wrong.

She reached her front door and pushed it open, kicking it closed behind her. Poor Aumery was almost asleep in her arms, and she murmured kind words to him as she took him up to her little chamber. At her bed she pulled the blanket across and kneeled gingerly, aware of the child's weight. She laid him down on the blanket and wrapped another over him to keep him warm, then pulled the string to raise the shutter in its runners, hooking it over the peg in the wall above, and softly walked from the room.

Downstairs again, she built up the fire and got it going. It took some while, and when she had a good blaze, she set her tripod over it and hung her pot dangling from the chain. She was standing and stirring the pot when Alexander arrived home.

'What would I do without you?' he sighed. 'Already preparing food, even after a day like this one.'

'Are you hungry?'

'A little,' he lied. The sight of Muriel and poor Hamelin had quite ruined his appetite. A death so close to a man's own family was devastating.

He'd tried to seek out his brother to offer his condolences, but Serlo was so far gone, he scarcely knew Alexander. He just apologised drunkenly for stealing so much money in tolls, and went on to curse the slut Athelina for not paying up on time. 'It was all that bitch's fault,' he had said, weeping.

Alexander rubbed a hand over his head. There was a pain behind his eyes. Another child dead, just like the other. Poor, poor little Danny. Serlo should have been more careful, but he was so taken up with his own problems, he forgot his duties to others. And he *never* took responsibility for his actions. It was always someone else's fault.

Looking at him, Letty saw the tears in his eyes. 'Oh, my love, I am so sorry!'

'How can God take away a lad like him? Only a matter of months old, and he's gone. It's . . . oh, dear Lord!'

She knew that he had been going to say 'unfair', but that was a word they both avoided. Life *wasn't* fair – they knew that. Yet there was no denying that Letty would dearly have liked God to have given her Hamelin. She could have taken him in and protected him. There was no need to snatch him away so cruelly.

'Thank God,' she said, 'the poor boy was baptised.'

'Yes. At least that will be a comfort to poor Muriel.'

'Darling heart, don't trouble yourself,' she said kindly. 'There is nothing we can do in such matters but pray for his soul, and for Muriel's recovery, and help her to continue life. We don't want another suicide.'

'Hadn't you heard?' he asked sharply. 'They are saying that Athelina's death wasn't suicide at all. They think she was murdered.'

She could feel his eyes on her as she returned to the pot and stirred it. After a while she asked: 'And do they know who did it?'

'No.'

She nodded, but when she looked up, she could see his face, and knew what he was thinking. He was sure he knew who had killed poor Athelina, she thought to herself sadly.

They both did: Serlo.

Chapter Fifteen

'Do you think Richer will do something stupid?' Simon asked Baldwin as they walked away with Sir Jules.

'He is in no fit state to hurt Serlo,' Baldwin said. 'In fact, in his present condition, I would expect the miller to thrash *him*.'

'Would you care for some food?' Sir Jules said.

'Perhaps later,' Baldwin said pensively.

'That means at some time when he realises he hasn't eaten for a month or more,' Simon said caustically. 'For my part, I'd enjoy some cuts of meat with bread.'

'There is so much to do,' Baldwin objected. 'We have to speak to as many people here in the vill as possible, then perhaps go to the castle and question the men there. We should also travel to Temple to interview the priest there, find out what he thinks of Adam.'

'You don't believe him?' Sir Jules asked. His young face was already troubled, but on hearing this his eyebrows shot up almost under his unkempt hair.

'I don't *disbelieve* him yet,' Baldwin corrected him. 'But in a situation like this, with a woman murdered, it's first necessary to hear what people have to say about the matter, and then pass their evidence through the most effective sieve available – the mind. If one man says a thing is so, you trust him until you hear a second say that it is *not* so; then you ask a third, and see what *he* says.'

'And if two men say a thing is so, and the third doesn't, you assume the latter is the liar, so he's the killer,' Sir Jules said dismissively. If this was the sum of intelligence that these two could bring, then they were little more use than himself, he reckoned.

'No. Then you find others and learn why any of them could have lied, whether they hate each other, so that two were putting the blame on one innocent, or whether all were wrong and were giving evidence based on bigotry or stupidity,' Baldwin smiled. 'There is rarely an easy path to the truth with a murder of this type. It is always a matter of balancing facts and using intuition. But one way in which to gain knowledge and base intuition upon fact, is to ask all the people you may about the folk involved.'

'And then ask more,' Simon said, adding, 'but we can plan who we need to speak to over ale and pie.'

'You are incorrigible, Bailiff,' Baldwin said, but he chuckled. 'Let us find our way to the alehouse.'

'It's this way,' Sir Jules said. He was still confused. 'What would you hope to learn from the priest at Temple, though? The man here appeared honest enough to me.'

'And to me,' Baldwin acknowledged. 'Yet his evidence should be tested, just as Richer's must be. Why, for example, did Father John evict the girl Julia, who now lives happily with Father Adam? Was it bigotry, or was there another reason? We have to find others in the vill who can vouch for him.'

They had reached a long, low cottage with three unglazed, barred windows open to the road. From inside came the smell of good clean woodsmoke and sour ale. 'Shall we try our fortune here?' Baldwin asked tentatively. There was a bush tied to a pole beside the doorway, which proved that there was ale ready to be consumed, but Baldwin couldn't help but reflect on the semi-poisonous brews he had been sold in the past. With a sigh he recalled the strong wines of Galicia, the sweeter and more refreshing wines of Portugal, and the delicious black olives. They were a delight of which few men or women of England could have dreamed, and he knew that he was now spoiled for ever.

The others had entered, and reluctantly he ducked below the lintel and followed them.

Lady Anne was happy to see her husband return, even though he was late for their usual meal. 'My love, are you hungry?'

'I am ravenous.'

She kissed him, then called for the servants to bring the food. Like a good wife, she had not eaten while he was out, and she was glad to see the plates of meat arrive with a loaf ready sliced, the crusts removed by her panter. Nicholas said grace, and then the two set themselves to their task.

Anne herself was voraciously hungry, and it was only after she had taken the edge off her appetite that she could pay attention to her man. It was often the way, she had heard: sickly and repelled by food all morning, then starving and vexed all afternoon. At least her appetite had not been altered by pregnancy. One friend had told her that she desired only bloody pork, eaten raw, while another discovered the delights of charcoal. 'Charcoal?' Anne had demanded. 'You're joking!'

'With gravy, of course,' her friend had replied distantly.

She was tempted to mention this revelation to Nicholas, but something about his demeanour told her that he was in no mood for pleasantries. 'You are very upset?'

He looked at her and smiled, but his face was quite pale. 'I am sorry, my love,' he said, his eyes going to her bump. 'Are you all right? I don't want to trouble you.'

'I am all right,' she smiled. 'Please tell me.'

He nodded. 'It's Athelina, of course. Her corpse and those of her boys were hauled out for the jury, but as we were proceeding, Keeper Baldwin and Bailiff Puttock suggested that she was herself murdered.'

With a flare of pride, Anne recalled that it was she herself who had pointed out the grazes on the corpse's throat. 'Who could have wanted to kill her?'

'A rapist? Someone who thought she had money to steal?' he guessed, and then waved a hand in frustration. 'Who would think that!'

'What of poor Aumery?'

'I forgot you were there.' He studied her face a moment, anxious not to alarm her in her delicate state. 'It was all Serlo's fault. The idiot left the children with his sick wife. The family pig got in, and knocked a basinful of boiling pottage over little Ham. The poor lad was dead in an instant.'

'Oh, poor Muriel!' She put a hand to her breast to stop her heart's fluttering, but no matter what she did, she could feel the beat racing. As if in sympathy, her baby gave a convulsive kick. Perhaps he was simply complaining, she thought, and then she felt her mood lighten. By now she was quite certain her child would be a boy. That was wonderful. Her husband would be delighted to know that he had an heir.

But then, looking at him again, she knew that this was the wrong moment to share her pleasure. 'My love, you are very upset by all this, aren't you?'

'Yes, of course,' Nicholas said heavily, his face still troubled. 'But talking of Serlo – what did he want with you? I saw him approach you at the inquest. What was that about?'

She smiled at him, but it was some moments before she could trust her voice. 'Why, nothing, dear. Nothing at all.'

Warin had stood at the back of the inquest, but left long before the arrival of Muriel with the body of Hamelin and the revelation about Athelina's death. He had other work to do. Behind the churchyard he had left a horse. He went there now, and mounted it.

From the churchyard where the inquest was being held, the road led northwards past the spring called the Holy Well. It joined up with the road to the moors after a while, a long road that opened out after a quarter mile or so, away from the trees and low bushes that lay about the vill itself. Here the land undulated more smoothly, with sprinkles of bright yellow where the gorse flowered. Warin stopped once, staring about him at the view, and then took a deep breath before setting off once more.

His path took him up past the fields at Colvannick, and then on towards the vill of Temple. It was a place with which he was well acquainted, and he glanced at the fields approvingly. The harvest had been good this year, and it was pleasing to see that it had all been collected before the weather worsened.

The road to Temple was over the top of the moors, and he could feel the hot sun burning into his back. He took a drink from a spring at a high point, from where he could stare back towards the vill. The church stood proud of the landscape all about, a tall steeple with little decoration, a clear marker for those who had faith so that they knew where to go. Even the poor traveller who was desperate for a chance to pray, or perhaps merely seeking warmth and shelter, would be able to see this building from miles away. After crossing the worst of the moors, a traveller would be glad of such a sight.

And in the other direction there lay the strange little manor, once a part of the great organisation that owned so much of the country: the Knights Templar. Now destroyed, the Order existed still in stone and mortar in a thousand little manors and chapels up and down England. Across Europe most had been handed to the Hospitallers, in compliance with the Pope's orders, but in England, the King preferred to protect them. He had kept several of the manors for himself.

This was not one of them, though. Too small to interest the King, it had been absorbed by a knight who had given Edward good service, as Warin knew; perhaps he was the only person in the Earldom of Cornwall to know that. But he had good reason to know. The new owner had instructed him to come here and look at the place, evaluate its worth, and decide what should be done with it.

That would not be too difficult, but the second of his tasks was to assess the loyalty of the men of the county, so far as he could. Not because Warin was a spy by nature, but because there must be one man in whom Sir Henry of Cardinham could trust, and who better than bluff, honest Warin?

Warin knew why he had been picked for this job, but he was also aware of the desperate need of Sir Henry to know the mood of the county. A single man could be an irritation in a vill; a vill like Cardinham in revolt could prove to be an annoyance for the Sheriff; a few places like Cardinham rising up could mean a civil war.

Many of the men from the Marches had been arrested and thrown into the Tower or executed since the last abortive uprising. The King had been defeated and his most trusted aides exiled, but then he had planned, as only a man like he could.

Warin was no cretin: he knew how devious King Edward II could be. He'd seen Edward and his lover, Hugh Despenser, plotting the overthrow of one man after another, even to the exclusion from his affections of his own Queen. At the first opportunity, Edward had baited his trap. One by one, the men who could have threatened his power were caught in his nets, even the most powerful, Lord Mortimer of Wigmore, who now mouldered in the Tower of London. He had been arrested eighteen months ago, and at first was threatened with execution, although he was later reprieved. However, Warin knew that Hugh Despenser, the son of the Earl of Winchester, was pissing in the King's ear again, demanding Mortimer's death.

Mortimer, as Despenser knew, was a risk as long as he was

alive. One of a few men who were competent to lead others, as he had proved in Ireland, he was a threat to the rule of the Despensers. For that reason, Roger Mortimer would be dead before the end of August. That was the rumour. Despenser had demanded his head.

In this year of 1323, the Despensers, father and son, held sway. There was no theft, no act of brigandage, no extortion, which could persuade the King to remove them. Of course, it was likely that the King didn't hear the murmurings of unrest. All the reports he received came through his most trusted adviser, Hugh Despenser, and all Hugh ever wanted was more money, land and property. The man got away, literally, with murder, since none would dare to speak ill of he whom the King most trusted – and loved.

Another reason for Warin's being sent so far from the court was to protect him in the event of a fresh coup in the King's Houschold. Such things, Warin knew, could suddenly spring up. In the last decade he had seen the deaths of many men. And when such men were executed, they left behind them the disgruntled and the avaricious, who craved vengeance or their own rewards. Knowing this, Warin was only too happy to be away from court.

Especially now, in mid-August. If the rumours were true and the traitor Mortimer was to be executed later in the month, Warin knew that the end of so powerful a nobleman, once the King's trusted friend and ally, could cause mayhem on a scale unforeseen by either Edward or Despenser. London no longer felt like a safe city. The apprentices were always an unruly band, and just recently they had been worse than usual. There had been reports of gangs of them wandering the streets just before he and Richer had left Kent.

He clattered along a stretch of almost metalled track, and then found himself on a well-made road which, although it had not been properly maintained for some while, was still perfectly usable. This took him past a few small buildings, and then he was in a wooded area. The road led on straight ahead, but he took a well-used track southwards, and here, a short way down the path, he found the church. He swung himself down lightly, and tethered his mount.

It was a small church, some six and twenty feet long, maybe fifteen wide. The altar was a simple slab of moorstone, while the walls were decorated with vivid scenes from Hell: there were beasts of all sorts, reptilian, human in body but with animals' heads, or scaled and twisted, all wielding tridents and bills, pushing the wailing, weeping naked souls of the damned into the flames of the pit.

Warin studied the pictures with some interest for a few moments, but then he heard a cough, and he looked up to observe a slender figure beneath the small tower. 'Godspeed, Father.'

'Godspeed, my son. If you wished for a prayer on your journey, I can help you shortly, but . . .'

'No, Father John.'

'You know me?'

'I have heard much about you. I am not here for a prayer,' Warin said. He watched as the priest approached him, smiling a little uncertainly.

'No? Then how can I help you?'

'You can talk to me about the wench living with the priest at Cardinham, for a start,' Warin said, and then he smiled wolfishly as Father John's smile froze on his lips.

Chapter Sixteen

It was no noisome hovel, this tavern, but as soon as Baldwin, Simon and Jules entered, the lusty singing and roaring which they had heard from outside died down and the whole room became as quiet as a church at dawn.

There were many vills where those in a tavern would behave in a similar manner, but here, Baldwin was sure that there was a reason other than the usual one of local suspicion of foreigners. Here it seemed more likely to be alarm at finding three men-at-arms in the doorway.

That was true except for one man: Serlo. The miller was slumped on an old barrel, his legs spread wide and a pot gripped in his fist. About him was a small group of local men, from the look of them.

'What, come to demand more questions of me, have you?' he slurred rudely at Baldwin. 'Thought you'd get a poor miller when he's down on his luck and his brat's been scalded? Or do you want to accuse me of his murder – is that it, you curs whelped by devils!'

Baldwin set his jaw and walked to a heavy table, sitting with his back to the wall so he could see Serlo and the door. He could not blame the man for his mood after all he had endured that day, but he wasn't sure that Simon or Sir Jules would be capable of controlling their anger should Serlo continue to insult them. He considered walking out again, but to do so would leave them open to ridicule. Their offices required respect.

In preference, he beckoned the only woman in the place. She made to go to him immediately, wiping her hands on a grubby cloth bound about her middle by a piece of string. 'Master—' she began anxiously, but he cut her off.

'Mistress, fetch me a jug of your best wine, and my friends here will have . . .?'

Sir Jules ordered wine, but Simon, who was desperately thirsty, demanded a quart of cider. When they had done, Baldwin leaned forward. 'Mistress, we shall be here for one drink, and we shall not leave under the threats of the miller, but please order him to be silent. We are officers of the King, and if he abuses us, we shall have to respond.'

'I'm sure he's not serious, master,' she replied, wiping her hands more vigorously in agitation. She was a pretty woman, Baldwin thought, with a round face, bright blue eyes and hair the colour of straw at harvest-time, more yellow than gold, which hung in natural ringlets about her features, unflattened by her coif. 'He lost his son today and—'

'We know, but he cannot insult a Coroner and a Keeper of the King's Peace with impunity. Make him silent, or command him to leave.'

'I will.'

She threw Serlo an anxious glance and made her way back towards him. She had set up her bar at the far end of the room, near to where he sat, and as she served the cider and drew off two jugs of wine, she leaned towards Serlo and spoke.

There was silence. At first Baldwin thought that the man had taken the hint and would leave them in peace, but then he saw the slow dawning of anger on Serlo's face. The miller reddened, then his scowl grew into a ferocious glare. He said nothing, but sat staring fixedly at Baldwin and the other two while the woman served them.

She returned to the table and set their drinks before them,

saying in an undertone, 'I hope he'll be sensible, master. Don't think too harshly of him. He's been very unlucky today. To lose a son . . .'

'We all know of his misfortune,' Baldwin said, 'but he must respect our offices, whether he likes us or no. Make him remain silent like this, and we shall leave as soon as we have finished our drinks, mistress.'

She flashed him a smile. 'You can call me Susan, master. Everyone else does about here.'

'Thank you. Tell me, Susan, how has he been? He looks as though he'd like to begin a fight. Is that how he reacts to ale?'

'In all truth, yes.' She allowed her gaze to float over them. 'I don't think he'd try his luck with three armed men though, Sir Knight.'

'You may call me Baldwin,' he said. 'Well, that at least is a relief.'

'He's a bully, Sir Baldwin. The only person who's likely to feel his fist is his wife.'

She spoke with some contempt, and Baldwin thought to learn more if he could. 'This Athelina: I heard that she was widowed some nine years ago. Yet she still lived in her own little house. How did she support herself?'

'Not in the usual way,' Susan said with a broad grin. 'Any man asking Athelina to whore for him would end up with a blackened eye, no matter what some men might say.'

'He has made some comment about her?' Baldwin enquired, seeing her gaze harden as she glanced at Serlo again.

'He was talking in his ale earlier, that's all. Said she should have whored and paid him that way for the house. He's all mouth when he's been drinking. I think it's because he never had a mother. His own died when he was a babe, and he was brought up by his brother.'

'A hard life for a child,' Baldwin mused. 'This Athelina . . . if she didn't rely on the old profession, how did she earn money?'

'She enjoyed the support of the church. And there were the gleanings, alms, money from the castle. Many here are very poor, so she often went to the castle.'

There was a subtle alteration in tone that caught Baldwin's attention. 'So she would go to the castle for food and perhaps . . .'

Susan smiled again. 'Like I said, no whoring for Athelina. No, she was the sort of woman to give herself entirely, never by halves. She loved her old man, Hob, and when he died, she never looked at another local man again so far as I know.'

Baldwin thought he caught that curious intonation once more, but as he glanced up at her, her face hardened. 'Perhaps Athelina had a lover, one who was not a "local man"?' he wondered. 'One of the castle's men-at-arms?'

'Perhaps. She was still a handsome woman.'

'How could she afford the house? The miller over there was apparently making money from her, and the first reason why everyone assumed that she had committed suicide was her inability to pay an increase in rent. How did she manage to pay before?'

'I don't know,' the alewife said, making as if to leave.

'Wait, Susan,' Baldwin said firmly. He remembered the Coroner, who sat silently without evincing the faintest interest in the conversation. 'We are investigating a murder, and *the Coroner here* is interested in all aspects of her life.'

Sir Jules coughed slightly to hear this. He had been enjoying his wine without being plagued by questions he must ask or people he should see. When Baldwin started questioning this maid, he had thought it was because the knight was interested in her for himself; he hadn't realised it was in order to further the inquest. So far as he was concerned, the investigation could wait until his official inquest. All this was speculation, nothing more. He tried to appear interested.

'So, Susan,' Baldwin continued, 'do you know how she earned money before?'

'No,' she said, a hint of sulkiness in her tone. 'It wasn't my business. All I can say is, she was fine until a year or so back, and suddenly life was more difficult. Recently she'd been worried about money.'

Sir Jules decided to show he was also listening and wiped his mouth. 'So you think that she might have grown despondent about money, and that made her occasionally lose her reason?'

'Maybe. Sometimes.'

'And what about the boys? How were they?'

'They were worried about her, I suppose.'

Sir Jules said, 'If she was murdered, who was most likely to kill her?'

'I don't know.'

'What of the miller there?' he asked. 'He's a bully, cruel by nature. He could beat his wife, you say, but he holds his tongue against us – he sounds just the sort of man to kill a defenceless woman. Maybe this mention of whoring is because he desired her?'

Baldwin shook his head. 'What do you think, Simon?'

'I think he had no reason to kill. Perhaps he desired her, but so what? He probably desires you too, Susan. You've certainly the looks and figure to make a man love you . . .'

She dimpled.

'But,' Simon continued, 'there would have been no purpose to his hurting her. He wanted her money, didn't he? Anyway, she started getting strange a while ago, before Serlo increased her rent, which shows that there was something else that made her depressed.'

'I agree,' Baldwin said. 'Whatever caused her to start to lose her mind may have had a direct influence on her end.'

'But it may have nothing to do with her death,' Sir Jules said. 'After all, it could be a rapist who wanted her and decided to take her, with or without her agreement. Serlo the miller would be that sort of man.'

'It's possible, yes,' Baldwin said. 'But I think we would be remiss not to investigate all the possible solutions. And the fact of her melancholy is curious. You are sure, Susan, that you weren't told why she was so suddenly afflicted?'

'She wasn't the sort of woman to confide in all and sundry,' Susan said and went to serve another customer.

'Should we question that miller now?' Sir Jules asked.

Baldwin was tempted to say yes, but a glance at Serlo dissuaded him. The man was sitting slumped, head hanging miserably. Every few moments he would shake it as though in disbelief. He was past rage at the world, and now was sunk in grief.

'No. He's consumed too much ale. Wait until tomorrow. We can ask him then, before the inquest of his child.'

'So we have learned a little today,' Simon noted. 'She was desperate for money. Fine until a year or so backalong, Susan said. Since then, the money dried up.'

Baldwin nodded. He glanced at Sir Jules. 'What do you think?'

'Me? Nothing. Let's wait until we can hear what others say.'

Baldwin stared at him a moment, then looked to Simon.

'Yes,' Simon said. 'I think we need to find a lover.'

'A man,' Baldwin said, 'who could afford to support her and her children, who had the inclination to protect her and who, roughly a year ago, lost interest in her.'

'He found a new lover,' Simon guessed.

Jules narrowed his eyes. 'He might have got married.'

Baldwin considered. 'If he was enjoying himself with Athelina, would he have had time or inclination to woo another? I'd think it unlikely. And he'll not be young. She wasn't, and a man seeking a mistress almost always looks for a woman younger than himself.'

He stood and left some coins on the table before leading the others from the room. As they reached the roadway, the noise began to build again, with a harsh voice speaking, then a burst of raucous laughter. It was tempting to return inside, but then he reflected that there was little he could achieve. Perhaps he could have Serlo thrown into gaol, but that itself could serve no useful purpose. Or so he thought.

Later he wished that he had done exactly that, but of course by then it was too late.

Susan could see that Serlo was now very drunk indeed. It had grown dark outside, and as he drank, he grew more and more depressed.

'She can't love me any more. If she ever did before, she won't now, will she? I love her, too. I loved Aumie and Ham, and now Ham's dead, what'll Aumie think of me? He'll blame me too, won't he? All I wanted was to have a good family, but it's all gone. All gone! All because I couldn't find anyone to look after them while Muriel was in her bed. How was I to know Ham would be scalded? I couldn't tell.'

She knew his complaint was reasonable. There were few men in the tavern with them who wouldn't have done the same; leaving their children alone, hoping that they would be sensible enough to avoid any danger. But it was a lot to expect of a crawling baby and a boy of four.

It was odd that Athelina's boys hadn't been able to call out the alarm. They were, after all, aged twelve and ten. Had they died first, or had she? Faugh! It was a horrible thought that she could have walked into her house and found both murdered, the killer still there. No woman could do much if she walked in on such a scene. Except . . .

Susan considered herself ordinary enough, not dissimilar to Athelina in many ways. Surely if she had walked in to find a man doing that to *her* children, she'd have screamed and attacked. He'd have scratches all over his face, and even if he killed her afterwards, he'd remain hurt. However, no one in the vill had shown any such marks. Perhaps she had just fainted. Maybe that was it. She collapsed as soon as she saw her boys.

Or perhaps she was dead first. The two lads were out, and she was killed first, the boys next. But how could the killer have kept them both quiet? They must have screamed and shouted and struggled.

That was when she had the disturbing thought. It made her stop in her tracks, and as she stood, staring into the distance, she heard Serlo slurring coarsely.

'Well, Sue? You want something? Looking for a man to tire you? I'm the one. Other men can't sire a single child, but I managed two in three years. My seed's good.' He belched, and she turned to him with exhaustion tinged with anger.

'You think you could raise more than a finger? I need a man to satisfy me, Serlo, not my own ale!' There was a drunken chuckle which ran about the room as the other men appreciated her joke. She was angry enough to make mention of his son's body cooling in the church, but she stilled her mouth.

'Go home, Serlo,' she told him. 'You'll have a hard day tomorrow, so go home now and sleep well. Angot, you look after him, eh? Make sure he gets there safely.'

There was a lot of argument at that, and some of the other men disputed her decision to close the doors, but she was tired.

She was also very worried by the revelation she had just had. The idea that the children could have been silent when the murderer entered left her thinking she could guess who it might have been.

No, not worried. Petrified.

'Come on, old Serlo,' Angot said, and hiccuped softly into the night.

It was much later than usual for him to be out. Usually he'd be up until dusk, and then he'd be off to his bed as darkness fell. Not much else to do. And Bab was a cheerful sort, thank God. Some men had wives who moaned and complained about their lot all night, but Bab was a good wife. She was happy to let him do as he wanted. She'd be there now, waiting for him to come home. He burped. She wouldn't be over the moon if he let it out that he'd had a gallon or more of Sue's best ale, mind. Better explain it was 'cos of poor Serlo.

'Come on, poor old Serlo,' he said companionably. 'Time to go home.'

They had almost reached the bend in the track where the stream met it, more than halfway from the tavern, but it had taken them much longer than it would usually. Angot looked up and saw that the sky was clear. Above the trees the stars glittered and shone like pinpricks through a black veil. He had to pause, staring up in awe. God must be wonderful to have created that, he thought. Vaguely, he acknowledged that he wouldn't have had any idea where to start. It was lovely, though. As a small silver fleece of cloud sailed across the sky, passing near to the moon, he felt his heart expand in pleasure at the beauty of the sight. And Bab would be lying on their palliasse back home, waiting for him.

'Come on, old fellow! Time for bed.'

Serlo was dragging his heels, leaning on Angot and breathing stertorously, and from what Angot could tell, sweating profusely. No surprise there. The miller always sweated a lot. Usually smelled like a rancid stoat, too. Never bathed, and his armpits were foul enough to be classed as weapons. Now, though, he appeared to take offence at Angot's words.

'Keep off me! You think I need help? Sod you! You go home to your wife, and leave me alone. I'm not in need of help from the likes of you. Think you're so sober you can lead me like a pony? I'm all right!'

He staggered away from Angot, reaching out to grab a tree's branch as he did so, the breath groaning in his throat, and he cursed bitterly as he started to retch.

'Let's get you home, Serlo.'

'*Fuck off!* Leave me to myself, you prick! Get yourself off to your own home and leave me alone!'

Angot put out a hand to him, but Serlo slapped it away. In truth Angot would be happy to go. There was little point in his staying here if the miller didn't want him. He shouldn't leave Serlo in this state though, he thought as the other man brought up much of his ale, vomiting it in among the trees and swearing again as he wiped his mouth on his sleeve. 'Christ Jesus! That ale was bad.'

'Come on, let me just help you to your door.'

'*Go away!*'

Angot reflected that he had done the best he could. He shrugged, a little pointlessly since Serlo was throwing up again and not even facing him, and then he turned on his heel and stumbled away from the place. If he was quick, Bab would still be awake. It was a lovely night, after all, he thought to himself. A lovely night.

And so it was. The crescent moon was waxing, and the sky was alive with stars. Bats hurtled across the sky in search of their prey, and over the meadows there glided a white wraith, a barn owl, which plummeted as silent as starlight upon a shrew, and then, with an effortless waft of wings, rose again to lift over the trees at the edge of the meadowlands. There he perched on a branch and devoured his meal.

Afterwards, he remained there, watching, his enormous eyes blinking slowly as he digested his food. He was above all the little creatures of the wood. He cared not for the souls of the animals which scampered and tussled below him. Although in human terms he was the king of all birds here, he had no interest in any other creature, other than those which he might consume.

He saw the shuffling, stumbling shape of Serlo, and he saw the other figure step out from behind a tree. As the knife rose, the blade shining with an oily perfection under the moon's silver light, he blinked, but only once. He watched the blade fall, heard the loud hiccup, the whimper, and the sound of blade striking flesh – once, twice, thrice, and once more for luck. He observed the figure of Serlo crawling on as the life drained from him, saw the man walk alongside and kick him viciously in the head and saw him kick again at the dying man's flanks. He saw the blade come down again, the fingers knotting in Serlo's hair, yanking the miller's head back to expose the throat, and saw the blade swipe cleanly across, like a scythe taking the corn. And then there was silence, other than the loud rasping breath of the killer. Soon even that was gone as the man picked up Serlo's corpse and carried it down towards the mill.

The owl remained there watching impassively. It was only when he heard a strange rumbling noise that seemed to transmit itself through the ground and up through the trunk of the tree, that he stirred himself and peered about him. Then, a few moments later, he saw a small mouse pushing its nose through the stems of grass at the edge of the meadow.

He glided down once more on assassin's wings; as efficient a killer as any human.

* * *

It was late when Richer got back to the castle. Thankfully the door was open still, even though it was long after dark, but here in the wilds, the gate was often left ajar. Inside his hutch-like shed, the gatekeeper slumbered, snoring and whistling, and Richer tiptoed past, rather than waken him.

'You have been gone a long while,' Warin said as he entered the hall.

'I have been sick. A severe headache . . .'

'It's curious,' the squire said. He was sitting at a table, and now he leaned forward, elbows on the table-top, staring at Richer unblinking. 'I have known you many years, and in all that time, you've never had such bad headaches – but today you refused to join me because of one, and you say you've suffered a worse one since.'

It was true. The headaches had been at their worst when his family had all died, but had reduced in severity over time. 'I don't understand it either,' Richer shrugged. 'They haven't been so bad in years. Today I could hardly see for flashing lights and poor vision.'

'Very peculiar.' Warin stared at him with a strange look in his eye. 'So long as you're sure there's nothing else the matter?'

'What else could be wrong?'

'Perhaps you're upset over this dead widow? Or could it be something else?'

'You mean the King's murder?'

Warin's eyes hardened. 'Not so damned loud, fool!' he hissed. 'Do you want the whole castle to hear you?'

Richer shook his head, eyes shut. 'I can't think straight while my head's like this. All I meant was, while the King was planning to murder the Lord Marcher.'

'He intends to execute a traitor, that is all,' Warin said flatly. 'Mortimer raised his flag against the King's friends and officers. That makes him traitor.'

Richer nodded. It was too late and he was too tired to argue. The flickering candles in the hall were making his head start to feel odd again, and he had no desire to be caught here with a fresh migraine. 'Did you learn all you sought?'

'The priest agreed to my proposal, yes. And he'll keep his mouth shut. There were some interesting snippets about the people in this vill though – especially Father Adam.'

'What sort?' Richer asked.

'The man is a sodomite,' Warin smiled. 'So he's another one we can count upon!'

Chapter Seventeen

Simon and Baldwin were woken the next morning by the sudden eruption of noise as the little fortress's servants began to rouse themselves.

It was something that Simon reckoned he could never get used to, this infernal din heralding each new day. To Baldwin it was as natural as breathing, and he lived with the row perfectly happily, but Simon groaned as the men entered the room, chatting loudly about their plans for the day, issuing orders as they went about which horse was to be taken for exercise first, whether the bitch was going to pup today or hold back for another, whether the falcon with the lame wing would recover, and then the more crucial decisions, such as should the red calf or the black one with the lighter flank be pole-axed today. All the Bailiff wanted was to pull his cloak back over his head and return to the arms of Morpheus. (Simon had no idea who the man was, but he'd heard Baldwin mention him before now, and he liked the sound of the phrase.)

When at last he sat up and pulled on his clothes, the hall was already almost filled. At a nearby wall, Baldwin sat slouched, his face dark as he stared into the distance. Gervase was sitting at a bench on the dais, dealing with the hundred and one little decisions which, as steward here, he must make each day, and not far from him, forlorn and chewing a fingernail, was Jules. His disconsolate clerk peering at his master with a look of impatience on his face.

Simon ran a hand through his tousled hair and felt a slight tension in his left shoulder. It was always the way when he slept on a bench. The damn things were too hard, but he supposed in a little place like this, he was lucky to have been given a bench to himself. All too often even a notable guest might be forced to sleep on the floor in a castle this size. It was good that the lord and his wife at least had their own chamber separate from the men here in their hall. Most modern castles were built this way, as Simon knew, because with so many hired men-at-arms, it was safer for the lord and his lady to be segregated in case of treachery. Things were no longer, as Baldwin was so fond of saying, as they used to be, when each warrior gave his oath to support and protect his lord for as long as either lived. There was no need for payment in those days – the man served his lord and in return he received food, shelter and clothing. Nowadays, the bastards always wanted money.

Simon's mouth tasted foul. Last night, Jules and he had discovered a joint attraction for the red wine Gervase had stored in the buttery. It was flavoursome – powerful and sweet – and although Baldwin had retired to his sleep before long, Simon and Jules had remained in the corner, talking. Now his mouth tasted like the inside of a chicken house. He needed water to sluice it clean. A little meat to chew on would help – as would a pot of cider.

Outside he ducked his head under the water in the trough and came back up blowing and shaking his head like a dog. *God's heart*, but that was cold! Still, at least the wash was refreshing, and he took off his shirt and used it to dry the worst of the dampness. Returning to the room, he saw that Jules was talking to Gervase now, Baldwin listening intently.

'What is it, Baldwin?' he asked heartily. His belly rumbled and he thought of breakfast again.

'There is a possibility that the inquests will be swiftly completed,' Baldwin said quietly.

Simon stared at him. 'How so? If there was murder, we'll have to find out who could have killed her.'

'The good Coroner has many other calls upon his time,' Baldwin said sarcastically. 'He feels this affair is not important enough to hold his interest. He wishes to be away.'

'The ignorant puppy!'

'No, sir.'

Looking to his side, Simon saw that the Coroner's clerk had joined them.

Roger continued, 'I fear it's more difficult. This morning we have had a message from the Sheriff. A prisoner of the King's has escaped from his prison and we're commanded to raise the Hue and Cry and catch him alive or dead.'

'Who is this terror?' Simon asked with a frown. For a man to escape the King was unknown. Surely the fellow would be recaught soon, but the fact that he had caused messengers to be sent all the way here spoke of the man's dangerous reputation.

'Lord Mortimer of Wigmore. He has escaped from the Tower of London, apparently.'

'My Heavens!' Baldwin breathed. 'No one escapes from the Tower.'

'Not for ever, no,' the clerk nodded.

Simon shot a look at Baldwin, and he saw his friend's head shake. They could not discuss the matter in front of a stranger. It was one thing to enquire about the circumstances, but any speculation would have to wait until they were out of earshot of this clerk. Since they had returned from their pilgrimage, it had become plain to both that it was all too easy for a man to be heard by a fellow talking insolently about the King or his friends, or speaking in support of a man whom the King now considered his enemy. A man who wished to keep his head would refrain from commenting in public.

'So will you be leaving shortly, Roger?' Baldwin asked.

The clerk pulled a moue and shrugged. 'I don't know. It seems madness to me, because there is clearly much to investigate here, but whether it was a murder or a suicide, the most important thing is to keep the records. Once we have the story written down, and the value of the fines, we can move on to the next matter. The child's death was sad, of course,' he said, his face growing still more cadaverous, 'but at least that will be straightforward. The pig will be *deodand*, for it caused his death.'

'Accidents will happen,' Simon said heavily. 'It's better than some: last time I was involved with a pig causing death, the damned thing had entered a house in Exeter and eaten a baby before the mother's eyes.'

Baldwin said offhandedly, 'It is a great shame, but as you say, if your master cannot find the murderer, I suppose the record is all that matters.'

'That is not what I said,' Roger began, but then he peered at Baldwin with a sharp eye. 'Hmm. You're a sly one, I see. Perhaps a little further enquiring wouldn't go amiss.'

'I don't understand,' Simon began, but both ignored him.

Baldwin said, 'So Mortimer is free. That will be a sore irritation to the King.'

'I should think so. He was a doughty warrior in the King's service – before he turned traitor, of course,' Roger said.

'So your master will be needed immediately at Bodmin, just in case Mortimer has come all this way?'

The clerk smiled. 'You are a determined man, Sir Baldwin.'

Simon frowned: he could recall the tale of Lord Mortimer. He was a Marcher Lord from the Welsh borders, installed there thanks to his grandfather's devotion to the King's own grandfather, Henry III. It was Mortimer's grandfather too who had rescued the young Prince Edward, later to be the present King's father, Edward I, from Simon de Montfort's men; he later helped the King to win the Battle of Evesham. It was Mortimer who had killed de Montfort's ally, Hugh Despenser. When his men won through to de Montfort himself, pulling him from his horse and hacking his head from his body, then draping his testicles over his nose, Prince Edward had ordered that the skull was Mortimer's property, and the skull remained as a proud memento of the victory at the Castle of Wigmore. Simon wondered what had happened to the testicles.

Thus were the seeds of Mortimer's destruction sown almost a quarter century before his birth. There was a bitter enmity between the Mortimer family and that of the Despensers.

Roger Mortimer had been a close friend of the Prince who was to become Edward II, and through the early years of Edward's reign, Mortimer had been his most devoted lieutenant, supporting him even through the years of Gaveston's ascendancy when others deserted him. When the Bruce sent his brother to Ireland to disrupt the English territories there, it was Mortimer whom the King sent with the host, and when the Scottish invasion force was destroyed, he became the Justiciar in Ireland, ruling in the King's name. Until three years ago, Mortimer was the King's most trusted servant.

That changed when the Despensers began to encroach on the Marcher lands. One of the lords most affected was Mortimer, and at last, provoked beyond reason, Mortimer rose up in arms with the other Lords Marcher. They took arms against the Despensers, not the King, and when the King's standard was raised against them, the Marchers stopped fighting and surrendered. As a result, Roger himself was taken and had mouldered in the Tower for eighteen months, since the momentous events on the Welsh marches.

And now he had escaped: the man most feared and detested by Hugh Despenser. It was no surprise that the King and Despenser wanted his head. If Mortimer escaped permanently, he would prove a powerful enemy.

'Christ Jesus,' Simon breathed. 'I hope there won't be another civil war.'

The clerk Roger crossed himself. 'So do we all,' he intoned.

All could remember the tales told at firesides of those terrible times when Henry III fought de Montfort up and down the kingdom. There was scarcely a family which didn't lose men in the battles that ranged all over the land from Lewes to Wales only fifty years previously.

Baldwin frowned. 'He isn't here, though, is he? And I believe the death of this woman and her children is enough of a concern. A man like Mortimer may be able to unsettle the realm, but revolt starts because of injustice. If we allow injustice here, and don't seek the murderer, it will be as a pebble at the top of a hill which rolls and starts a landslide. I think Jules would be better served remaining here and learning the truth.'

Roger the clerk gave a half-smile. 'I shall speak to him.'

'Do so. And I thank you. Godspeed.'

Baldwin watched the clerk walk slowly towards the men at the table. 'He is a shrewd one, that fellow.'

'Why do you say that?' Simon asked, baffled.

'I think that he has his post because he is interested in justice. Of the pair, he is the man with the understanding and authority. Jules is a pleasant young fellow, but he is an appointment made by the Sheriff – I expect his father is in the King's Household. It is Roger who records the crimes and instructs his master in what to ask. I think he could be a most useful ally in our investigations.'

Letitia was walking along the lane from her house towards Serlo's. She carried a basket containing some bread and an egg, and was readying herself to be pleasant to the man. Apparently he had been at the tavern until some ridiculous hour of the night, and now he would likely be incapable of rising from his bed, like the hog he was. Lazy devil!

Well, she wasn't going to let him stay there. He had a duty to the memory of his son, and a responsibility to his wife and remaining son. Letitia wasn't going to let him lie about indolently and bring any more shame on himself and poor Alex. She'd stop his sulkiness if she could, and if she couldn't, well, she'd make his life as miserable as only a woman who knew a man's weaknesses could.

The stream was loud down here. On the left the trees were taller than at other places, fed from the constant supply of water, and the bushes and ferns in among them were thick and impassable. It was a pleasant, secluded area, she reckoned, just as the mill's setting was pleasant – but not as a place to live. She liked being in the centre of things. It was alarming to be so far from people, isolated. Although it was only a half-mile from her house, she felt that this valley might have been a hundred leagues away. It was so green, so damp, so noisy with that stream . . . she could have been anywhere.

There was a place where the ground was stirred, and the soil was black with moisture. She hadn't noticed this place before, but it was a strange thing about this trail: every so often a patch of dampness would appear. Today she scarcely noticed this new one.

The mill stood, as she had expected, silent; the wheel was stationary, and from inside came not a sound. All she could hear was the chuckle and slap of the water, and the regular snorting of the old sow demanding her food, unaware of her crime. There were chickens scrabbling, too, but since they were all youngsters from Letitia's last brood, she knew that none were laying yet. The fox had got in among Serlo's last flock one night when he had been drunk again. Luckily not all the birds had been killed, but those which hadn't had been traumatised and wouldn't lay again. They had to be culled. At least they could be eaten. Those which the fox had killed and left had to be thrown away. If a man ate a chicken which had been killed by a fox, he would become very ill indeed.

'Serlo! Wake up!' she called, walking into the house, but there was no sign of him there. She went to the sleeping area, but the bed was as it had been the day before, when she had come in here to find Muriel wailing and keening, rocking her dead child.

The memory made her shiver. Thank God that little Aumery was safe at her house now. She put the basket down then crossed the yard to the mill itself. Pushing open the door, a sense told her that there was something wrong, but her rational mind ignored it. She felt the chill in the place, but told herself that was the water nearby. Mills were always cold. She could smell the tinny odour – must be the grease Serlo used to keep the machinery working. She saw the blackened mess on the floor: her brother-in-law was a lazy devil who hadn't cleaned the place in ages. She heard the scatterings of the rats' feet, and tutted; she had reminded Serlo time and again to purchase a cat to keep the vermin from his grain stores.

Only when she had walked right inside did she see his legs by the machinery, and the mashed-up mess that was his head. Even then her mind refused to respond. It was only when she was halfway home that her mouth sprang open as though of its own volition, and she began to scream and scream and scream . . .

Warin was already awake and had been out on his destrier for a five-mile ride before Simon had heard the first sounds of morning. Now returned, he left his mount with one of the stable-hands and strode towards the hall.

'A good day, Squire.'

Warin turned and gave a slow smile. 'I thought it was my duty to be the man who sprang upon you, Richer.'

'It's good to know there are times I can still make you jump,' Richer said, and let himself down from the wall on which he'd been sitting. 'Had a good ride?'

'Fine. I think he'll need a new shoe on his for'ard left hoof. It's coming loose.'

'The smith here's a good lad,' Richer said. 'I am sorry for last night. I don't know what the matter was with my head.'

'Is it better now?'

Richer pulled a face. 'After one of my migraines, it feels as though another threatens for days afterwards.'

'Let's hope there isn't another, then,' Warin commented. 'Later today we should practise with our weapons.'

'Not today, please. I am still a little enfeebled.'

'Yes, today. You need your practice and so do I.'

Richer pulled a face and was about to respond when there was a sudden commotion behind them. A young lad had run to the gate and was gabbling to the gatekeeper.

'I don't care. I got to speak to the Coroner – I got to!'

Sir Jules had tied on his sword-belt as soon as the lad, Iwan's grandson Gregory, had told him of the body.

He found it hard to believe: five deaths in a matter of days. To have another corpse on his hands was far more than he had bargained for. 'I'm not up to this,' he muttered to himself as he followed the boy to the vill.

'Sir?' Roger enquired.

'Nothing.'

There was no way he'd admit to his clerk that he didn't feel up to the task ahead of him. A knight always knew his own mind and his abilities as well as his responsibilities. Jules was fully aware of his duties. He had been given them by the Sheriff, his father's old friend, and he had intended to show himself competent, but that was before all these deaths. A hanged woman and her dead sons, that was all he had anticipated here; now he had a scalded brat and a dead man as well. There was something evil at work here in the vill.

For a moment he wondered about asking Roger for his advice. There were cases of demonic possession, he recalled. Sometimes a woman was found to be a witch, or a man was discovered to be possessed. Terrible thought. It quite made his hair stand on end to think that he could be looking into a case like that. 'Oh God, please help me,' he murmured.

'Sir?'

'Oh, nothing.'

As the lad took them through the middle of the vill and down the lane to the track that led to the mill, Sir Jules could hear Sir Baldwin muttering away to his friend behind him. Christ's pain, it was bad enough having Roger here with him, watching his every move without those two coming along for the ride. Good God, what had he done to deserve this?

Sir Jules felt he had good reason to be discontented. What had been described as a pleasant little job with good remuneration, when the good Sheriff had offered it to him – as a mark of respect to his father, true, but Jules wasn't going to look a gift horse in the mouth – the idea had been that this little sinecure would provide some welcome additional funds. For a young knight, that was always agreeable. And to be fair, there weren't that many knights in Cornwall who could take on the task. Especially since the last cull. Kings would keep removing all Coroners *en masse* from their duties just because of the odd complaint and accusation of fraud. Of course there was fraud! How else was a man to survive?

But he had three poxed experts on his tail now. It was not enough that he should be forced to actually view these bloated corpses, now he was lumbered with a team of men who actually wanted to find the murderer or murderers, rather than taking the fines and forgetting about it all.

He felt very small and insignificant, but also under a great deal of pressure. He was only a young man. Most fellows his age would have been lucky to have been made squire, but here he was:

a full, belted knight. And in the presence of three men who were clearly more experienced and capable than he. It was a miserable position in which to be placed.

The mill loomed ahead, a squat black shape seen through the trees. He splashed on through the little puddles, feeling his head sinking on his shoulders like a tortoise. He'd seen one once when he was a lad, and the sight of the creature pulling legs and head into its shell in such a cowardly fashion had made him laugh at the time; it had certainly never occurred to Jules that he could ever liken himself to that same tortoise. He knew even then that he was to rise to greater heights than any of his companions.

It hadn't happened though, had it? All through his training he had been a competent, unadventurous but skilful enough fighter, whether with lance at quintain, with sword, or staff. Yet as soon as the targets began to fight back, his martial spirit dimmed. There were men he fought who would think nothing of slaughtering him for an insult. Now, for him to take offence at some fool's words and draw his sword, that was one thing. Many a peasant had learned to apologise to him, when a six-pound piece of sharpened steel was held at his throat, but when a similar, unrebated block of steel was held at Jules's own neck, when it was flashing and gleaming in silver-white circles whipping in close to his face or his belly in the ring, that was when his ardour started to fade. To practise at weaponry was one of the duties of a warrior, but it was disquieting that a blade could lop off an arm without effort.

No, his warlike spirit was dissipated in the reality of a hot, sweaty metal suit on a dusty training ground. More, it was pounded out of him as his body was hurled to the ground by an opponent's lance; it was drawn from him as he lay on his cot at night with tears streaming at the futility of his calling, as the bruises worried at him, the sores chafed and the blood of his wounds stung him. As his love for display and glory had faded, so had his father's contempt for the King grown. Now even his father insisted that he shouldn't risk his life in challenges and duels, which was why he had been given a job in which his brain could be used, rather than his arms.

Except he wasn't as clever as his father thought. He was as incompetent a Coroner as he had been a knight.

'Sir Jules! Wait one moment.'

'Yes, Sir Baldwin?' He was glad to have his thoughts interrupted, but he couldn't help a slight petulance as he stopped and turned to face the man.

Sir Baldwin was staring down at the dark puddle in the roadway.

'It may be nothing, Sir Jules. It may be nothing.'

Roger the clerk was already down on one knee, poking a finger into the soil. All the path here was wet, as Jules could see for himself, and he wondered what could have intrigued the two. As Sir Baldwin dismounted and crouched, Jules caught sight of a similar look of bafflement on the Bailiff's face. Simon shrugged as though to say, 'Best not to ask what they're doing. They'll let us know in good time.'

Baldwin and Roger were rubbing their fingers together and sniffing them. Both stared at each other for some while before standing again.

'Well?' Jules asked.

'It's hard to be sure. The soil is dank and smelly here, but I think that there's lots of blood,' Baldwin said.

Roger had found something else, and he held it up now. 'Look.'

'A clot,' Baldwin acknowledged. 'You are observant, Clerk.'

'I take that as a compliment,' Roger smiled, ducking his head. Then his face hardened. 'If a man was killed here, the water seeping through the soil would have washed most of the blood away before long. There must have been a great deal of blood here in which case, and not too long ago.'

Jules was staring from one to the other. 'What made you notice this? I can see nothing on the ground even now.'

The clerk gave an apologetic little cough and pointed to his legs. When Jules looked down, he saw that the calves of his hosen were tinged pink.

'We saw it when you splashed through the blood, Sir Jules.'

The knight stared at him for what seemed a long moment, and then stepped into the river to wash his hose.

Chapter Eighteen

It was sad to see how crestfallen Jules was when he saw the state of his hosen, Roger thought, but the man was a fool. Most Coroners were, apart from the ones who had agreed to the position purely for the profit they could make. Those were the truly contemptible ones, the men who'd sell their office and their honour for a few shillings, perhaps even seeing to the execution of an innocent man and the ruin of his family to line his own pocket. And letting the guilty go free, more to the point.

Roger had firm opinions on the law; he thought that the realm, indeed the whole of Christianity, could only function when criminals received their just reward. If the guilty could buy freedom from punishment, the King's law was a nonsense and the poor must lose faith in it. When that happened, the country would fall into anarchy.

Roger was a thoughtful man. He considered many things: why the sky was blue, how the stars were held in the sky, how a plant knew to grow upwards, instead of upside-down . . . there was much to study and wonder at in the world. Yet he was unceasingly astonished by the failure of other men to look at things with the same attention to detail.

Sir Jules here, for example: a man born to wealth and power, clearly not one of those mad fighting spirits who'd take a lance to a stranger as soon as shake their hands, but nonetheless, he was not nearly observant enough for his post. The job required a man who would look carefully at the facts of a case, someone who would listen and weigh the evidence before leaping to judgement.

There could be much to listen to today, he thought.

Sir Jules had reached the mill's door, and was waiting for them. Roger allowed Baldwin to go before him, and then followed. The Bailiff was polite and stood away so that he could enter, and Roger smiled to himself. The man plainly wasn't that keen on corpses.

The room was dark, the night's shutters still locked in their wooden runners. Sir Baldwin walked slowly about the place, reaching up and unhooking their strings. All were vertical-drop shutters, held up over the windows by a cord with a loop that hooked over a nail in the wall. As Baldwin pulled the strings, they dropped in their channels to rest on the floor, and daylight began to flood the place.

It was, like all mills, immensely dusty. As the sun's rays slanted inside, each window created a bright shaft of whiteness, a cone filled with tiny motes moving in the warmth. Baldwin's passage took him down the longer side of the room, walking away from the doorway, disappearing as soon as he was beyond the second window, hidden by the whiteness. Then he slowly returned, and Roger saw his shape form like that of a wraith, walking in the shadows between light-shafts, reappearing as he stepped into sunlight.

Serlo's body lay sprawled, mostly upon the floor, arms loose, his head resting upon the wheel of his great toothed cog.

Behind him, Roger heard the quiet, 'Christ Jesus!' as Simon took in the sight.

Roger couldn't blame the man. It was enough to make even him gulp. Serlo's head had been caught by the teeth of the cog, and pulled around until the teeth from the vertical wheel above, driven by the water wheel outside, had met it. As soon as the hardwood teeth had found his skull, they had crushed it. The right side of his head was gone. A bloody mess had exploded against the machinery and over the floor where his brains had been expelled, and his eyes were forced from their sockets. One dangled by a cord about his cheek near his wide-open mouth.

Jules had entered quickly, and now he left at the same speed. There was a dry swallowing from Simon as he took in the scene, but Roger was glad to see that the Keeper merely stood back from the corpse with a pensive frown. He made no move to touch the body, but stood with his chin cupped in one hand, the other arm around his breast, the hand under his armpit.

'Roger, can you see his throat?'

'It's been cut, has it not?'

'The cause of the blood outside?'

'Perhaps.'

'And then his body brought in here – for why? What possible reason could someone have for leaving his body here in this state?'

'My Christ! Serlo? *Serlo? SERLO!*'

And Roger found himself thrust aside as Alexander barged into the room, his mouth wide in dismay, and sank to his knees sobbing beside his dead brother, scrabbling at the body as though trying to pull Serlo from the machine.

Simon grimaced as he helped Roger to remove Alexander from the room. The man had fallen into the pool of gore about Serlo's body, and he was covered in a bloody mess.

'He was my brother, my only brother! I loved him! Who could do this to poor Serlo? He was an innocent! Poor boy! I had to look after him from when he was a baby, you know. I washed him and cleaned him and helped feed him – and all for what? So a madman could come here and kill him! Oh, my poor brother! Oh God, why Serlo?'

There was much more in the same vein, but Simon ignored it. The blood all over the man's tunic and shirt was mingled with streaks of flour, forming a repellent dough, and the Bailiff wanted to get away and wash his hands in the stream. In any case, there was no time for such maunderings: Simon had a duty to see whether he could learn anything from the man. 'Your brother: did he have any enemies who could have sought his death?'

'There are always people who'll moan about the miller,' Alex said, sniffing back the tears. 'Of course there are! But who would do *this*?'

'Why should people always complain?' Jules asked. He had rejoined them, but was looking queasy and stood with his head averted from Alexander, as though the mere sight of so much blood would make him vomit once more.

Simon explained. 'Because of the multure, the portion of flour paid for the use of the mill. People are often jealous of the miller's tenth.'

'Yes. Just as they hate me for keeping the farm of the baking ovens.'

Roger nodded. This was the usual way of things. The lord built, or allowed to be built, the tools which his peasants needed, and in return they paid for the use of them. It seemed as though the two brothers had a near monopoly of the bread-making process, a sensible venture for forward-thinking men.

Alexander was sobbing again. 'To kill him like Dan, that's sick!'

'Who's Dan?' Simon demanded.

Perhaps it was the sharpness in his tone, but Alexander looked up at him, and in his eyes there was fear. 'Serlo had an apprentice called Dan. Last year, Dan tripped and fell into the machine, just as Serlo has there.'

'Perhaps someone blamed Serlo?' Simon guessed. 'Was he a local boy?'

Alex looked away. 'Serlo took him in to teach him a trade. I don't think he had any family.'

'No father, no brother to avenge him? Not even a sister?'

'No. When his mother Matty died, Serlo was the only family he knew, poor devil. Poor Serlo! He did all he could to help the fellow, and look at what's happened!'

'What of others? Can you think of anybody at all who might have wished to hurt Serlo?'

'Who would want to hurt him? He was a good man,' Alexander said.

Simon watched him closely. There was a strange frown on Alexander's face, as though he was unsure of himself. He reminded Simon of witnesses who had said too much. And then there came into his eyes a curious intensity, like a man who realised that something at the edge of his memory could have a bearing.

Then Alexander's face broke again and he wept, his whole body shuddering. 'No! I can't think anyone would hate my brother enough to do *that* to him. The poor fool!'

Simon was glad when Baldwin and Roger appeared in the doorway, pulling it shut behind them. The Coroner had gone off to sit on a tree stump, his head in his hands. Simon instantly thought that he had been throwing up again, but then he saw that the Coroner was perfectly well. He just looked sad, like a man who was struck by the fact that he must suffer whatever trials were thrown at him. From Simon's perspective, all he knew was that *he* would have been violently sick, had he been forced to go nearer the body in the mill, and that he had never missed his wife and family more than he now did. God knows how that poor wife of Serlo's had reacted on hearing this news. What with the death of her baby, and the grievous wound on her head, it was enough to kill the woman.

It was Baldwin who spoke first. 'Coroner, that man was murdered. His throat was cut, and he was stabbed several times beforehand.'

'Stabbed and his throat cut,' Jules repeated and shook his head.

'*Tut!* What is a man to make of something like this? In God's name, I can understand someone taking a dislike to the fellow – I could see yesterday that he was a rough, brawling sort of churl – but to slaughter him like a Moor and then savage his skull in this way . . . That is pure evil.'

'Or proof of a man's hatred,' Baldwin said.

Simon interrupted. 'Alexander here says that a boy was killed in that machine a year ago – a lad called Dan. But he was an orphan, so there's no one to avenge him.'

'There is always someone,' Baldwin said.

'Richer!' Alexander breathed. At first, Simon wasn't sure he'd spoken, but then he spoke louder. 'Richer atte Brooke! He always hated Serlo. From when they were children, they loathed each other. Richer could have wanted to do this. He *did* do this! It must have been him.'

They sent Roger to the castle to fetch men to carry this fifth body to the church, Baldwin thinking it would be better for them to wait at the mill with Alexander, rather than let him spread wild allegations. It was bad enough that the place was riven with suspicion after the death of Athelina, without having a man in a frenzy of grief accusing men-at-arms at the castle of murder. There were easier ways of causing a breach of the King's Peace, Baldwin considered, but not many.

Jules still sat staring at the ground as though in a state of shock. Baldwin had seen men react in this way before, especially in war. They sometimes lost all reason, lost that detachment which is essential for anyone who must lead others into battle. Some, when the weight of decisions grew, would lose themselves in actions which they could comprehend: a man who had been trained as a knight would leave the command of the battlefield to ride in combat himself, risking his own life and the lives of those who fought for him; others of a religious bent might retire from the field and find a welcoming altar at which to pray. There were many kinds of breakdown for a man who was unused to power, or to the appalling turns of circumstance.

Baldwin could feel sympathy for Jules. The post of Coroner was one for which he was neither intellectually nor emotionally suited, in Baldwin's opinion. As for Roger – now there was a man who could be an influence for good!

'There is so much to do!' Jules said with a note of despair. 'I had more deaths to view before ever I left Bodmin to come here, and now look! I've found me another damned corpse!'

'You had other bodies to go to?' Simon asked.

'Yes.'

'Then send a message to Bodmin, and have a man go to the places where you were due to visit. Better, have a message sent to another Coroner. You can be sure there are none who will be so engaged as you today. When you have done that, you can concentrate on these killings.'

Jules glanced at him. 'What of Mortimer? I'm ordered to raise the Hue and Cry.'

'I know who's responsible for these murders, Coroner.' Alexander's face was impassive, but the eyes moved about the area like a frighted stag's. 'It was that poxed cur, Richer. He came back here after many years away, and within a few weeks, here we have the death of my brother, whom he detested, the death of the woman whom he lusted after, and her children – the remaining insult to him since they were sired by another on the woman he had thought was his own. Richer atte Brooke, he's done all this. No one else.'

'Why do you say he hated your brother?' Simon asked. 'What reason did he have?'

'I don't know. My brother was a decent, hardworking man. Why should anyone have anything against him?' Alexander demanded, turning his red-rimmed eyes upon Simon.

Simon couldn't answer while confronted by the brother's grief. It would have to wait a little while. 'Was this apprentice Dan related to Richer?'

When Alexander shook his head, Baldwin said, 'Simon is right, Coroner. You should be here to resolve these matters. A messenger can go to the Sheriff and raise the posse against Mortimer while you remain.'

'Very well. I shall do so – then perhaps we can complete the inquest into the woman, and Serlo as well.'

Simon and Baldwin exchanged a look. Before they could speak, however, Alexander was on his feet, his face suddenly red with rage.

'What? You think you can dispose of my brother's murder like some whore's death? You think I'll let you rush through some decision just so that you can leave the matter and our vill and get on with investigating some other death which is more lucrative, or interesting to you? What is it? You have too many wealthy men dying, do you? Can't spare time for the likes of us, is that it?'

Sir Jules held up a hand, his face darkening. 'No, not at all, but there's no reason to hold me here if there's a simple answer.'

'Simple? Yes, it's simple enough. Arrest Richer atte Brooke and order him to be held until the Justices get here.'

'That's not what I meant.'

'It's what *I* meant!' Alexander spat.

Simon stepped between the two. 'Wait! Alexander, we won't achieve much if you spend your time insulting the Coroner. Coroner, I think it might be best if you were to delay the inquests until we have conducted some more enquiries. First, we have to learn whether there actually was anyone who had a reason to attack Serlo . . .' He paused when Alexander drew breath. 'Constable, I know what you're going to say, but I for one am not convinced. You can raise trouble if you wish, but if you really want to find your brother's killer, leave the matter to us. We're used to investigating murder.'

Baldwin nodded behind Alexander, and Simon was grateful at least for that, although his own words depressed him. He wasn't of a mood to seek out another killer. Already in the last few months he had sought murderers in Gidleigh, in Galicia, and in Ennor. All he wanted was to be able to return to his home, far from the air of menace that seemed to permeate the vill of Cardinham. This mill in particular felt evil. It wasn't only the body in the millhouse itself, it was something about the whole place, as though the soil itself was tainted. As it was, he told himself. The soil was polluted with the man's blood, while the mill had been the instrument of his body's desecration.

All he wanted right now was to be home again, his beloved Meg cradled in his arms, and to be far from death and hatred. But his own words had already condemned him to remaining here for at least a little while longer.

Chapter Nineteen

Baldwin was interested in the period between Serlo's leaving the tavern the previous evening and his actual murder. When Roger returned with a cart and some of the men from the castle to take the body back to the vill, Ivo was with him. He immediately walked over to Baldwin.

'Sir Baldwin, I thought you ought to know—' he began.

'Not now, man. I am busy,' Baldwin said without turning.

'This is only quick: rumour is, Athelina was having it away with a rich man, and she is dead because he dumped her. She'd been trying to get him back, see. Maybe he was angry that she kept pestering him.'

'Do you know who he is?'

'No. Julia didn't tell me that.'

Baldwin thanked him and filed the information away for later. Soon the cart was rumbling back towards the vill, Roger going with it to guard the body, Alexander bringing up the rear. When they were alone again, Baldwin suggested that they might sensibly begin their investigation into Serlo's death at the tavern.

'What of the dead child?' Jules asked with a frown. 'At least we could dispose of that inquest swiftly enough before looking into this latest murder.'

'I think not,' Baldwin said with a short sigh. 'The child is a straightforward matter, but you still need witnesses.'

'Yes.'

'There are two: his four-year-old brother, and his mother Muriel who is not only distraught at losing her son, but also has a debilitating injury. Now she has lost her husband as well. I feel it would be too unkind to impose a Coroner's court on a woman in such affliction.'

Jules grimaced. 'Perhaps it would be a little unfair – yet I should seek to close at least *one* case.'

Baldwin nodded. Then he peered at Jules from the corner of his eye. 'Of course, it's possible that the murders weren't committed by the same man.'

'Unless Alexander's right,' Simon mused. 'And Richer *was* responsible for all.'

'You really think he could be guilty?' Jules scoffed.

'I consider it entirely unlikely, but possible,' Baldwin said briskly. 'Which is why I think that we should speak to Richer urgently, as soon as we are done at the tavern. If Simon can imagine Alexander being right, you may be assured that others in the vill will feel the same, and that could lead to more violence.'

Jules nodded, and soon they were walking back towards the vill.

On the way, Simon couldn't help but notice Alexander. He stood outside the last home at this side of the vill, and on seeing the three, he quickly withdrew. Simon was sure that it was his own house, and he studied it with interest.

The Constable's dwelling was much in the style of a large Devon longhouse, but with more outbuildings, as befitted a wealthy man. And it was no surprise that he was wealthy, Simon thought. Money grew money; Alexander had helped Serlo buy the mill, so the two controlled all the flour used in the vill; the Farm of the Ovens was owned by Alexander, so every loaf baked brought in more money. Every loaf baked meant payments to Serlo and Alexander. That was surely a cause for bitter resentment.

Comparing Alexander's wealth to the general poverty all about, Simon wondered whether jealousies had sprung up between the Constable and his neighbours. Perhaps that was why Serlo had been so arrogant, because he felt secure while his brother ran the place – and if that was so, maybe someone had attacked and killed Serlo in order to get back at Alex. It was astonishing the lengths to which some men would go in order to gain revenge on another. Simon decided he should mention it to Baldwin later.

The tavern was a welcome sight. As soon as Simon saw it, and smelled the odour of pies and meat, he recalled that he had not yet broken his fast. He shot a look at Baldwin, but his friend was peering down at the ground before him like a man who was about to launch himself on the most important journey of his life and who doubted whether he would ever see these stones and pebbles again. There was an air of anxiety about him which Simon had not noticed before, and the sight gave him pause for thought. If the murders here were enough to make Baldwin pensive, Simon was justified in being worried.

'Wine!' Jules shouted rudely as soon as they entered.

Susan glanced at them with a frown. Sighing without pleasure, she crossed the floor to them. This early in the morning, the place was empty, apart from two grim-looking customers at the bar, to whom she had been talking.

'You don't have to shout, and a little politeness would cost you nothing, my lords,' she said stiffly.

Baldwin smiled up at her. 'Susan, could we prevail upon you for three goodly jugs of your finest wine, as well as a little bread and meat?'

'Yes, of course, Sir Baldwin,' she said with a glance at Jules that could have frozen an ocean, and left them to fetch their order.

Ignoring her, the Coroner said, 'What is your opinion, Sir Baldwin?'

'I say that we should question all about Richer's dispute with Serlo, and see whether there could be some link between him and these deaths, if only to prove that Alexander's accusations are false.'

'Why should we bother wasting time on such matters?' Jules snapped. 'We should only trouble ourselves with those issues which have a direct bearing upon the murders, surely?'

'You are a Coroner,' Baldwin said mildly, 'and must focus on the discovery of the killer so that the Justices know whom to execute, as well as keeping a track of all the fines and forfeits for the law. I am a Keeper of the King's Peace. I am keen to prevent *further* bloodshed; that is *my* focus. If we find the killer, but do not prove that Richer was innocent, we shall be leaving trouble behind when we depart, and that will mean Alex or Richer may soon die, and you will return. I trust you do not wish that?' he added with gentle sarcasm.

'In the name of my mother's sire, *no*!' Jules stated.

'Then we should learn all we can about this enmity,' Baldwin said, and leaned back against the wall as he awaited Susan's return.

As soon as she had served them a platter piled with cold meats from the previous day's cooking and a pair of loaves fresh from the oven at their side, Baldwin asked her to fetch a cup for herself.

'I don't have time for wine at this time of day, Sir Knight,' she said pleasantly enough.

'Today you do,' Baldwin said, a hint of steel in his voice.

'What makes you say that?'

Simon answered her. 'You were discussing the reason why over there with those two men, weren't you? This is about Serlo.'

'There are others you can ask.'

'I suppose this bread came from his brother's oven?' Simon enquired.

'Not his, no! The lord's! Alex just takes our money to use it,' she said bitterly.

'Would someone kill Serlo because of Alexander's Farm of the Ovens?' Simon pressed. 'Or would they kill him because of his own farm – the mill?'

'Why would someone kill him for that?' she demanded with a twist of her lip.

'If he was taking more multure than he should, people might have rebelled,' Simon guessed. 'Someone could have grown hot-headed.'

'I don't know anything about Serlo's death,' she said, and would have turned away, had not Baldwin gripped her forearm, not harshly, but tightly enough to keep her there.

'Maid, we have to ask questions about his death. You know that, and you know why: to stop unrest in the vill. Please help us.'

She stood with her chin high, but then gave a slight nod and accepted the space on the bench which Simon indicated for her.

'Serlo was here last night,' Baldwin continued when she was seated. 'Did he leave here alone?'

'No, he went with Angot,' she said. 'I told Angot to get him home safely, because he wouldn't make it there on his own.'

'Angot is here?' Baldwin enquired, looking at the two at the bar.

'Yes. He's there.' She pointed.

Baldwin beckoned the man, and soon Angot was behind Susan, standing nervously with a pot in his hand. 'You helped Serlo home?'

'Yes, I took him home.'

'All the way to his door?'

'Nearly,' Angot admitted. He was terrified as he spoke, knowing that he was the last man to see Serlo. He briefly explained why he had left Serlo on the way to the mill. 'He didn't want my help any more. He was bitter. Turned very nasty.'

'How was Serlo when he left here?' Baldwin asked Susan.

'Very drunk, but what else would you expect? His son was dead.'

'Whom do you know who might wish to kill Serlo?' Simon asked Angot outright, waiting to hear Richer's name.

The man shrugged. 'He was a miller; always took his tenth of the grain, and sometimes, when the customer wasn't watching, he took more. That didn't exactly make him popular.'

Simon nodded. 'What of the tolls? He was taking gifts from travellers, wasn't he?'

'Yes. He was always short of cash lately.' Angot pulled a face. 'Since Dan's death, he'd been hit hard with costs. He had the *deodand* to pay, and the funeral, as well as replacing broken bits of his machine. It's all expensive.'

Baldwin nodded. 'I see. In your opinion, is there anyone in particular who might have wished to see him dead?'

Angot laughed shortly. 'He managed to insult loads of people over the years.'

Susan chipped in: 'He took his brother's position seriously. If a man insulted Serlo, he insulted Constable Alexander. Serlo was so used to being related to the most powerful man here, he thought he could get away with anything. And Alex saw to it that he did, generally.'

'It's not just that,' Angot said, gaining confidence now. 'He put on a bold front, but he wasn't brave himself. He was a younger brother, you see. Alexander was his hero, he looked up to him all the time, and he wanted to prove himself to Alex. The trouble was, anything Alex touched turned to gold, while everything Serlo tried failed. All he could do was mill. Everything else was a disaster.'

'Alexander alleges that Richer atte Brooke could have been responsible. What do you know of that?' Baldwin asked.

'Richer?' Susan said, and she began to smile disbelievingly, but then she recalled Serlo's words the previous day and the smile died on her lips.

'What?' Baldwin pressed. 'You have remembered something. What is it?'

'It was something Serlo said yesterday. Richer came in, but when he saw Serlo, he turned to leave; said he'd go, to save Serlo further grief. But Serlo said something . . . I can't recall exactly, but it was something about he'd only lost one boy, while Richer had lost all his family. It made Richer go quite pale as he walked out. Did you hear that, Angot?'

He shook his head. 'I was drunk.'

'What did you think Serlo meant?' Baldwin enquired.

'He was implying that he might have had something to do with Richer's family's death. I don't believe it, but there was something in Serlo's voice as he saw Richer going: cruelty, you know? And there have been rumours for a while now.'

'Rumours of what?'

'That Serlo was up near Richer's house on the night of the fire. It was long ago, and I was only a child. But I can remember Iwan telling someone about seeing Serlo up there on that night.'

'So he *could* have been guilty of arson; he *could* have killed all Richer's family?' Simon breathed.

'No!' Angot protested. 'He could bully to get his own way, but kill a whole family? Never. Anyway, I think it was him went to the field to call the rest to help with the fire. Why'd he do that if he was the arsonist?'

'We cannot ask him now,' Baldwin sighed. 'Susan, if you're right, do you think Richer could have heard him and guessed what he . . . wait!' The sight of Richer, sitting with his head in his hands came back to him, and he knew that the question was unnecessary. 'This was mid-afternoon? A little before we came in?'

'Yes. Quite early in the afternoon.'

Baldwin stood. 'I think we should go and seek Richer.'

Simon looked down at the plate of meats. 'Yes. In a moment.'

'No, now, while the scent is still fresh,' Baldwin said, and started towards the door.

'Fine. You go, I'll have some food first.'

'Can't you get something later?' Baldwin asked, a trace of peevishness in his tone.

'No,' Simon said bluntly, taking up a slice of meat and studying it with satisfaction. 'And neither can the good Coroner, so sit down again and wait a short while. Susan, you cook a good piece of beef!'

Richer was sitting outside the castle's hall on an old saw-horse which the grooms used to polish the saddles.

He had tried to eat, but his belly was too weakly today. His humours were all unbalanced since hearing of the death of Athelina. It still seemed incomprehensible to him that she had been taken away just at the time when he was hoping to marry her at last. Most of the time he had little fragments of thoughts, things he would like to talk to her about, half-born ideas that he squashed. He was used to death, God knew, but he couldn't really believe that she was gone. She was so vital, so vivid . . .

'Richer.'

He opened his eyes, to find himself confronted by the Coroner, the Keeper and the Bailiff. The elderly clerk was standing behind them.

'Godspeed, friends,' he said without pleasure.

'We have some questions for you. Have you heard the news?' Baldwin said.

'Yes. It's . . . um . . .' Almost too late he realised that he should say nothing that could show his personal allegiance. 'Astonishing.'

'What do you know of it?' Coroner Jules said quickly, like a man who was determined to get a word in before others took over the conversation.

Richer was irritated by his manner. He had better things to consider, today of all days. 'The same as you, I suppose. Why?'

'We've heard you may have been responsible.'

Richer almost smiled, thinking this was some form of pleasantry at his expense, but it faded when he saw that they were all watching him with unreserved gravity. 'How could I have been involved? I've been in the castle for a few weeks now. It would take an age to ride to London and back.'

Simon blinked, then looked at Baldwin, and suddenly gave a laugh. 'We are fools! We came here asking about news, and all friend Richer can think of is the escape of Lord Mortimer from the Tower! No, Richer,' he continued, his smile disappearing like the first waft of smoke from an open fire on the moors. 'We wanted to hear about Serlo. What did he have to do with you?'

'Serlo?'

'He was murdered last night. Stabbed, and then his head thrust into his machine and crushed,' Baldwin said bluntly. 'We have heard that he suggested last afternoon that he was in part at least responsible for the death of your family.'

'Surely not!'

'He said so as you walked from the tavern, did he not?'

'Was that it? He did say something as I left. I paid him no heed.'

'Yet a short while later I saw you, and you had suddenly developed a bad migraine. That is a strange coincidence – a man hints that he killed your entire family in an arson attack, and although you didn't hear him, you nonetheless have a terrible head only a short while afterwards.'

Richer closed his eyes. There was a prickle of pain behind his right eye, at the very back of the socket. Christ Jesus, he hoped it wasn't another damned migraine coming on! 'Sir Baldwin, I know you are right to be suspicious, but I walked from the alehouse in order to avoid a fight with Serlo. He made some comments as I left, but I chose not to pick a dispute with a man who had just lost his son. He had his grief, and I had mine from losing Athelina. I left the tavern and a short while later, as you say, I had a terrible migraine. Perhaps it is a coincidence that the two should have been unrelated, but I cannot help that. I cannot change facts. I deny having had any part in that man's death. Why, I knew nothing of it until you informed me just now!'

'You were at daggers drawn with him when you lived here?' Simon asked.

'Yes,' Richer growled. 'But that was a long time ago. I confess that I hated him for what he did to others. He was a bully, but that doesn't mean I wanted his death.'

'If Serlo had committed arson upon that house,' Baldwin said, 'you would have had double the reason to detest him, wouldn't you: for killing your family, and for losing you your chance at marriage. Is that what you thought last night?'

'I told you I had nothing to do with his death. I couldn't. My head was too bad. Can you imagine a man with a migraine being capable of attacking another? It's ridiculous.'

Simon, whose ruddy face spoke of his own rude health, said, 'Why? It's only a headache, isn't it?'

Richer stared at him with disbelief.

Roger had been quiet, but now he looked at Jules and Baldwin, and said, 'I do not understand why the miller should be thrown into the machine after he was already dead.'

Richer shrugged. 'He was a miller – maybe the murderer thought it would look like an accident.'

'Hardly. He had already all but cut Serlo's head from his shoulders,' the Coroner said, shuddering at the memory.

'We have heard that a boy fell into his machinery in a similar way,' Baldwin said. 'Over a year ago, that was. Have you heard about this?'

'A boy falling into the mill?' Richer shook his head.

'It was a lad called Dan,' Baldwin prompted him.

'I've been away for fifteen years. If he was apprenticed to Serlo, he was likely born after I left here,' Richer pointed out reasonably.

'Sir Baldwin! Ah, I am glad to find you.'

Baldwin's eyes rolled heavenwards. 'Ivo,' he said, attempting a false heartiness. 'How pleasing to see you again.'

'You know, I've got to get home before too long, Sir Baldwin,' Ivo said. 'I didn't agree to stay with you all year, only for a journey to Lydford. I didn't think I'd be stuck here like this.'

'You will be compensated,' Baldwin said.

Simon grinned. Baldwin sounded like a man about to grind his teeth. The thought of Ivo rambling on with his foul stories all the weary way from here to his home clearly pained him deeply. Lydford, he thought. Where his wife and daughter and son all waited for him. Suddenly the loneliness of separation attacked him with renewed savagery. It seemed as though the nearer he came to his home, the longer this journey took.

His mind was on his wife as Baldwin told Roger all they had learned about Dan the apprentice from Alexander. Afterwards Roger stared up at the hall, narrowing his eyes thoughtfully. 'Perhaps there is a hint there. The boy Dan had a mother, Matefrid or Matty, but no father.'

'What of it?' Simon asked, still thinking of Meg.

He felt slow on the uptake when Baldwin nodded thoughtfully and said, 'You may have a point, Roger. That is another avenue we should investigate. And meantime,' he continued, looking at Richer, 'I should remain here at the castle, if I were you.'

'Are you threatening me?' Richer demanded.

'No, but at present Serlo's brother is convinced that you murdered his brother, and if you go to the vill, your life will be worth very little. Stay here, or run the risk of death!'

Chapter Twenty

'So what did you mean?' Simon asked as they watched Richer angrily stamping towards the hall's bar.

Baldwin glanced at him. 'We know of Athelina, widowed but supported by a man who has now deserted her; Adam's maid, with child but without a husband – presumably her lover deserted her; now we hear of this third woman, Dan's mother, again with no one knowing who her son's father was. A string of coincidences.'

'There are some women who never marry,' Roger said.

Simon shot him a look. 'You mean she was the local . . .'

'No,' Roger smiled, guessing where his mind had already led him. 'I mean she could be one of those unfortunate women who believed her lover when he swore marriage to her. She was given the word of a man who was less than honest, and became pregnant only to learn that her sworn husband decided to deny his oaths, or ran from his responsibilities.'

'Or he was a wealthy man in the area,' Baldwin mused, 'who could afford to risk her enmity. A man who might still be here.'

'Well, if you put it like that,' Simon said, 'the father could just have been a rapist who took her without her consent then denied it. Perhaps she didn't even dare to accuse him. When she realised she'd got herself in pup she didn't know what to do. Happens often enough.'

'A rapist or a deceiver; and a man who fled or a man who remains,' Baldwin breathed. 'Who can enlighten us?'

'At the inquest there was an elderly smith called Iwan,' Simon said. 'A smith would know all the rumours from the area going back many years. Might he know of Dan's father?'

'Yes,' Baldwin said. He was eyeing the man-at-arms called Warin, who stood at the stable, hands on hips, watching his mount being groomed.

'He's Richer's master,' Ivo said.

Baldwin didn't speak, but remained gazing fixedly at the squire. 'He is a dangerous man, that one,' he said at last, but wouldn't explain himself.

Iwan stood and stretched with a grunt of satisfaction. He had been taking a welcome rest from harvesting the oats. The sun was high, and he could feel the tingle of burning on his shoulders.

The sun was like a good forge, he thought, all concentrated power when you wanted it, in the summer. It made the crops grow, and put men in mind of a lithe and welcoming maid. All natural stuff. As far as he was concerned, sunshine was the essence of life. It worked on all animals, humans and plants, just as it did on metal.

He had a smith's beliefs. A priest could warble on about God and Christ and all the saints, but then he had never stood day after day beating steel into shape. He had no idea of the malleability of a solid bar when treated the right way. Metal reacted to heat just as men would, and just as a man and a woman would come together to form a child, so pieces of steel could be joined to create something new. It all came from the smith and his own abilities, just as God had used His own arts to form man. Iwan knew that in order to create, both men and God Himself must put something of themselves into the task. To Iwan, as to all good smiths, there had been given a certain ability. It made him more than an ordinary man, as though God had touched him and taught him his craft.

Yes, smiths were a race apart. And here, watching the oats swaying in the breeze, while young Maud lay sweating after being covered by her man near the great oak, he knew that the warmth was forging new creatures. It was the natural way of things.

He swept the stone along the blade of his scythe with smooth, rhythmic strokes, top to bottom, top to bottom . . . only stopping when he heard the hooves.

'Master Smith?'

'I was,' Iwan said. He had watched this man during the inquest, and rather liked the serious expression in those dark eyes. 'You're the knight.'

'I am Sir Baldwin. This is Coroner Jules and his clerk Roger, and my friend, Bailiff Puttock of Lydford. Smith, do you have a little time to talk with us?'

'Would I have any choice?'

'A man of your age does not need to ask a question like that,' Baldwin smiled.

'Which means I don't.'

'You have the choice. We are not here to interrogate you for no reason, but to ask for your help.'

Iwan eyed him again, then nodded and set his scythe down, sitting beside it. 'Ask.'

Baldwin had already swung from his mount. Now the others joined him as he hunkered down before the old smith. 'There was a lad who died in Serlo's mill. What can you tell us about him?'

'Dan? He was a good fellow. Son of Matefrid from Temple. Matty, we all called her. Lovely girl – beautiful. Died two years ago when the crops last failed, like so many.'

'Who was the father?' Baldwin asked.

'What makes you think I'd know a thing like that?' Iwan asked with twinkling eyes. He waited to hear the knight's response. He was in no hurry, and he was intrigued by Sir Baldwin's interest.

'I think a man like the local smith would hear all sorts of stories about the men and women in his area,' Baldwin smiled.

'I'm no smith now. Just an old peasant who helps his son with the fields.'

'Once a man has forged and harnessed fire, I think he can't lose the skill,' Baldwin said.

'There were tales about Dan's father,' Iwan nodded after some moments. ' 'Twas said, Matty had her boy sired by a rich stud.'

'You think it was a knight?' Jules demanded.

Baldwin held up his hand for silence without taking his eyes from Iwan.

For his part the smith sat relaxed and happy, ignoring the Coroner's expostulation, a cheerful smile on his weather-beaten face.

Baldwin continued. 'You don't think it was a knight, do you?'

'No. Where is there a knight about here?'

'But it was a man from the castle?'

Iwan shrugged, but his steady gaze was enough for Simon and Baldwin. They exchanged a sharp glance.

'There are two other women who've had lovers,' Baldwin said. 'Athelina had a protector, and Julia at the priest's house has a child.'

Iwan lifted his brows. 'Round here there aren't many men as would take on all that. It's said one man at the castle likes women, though.'

'That's very interesting,' Simon said. 'And you say Matefrid died before her son? She died two years ago, and he was crushed in the mill last year?'

'That's right.'

'If his father was alive,' Roger said slowly, 'he would surely have borne a strong anger against the man who was responsible for his boy's death so young.'

'*I* would,' Iwan agreed.

'Do you say that this man might have killed Serlo for an accident which happened over a year ago?' the Coroner asked doubtfully.

Baldwin raised his shoulders. 'It makes as much sense as anything else. What more can you tell us, Iwan Smith?'

'What more do you expect me to tell?'

'We would be grateful for your help,' Baldwin said. 'Serlo's murder was no accident. He was slaughtered like a bullock at market.'

'Ah? Some might say he deserved it.'

'Some might. Would you?'

Iwan slowly shook his head.

'What can you tell us?' Baldwin pressed him gently.

'When I was younger, Serlo and Richer had a fight or two. Richer was the son of a local man, a bright, clever fellow. By his efforts, they got money for theirsel's. That was good, but Richer was a bit loud, proud of his sire, like boys will be. He used to bully Serlo and laugh at him because of Serlo's father, Almeric. Richer's a year younger than Serlo, but no one could bully Richer, not even Alexander, because he was big enough even then. And then Richer got to want Athelina. Poor child.'

Simon was struck by the way the smile was wiped from the old man's face. It was like seeing a picture in the sand smoothed away by a wave. In that moment Simon had a feel for the man: so old was he, Iwan must have seen almost all his childhood friends and relations die, and now he was left, the last remnant of a happy tribe. He had his children and grandchildren, it was true, but without a man's childhood companions, what was he? A mere antique bobbing in the seas of history. And now he was seeing even youngsters die.

'Why "poor"?' Baldwin asked.

'Because she loved Richer back, but he left her here. It was a long while before she found another, Hob, who suited her. When she did, he died too soon, and since then she's been lonely.'

'She was murdered too,' Simon said quietly. 'Who could have done that?'

'If I knew that, I'd have killed him by now,' Iwan stated flatly.

Baldwin said, 'Tell me about Richer and Serlo.'

'Richer left because of the way his family were wiped out. One night late in the summer, when the harvest was in and the fellows were enjoying themselves with their women, his house caught fire. When they got there, all those inside were burned. It was Serlo gave the alarm. He tried to save them.'

'And?' Simon prompted. 'You saw something, didn't you?'

'No need to hide it now. I wasn't at the harvest. Before the fire I was down that way, near the house. It was dark: I couldn't be sure, but I thought I saw a man slip away in among the trees and I thought nothing on it. Later I heard Serlo had called on the rest of the men to come and put out the fire, but they were all drunk and stupid, and took their time.'

'So you think he may have had a part in the deaths of the atte Brook family?' Baldwin asked.

'A friend of mine also thought he saw Serlo hanging round just before the fire started. There weren't that many men here who are so broad but also so short, you see. Little while later, he saw him running up to the harvest, calling out that there'd been a fire, and everyone ran back. So, he wasn't there with all the youngsters at the harvest, and he came up to raise the alarm. Sounds like he could have been the one set fire to the place.'

'We have heard that he hinted at something like that to Richer last night,' Baldwin said. 'Perhaps he was taunting him.'

'If so,' Simon considered, 'he succeeded. It looks as though Richer might have killed him.'

Baldwin frowned. 'And yet why should he have done so in that manner?'

'What was that, master?' the old smith asked.

'Serlo was killed, but then his head was deliberately crushed in the mill-wheel, just as the boy Dan's had been.'

Iwan stared away down the gently sloping hill towards the vill. 'So, likely it was the boy's relation, or friend of his father or mother who killed Serlo?'

'Or his father himself,' Simon pointed out. 'We don't know who his father was, after all.'

'Why should Serlo do that to Richer's family?' Roger wondered, still harking back to the fire. 'What could drive a man to such a barbaric act?'

'Perhaps it was retaliation for some other slight?' Baldwin said.

Iwan nodded slowly. 'It was only a little while after Serlo's father Almeric lost a sheep. It strayed out from his fold and onto the lord's land, and was forfeit because it ate his crop. That was a bit of a laugh for most of us hereabouts, but Richer, he liked it more'n most. He laughed loudest whenever Serlo was about, and that hurt Serlo. He was always irresponsible, and who knows? He himself might have left the fold open so that the beast could escape. Anyway, Serlo got thrashed, and Richer made fun of him. That could have been enough.'

'Serlo wanted to make Richer suffer the indignity and ignominy of failure and disaster,' Baldwin nodded. 'It is possible.'

'But how does that measure up with the dead boy and Serlo's head being crushed?' Simon demanded. 'There are too many threads to this tapestry, and none seem to lead to the full picture.'

'True enough,' Baldwin said. 'Master Smith: this woman Matefrid. Whom could we ask about her?'

'The priest might be able to help you.'

'Who – Adam here at the church?' Simon demanded with surprise. 'What could he know of this woman?'

'Not him: the other priest. Matty came from Temple, see. Father John may know something about the apprentice, if only by rumour.

He was helped to win the place by Sir Henry – although it's said that he was a Lancastrian.'

'Who, the priest was?' Roger asked.

'Aye, so it's said,' Iwan nodded. 'He's a priest though, so it's none of my affair.'

But it was a matter of interest to others, Simon knew. Thomas, Earl of Lancaster, had died after Boroughbridge, and his leading adherents slaughtered, because the King wanted no one to survive that war who had ever held arms against him or his friends the Despensers. Even a cleric could be fearful of past loyalty coming to light.

Simon glanced at Baldwin, but he saw that his friend's thoughts were elsewhere.

'Temple?' Baldwin repeated mildly, but Simon saw how his eyes lit up at the name. There were many manors up and down the country which had been owned by the Knights Templar, and Baldwin loved to visit their churches, reminding himself of his own past serving in the Order.

'It was where the pagan knights used to have a small manor,' Iwan said dismissively. 'The manor's still there, if the heretics are gone.'

'Thank you,' Baldwin said, but with considerably less warmth than before.

Richer was still fuming when he left the bar of the hall, wiping his mouth with the back of his hand, and almost strode into Warin outside.

'Whoa! Watch where you go so carelessly, friend Richer,' Warin cautioned. 'Where do you go in such a fury?'

'Nowhere!' Richer declared bitterly. 'I am not permitted.'

'By whom – Nicholas?' Warin asked with some surprise. 'Do you care what he says, when you know your position?'

'Not him, no. It's that knight and his friend the Bailiff,' Richer said sourly. 'They all but accused me of murder. Have you heard about the miller?'

'No. I have been considering other matters,' Warin said loftily. 'Why – what's happened to him?'

'Murdered, apparently, and his head thrust into the machinery of that damned mill of his. Someone took umbrage at his corruption, I daresay, and now the knight and Bailiff are trying to convince the Coroner that I was responsible.'

'Why should they do that?' Warin asked, but there was a certain quiet intensity to his voice, like a man not wholly convinced of his companion's innocence.

'Because of our past,' Richer said. This was painful. He put a hand to his temple. There was almost a feeling of regret at the passing of another soul from his youth. And he was aware that his story must make him appear suspicious in any man's eyes. Still, he must trust his squire. Warin was his master: if Richer couldn't trust him, he could trust no one.

'When we were lads, we neither of us liked each other. By the time we were old enough to fight, we would scrap at any opportunity. We'd do anything which might upset the other. Once . . . I can't hide it from you. Once I released one of his father's sheep from the fold. The beast escaped onto Sir Henry's lands and was forfeit. That gave the vill a good laugh for months. Everyone knew how dissipated and ridiculous Serlo's father was, and seeing that he could lose his own sheep made everyone amused.'

'Other than Serlo and his brother, I assume,' Warin said flatly.

'Well, yes. They weren't happy, obviously. Both were beaten by their father, because he thought Serlo had left the gate open, and Alexander tried to protect him.'

'So your enmity grew because you had lost his family their wealth?'

Richer winced at Warin's cold tone. 'I suppose so. Until my family died and I fled.'

'So he won,' Warin said wonderingly. 'I suppose that's what people might say, that you fled, leaving him the victor, and that when you returned many years later – *now* – you were determined to take your revenge.'

'Except you know that's nonsense.'

'Do I?'

'Of course! I couldn't have killed the man. I've killed before, but never like an assassin. Only ever in a fair fight.'

'Then you should deny it,' Warin said. 'Else the people of Cardinham will say that you are guilty. Why should they say something like that?'

'There is one more thing,' Richer said slowly.

'Aha! Isn't there usually one more detail?' Warin said lightly. Then his voice hardened. 'What?'

'Apparently the night before he died, Serlo implied that he himself set fire to my parents' home.'

'He suggested that he was guilty of arson and murder?'

'It is what is being said, apparently.'

'*Apparently?*' Warin's face was like flint. 'How did you hear this?'

'The Coroner and that knight Sir Baldwin. They told me today.'

'Did you hear Serlo say this?'

Richer looked away. 'I was there when he spoke, but I swear on my mother's soul that I didn't understand. I saw him in the tavern, and left; he was grieving for his son.'

Warin smiled unpleasantly. 'Why leave? To seek a suitable ambush?'

Richer glanced at him. 'Warin, this is serious.'

'I rather think so,' the squire agreed. 'If people believe you killed him, it would not reflect well on us here at the castle.'

Richer stared at him open-mouthed, and then turned his gaze towards the gate to the castle as though he could look through it and see beyond it to his old home, the timber-framed house with the wattle and daubed walls substantial enough to keep out the worst of even a cold winter. He could see it again in his mind's eye, feel the leaden mass in his belly as he saw the flames dancing like frenzied devils all about the roof, the thick coils of smoke rising, green and faintly luminous from the damp thatch . . . He could hear the screams again as though it was only last night. He could hear them . . . Christ's pains, but he could hear them yet!

'If you did murder him, I suppose many could honour you,' Warin said absently, as though it was of little significance. 'Although some will not.'

'Alexander.'

'Precisely. He will want to have his revenge upon you for daring to level the score. And I don't think we should permit that. So you would be well advised to prove that you feel you have nothing to hide.'

'How can I do that?'

'We shall go to the vill and demonstrate that you aren't evading capture by hiding behind the Coroner's hosen.'

'If I do that, I may get killed,' Richer said with deliberation. 'You are gambling with my life, Squire.'

'Better that than bringing the castle and all within it into disrepute,' Warin snapped. 'We cannot afford that. *I* cannot. Especially now.'

Richer nodded sourly. 'Not with Mortimer free.'

Warin glanced about them and then muttered angrily, 'Keep your voice *down*, fool – unless you want me to still it for you!'

Chapter Twenty-One

This, Baldwin thought, jogging along on his horse, was the sort of manor he might have retired to, had his Order survived. Far from anywhere, deep in Cornwall's bleak moors, with no opportunity for temptation by women, gambling, gluttony or sloth. The life here would have been harsh, but attractive for all that.

Temple church was a pleasant block in grey moorstone, and there was a small vicar's house, a well-thatched hovel, nearby. Built on the side of the hill, the church enjoyed views over the tree- and field-studded lands south and east, and moors beyond. Here any wind from the sea would rush straight up and whistle about it.

But Baldwin was sure that he would have enjoyed life here as a *corrodiary*, a pensioned Templar Knight. For a Poor Fellow Soldier of Christ and the Temple of Solomon, this would represent final security after the trials of a life in the centre of the world, in the deep deserts of the Kingdom of Jerusalem. A life of fighting in the brutal dry heat of the lands about Jerusalem, or the still more daunting city states near the coast. It was there that Baldwin had chosen to join his Order, when the Templars saved him after the ferocious battles for Acre, when the Kingdom of Jerusalem and the whole of the Crusader lands of *Outremer* fell to the Egyptian Mameluke hordes.

He could recall the fighting: the screams, the blood, the chunks of flesh hacked from still-living bodies like joints butchered from a carcass and left tossed to the ground for the dogs. Fighting while the sweat ran in rivulets down his brow, down his back, down his breast. Fighting while he gradually lost all hope. Fighting while his strength ebbed, while his parched throat pleaded for a moment's rest so he could take a slurp of anything to ease it. Fighting while his friends died around him. Fighting even when he could scarcely remember why he was there, why he had travelled all that way.

He shivered at the memory of those friends and comrades. Bodies of men he had known lying at the foot of the city's walls. Some had become friends after the arduous journey from England, going like him to protect God's lands from invasion. They had set off full of enthusiasm: hopeful, intrepid men, but when they arrived, the place was all but lost, and they began to die. Some sickened, losing their energy with their diarrhoea, and more fell as the arrows rained down, or as their legs were hacked from beneath them. Too many to remember. It was one thing to see an unknown dead Christian; infinitely worse when the man was a companion who had bought a drink, or spoken kindly and shown honour.

Baldwin could recall so many faces among the dead. In the desert their faces were ravaged by the heat, desiccating and mummified before they could rot, while those who fell in Acre seemed almost to melt in the humidity of the coast.

Yes, he could easily believe how calming this place would have seemed to him, had his Order survived long enough to permit him to come here as an old man. A cool place, in which sudden death and the odour of decomposing human flesh was unknown. A land in which the rain fell gently as rose petals; no parched throats here. A green and lovely land.

'Baldwin?'

Simon's concerned voice brought him out of his reverie, and he gave the Bailiff a shamefaced grin as he kicked his horse's flanks and led the way the last few yards to the church.

The priest was nowhere about. Worse, Baldwin had expected the interior to be clean and tidy. Instead there were signs of neglect. The floor bore leaves and dirt which should have been swept clean, and when Baldwin glanced about him, there was a subtle impression of mess. At the altar, the cloth was slightly skew-whiff; a candle had been knocked and leaned drunkenly from its candlestick. Neither was significant, perhaps, but they indicated a hint of slipshod care towards the building that rankled with Baldwin. And then, he had to shrug as he recognised the injustice of him, a renegade Templar, a man who was a criminal because he had betrayed his oaths, thinking less of a priest because he was late to sweep his floor, had knocked a candle with his elbow after Mass, and had managed to catch the altar-cloth as he made his way from the church.

Baldwin left the building, glanced towards the little home and walked to it, rapping sharply on the door.

Made of planks of elm nailed onto a couple of horizontal bars, the door moved alarmingly as he knocked. Listening, Baldwin was sure he could hear a snore. It made him frown. First the effeminate Father Adam at Cardinham, now this. His mind flew back to the church. The man hadn't done a thing in there yet today, and that was scandalous. He was lazy and degenerate, as Baldwin had first thought. Well, he would learn that a knight would brook no such sloth!

He thrust at the door firmly. It creaked as the peg which held it closed stopped it, but the creak became a loud crack as Baldwin angrily kicked it open. It bounced back against the wall and trembled as though it had the senses of a man and felt terror at his rage.

'Priest?' he roared. 'Where are you?'

There was a sharp gurgling sound, and he peered into the gloom to see a quivering figure sitting bolt upright on a palliasse. The reek of sour ale permeated the entire house, and he curled his lip at the odour.

'It is almost afternoon, priest,' he said, and was just in time to move aside as the pathetic creature vomited over the place where he had stood.

Father John opened his eyes blearily and wiped his mouth. God's bones, but it was hard to keep the stuff down nowadays. Gone were the days of his youth in Oxford when he could quaff a gallon of ale at a sitting, near enough, and wake refreshed. Now he had to sleep for practically a whole day. Not that it stopped his feelings of dullness and general lethargy.

'Since you have chosen to enter already, Lording, I suppose there's little point in asking you in,' he said acerbically, eyeing his visitor without pleasure.

The intruder looked like a knight from an old romance: tall, well-formed, with little of the belly that a man might expect by his age. If anything the fellow had the look of a much younger man, although there was something about him which looked curiously out of place. Ah yes, the beard. A strange affectation, John considered. Why a man would wear a half-beard like that was beyond him. Perhaps a full-blooded chest-long beard would be all right, or none whatever, but this thin covering over the line of the jaw was plain silly.

Another wave of nausea smothered him for a moment. When he could open his eyes again, he saw three others: another belted knight – a younger, more disdainful fellow; also a rather scruffy-looking, big-built man who scowled at him darkly, and a clerk. Oh, God in Heaven save me from clerks! he thought. Weren't there enough of them in places like London and Oxford? Did the Good Lord have to send them here to the moors too?

'Ach! My mouth tastes dreadful!' he muttered, and went outside. His trough was at the rear of the churchyard, and he plunged his head into it, coming up with a great exhalation.

He smiled for almost exactly three heartbeats, thinking how refreshing it was, then puked again, thankfully missing the trough.

'You have missed your Mass, Father.'

He turned and studied the tall knight. His belly was roiling like a boiling pan, but he felt better nonetheless. 'Sir, I don't know who you are, though I'm sadly afraid I'll soon learn – no matter! I perform my functions here to the best of my abilities. Poor they may be, but occasionally, like last night, if I am out of sorts, I will pray to God and He will give me dispensation to miss an occasional service. If He feels able to allow me some peace, I see no reason why I should take complaints from a man like you, whom I neither know, nor wish to know.' He sat back on the edge of his stone trough as a shiver ran through his frame. Soon, very soon, he would need to be sick again.

'I am Sir Baldwin de Furnshill. What were you doing last night to cause such a foul illness in your belly?'

'Perhaps it *is* your business, but . . .' John pulled a face and considered before shaking his head. 'No! I can't see it's any business of yours what I may or may not do when I have a few moments to myself.'

'Really?'

John's eyes widened as the man lunged at him. A fist gathered up the robes at his shoulder and lifted him bodily from the trough. 'Don't bandy words, *priest*! A man was murdered last night! I want to know what made you turn to your drink. The sight of so much blood, or the feel of it on you?'

'Where is this blood?' John asked rhetorically, glancing down at his robe so far as he was able with the knight's fist bunching at his chin. 'I see none. Granted, I do have some puke on me, but that is an occupational risk of drinking.'

'Do you care nothing for the dead man?'

'Perhaps if you told me who it was, I'd be able to say. If at the same time you were prepared to release me, I might feel disposed to discuss my feelings with you.'

'The miller: Serlo from Cardinham.'

'In truth?' John asked. 'A shame, I suppose. Although he wasn't the sort of man to be missed by many.'

'You seem callous, priest,' said the second knight.

'Should I pretend affection? He wasn't from my flock and I won't miss him.'

'You should be more helpful,' Roger grated. 'My master here is a Coroner. We could insist you answer our questions on oath.'

'I am a priest. I don't have to respond, even to a Coroner.'

'We have heard already that you are a supporter of Lancaster. How would it be if we were to spread news of your loyalty?'

John gave him a hard stare. 'It wouldn't change my attitude to my flock, clerk. I'm not the sort of man to be scared by threats like that and I am surprised that you should suggest I could be.'

Baldwin released him and John motioned to the trough. 'May I sit again?'

'If you wish,' Baldwin said, but there was a half-grin on his face, acknowledging that there was little point in attempting to scare this man. Father John would be resistant to all threats . . . and yet there was something in his eyes that looked very much like fear. Baldwin studied him more closely. Many a man who was unused to killing would drown the memory in wine or ale, as he knew; some would get themselves drunk in order to steel themselves to the task of murder. 'Did you see Serlo yesterday?' he asked.

'No. I was up here all day,' John said with a twist of his mouth as he burped uneasily. 'And all night.'

'You were upset?'

'I was lonely,' John said with perfect honesty. 'I often am.'

Simon stepped forward. 'I am Simon Puttock, Father. We have

heard that a girl, Julia, who is living with the priest in Cardinham, came from here.'

'If by that you mean to ask, was it I who put her in pup, the answer's no,' John said testily. 'Nor was it Father Adam. Another man did that to her – or with her, I suppose,' he corrected himself. 'I don't think there was any coercion involved. Just subtle words and a certain kindness to a young and impressionable woman.'

'Perhaps the promise of a marriage?' Simon asked. 'It's what all too often happens, and then the man bolts like a cat with his tail on fire when he realises she's with child.'

'Perhaps.'

'You can't tell us?'

John looked up at Simon. 'Perhaps I could, but I don't betray the confessions of my flock to men who barge into my house, no matter how wellborn they may be.'

'What do you fear?' Baldwin asked.

'I fear giving away information that could cause trouble for others. It is not my place to cause other folk problems,' he said coolly.

'Very well,' Baldwin said. 'Perhaps you can answer some other questions, though. We have heard of a woman, Matefrid, who is dead. Her son died in the machinery of Serlo's mill. Do you know of him and her?'

'Danny and Matty?' John recalled with a smile. 'Lovely folk. Good-looking, too. It was a great shame. Horrible death, and made worse by the way that Serlo ranted afterwards, claiming that the boy was no more than a cretin. It didn't endear him to many people. Mind, it was an appalling fine that the Coroner imposed upon him.'

Jules glanced at Baldwin in response to his enquiring look. 'Before my time,' he said.

Simon had heard something in John's voice. 'You say Serlo ranted afterwards, but you don't seem to condemn him.'

John shrugged. 'I'm the youngest of five brothers. The oldest has the manor, the second and third died, the fourth was born a fool, and I was told I had this vocation. I always looked up to my older brother and in return he defended me from all my foes. I think Serlo was the same as me in many ways; the only difference was, I grew independent, but Serlo was always in his brother's shadow. Was he an evil man? I knew Danny while he worked for Serlo, and he never complained. If anything, Serlo was kind towards him, but that doesn't mean he knows how to describe his feelings. He was out of his depth when Danny died, and he presented himself as a tough man of business. It was all he knew.'

'Who was Dan's father?'

'What is it with you and paternity?' John demanded. 'Do you mean to accuse me of fathering all the bastards in Cardinham and Temple? Anyway, I don't know. There were rumours, though.'

Simon snorted. 'We've heard some. A man from the castle.'

'So I believe.'

'Our interest lies in the other women here: Athelina was supported by a lover, as was Julia, whom you threw from the parish, and also Matty.'

'No one threw Julia from here, she was offered an opportunity to go nearer to her lover and took it.' He was still a moment, then added, 'I heard her say once that her lover was Athelina's too, but that he stopped supporting Athelina when he fathered Julia's child.'

'That would explain why Athelina found money coming scarce,' Simon noted.

'And why she started going to the castle to demand more,' Baldwin agreed.

'And possibly why she was killed,' Jules concluded. 'Come! Let's return and see if we may learn who this man was.'

Roger and Sir Jules span on their heels and left.

'What's their hurry?' John muttered.

'The good Coroner needs to return to Bodmin,' Baldwin explained. 'It's this escape. He wants to be back with the Hue and Cry.'

'What escape?'

'Lord Mortimer has escaped from the Tower of London,' Baldwin told him, but then he murmured, 'Friend, what scared you so last night?'

John paled. 'Why should anyone have scared me?'

'You drank to excess like a man who was living in terror.'

'You imagine it.'

'Could Dan's father be alive still? Might he wish to punish Serlo for Dan's death?' Simon asked.

'I suppose it's possible – but who can tell?'

'You know of no surviving members of the boy's family? No uncle or brother who could desire revenge?'

'What do you ask all this for?' John said as the acid bubbled into his throat again. He swallowed hard. 'The man's dead – isn't that enough?'

'No. He was killed and then thrown into his machine, like the apprentice Danny,' Baldwin said. 'Had you heard about Athelina?'

'I'd heard she was dead.'

'Murdered as well. Perhaps these murders are connected?'

John stared out over the valley to the south. 'The man was never here, but he confessed to another cleric. I can't betray that confession. Matty was a good girl, but trusting. I suppose Julia is a little like that; Athelina as well. All fell for kind words and hints of possible marriage. All were used as wives for as long as it suited their lover.'

'Matefrid remained here,' Simon noted, 'but Julia left. Why was that?'

'Matty wanted to stay and raise her child. Julia was still seeing her lover, and it was more convenient for her to be nearer the castle. There is one thing, though . . .'

'What?' Simon asked.

'I heard that Julia has been abandoned by him too. She may be willing to help you, if she wants revenge on the man. After all, when he dropped Athelina like a hot stone, she became vindictive about his promised money – and who can say but that Julia won't feel the same?'

On the journey back to the castle, the men were quiet, mulling over John's words. As the priest had suggested, they must speak to Julia and see whether she would tell them who her lover had been. He could be the key to the deaths; indeed, he might be the murderer of Athelina and her children.

Clattering up the path to the castle itself, Simon sat more upright in his saddle. If this matter could be resolved speedily, the Coroner would conclude his inquests, and they could all go home. Back at last to Simon's family, he told himself, and in his mind's eye he saw a delightful picture of his wife.

Glancing across to Baldwin as they rode in through the main gate, he saw the same easy smile on the knight's face. He too was missing his wife, the Lady Jeanne, and the chagrin he would feel at failing to complete this investigation must be leavened with the knowledge that he would see his lady that little bit sooner.

Aye, Simon thought, it was good to have a wife.

And then that niggling sensation returned to him. A feeling that he was being less than honest to himself and to his wife, let alone to the memory of the dead women and their children. He was not concerned about Serlo, for the miller had been a brutish man, prepared to use violence against anyone smaller or weaker than him. Although the priest John had implied he might have been different, no one else thought much of Serlo. The miller seemed to have shrugged off the death of his apprentice, but had harped on about the cost of it – the fines and expenses he must suffer. John could argue that Serlo was misunderstood, but as far as Simon was concerned, Serlo was a nasty piece of work who was no loss to anyone. It didn't matter if his killer wasn't found.

Yet Serlo had been murdered. His death was a crime.

Surely Simon could forget this case and return to Lydford. It was what his wife deserved.

But Meg, were he to die, murdered, would at least expect someone to try to find the murderer. If a man were to kill Simon's son, he would like to think that someone would be prepared to seek the killer, even if that son were a brute. It would be intolerable to think that he would go unrevenged, that no one would seek to impose justice of some sort.

With a grunt of irritation, he realised that he could not give up the matter just yet. He must persevere, do all he could to learn what had really happened here, and even if he discovered who had killed Athelina, he must also try to find Serlo's killer.

Simon could not flee homewards yet.

John cleaned himself again at the trough, and busied himself about his little church to keep his mind from less pleasant thoughts.

He might have to leave this place. If the truth was to be released about his support of Earl Thomas's family, there was no escape, and John didn't trust that clerk, Roger. He rarely trusted any clerks, but the man with the Coroner seemed to have no sympathy. John would be better – safer – in a convent. Whether or not Sir Henry sought to have him removed was irrelevant: the fact was, the King could make life here impossible for him. He'd ensure that another man was put in; a friend of his own, or of the Despensers, would find themselves enriched.

How had news of his loyalty been spread? he wondered again. Could Adam have said something to Roger? No. But if the clerk had learned of John's secret, could he not also have learned of Adam's?

John had little cause to love Adam, and yet the fellow didn't deserve the fate reserved for men like him, inside or outside the Church. Perhaps John should give him some sort of a warning? Tell him to beware?

The march to the alehouse felt longer than usual to Warin. Usually, his boots and sword were enough of a proof of his authority, and people moved out of his path, averting their eyes in case they might give him offence, but here, today, there was an air of rebellion.

It was just as he had feared! The folk all thought the murderer was someone from the castle. Worse, they remembered the enmity between Richer and Serlo. Richer was the man who had loved Athelina, but who had lost her; he was the one who had threatened Serlo over his tolls, who had threatened to get the man ruined. Now that Serlo was dead, it was scarcely surprising that people thought he must be guilty. God's teeth, even Warin thought him the obvious suspect!

Richer could survive the accusations. If he could stand his ground and absorb the verbal attacks of Alexander, he could stay on at Warin's side, but if he failed, Warin would find a new man-at-arms. Alexander might try to have Richer taken and held in a gaol, but he would never risk offending Warin. A Constable didn't pick fights with a squire, when all was said and done. No, Warin and Richer together should be able to defend themselves against a few malcontents. It should be all right.

But the atmosphere as he approached the vill was grim. Suddenly Warin wasn't sure that he had chosen the most sensible path. It was only a few years ago in Courtrai that a bunch of peasants had taken on a French army and destroyed it, killing hundreds of knights and taking their golden spurs to hang in their churches. English peasants weren't so bold as that, nor so competent, Warin told himself. But as he walked, his hand remained on his belt, near his sword, and when he saw a farmer spit in his direction, that hand began to shake a little.

Chapter Twenty-Two

Ivo watched them arrive back at the castle with a sense of mild disappointment. He had been hoping to get away from here before they returned, but that looked impossible now. Still, being an optimist, he felt sure he'd soon be able to nip down to the vill and see Julia.

So far he'd been quite lucky, hanging around in the vill at every opportunity since he'd first met Julia. He had discovered her route to the Holy Well where she filled her buckets every day, and had carried them for her, and she'd rewarded him after the inquest with a tussle and grope in her room. He was hoping that another trip to town might produce better results. Country wenches were sometimes all for it, but a few like this one needed nurturing, he reckoned. Hey, that was part of the fun though, the thrill of the chase. It was less exciting when the draggle-tail agreed immediately.

He ran out from the stable where he had been loitering, and took hold of Baldwin's reins while the knight dismounted. 'Sir? Did you have any joy?'

'What are you doing here?' Baldwin growled. 'Have you no duties to attend to?'

'I think everyone is waiting to hear what is happening. A fresh messenger has just gone up to see the castellan. How was Temple? Did you learn much?'

'A little, maybe,' Baldwin said tersely. He nodded to the Coroner and Roger, who walked their mounts straight to the stables, not wishing to discuss the matter with a mere hobbledehoy like Ivo. He was completely beneath Jules's dignity, of course. For his part, Baldwin could easily comprehend his feelings.

Ivo recalled something. 'Maybe you should ask Squire Warin, the friend of Richer, if *he* saw anything. I saw him going up towards Temple last evening while you were at the inquest'.

'Squire Warin,' Simon mused. 'Richer's companion. Have you heard anything about him? He isn't a local man, from his accent.'

Ivo shook his head as he stroked Baldwin's horse. 'No. He's a man-at-arms who came back here with Richer a short while ago. No one here seems to know much about him. Regular mystery, he is.'

'A close friend of Richer?' Simon wondered.

'Seems close enough . . .' Ivo said, but added, 'for a man who's Richer's master. That Richer's just a mounted warrior, when all's said and done. They've been through some things together, though.'

'Why should you say that?' Baldwin asked.

'Just looking at them, you can tell. They mix with others when they want, but not too often, and more often they'll stay together talking low, away from anyone as might listen. They seem to trust each other, though. Warin often seems wary of others, but he'll go to talk to Richer; Richer looks to Warin when he feels threatened, too.'

'You've seen him threatened?' Baldwin asked.

'When you were with him this morning,' Ivo said. 'Soon as you were gone, he went to the bar for a whet, but when he came out, he saw Warin and the two of them went into a little huddle to discuss things. It's not the first time I've seen them do that.'

Baldwin and Simon exchanged a look. Simon was interested in what the lad had said, but he could see Baldwin was reluctant to discuss matters in front of Ivo. He hadn't got over his initial revulsion during the ride here. In case Baldwin was going to forget the information, Simon said, 'We've heard from the priest at Temple that the maid, Julia, has taken up with the man who was supporting Athelina.'

'Yeah. But she wouldn't tell me who it was,' Ivo said. 'Why, do you want me to see if I can persuade her?'

Baldwin grunted. 'If you can find out, it may help us. Otherwise we'll have to talk to her. Now, can you take our mounts for us and get them groomed?' When Ivo had gone, he continued: 'It seems curious to me that Warin and Richer should have turned up here just before these killings began. All those years away, and presumably this vill was quiet enough, with just the odd accidental death, like Serlo's apprentice, and now suddenly there is this rash of murders.'

The Coroner rejoined them at this moment, accompanied by his clerk. 'What is this? Don't tell me that odious little man had something useful to impart?'

'It is curious,' Baldwin said coolly, 'how the shabbiest fellow can occasionally point the way. Take this one: he says that Richer has a good friend who is a squire. The two arrived here together, apparently, and are close companions. Even now they discuss much together.'

'You make them sound like confederates!' Jules said. Roger said nothing, but his eyes were heavily lidded as he watched Baldwin.

'Perhaps I do,' Baldwin said. 'It is natural that Richer should come here because of his childhood; a man will often return to the place of his birth – but what is his companion doing here?'

'Surely no man of any intelligence would think of returning to Cardinham!' Jules said dismissively. 'This fellow Richer could have made himself wealthy elsewhere if he had had a mind to work. Why come *here*?'

Baldwin swallowed his anger. He himself had returned to the manor where he had been raised when the Temple was dissolved. There was nowhere else for him to go. Of course, like all aspiring knights, he had been brought up elsewhere, in a household where he could learn his duties and skills, but still he had wanted to return to his birthplace. It was just as well he did so too, for only when he arrived there did he learn that his older brother, who had inherited their father's estates, had died, and that he was now the lord of the manor.

'Some,' he said, 'would surely look upon the place of their birth with affection. Even this man Richer, who had seen his family die here, must have felt a strong tug. And if his friend was in any way troubled, it would be natural for Richer to bring him here as well.'

'Come now! If this fellow Warin is the more senior of the two – and you say he is a squire? – he would have suggested a place for them to go,' Jules said.

'Unless,' Roger put in, 'Warin had nowhere to go.'

'What do you mean?' Baldwin asked.

'If a man sought to evade justice, this vill would be a good, secure hiding-place,' Roger said, and then he set his head on one side. 'I recall Richer, when you spoke to him earlier, immediately saying that he could have had no part in the freeing of the man Mortimer from the Tower, for example.'

'So?' Baldwin pressed him.

Jules intervened, frowning darkly. 'Surely you don't mean that this man could be . . . But as he himself said, it would take days to get here after leaving London.'

'We don't know exactly when Mortimer escaped from London,' Roger said reasonably. 'It could be that he was out of prison weeks ago, and news has only now filtered here. We are not,' he added, gazing about him, 'on the main thoroughfare. We are beyond those lands which most would consider civilised.'

Simon was grinning. 'You mean to say Squire Warin could be Lord Mortimer? But he's one of the most famous men in the country! How could he hope to travel here without being seen?

His face is well-known, surely? He was one of King Edward's most trusted advisers and friends!'

Roger said grimly, 'And now he is a homeless wanderer, accused of Grand Treason, reviled by the King, detested by all who may come across him. He—'

'Yes, I know,' Simon interrupted. 'But surely he couldn't hope to walk abroad without being recognised and arrested.'

'He has gone somewhere,' Roger pointed out.

'He will have gone to the Low Countries,' Baldwin said with certainty.

'Would *you* recognise him?' Roger asked Simon.

'Me? *Me?* Of course not! I've never been to London or York,' Simon laughed.

'Nor would I. Nor any man here, I should think,' Roger said pensively. 'So this would be a perfect place for such a man to conceal himself.'

'This is ridiculous!' Simon expostulated. 'Here we are, three King's officers and a clerk too, and although we know a man should be taken, none of us can tell whether this man is in fact the one whom we seek! Coroner, do you have a description?'

'There may be one waiting when I return home to Bodmin,' Jules said. 'But I've heard nothing of this since I came here.'

The four men stared at each other, and then Baldwin gave a secret grin and resorted to studying the ground at their feet rather than meet the others' eyes. The other three felt the same trepidation at the thought that the kingdom's most notorious criminal could be here with them, but, for his money, Baldwin was quite sure that Mortimer had fled across the Channel. From the Tower it would be easy to climb into a small boat and take off along the Thames to meet with a larger ship to cross to the Continent. Far safer.

Some delight was afforded him in the expression of alarm on Sir Jules's face, although he was more amused still by the look of doubtful horror on Simon's.

'There is little chance that this Squire Warin is Sir Roger Mortimer,' he said at last. 'But I for one would be glad to learn what the man has to say about his presence. Who is he, and why is he here?'

At that moment, the focus of Sir Baldwin's interest was in the vill with Richer; the two men were strolling along the roadway towards the tavern. They passed the lane which led down to Alexander's house and the mill, and soon after there was the church. Richer was tempted to enter, but Warin reminded him that Serlo's widow would probably still be inside, watching over the body of her son. Richer regretfully agreed to go there later, when the woman had gone home.

At the point where they must turn right to go to the tavern, Richer stopped and glanced back the way they had come. He was almost sure he saw a figure dart in among the shrubs and bushes which lined the roads, and for a moment, he nearly called Warin's attention to it. However, the squire was already striding towards the alehouse, and Richer told himself not to be such a fool. It was his nerves, that was all. He was anxious because of the way his old enemy had suddenly died, leaving him as the clear suspect.

Richer was still shocked by the idea that Serlo could have fired his home and killed his family. Although he hadn't admitted it even to Warin, those words of Serlo's *had* brought on his migraine with full force last night. It was appalling to think that the devil could have wrought such damage. As the eldest, Richer had gone off to celebrate the finish of the harvest, while the others remained at home. They'd already taken too much cider and ale at the other parties and the castle's own banquet for the vill.

Strangely enough, Richer could still remember some of those other parties, even though they took place so long ago. He often found that: he could bring to mind events of ten or even twenty years ago perfectly clearly, while forgetting those which happened last week or last month. At least there was some solace in recalling the past: the sweet taste of Athelina's lips, her lightness when he picked her up, her agility and her laugh, somehow innocent and exciting at the same time. Christ, how he had adored her! And just as he thought that they'd be partners for life, she was snatched from him . . .

During those sixteen years away his life had consisted of endless journeys with his master to the separate manors which made up Sir Henry's demesne, enduring rough roads, lousy food, worse ale, and all in the name of his master without benefit to himself. Coming back, all that had been supposed to change; Richer should soon have found himself in a stronger position, and might even have been able to plan a marriage – and now he might lose his position and future because of damned Serlo again.

Warin was not concerned, from the look of him. He was an odd one, though. Richer had often wondered exactly where he stood in Warin's mind: a mere churl who could be discarded at a whim – or a trusted companion? Until this last week, he would have said definitely the latter. They had been through fire and war together, experiences which forged a strong friendship. Yet Warin was always aware of his position in the world, and a man like that would find it difficult to maintain a solid bond even with the comrades of his youth. Richer had been a close *mëat*, or mate, as they said in the North, but now . . . Warin seemed ever more acutely aware of the problems of his position. He trusted Richer usually, but for how much longer was a good question.

The sun was still high in the sky as they walked along the roadway, and Richer could feel the heat seeping through his tunic, but for all that, he knew that a part of his warmth was caused by the accusing stares of the householders.

Before they passed the church it hadn't been so bad. There had been men splitting hazel in a copse, and they'd stopped to stare as Richer walked by, but here, in the middle of the vill, it was worse.

A woman appeared in a doorway, only to slam it shut, as though to prevent any trace of Richer, even his shadow, from entering her room. At the top of the lane there came the sounds of women at work. There were many gathered at the Holy Well, and from the bottom of the road Richer could see the women walking back with filled pitchers in their arms, but all laughter ceased when they saw Richer. Their eyes followed him and Warin as they turned right to go to the alehouse, but even when they were out of view, Richer heard no return of their gladness. There was only a deathly hush, like the silence before a battle.

Warin as usual appeared unaware of the tension about him, but Richer could see that his master was keeping a keen eye on the woods and hedgerows about them, making sure there was no risk of some grubby-arsed villein taking a pot-shot at them.

The alehouse was a reassuring sight. Richer felt calmer just seeing it; it was so much like the house in which he had been born and raised, the one in which his family had perished. Suddenly he was struck with a premonition that, should he enter, he would suffer the same fate. Greyness swam before his eyes and he stumbled and all but fell.

'What is it? You aren't scared, are you?'

Richer felt the quick grasp of a fist at his upper arm, and the shock of the jerk as he was caught. The mists cleared and he grew aware of the sun again. As though to soothe his fears, a thrush began to sing in a nearby tree.

'I'm all right.' He released his arm from Warin's hand.

The squire's face was dark with suspicion and concern. There were deep gashes at either side of his mouth; now his brows came together. 'Keep with me, friend. Together, I can protect you. Apart, I don't know. Stay with me. We can face down your accusers and make them retract.'

'Yes,' Richer said, but he had already seen his ruin in Warin's eyes: the man thought he had killed Serlo. For Warin, it would be possible to defend Richer against the charge of murder if Richer could face down the men of the vill, but if Richer failed, Warin could do little to help him. His master couldn't protect him. Not now. Perhaps never again.

That reflection brought tears to Richer's eyes. Loathed by the people among whom he had grown, now he had lost the support of the man for whom he had worked more than ten years past. He would surely be killed here.

If he were to die, he could at least do so with honour, he told himself, and he forced his chin a little higher, fixed a look of pride upon his features, and pushed the door wide.

If his own master chose to discard him, he would at least make the whole vill remember him for a long time to come.

Lady Anne walked about her small orchard trying to settle her spirits, but it wasn't easy. The child in her belly was squirming and kicking, apparently aware of her unease.

She knew the pressure on her husband was immense. When messengers came to speak to him, they often passed on snippets of information which could be fascinating to a man so far from the centre of politics and intrigue. Or woman, of course.

Many believed that a King's court was a hallowed place in which beautiful men and women engaged themselves in courtly love or discussing great affairs of state, always rational and reasonable, always patient and purposeful.

She knew better.

Any great man's household was like another's, and the way a man got on was by stabbing others in the back, literally or metaphorically. In the King's Household, the currency was favours and power, the same as anywhere else – the only difference being that the winnings were more tempting.

All knew that the King was in the grip of a devious and mendacious politician who would stop at nothing. If he thought he could get away with it, Despenser would be happy to slit the King's throat and take his realm. As he had already done with Mortimer's lands.

Poor Mortimer. Once so powerful and trusted, now an outcast. He had lost his lands and his castles, but at least he was alive. Perhaps he could build a new life.

The messenger today had told of Mortimer's daring escape, and the instruction brought was: arrest or kill him, but bring Mortimer to the King. Traitor and rebel, he must suffer the punishment due for his crimes. All the realm knew that his offences were against Despenser, not the King himself, but that was enough. *Despenser* had decided he must die.

Nicholas walked in and went straight to the jug of wine at the table nearest the fire. He poured himself a large cup and drained it in three gulps before sitting and pouring a second.

'My love?' she said. 'What did the messenger say?'

It was painful to see her man in this sort of mood, gruff and unresponsive, but when she had seen Nick's face blanch as he read through the message, she had known that the news was evil. Especially when he took the messenger into the solar to question him further.

Nicholas grunted. 'It's worse than I thought. No one knows where Mortimer is; the King has sent men all over the realm demanding that all strangers be questioned. It seems he believes Mortimer will try to make his way to Ireland. He was respected there after he rebuilt the country once Edward Bruce, the invader, was killed, and the King fears he may build an army. That means he could be around here. It would make sense for Mortimer to find a ship from Wales or Cornwall; to reach Ireland from Wales, though, he'd have to pass through Despenser's lands, so that's not likely. No, I think Cornwall would make most sense. That means he could well pass by us. And God help us if he does and we don't catch him!'

Lady Anne nodded, but she wasn't persuaded that this was the real reason for his black mood. She knew her husband too well after six years of marriage; he had never fooled her. She went to him now and placed her hands on the back of his neck, kneading his muscles firmly, the way he liked it. Then she leaned down and kissed his head. 'Come, my love. What is it that concerns you so? Is it him, or is it the other one?'

He stiffened under her hands, but then gave a low, reluctant chuckle. 'That is the trouble with you, woman, you always read my mind. Yes, it's Richer. I don't know what to do about him. I am sure he is innocent and he deserves the opportunity of remaining with Warin. After all, he was sent here with the squire, wasn't he? Sir Henry must trust him; so should we.'

'If your trust is misplaced, we could be risking other lives,' Lady Anne said gently. 'Richer may have slaughtered not only Serlo, but his past lover, Athelina, and her children.'

'That wasn't him,' Nicholas grated, and she felt his muscles tighten again.

'Perhaps you should make the Coroner aware of our doubts?' she suggested. 'He can take such action as he deems fit.'

'You wish to have Richer hanged for something he didn't do?' Nicholas demanded.

'No, of course not.' Anne withdrew. 'My love, I only seek to help you, you know that.'

He held his head, then shook it, like a dog clearing its brow of water. 'Yes, of course I do.' He finished his wine, turned and pulled her down to him. His lips tasted of the strong, sour wine, but she revelled in the flavour. She did love her man when she was with him like this.

As she smiled down at him, his face on a level with her breast, he gave a wolfish grin and buried his nose in her cleavage, rubbing his stubbly jowls up and down. She squealed and drew away. 'Enough! Husband, you have work to do.'

'Aye, I know. And you must rest,' he said seriously, a hand patting her belly. 'I don't want you overdoing things. Take care of yourself for the child's sake.'

'I will,' she promised as he rose and left the room.

She stood a while, her hand on her belly, smiling with satisfaction. Her man was prey to concerns at times, but her duty was to remain calm. She must uplift his spirits.

It was so sad she couldn't tell him of her past. He knew much, of course – especially about the death of her parents and the hideous journey here with the lascivious friar – but nothing about that period of her life as a whore. She wasn't sure he could understand or forgive that, any more than he could forgive her brief affair while he was away.

Yet it was all too natural that she should have panicked, convinced that he was dead. And seeking another man who might protect her had seemed so sensible. A woman who was without a husband or wealth was a woman in danger. She couldn't return to the brothel; she would rather cut her own throat.

Outside there were voices, a relief from her grim thoughts, and she stood on the threshold from where she could see into the yard.

With a flicker of interest she saw that Sir Baldwin and his taciturn friend the Bailiff were both there, and she decided it would be diverting to learn how the two had fared. She knew they had ridden to see Father John at Temple that morning for there were no secrets in a small castle.

Standing on tiptoes, she waved to Sir Baldwin. The two men exchanged a glance, seeing her beckon, then she saw the Bailiff shrug and both made their way across the yard. Soon they were in the hall. She indicated the replenished jug of wine and cups, then took her own seat near the table. The two bowed and sat on a bench, filled cups in their hands.

'Sir Baldwin, Bailiff. I heard you had travelled to see that odd fellow at Temple. Tell me, did he help you?'

It was Baldwin who responded. 'Alas, he was little aid. He considered our questions impertinent, or perhaps he thought we touched on subjects which were more the domain of a priest than a King's officer!'

'John is very sure of himself,' Anne agreed. 'He is closely allied to the King's cause, you know. His father died at Bannockburn, I believe. In any case, most priests would be reluctant to speak of their feelings about the miller. Most had reason to dislike him.'

'You too?'

'Oh, that's different!' she laughed, but there was an edge to her amusement. She hadn't expected him to spot her weakness quite so swiftly. Yes, she could easily have killed Serlo for his attempted blackmail.

'Do not fear, Lady,' Baldwin said. 'You didn't kill him. In your present condition you would be quite unable to drag him along the track where he was killed and push him into his machine. I doubt whether you could have done so before you were pregnant, but it would be impossible now.'

'I suppose I should be glad you feel so,' she said with a hint of sarcasm. It was hardly chivalrous to speak to a woman in such a way.

'Of course you could've paid someone else,' Simon said.

She gazed at him, appalled. 'You surely don't . . .'

'No, of course not,' Simon said with a smile. Yet she noticed that he did not spell out exactly what he didn't believe.

'This Serlo was hated by all,' Baldwin mused. 'Which makes it hard to find his killer – unless his murderer was related to his apprentice Dan and this act was motivated by revenge. But I understand there are no living relations.'

'I believe not,' she agreed.

'A lad doesn't need to be related by blood to be loved,' Simon said. 'Maybe it was a jealous rival in love. Could a woman have killed him?'

'He was surely too young,' Anne chuckled. 'He was only seven!'

'All right,' Simon tried. 'Perhaps a woman attacked Serlo because Serlo had killed her lover.'

Baldwin shot him a look. 'Think about her dragging the body to the mill. Few women would be strong enough.'

'And setting it off,' Anne said. 'Surely only someone who knew about the mill would have been able to set the mechanism going.'

'Hardly,' Simon said. 'I daresay I could start it myself. Mills aren't complicated devices and many will watch while the grain is milled, both to gossip and make sure the miller is honest.'

'That is an interesting thought,' Baldwin frowned. 'Gossip is useful currency anywhere . . . perhaps Serlo learned something about others in the vill, and was killed to silence his mouth?'

Anne felt her heart freeze. For a moment she thought she must collapse, and her pallid features caught Simon's attention.

'My Lady, we have upset you with all this talk of death! Please let me fetch you some wine.'

'No, no,' she protested, telling them that it was nothing, a mere passing faintness. Her child . . .

'Ah yes,' Baldwin said with a smile. He lifted his cup and drained it. 'I hope your child brings you as much joy as my own did me.'

He was surprised to see her colour, but thought that it was simply the pleasure of a young woman to be so honoured by two rugged old warriors like Simon and him. The truth would take time to occur to him.

Chapter Twenty-Three

Inside the alehouse it was dark and gloomy. Richer entered with his chin high and his hand near his sword's hilt, stopping at the doorway to the screens passage, staring about him.

This early in the evening, only a few men stood with pots in their fists. One, Angot, was merrily drunk, sitting on the floor near the bar and humming a tune, occasionally breaking into a bawdy song when he could remember the lyrics, and then laughing uproariously.

Two men were strangers and watched Richer with unconcealed surprise as others glanced his way, and then swiftly averted their gaze, suddenly finding the ale in the bottom of their cups a source of fascination.

Susan went to see him, hissing angrily, 'Richer, what're you doing here? By my mother's soul, I thought you'd have more sense, man! Go back to the castle before Alexander hears that you're here! Quickly: *go!*'

'I am going nowhere. I didn't kill Serlo, and I won't skulk in the castle like a felon seeking sanctuary. Fetch me ale, Sue. Wine for my master here.'

'Why, so you can be hanged from my lintel?' she countered. 'Get back to the castle until they find out who did kill Serlo.'

'And if they don't, what then? Shall I remain there for ever? If I hide away, people will think that proof of my guilt.'

'Can't you talk sense to him?' she demanded, turning to Warin in frustration. 'He's your servant, isn't he? You have a duty to protect him, in Christ's name!'

'I'll have wine; he'll have ale. We'll be at the table there,' Warin declared, pointing to a table at the far wall.

Richer nodded. It was well-chosen. There was no window behind. Both men could command a view of the entrance, with no risk of an assassin behind them. On the other hand, there was no means of escape, either. He slapped his hand on his hilt and marched to the table. Grabbing a bench, he kicked it against the wall and dropped down on it.

There was a curious feel to this, as though he had been in this situation before, and then it came to him. Many years ago in Wales, he was a part of the garrison of the King's new castle at Ruddlan. The country had only recently been pacified, and the men living there detested the English with a passion. For Richer back then, in 1312, it was hard to imagine that the peasants could rise against their lawful King, Edward II, but they did. And Richer and a friend were caught up in it.

He and his friend had entered an alehouse like this, and just like this one, the atmosphere had chilled as they walked in, all conversations stopping. Yesterday the place had gone quiet because Serlo was in the corner; now it was quiet with fear. The folk knew that Richer was a fighter and dangerous, but they also knew that Alexander wanted to capture him and take him to the nearest tree to hang.

In Wales there had been rumours that one of the castle's garrison had raped a local girl, and the vill's men had gathered angrily, waving weapons and shouting for revenge against the 'invaders'. As if Richer and his companion (he couldn't recall his name; it was so long ago now) were invading! They were subjects of the same King.

The mob had appeared at the tavern before Richer knew what was happening. There had been a window behind them both, and as soon as they saw the men pouring through the doorway, his friend pushed him to the window and helped him up and through.

273 of Death 273

Richer had drawn his sword the moment he was out, but even as he turned to help his friend, he saw the blood splash against the wall. The other man turned once, his eyes desperate, and bellowed to him to run and escape, and then he was borne down by the press of bodies.

Later he saw the body. It had been left dangling, naked, moving gently in the breeze, a bloody mess where his genitals had been. They had been hacked off and shoved into his mouth where they remained, protruding obscenely. The swollen face and bulging eyes seemed to look at Richer accusingly. He still saw that face in his nightmares.

This alehouse had the same feel. There was anger in the air, a tension like an over-filled bladder, that needed only a sharp blade to release it in death and fury. Richer knew that he was that blade. Unless he was careful, he might precipitate a disaster.

Warin sat next to him on the bench. 'And now, old friend, we wait,' he murmured.

Letty was much recovered now. At least, she thought she was. Letitia knew she was fortunate enough to have the constitution of a man, and a stronger man than most who lived here in the vill, but even so, the shock of seeing that terrible wreckage lying among the cogs had almost given her a brain fever. She had needed to return home and rest. Awful, too, considering how Alexander had needed her. Poor Alex! He'd seen Serlo lying there. If only she had controlled herself better, rather than screaming and bolting like a pathetic child.

That was how Alex learned of Serlo's death: she'd collapsed at her door and Alex had taken her in and seen to her before going to the mill. Unlike most men, who would have left their wives and run, Alex was organised. He first sent a man up to the castle, then called on two women to come to the house. Their maid had also helped, and before too long Letty was back in her bed, Jan applying a damp cloth to her forehead. And only then had Alex gone to see his brother.

Aumery had been lying near the fire overnight, and exhaustion had prevented his waking this morning, but he was truly awake now, and like any little boy who had witnessed a dreadful event, he wept and started to cry for his mother. Letty was forced to rise from her palliasse and catch him, taking him back to bed with her.

Then Alex returned, blanched and shaking; he looked like an old man. To see a brother crushed so brutally was a truly hideous experience. Stoically, Alex tried to conceal his feelings. He was never one to wear his pain on his sleeve. A man brought up apart from others, motherless, beaten and shamed by their father in poverty, he had only ever known self-reliance. All his love had been devoted to his brother – until he married Letty. She felt guilty that he must look after her, but she was also glad; he could concentrate on her and save his own grief for later.

She rolled over when she had managed to comfort Aumery enough to leave him alone, and saw her man at the doorway. 'Alex? Are you all right? Come and let me hold you.'

'I am all right.' He didn't turn to her, but remained staring out at the roadway.

'I am so sorry!'

'I know you never liked him – many didn't. He was always an aggressive fool: a bully, and in many ways a coward. Perhaps it was my fault. I used to spoil him when he was a child. I'd take the blame for his faults and take his punishment too, just to protect him. If I'd let him stand on his own, perhaps he'd have learned to win friends.'

'You did all you could,' Letitia said, shivering. She pulled a rug over her nakedness and stood. Tucking Aumery in, she exhorted him to close his eyes.

Alex continued, 'It was never enough though. And then when we grew, and I started to make a decent fist of my life, he still wanted to be molly-coddled and swathed in my love. Whatever I did, he thought was good, but he couldn't copy me. Running the mill was the limit of his abilities. When he tried to make his own way, he failed.'

'In what way?' she asked. She had walked to his side and now she wrapped her rug around him as well, enclosing him in her own warmth.

'Look at the matter of the tolls. How stupid, taking gifts to let people use the bridge when the castellan and steward must have seen what was happening. Soon they must have taken action against him for that. It was too flagrant. And it defrauded us, too! His own family!'

'I am only surprised that they hadn't already taken action against him,' she agreed, tight-lipped. No matter how hard she tried to think kind thoughts about Serlo, when all was said and done, he was an aggressive idiot, just as Alex said.

'And as for his talk about Athelina . . . I could have hit him for what he said about her.'

Alex remained silent for a long moment. In the circle of her arms, Letty could feel his heart thundering like a destrier's after a race, and then she felt the catch as he sobbed.

'And then he made more enemies . . .'

'It's all right, Alex. Alex, my love, come!' she crooned. If only they had been able to have their own children, she thought as she turned him gently and rested his head on her shoulder. She let her cheek touch his and smiled. At least he was letting the anguish out. That was bound to be good for him. He couldn't stop up all his feelings all the time. Now that fool of a brother of his was dead, perhaps Alex would be able to find some rest. The last link with his miserable childhood was gone. 'It doesn't matter now,' she murmured.

'No. All that matters is, Serlo's dead. That's all that matters,' he said dully.

There was a loud sobbing from the bed, but neither moved. Poor Aumery would have to grow used to his loss, just as would Alexander himself. Both had lost their brothers.

She saw a figure approach and shook her head at the man, but even as she did so, Alex felt her movement and turned to face the door. There, shame-faced, was Wal from the farm near Holy Well. He shuffled a little under Alexander's fixed stare.

'Constable? Sorry to hear about Serlo. Some of us, we reckon it's terrible what that bastard's done.'

'Thank you. He'll pay.'

'He's at the alehouse now. We'll help you, if you want.'

'He's come here? He's flaunting himself in my vill?' Alexander demanded, aghast.

Letitia clung to him. 'Alex, don't do anything – the Coroner and his friend will arrest him and see that he's punished. Don't go there, it'll only end in you being hurt!'

'Me? Hurt?' Alexander gave a hollow laugh. 'I have no children, no brother, no hope. All I have created will die with me.'

'There's me, Alex, and there's still time! If we pray, He may send us a child to—'

Alex made a small gesture of dismissal. 'We shall never have children, my love. And justice must be done. It was that son of a hog who killed my brother,' Alexander said. 'And now he will pay!'

Sniffing, Aumery watched as his uncle left. His father had spoken about the lady at the castle, as if the secret was important. 'If he learned that another man knew his wife,' his father had said, 'it would be terrible.' Aumery was not to speak about it, or his father would kill him. Now his father was dead.

He sobbed again. The rock of his life was gone, as well as his baby brother. He felt very lonely. He wanted his mother to come home and cuddle him. It was a relief when he felt Letitia's arms go about him. 'It's all right, Aumie. Auntie's here. Don't worry. Poor Aumie. Soon I'll take you to your mother, all right?'

Yes. That was what he wanted. Then he thought: his father was dead now, so he was master of the house. He was responsible for his mother, and he must protect her. He was big enough. He was nearly four years old.

Daddy was dead. So was Ham. He sobbed again and hid his face in his aunt's rug.

'There is no sign of Squire Warin or the man Richer anywhere,' Baldwin said. 'Have you sent them on an errand?'

Nicholas eyed him distractedly. 'No. They may have gone out for some exercise.'

'No,' Simon said bluntly. 'We've asked the grooms. All the mounts are there.'

They had gone to ask Ivo – against Baldwin's better judgement – but all they had learned was that Warin and Richer had left the castle on foot. Sir Jules volunteered to seek them, and Simon and Baldwin gladly accepted his offer. Both were finding the Coroner's company tedious. Baldwin, watching him leave with Roger, had a fleeting sense of compassion for the clerk, along with gratitude that it was not his task to look after the Coroner – and gladness that someone else was there to protect the young man from his blunderings.

'I am concerned that Richer in particular might be in danger,' Baldwin said. 'He was known to dislike Serlo; if the Constable should take it into his mind to challenge him, or worse, attack him, there could be bloodshed.'

'True,' Nicholas said heavily. Since the death of Athelina, he had been prey to appalling doubts, and he was aware that his attitude must seem peculiar to these men. How could *they* understand!

'Are you quite well?' Baldwin asked.

Nicholas looked at him sadly. 'I would see the boy safe, if at all possible,' he said.

'Boy?' Baldwin asked, confused.

'Richer atte Brooke.'

'We shall protect him if we can,' Baldwin said, but then he took a second look at Nicholas's face. 'But if you know something which may help us, you should tell us now. You *do* know something, don't you? Tell us, please!'

Yes, I should. But how can I tell you the truth without earning your condemnation? Nicholas thought to himself. He rose from his chair, went to the door and called to a servant. 'If anyone wants me, tell them they'll have to wait,' he ordered. 'I want no one to come in here until I say so.'

'Yes, sir.'

'Go!'

Nicholas returned to his table and poured himself a mazer of wine. Standing with it in his hands, he began to speak, not once glancing at the other two men.

'When I was a lad, I was a cause of shame and embarrassment to my father,' he said at last. 'He was a cobbler, a simple but cheerful soul who wanted me to follow him. I hated the thought of being apprenticed; instead I set my heart on higher things. So when the King's Sergeant came asking for men to join his Host, I volunteered.

'I'd always been a hearty lad, full of piss and wind, and when there was ale flowing, I was there, mouth agape to drink it. After taking my fill, more often than not, I'd get into a fight. Many's the time I've been knocked sideways by someone bigger than me,' he said nostalgically, 'but I usually got my own back on the bastards.

'Anyway, I left my home and went with the King. I fought well in his service, and I made my way through his forces. Lord Henry was my master, and as he grew from squire to become a belted knight, I grew with him.'

Baldwin nodded. 'It is the way with warriors.'

'Yes. Still more so when they have been involved in evil.'

'What do you mean?' Baldwin asked sharply.

'When we were sent to subdue the Welsh, we had a hard time of it. They captured the King's baggage train, and we spent a miserable few weeks in Conwy waiting for ships to come with food and drink. God bless the old bastard's memory! The King was always a warrior first and politician second: he knew what it was to fight. When his supplies of wine were down to the last gallon, he insisted that it be shared among the men with him. While we waited, we were forced to go and seek provisions. We had to take whatever we could, before the enemy could starve us. You are a knight, you know what war is like!'

As he turned to look at Baldwin, he saw the cold expression on the other's face. Baldwin looked like a man who had been turned to stone.

'Yes, I have seen war,' he replied, 'yet I never robbed the poor unnecessarily. We always took what we needed at that moment, and left enough for them to survive.'

'Enough? What is enough for a peasant?' Nicholas cried He flung an arm towards the south. 'Look at them! They have a hard time feeding themselves when the weather's good, let alone when it's foul. There's never enough to fill their bellies. They survive when they're fortunate, but more often they starve. What we did was wrong, perhaps, but we were at war.'

'You robbed them and left them nothing, then?' Baldwin asked.

'We took what we needed.' He remembered the flames. When he closed his eyes, he could see them lighting his inner lids with amber vigour. The horror was still foul even after so many years.

'We were told to fetch food from a vill a few miles from the castle. It should have been an easy job, but the land wasn't safe. You know how these things go: occasionally sling shots, some arrows. A companion of mine suddenly fell, an arrow in his throat.

That kind of thing wears you down, and I never had a good temper. I was in charge of the *chevauchée* because I was the more senior man there, and I grew more and more bitter and vengeful. The people were spiteful. Rebellious to the last, damn them all!

He paused for a moment, remembering. 'We rode into the vill and as we entered, I saw some men with . . .'

Weapons. That was what he'd thought. They looked like the long bows which had been plaguing them all day, and he'd felt his bile rise to see these peasants flaunting their treachery. What could a man do? He ordered the charge, and spurred his horse on in a moment.

It was like a dream, or so it felt now; a slow-moving dream in which he wallowed onwards through treacle, his mace in his hand. The men turned and saw him, their faces blank in terror, and then one dropped his weapon and darted away, ducking under the lintel of a nearby cottage; a second slowly stepped backwards, appalled; the third stayed put, no fear on his face, only bovine resignation. And then the scenes came with a vividness that still woke Nicholas in his dreams.

The nearer man was felled by the iron mace, his skull so completely crushed that the spikes caught, and when Nicholas twisted it free, it pulled great slobbery lumps of brain with it. Blood dripped on his arm as he rode at the second man. He was still there, a look of pleading in eyes filled with tears. Nicholas saw his hands come up as though in supplication, but Nicholas knew no compassion. The mace swung, and the spikes raked down his cheek, puncturing his eyeball, which turned to a bloody mess in an instant. A second swing and his face dissolved: the steel hit his nose squarely, smashing his features.

His bloodlust was still with him. He threw himself from his horse and pelted into the cottage. There was a naked woman with a rug over her breast, but he thrust her aside and he stood, breathing like a horse after a gallop, until he heard the sobbing.

Pulling away a curtain, he found the two children hiding in a recess in the wall. They stared at him, eyes wild like dogs with the rage, the drooling disease that made men fear water even when they were dying of thirst.

He reached in, hooking out the first, slamming the figure to the floor with a blow from his mace, then grabbed the other, lifting the mace high over his head to kill, when the bare woman grabbed his arm.

Christ's bones, but she had some strength, that woman! She grabbed him so hard, he thought he must have his arm wrenched from its socket, and when he turned to face her, he saw she gripped a knife. He shattered the hand with his mace, the spikes ravaging her wrist, tearing down her hand and pulling off her thumb and forefinger. Still she came at him, a terrible expression of hatred on her face, eyes quite mad, mouth spitting in that lunatic gibberish they called a language! He swung again, and the fury and hatred died with her.

Turning to the last, he saw that he was too late. The figure had snatched the dagger from the floor, and had already used it on himself, thrusting it into his own breast. Except now he could see more clearly as the red mist left him, Nicholas saw that this was no warrior but a slim girl. Probably the dead woman's daughter Only thirteen years or so. Not more.

The boy at his feet was the one who had ducked inside, but now Nicholas looked, he too was hardly more than a child. He was her son. The woman herself was older, more worn, but there was something about her; the sweat and stench of the cottage was not just from the odour of animals or rank humans, it held something else, and when he looked at her more closely, he saw that she had a disease.

'We went into the vill, and they had some people there,' he said at last. 'I had ridden with the men for miles, with bowmen taking their chances at us all the long way, and when I saw three men with bows in their hands, I thought these were some of those who had been attacking us. I rode them all down. A woman tried to protect one, too, and I killed her.' He swallowed. It hardly expressed the reality of the slaughterhouse that was their home. 'When I looked later, it wasn't a weapon. They were all playing with wooden lances. Toys.'

'You killed them for playing?' Simon asked. His face registered incredulity.

'We rode in, we saw what we thought were weapons, so we protected ourselves,' Nicholas declared stiffly. 'If it helps you, Bailiff, I have ever seen those faces before me in my nightmares. We fired the place once we had taken all we could.' It was all he could do not to order that the vill be razed to the ground, he felt it to be so vile, but instead he ordered that the carts be filled, and while the sullen villagers watched, he took the first of the burning torches and threw it into the cottage, watching as the flames grew, the smoke rising, first green and yellow and foul, then thick and blue-black, the stink of burning flesh disgusting on the evening air. And they had left. But Nicholas bore the scars. He always would.

'What has this to do with us now?' Simon demanded harshly.

'I left there soon afterwards. I grew ill with a sickness. Henry my lord was unwell too, and he and I left Wales to come here, to his home, to recuperate. It was here that I found some peace.'

'With a woman?' Baldwin asked, glowering.

'She was willing!' Nicholas protested at Baldwin's tone, and then his eyes dropped. 'When she conceived, I was delighted. My own child. And I saw to it that she and her family were looked after. When she decided to marry, I gave her money to help. Later, she and her husband and all their children died in a fire. Only my son survived, and he fled, but I was able to ensure that he wasn't chased for being a runaway serf. Instead, I had him guided into the arms of Sir Henry's retinue, where he was protected. He learned his skills as a warrior, and later he could come home again.'

'This was Richer?' Baldwin continued relentlessly. 'You are his father?'

'He is my only child.'

'Be glad you have another coming, then,' Baldwin said remorselessly. 'Because I swear, if I find he is the murderer, I shall see him hanged.'

Nicholas stared at him, wanting to demand sympathy, but couldn't. After a moment, he looked away again, and prayed that Richer might be safe.

Chapter Twenty-Four

Warin was noble by birth, and certainly didn't fear this rabble. They made him want to laugh. There was none among them whom he would be concerned about individually, he grew aware of their eyes moving from one to another, like a pack of dogs working up the courage to make an attack. That was less amusing.

He couldn't really permit them to take Richer, no matter what he had said before. Richer was his servant, and no one was going to take him against Warin's will. The squire was more than powerful enough to prevent a small group from lynching his man. Still, he must also be seen to be fair. He didn't want to be thought of as harbouring a fugitive from justice. That was not the way to gain the respect of the peasants.

A strange place this, when tempers were hot. The alewife was serving with a face like a wet week in Wales, while men fingered their stubble or hunched their shoulders and glowered.

In the far corner was an old man, hard to see at the other side of the room, just a dark smudge with eyes that twinkled as the firelight caught them. Then he sat forward, and Warin recognised Iwan. The old smith didn't look away, but met his gaze calmly, a massive pot in his hand. Then he smiled, but somehow he still looked threatening. It was the eyes, Warin's father had once said: the eyes told you about the soul. Watch his eyes and you'd see the attack before his hands could move. Warin wouldn't want to have Iwan as an enemy . . . at least not if Iwan was younger.

Richer was anxious: Warin could sense fear oozing from his pores like sweat. Couldn't blame him. This was the most dangerous situation Richer had ever endured. Going into battle with friends at his side was one thing: sitting and waiting for a man who was sworn to see his destruction while on all sides his enemy's friends fenced him in, that took courage.

And conviction, of course. Perhaps Richer wasn't the murderer. Attacking a man in the dark was not his way – but the question was, would the people here believe that?

A sudden hush smothered them. The fire sparked, and Warin saw the smoke gust up and through the window. At the door, men moved aside, and there in the doorway stood Alexander.

'So, *murderer*! You thought to celebrate your success here, did you? Didn't think that there'd be anyone else here who'd challenge you?'

'I didn't touch him, Alex,' Richer said. There was an edge to his voice: partly fear, partly anger, but only the fear was heard by Alexander's men.

Warin could read their minds. These folk were like cattle. The strongest man in the room today was the Constable, and he could herd them. He was strong because of his hatred, sincerity and rage. Today all the men would follow him.

'You didn't *touch* him? Was it your knife, then? Did it leap from your belt, slash his throat wide, and carry him to the mill to be draped over his own wheel?'

'I had nothing to do with his death,' Richer said.

'You had no reason to murder him,' Alexander said, stepping forward slowly, his head jutting pugnaciously. 'But you did anyway. You waited until his mind was weakened by seeing his poor boy, my nephew . . .' His voice was choked suddenly, and he had to break off, while fresh tears flooded his cheeks. 'While his wife was still inconsolable with grief, you slaughtered him!'

'It was not me!' Richer declared again, and he held out his hands in an impassioned plea to the men about him. 'Look at me! I'm *Richer* atte Brooke! This is my place of birth! I'm no murderer!'

'You say one of us is?' a voice sneered, and Richer sensed his master stiffening.

Richer felt it too. There was passion in the crowd. Richer could hear low, bitter mutterings. They were like the apprentices after the ale had flowed too freely in the taverns; a mob that hunted in a pack, attacking anyone in their path, whether an enemy or passer-by. None was safe when the mob prowled. These usually submissive peasants had been welded together by a sense of injustice; few might have liked Serlo, but he was at least one of them. In comparison, Richer was a stranger after running away fifteen years ago.

They were ready to tear Richer to pieces with their bare hands. There was a blow at his shoulder, and a heavy earthenware pot fell and smashed on the floor A platter span across the room: it slashed a cut into his cheek and bounced from the wall behind him. A metallic rasp spoke of a blade being pulled from a wooden scabbard, and Richer knew he must die. Next to him, Warin drew his own sword and the polished blade gleamed evilly in the dimly-lit room.

Warin bared his teeth. He hadn't expected violence to flare so swiftly, damn it! He'd wanted to use his authority to persuade the men in here that Richer was innocent, but events had moved too quickly. Now it seemed certain that Richer must die. In a moment the hot rage in his belly was fired, but now, seeing the churls baying, Alexander's pale and resolute face approaching, he felt his ire fade and a strange new sensation take its place: fear. He had brought his servant here to save him, and instead he had escorted Richer to his doom. Richer was stunned by a jug hitting his head, his sword still sheathed. Warin shouted: 'Richer! Defend yourself!'

Other voices took up the cry of rebellion. 'Catch him – let's string him up! Who else could have wanted to have Serlo killed? Only you, Richer!'

To Warin's surprise, a loud, calm voice answered. 'Oh, I reckon any man here who took oats to be ground and found his grain had melted away when his back was turned. Serlo was good at taking more than his multure.'

It was old Iwan. He had remained at the back of the room when the men pressed forward to encircle Richer and Warin, but his voice was clear through the baying of men become animals. He was staring at Alexander with a fixed intensity.

Alexander glared and pointed a shivering finger at him. 'Don't speak ill of the dead, old heretic! You never liked him, did you? Leave his memory alone, lest you have cause to regret it later!'

Some of the men were readying to spring on Richer and Warin, but some, if only a few, were glancing from Iwan to Alexander. They wore puzzled frowns, like men who were recovering from a strange dream.

Iwan's eyes narrowed as though in amusement at some joke the others hadn't seen. His posture, though, was not that of an ancient, but of a warrior who was capable of teaching a man half his age many lessons. 'Do you think to threaten me?'

'Don't push me, old man!'

'Alex, boy, I reckon 'tis time you was goin' home.'

There was a chuckle, instantly stilled, but Warin saw some faces lighten for a moment. Then another rolled his eyes ceiling-wards, and Warin realised that Alexander had lost the momentum of the crowd about him.

'Shut up, Iwan! I've got business here.'

'Alex, I'll ignore your manners, but I call on the tithing to witness you're breaking your pledge to hold the King's Peace. You may be the Constable, but that don't put you above the good King's laws. You're trying to raise a mob, and I won't let you.'

Those words made some men take pause. A fellow at the back moved a little away from the men ringing the two. He was less reluctant to join in.

'You can't stop me!' Alexander spat.

'Oh I can, Alex,' Iwan said, crossing the floor until he stood with Warin and Richer. He frowned at Richer. 'No one can really believe that this man's guilty of murder. We all remember him: he's one of us.'

'He hated my brother!'

Alexander's voice was taut with emotion, his face pale, but although he held out his hands in appeal to the men about him, they didn't return his gaze. There was some shuffling in the dirt of the floor. Two more men left the crowd, joining the first, who now stood at the doorway. The three exchanged a look, and then darted out. The door slamming made more men glance about them, and some noticed the gape and looked more anxious.

'He didn't get on with Serlo. Like I said, many didn't,' Iwan agreed. 'That's no reason to murder.'

'Serlo told him,' Alex said quietly but venomously.

Iwan cocked his head. 'Aye?'

'Told him that it was he who had fired his house: Serlo burned it, killed Richer's family. He told him in this very tavern. You heard him!' he demanded, pointing at two men. They both looked away.

'That true?' Iwan said to Richer.

'No! I didn't hear him say that. I left the place when I saw him here, to save his grief.'

Iwan studied him intently for a few moments. 'It'd be good reason for a killing, if you had, but I don't reckon there's enough anger in you even now to do something like that. You might accuse him in front of witnesses, maybe even catch him and cal' on him to pull a sword – but not more than that. No, Richer's no murderer.'

'Out of my way!' Alexander snarled, and gripped Iwan's upper arm to shove him aside.

Warin saw it all, and it still astonished him, many years later. The older man's face emptied, as though all emotion had fled, and his left hand whipped around his body, pulling Alexander's hand away from his biceps. At the same time, his right hand snaked forward, grabbing the Constable's throat and pushing with all the force of his body behind his hand. Alexander was thrust back between Richer and Warin, against the wall, the air exploding from his lungs in a gasp of pain, and then he found himself inches from the ground, staring down at Iwan's face.

'Constable, I'll thank you not to push me around.' The smith smiled without humour. 'You could hurt a poor old man. Besides,' he added, 'you wouldn't want to tempt the vill to rise against the Lord's own son, would you?'

'What do you mean, the Lord's own son?' Alexander managed, trying to breathe. Iwan's fingers felt like talons of iron and he was growing light-headed.

'This man Warin. Take a good look at him, Constable. He's Sir Henry's boy.'

Anne saw Simon and Baldwin leaving her husband at the solar door when she entered the hall, and she could see Nicholas's tension as he stood there watching them go. Then, slowly, like a man who had aged ten years in as many minutes, he returned to the solar.

There was a fluttering in her breast at the sight. It made her realise just how fragile was his spirit nowadays, how fragile was her own security, and her hand went to her womb in a gesture that was growing habitual.

He had always been so confident in his power and position, and now that was fading. In some measure she felt it was his memories which plagued him still. They were growing in virulence recently, and there seemed nothing she could do about them; if anything, they appeared to grow worse when she was with him, as though her presence was a cause of shame and anguish, rather than a balm easing his pain.

He had been so happy to hear she was with child, yet more recently he had lost his vigour, especially since Athelina's death. In the last few days Nicholas had grown more inward-looking and less responsive.

Perhaps it was Warin. It was the problem with a yeoman like Nicholas running a castle. Squires like Warin were noble-born and might be knighted, whereas the likelihood of that happening to Nicholas was remote. He was a stolid, reliable man, and trusted by Sir Henry, but that was all. A man who held a castle for the King might win a knight's belt and spurs, but Nicholas was slowly rotting here. There was nothing for him.

Still, Nicholas had never suffered jealousy like that before. No, this was more like grief. Perhaps – my God, but her heart was fluttering fit to burst! – he had realised the child wasn't his!

Christ in Heaven! She had to consider! Quickly!

Serlo had threatened her with exposure, and Athelina had known. That was the plain meaning of his words at the inquest – but he hadn't had time before the end of the inquest to speak to Nicholas, surely? He'd stood there until his wife's appearance with his son's corpse, then he had run in a welter of panic and grief to the alehouse.

No, there had been no opportunity for him to ruin her marriage.

Unless Athelina had already done so, of course. When had Nicholas grown so withdrawn from her? Was it just after hearing of Athelina's death, or before, when he might have visited the woman and learned about his wife's infidelity? It was possible.

May be Athelina had told him, and he had killed her in a sudden rage. Just as he could have killed Serlo.

'My God!' she murmured.

Nicholas was being driven to distraction by something, she knew. She only prayed it *wasn't* her and her child. That would be too cruel.

Simon and Baldwin stood in the yard, but when Baldwin caught sight of Ivo loitering, he grunted, 'Let's get away from this place. It's making me choke!' and led the way to the gate.

Their path took them along the protected corridor that led out to the open air. A waft of breeze brought with it the stench of the shit-bespattered ground under the garderobe at the western edge of the wall, and without speaking, the two walked away from the castle and the foul smell.

Following their feet, the two trailed down the hill towards the vill itself. Here the land was much like Devonshire's, and Simon felt his heart being drawn eastwards again. He had endured enough travelling, enough death and hardship to last him the rest of his lifetime. The little house which Meg, his wife, had made so welcoming was never so appealing as now. He hoped his family were well. Praying for them was one thing, but there was no guarantee that God would protect them. Christ's bones, but he missed them!

At the bottom of the little hill were more trees. A charcoal-burner was camping there, and a stack of wood smouldered merrily under its covering of wet sacks. They walked on past and down to the small stream that chuckled its way northwards. Even the sound made Simon homesick: the stream was a tiny version of the water that thundered in the gorge at Lydford.

'I can make little of this,' he said, sitting on a fallen trunk. 'The folk here seem unsettled by the murders. There is much bubbling away below the surface.'

'Yes,' Baldwin agreed. 'There is much going on: Athelina's murder with her children, the priest's tale, Danny's death, crushed in the mill, and Serlo's killing made to look like his. And now Nicholas's story.'

'An odd little story, that. He wanted us to help protect his son, but there seemed something else in his manner. Does he think his son is guilty? How can that be? The first death was Danny's, which happened long before Richer arrived.'

'Not quite true, Simon. The first deaths were Richer's supposed family. It was their deaths which made him leave the vill, and now he's returned the killings have started again.'

'Iwan seemed to think Serlo killed them . . . many must believe he also got rid of Athelina and her children too because she couldn't pay her rent. Someone then retaliated and killed him.'

'So the connection is revenge. Perhaps it was Richer,' Baldwin mused.

'And perhaps there is no connection whatever. The fire at Richer's home was fifteen years ago. It stretches my credulity.'

'A man who lost his whole family would demand revenge,' Baldwin said.

'Surely he would have sought it before?' Simon grunted. 'God's teeth, Baldwin. There is an unwholesome atmosphere here. I shall be glad to get back home again.'

'A family perhaps murdered in an arson attack fifteen years ago; an apprentice killed by accident, perhaps: a woman murdered and her children slaughtered, definitely; and now a man killed and his body planted in the machine like the apprentice.'

'You forgot Serlo's boy.'

'I cannot believe that young Ham was a part of this,' Baldwin said. 'The lad's mother surely wouldn't have killed him. No, that was definitely an accident.'

'The people here thought that the apprentice was, too,' Simon pointed out.

'True enough.'

'So if that's the case, the killer of Serlo was merely saying that he was a lousy master.'

Baldwin frowned at the ground by his boot. 'Or that he didn't take enough care of his charge. Surely the most sensible explanation would be that the father of the apprentice considered Serlo too careless and decided to punish him.'

'If only we knew who the father was,' Simon said.

'The priest at Temple said it was a man from the castle,' Baldwin said.

'Who do you mean?' Simon asked, turning to him. 'Nicholas, the castellan?'

'He controls this castle and vill in the name of his lord; he has powers through his men-at-arms, and all would fear him if they lived within the reach of his arms,' Baldwin said. 'I should think that he would make an excellent suspect.'

'No. The man is honest, I am sure. There are others, though: I still want to know more about Squire Warin. That fellow seems less than entirely open.'

'Yes,' Baldwin said. 'And he's not in the castle. So let's see if we can find him.'

'Where are you thinking of looking?' Simon asked, reluctantly rising to his feet.

'There are few enough places in this vill to rest,' Baldwin said determinedly, rising to his feet.

The Lady Anne couldn't bear to see Nicholas, not now, while he looked so desperate. Instead, she went out to her orchard and little garden, seeking peace and tranquillity in solitude.

The orchard had been here for many years, a small space set aside for apples and some pears, but when Anne first arrived it had been terribly overgrown and ill-kempt. No one had pruned the trees in years, and the farther side of the orchard, which had originally been planted with cider apples, was filled with fallen boughs. Anne had set to with a will, having the dead trees cleared and setting out a number of low turf banks which could be used as benches in fine weather. It was to one of these that she walked now, sitting and staring back along the valley to the west.

'I thought I might find you here.'

She did not turn to face him. 'Gervase, I wanted some peace.'

'I think we need to talk, my love. There is much to discuss.'

'We lay together, Gervase. That is all. There is nothing to talk about.'

'And what if your child is born early? So early that even Nicholas realises it isn't his?'

That was her fear. To have been cuckolded might break his heart. 'I wish . . .'

'What?' he pressed. 'That you'd agreed to accept me before you took the older man's hand?'

She gazed at him stonily. 'I love my husband, Gervase. Don't deceive yourself.'

'I loved him myself,' he said earnestly. 'I still do, a little. But I adore you, my love. You should have taken me when we first met.'

'You had enough women. No doubt you still have.'

'No! Even Julia cannot tempt me. I won't have anything to do with her – I haven't seen her in months.'

'Athelina was still coming to the castle until recently.'

'She was trying to persuade me to give her money. I wouldn't, though.'

Anne looked up at him. His face was filled with a strange mixture of dread and yearning, as though he feared what she might say or do. 'Did she go to you and threaten us? Did she tell you she'd seen us lying together that day in the meadow?'

He waved a hand. 'Yes, yes. She said that, but it meant nothing. I told her I'd kill her if anything got out about it, and that was all.'

'She did see us, so Serlo told me the truth,' Anne said with a blank stare at the distance.

'Anne, why don't we run away from here? I can protect you! All we need is a small cottage somewhere away from Sir Henry's lands, and we can live decently enough. Perhaps I could find a new position as steward somewhere, and we . . .'

'What, run away?' she said, her mouth falling open in astonishment. And then, cruelly, she couldn't help but laugh at him.

'Do you really think I'd give up my warm home, my tapestries, my tunics – *my life* – to run away with an impoverished steward? My God, Gervase, you must be mad! I lay with you, and mind you hear me carefully, I lay with you that time because I thought my husband might be dead. I was lonely and desperate, thinking that I might have lost my only protector, and sought another man who could look after me. The only man about here was you; there was no one else. I do not love you, Gervase. I don't think I could. But if Nicholas was dead, I might have considered you as an alternative. That was all.'

'Our child, though. He's proof you love me.'

'He's proof that I lay with a man some months ago,' she said dismissively. 'If he is born early, I shall call in a midwife who'll swear on her parents' graves that the child is before full term and that I and the babe both need careful nursing. Nicholas will never guess. And you won't tell him anything, Gervase.' She stood and approached him slowly. 'Because if you do, Nicholas will destroy you utterly. He'll cut your ballocks off and stuff them in your mouth. So be very careful you keep your mouth sealed.'

'I wouldn't let news of this get out,' he protested, but he was shivering like a man with the ague.

'Be sure you don't,' she said, and then she faced him with a strange expression in her eyes. 'Do you mean to say that it *was* you? Did you murder Athelina and Serlo to keep this all secret?'

He was too appalled to answer. Instead, his heart bleeding with shame, sadness and bitterness at the rejection of his love, he let his head hang, and turned his feet back towards the castle.

Chapter Twenty-Five

While Simon and Baldwin made their way to the alehouse, Sir Jules and Roger had already passed through the vill seeking the Constable at his home.

Letitia answered the door without enthusiasm when she saw who stood outside. 'Coroner. Godspeed.'

'Good wife, is your man at home?'

'No, he's . . .' she glanced up towards the alehouse. 'He's gone out.'

'Perhaps we could wait for him?'

'He may be gone a long while,' she said evasively. She had only this moment returned from church, where she had deposited Aumery with his mother. A few prayers with them had initially soothed her, but this fool's appearance had unsettled her again. Where *was* her Alex? He wanted to see Richer dead, but please God, don't let him have had the chance. Please let Richer have escaped back to the castle!

Sir Jules pursed his lips. 'What would you say, Roger? Where can we seek the man?'

Roger smiled and bobbed his head at the woman, turning to gaze back down the track. 'Perhaps he has gone to the church to see his sister-in-law?'

Nodding, Sir Jules led the way from the house. 'We may also ask the woman Muriel whether she can help us.'

'I am not sure that this would be a propitious time to speak to her.' Roger was most reluctant to question a woman when she had just lost her husband as well as her son. The thought of interrupting her grief was sorely unpleasant.

'I hardly like the thought myself,' Jules said, demonstrating an empathy that surprised Roger. 'But I'm the King's man in this part of the county: I have two other corpses I should hold an inquest on, I've deaths here in this vill which I haven't satisfactorily resolved, and there is news of Lord Mortimer's escape! What must I do to return to Bodmin and normality? Clearly I must solve these cases to the best of my ability, and then take my leave.'

'We should speak with the Constable first,' Roger proposed.

'If he's at the church, we can do so. If not, the woman Muriel may know something. It is worth asking her. That is all I suggest – that we speak to her.'

'You could be adding to a mother's grief.'

'You are a Coroner's clerk, man! Aren't you used to grief?'

Roger studied his master with the attitude of a gardener surveying a colony of slugs in his cabbages. 'I have served as Coroner's clerk these last many years, and I have observed all forms of misery, of loss, of injustice, of devastation. I've seen more mothers grieving for their children, more widows bemoaning the loss of husbands, more sisters missing their siblings, than you have ridden leagues. Do not think to preach to me my duties, *Master* Coroner. I know them all too well.'

'Meaning you think I don't?' the Coroner bridled.

'Meaning I don't think it is yet right to intrude upon her sorrow.'

'Well, I do,' Sir Jules said firmly, and set off towards the church.

'Like many a bull-headed fool, you have less blood in your heart than does your damned sword,' the clerk muttered under his breath. 'God save me from men like you if I should ever need compassion!'

The Coroner strode straight to the door like a man who sought to complete an unpleasant duty with as much speed as possible. Roger uttered a short prayer for Muriel before he entered, crossing his breast in the manner of a priest helping a man at the gallows.

Inside, the church smelled of blood. Although the vill's women had tried to clean Serlo's body as best they could, the mess at his skull was foul. Roger could see the little patches of white where flies' eggs were already laid. Soon those heralds of putrefaction would hatch and begin the process of converting this corpse into dust as God demanded.

He knelt and bowed his head to the altar, crossing himself again, then stood and walked forward to the little group of people at the smaller body.

This, like Serlo's, was lighted by candles, but the tiny corpse was saved from the ultimate degradation by women who fanned at approaching flies and kept them at bay while Muriel knelt at her boy's side. Hamelin's face was undamaged and he simply looked like a babe fast asleep.

Adam was with her, and he had a hand set upon her shoulder in much the way that a brother would. It was good, Roger thought, to see a priest who apparently believed in the vows of chastity. This man did not look the sort who, in other circumstances, might allow his hand to fall and fondle her thigh or buttocks. If anything, there was a hint of distaste in his face – but Muriel was not looking her best. Although she wore a clean dressing about her head, she appeared pale and unkempt. Today of all days she had taken no care with her looks, and no surprise. The poor woman was, as Roger had predicted, all but beside herself with grief.

Seeing Sir Jules, Aumery snivelled and grabbed hold of his mother's skirts, as though he expected the knight to whip him like a cur from his path. The knight was an intimidating figure, without doubt, and as a lad even Roger would have been alarmed by such a tall, stern-faced man marching up to him. In Aumery's case, the appearance of dread was increased by his silence. Tears ran down his face from his wide eyes, but he made no noise, as though so much pain had been piled on his shoulders that even death itself held little fear for him.

His mother looked up on feeling her son tug at her skirt, and followed his gaze. She stared at Sir Jules unblinking.

'Good woman, I have to ask you about your husband. Do you know who killed him?'

Roger flinched at the sound of his voice. Usually Sir Jules was nervous in front of a crowd, but here, in among the women and children, he sounded like the worst chivalric bully. It little mattered that he felt deeply for Muriel, that he hated being here, that he loathed having to intrude on her grief: he felt it was his duty to demand answers, and so he would ask his questions.

'You come here to hector me?' Muriel asked hoarsely. 'Leave me to my poor angel! He can't be dead! He may wake yet. Look at him – he looks well enough. Perhaps he's only sleeping.' There was a panicked tone to her voice, as though she knew already that all hope was vain, but still she refused to admit defeat.

'Your husband was not liked. Most men here hated him. Do you know which could have killed him?' the Coroner pressed on, his left fist clenched about his sword-hilt as though it was the only thing that kept him upright.

'I know of no one who could have done this to us.' Muriel began to weep. 'No one could want to widow me. What have I done to be punished like this? All my life I've tried to be good. I've struggled to be a worthy daughter, then wife, then mother, and now all is taken from me!'

'Woman, the Church will protect you,' Adam said soothingly, patting her shoulder while glowering malevolently towards Sir Jules.

'Protect me how? If there's no food, I'll starve, and so will Aumery. Poor boy!'

Roger saw how Aumery clutched his mother's tunic, his eyes still fixed upon Sir Jules. There was terror in his face, the terror of incomprehension, of confusion. His mother was in such a lunatic, frenzied state, his father was gone, and his brother dead too. All in a few short hours.

'Sir Jules,' Roger whispered. 'We can do no good here.'

'Can you think of no one, woman? No one who could have done this to your husband?' Sir Jules pressed relentlessly.

She sobbed into her forearms. 'I know no one! No one!'

Aumery didn't quite understand what was happening. Father was dead, like the hog last year. That had died too. But Aumery wasn't sure what death was. Father had simply stopped being Father. He lay there like Father, but with his face blood-encrusted, and without the movement that made him Father. No noise, no breath. It was odd, and only scary when he thought about it. Hamelin was the same, all flat and breathless like a little doll.

Somehow Aumery was sure that it was this tall, intimidating man asking questions that so upset Mother. He was nasty; he was scaring Mummy, just like Daddy used to scare Aumery. Remembering that, Aumery felt a little quiver in his tummy. It wasn't nice to remember that. Daddy had told him never to mention it again. He said not while he lived. But Daddy didn't live. Rebellious and half-fearful, Aumery steeled himself, and then he glanced at his father's corpse before muttering his daddy's words like a spell.

Sir Jules saw the movement as Adam's head snapped around. 'What was that?'

'Nothing. He's confused. What can you expect when the boy's treated in this way while his brother and father lie dead before him?' Adam said scathingly.

'What did he say? Boy, what was that?'

Aumery swallowed, but the eyes of the Coroner were strangely intense and he couldn't keep it in any longer.

'It was the castellan. The castellan. Because Father said, "If he learned that another man knew his wife, he'd kill the man",' Aumery said defiantly.

Muriel sobbed into her hands now. Sir Jules looked to her, and waited, and after a little while she looked up at him brokenly. 'It's true: Athelina saw them, Lady Anne and Gervase, in the meadow while the castellan was away. My husband believed Nicholas would kill anyone who spoke of it.'

'Christ Jesus!' Sir Jules breathed.

Alexander gingerly touched his throat. 'You could've killed me,' he croaked sulkily.

'And you could have caused the death of your master's son,' Iwan said easily. 'Better bruises than a hempen rope. It gives terrible skin-burn.'

'I had nothing to do with your brother's death,' Richer said wearily. 'I was suffering from a migraine when I left here. Yes, I realised that he had said something about my family, but he didn't actually say he had killed them. He was taunting me.'

'So you saw little need for revenge,' Iwan nodded.

'That's right.'

Iwan allowed his gaze to drift over the men who still stood about them. No weapons were visible, but the old smith wasn't sure that they wouldn't reappear as soon as his back was turned. 'I was there at the harvest the year Richer's family died,' he told them all. 'The older folks like me were making sure none of the children grew so drunk they'd hurt themselves. I was up there, and I saw Serlo coming to join the rest of us. It was him gave the alarm, told us all there was a fire. When he shouted, I looked back, and there were the flames. God's holy pain, I could see them. Terrible, red flames through the trees, some appearing above the trees. I saw them, and that means Serlo could have been there; he could have fired the place.'

'You knew that and didn't say anything?' Richer demanded harshly.

'Easy, boy!' Iwan said sharply. 'I saw Serlo had appeared late, I saw him call the alarm and I saw flames. I didn't see him with a burning brand in his hand, nor did I see him throw a torch through your window. Maybe he simply saw the flames and ran to fetch us to help quench them.'

'Serlo was no murderer,' Alexander said, sniffing, his head hanging.

'So apologise to this lad, for suggesting *he* was,' Iwan said curtly.

'I don't know he didn't.'

'You don't know he *did*!' Iwan stated.

Alexander averted his head like a man who had been slapped. For a while he could say nothing. Then he gave a short nod of acquiescence.

'That's good,' Iwan said. 'Sue? Bring ale to celebrate this peace! The castle will pay, I reckon.'

Warin saw the shrewd old eye fixing upon him and gave a grunt partly of approval, partly of admiration. 'I think my father would be happy indeed to pay.'

'Thank you, master. I'm sure he will,' Iwan said as he held up his large pot for Sue to refill.

'So who else could it have been?' Alexander demanded quietly as men laughed off their tension and washed away their anger in good ale.

Iwan glanced at him over the rim of his cup. 'I was at home all the night, and saw no one. But I heard one horse passing late last evening.'

Warin flushed. 'That was me. I had gone to Temple to speak with the priest.'

'Now why would that be, master?' Iwan asked softly.

'I don't have to answer your questions, old man.'

'No. But I just saved your lives and probably the manor from ruin.'

Warin chuckled dryly. 'Father John at Temple owes his position to my father. My father suggested that I should speak with him. That is all.'

'All? Perhaps,' Iwan nodded. 'What did you speak with him about?'

'Many things. Mostly about the vill and the people here.' Warin met his gaze steadily. He was not going to discuss his private conversations, not even with a reliable man such as Iwan appeared to be. 'What else? Was any other man abroad last night?'

'No one I saw,' Iwan said.

'There was one.' Sue was passing them, refilling their cups from a large jug, and overheard their talking. 'A man rode past here a little before dark. It was long before Serlo left here, though.'

'It may have been the murderer, if he was prepared to sit and wait for a while,' Warin guessed. He glanced at Richer. 'Did you see anyone leave the castle?'

'Only you. And later I too thought that I heard a horse,' Richer said. 'But I didn't look to see whose it was.'

'It *was* you killed my brother,' Alexander spat suddenly. 'You may have convinced these others you're innocent, but I know the truth!'

'Oh, for God's sake!' Richer said wearily. 'Of course I didn't. Why would I?'

'Maybe you thought he'd killed your woman?' Alexander curled his lip.

Warin shook his head. 'I think you need to consider another man, Alexander. My fellow is innocent. I'd stake my arms on it.'

'Then who . . .' Alexander felt his breath stick in his throat as a fresh thought came to him. If Serlo had upset Nicholas because of some harm or insult, real or imagined, it was possible that Nicholas could have killed Serlo, or ordered another man to do so. If Richer was innocent, that didn't say the master was too.

'The murderer of Athelina must have known her and her sons well,' Susan remarked.

'Why?' Warin asked.

'Someone got in there and killed the boys first. Otherwise, one boy or both would have gone in, seen their mother hanging, and raised the alarm. If he killed the boys first, he could take them together, knock them on the head, and no noise. When she arrived, they were hidden.'

'Perhaps. So what?' Richer said.

'They knew him. Why else would they let him inside without fear?'

Alexander slowly lifted his head until his eyes were on Susan, and then he felt the slow thrill of understanding as she spoke.

'It can only have been someone they knew really well. Their mother's lover, perhaps. Especially if he was also an important official – someone from the castle.'

Alexander released his breath with the relief of finding the explanation: yes, one man could have killed Serlo to punish him for the death of his son, Danny. The same man could have killed Athelina to stop her demanding money. And Alexander knew who had the greatest reputation for womanising, who was the only man who could have wanted Athelina dead as well as Serlo: Gervase, the man who was seen making love with Lady Anne.

Sir Jules marched from the church with a feeling of failure. He had his duty, and he intended to perform it. Here in this vill was a murderer – a mass murderer, no less – and he would have the man arrested and amerced as soon as he could. Yes, he knew his duty, but he wasn't sure how he might execute it.

Christ Jesus, but there were a lot of men at the castle! He stopped as the thought came back to him. It was like a small tide washing over him, submerging his best intentions in a miasma of fear. To go against a man who had so many men-at-arms to defend him was madness itself!

'Sir Jules, are you truly thinking of going up there and accusing Nicholas to his face?'

'Hmm? Well yes, I suppose so, Roger.'

The clerk squinted at the sun, which was swiftly sinking towards the far hills. 'Then may I take my leave of you here? I shall return to the church and demand sanctuary from the priest. Or perhaps I should walk to Temple. That might be safer. There is safety in distance, I believe.'

'What? You must come with me to record my conversation.'

'You think so? I don't. No, I think I should avoid contact with you while you are set on the course of self-destruction,' Roger said with equanimity.

Sir Jules's jaw dropped. 'You are my clerk,' he managed after some moments.

'That's no reason for you to expect me to commit suicide with you! Dear God in Heaven! If you go there, and you are right and this man *did* commit these murders, he will kill you himself in his own defence, so that his accuser is no more. If he were innocent, I would expect him to whip your head off in a trice for being so gullible as to believe him guilty! Or to demand that any one of the six or seven squires he has in the castle do so for him. Many of them would be loyal enough for that little task, I should think. They all seem to respect and like him.'

'He has been accused. I am the Coroner, and I must—'

'The accuser was a *child*, Coroner. A small one, at that. You don't have to follow up the uncorroborated word of a minor.'

'He spoke with great conviction. I have a son, I know how they behave. That child made a convincing witness.'

'Perhaps so, but that won't keep your head on your shoulders, will it?'

'It would be the right thing to do.'

'So would many duties that are routinely left undone,' the clerk commented imperturbably. 'That doesn't change the fact that you'd be running the risk of death if you were to go ahead.'

'What would you have me do? Forget the allegation? Leave here and declare I could find no guilty party? Or would you prefer me to find another suitable culprit and take money from Nicholas in order to guarantee his continued freedom and supposed innocence?' Sir Jules demanded witheringly.

'Good God, Sir Knight, when did you stop thinking? You have a good intelligence, I am sure. Use it! Return to your original intention. Now you have a suspect, make use of your powers as a Coroner. Hold your inquests and demand answers from all whom you make attend. That way we may yet win through to an answer.'

'And if we don't?'

'If we don't, we fine the whole vill and go on to find our next body. *That* is our duty,' Roger said tersely.

Chapter Twenty-Six

Nicholas and Gervase, unaware of the ropes that were gradually being woven about their individual throats, were sitting together. They had completed their work when Anne walked into the room, and at once both men shot to their feet.

His wife smiled at Nick and he felt the warm flood of adoration flow through his heart once again. A look from her could make him so happy. He truly felt blessed with good fortune to have married her.

His sole regret was that he would not be here to look after her for very much longer. The pains in his fingers and hips were growing more serious with every passing year, and his back could be agony on occasion, as were the wounds which he had won in a lifetime's service to his master. There was always the knowledge that he had outlived most of his friends and even some of their sons. He was old; he knew that.

Whereas she was a fragrant, lovely young woman, succulent as a ripening grape. Just to see her was to love her anew.

She walked in like a youthful princess, taking her seat at the bench nearest the hearth, holding out her hands to the flames. For the last few days she'd said that her hands and feet were feeling a little cold, and that her feet were swelling. It had worried him enough to speak to the vill's midwife, but she reckoned that Anne was fine. She had even said that Anne appeared to be a little further on than she'd have expected, and suggested that the conception had taken place earlier than Nicholas and she had said, but he had to laugh at that.

Earlier? How could that be, since the child was the celebration of his return. After the last wars, Nicholas had remained with Sir Henry in his host rather longer than he'd expected, and when he returned, Anne had demonstrated how greatly she had missed him. She took not a moment's delay in pulling him up to their chamber.

And it was a miracle that this time his seed had fulfilled its destiny. They had tried to produce a child so often over the last six years that he had all but given up hope, but now, God be praised, his wife was proof that patience would be rewarded. Soon she would give him the son he so greatly desired.

He rose from the table and went to pour himself a little wine. Richer was still special to him, the bastard born of the luscious woman he had desired in his youth, but that was different from the feelings he had for Anne. She had sought him out and adored him as much as he did her.

Raising his mazer, he turned to toast her, and it was then that he caught sight of the steward's face.

Gervase was staring at Anne with an expression of longing so plain, he reminded Nicholas of a hunting dog he had once known, penned near a bitch on heat. The sudden memory of that scene was so comical, he chuckled to himself.

'Your expression, you know what that reminded me of?' he said, and explained. In the moment after he finished, he saw his wife flush, then go pale, and he saw the sharp glance she threw at Gervase.

The man, he realised, as a fist clenched about his heart, whom he had always thought of as his friend.

Sir Jules looked greatly annoyed, Baldwin thought as he and Simon approached Roger and the Coroner at the grassy bank near the church.

'I am decided. I shall continue with my inquest as soon as I possibly can.'

Roger looked at Baldwin with an innocent expression that the knight found entirely unconvincing.

'What is the reason for your decision, Coroner?' he asked, and then his face lengthened as he heard the man's reply. As Sir Jules came to the end of his tale, Baldwin glanced at Simon. 'This is interesting, Coroner,' he said, and explained what Father John had told them after Jules had left. 'Perhaps this confirms what the priest said – that Gervase has had many women, including Athelina, then Julia, but that he's recently thrown her over. I've heard from others that he might have a new lover.'

'Which could be Lady Anne,' Roger murmured thoughtfully. 'She could have insisted that he leave any other women.'

'Which is fine,' Simon said, 'but the child said that the castellan was guilty. That makes no sense. If Nicholas heard evil rumours, he might kill the adulterous couple, but why slaughter the mere witnesses?'

'I only repeat the child's evidence,' Jules said haughtily.

'You seriously tell us that this child, this *infant*, was a credible witness?' Baldwin asked. 'Enough for you to insult a man of Nicholas's stature? I find that more than a little surprising.'

'You are attracted to an abstract problem, Sir Baldwin,' Jules said with some asperity. 'This, for me, is a prosaic matter. We have bodies: a man and a woman and three children. These are issues of record. I am not interested in justice, my duty is to record the facts so that when the Justices of gaol delivery arrive, they can assess the guilt or innocence of the men put before them by the jury. All the time I am bogged down with this matter, I am missing others. Better by far that I should move on to the next. Especially while a traitor to the King is wandering the country-side.'

'So you will blacken the good castellan's name in front of his lord's peasants so that you can run off and look at other matters?' Baldwin asked silkily. 'Not to mention causing untold problems at the castle. What if Nicholas has no idea of the adultery of his wife? What if she is not guilty of adultery and these rumours are nothing more than that?'

'You say that, when both those who witnessed the steward and the lady rutting in the meadow are now dead? Surely it is this secret which is being concealed at the cost of so much death.'

Baldwin rolled his eyes. 'God save me from logical Coroners! Good Christ in Heaven, man. Two people saw Lady Anne lying with Gervase; the two people have been murdered – therefore they were killed because Lady Anne lay with Gervase. It is the same as saying this moth has wings; birds have wings therefore this moth is a bird. It is not logical.'

'You may not think so, but I disagree. I think it makes good sense, so I shall call my inquest now and finish the job.'

Baldwin licked his lips. 'Please, give me a little more time before you take this action. It is too drastic. I require another day to find the truth.'

'A whole day? Keeper, it's impossible.'

Baldwin glanced at Simon. 'At least talk with me for a little while. We can discuss the actual amount of time we have. Please, let me buy you a cup of wine to talk it through?'

Sir Jules threw a harassed look at Roger, who nodded encouragingly. Then, 'Oh, very well, Sir Baldwin, but only one drink!'

When Nicholas suddenly strode from the room, Anne could see that something had upset him, and she had an unpleasant suspicion that he had read her look. She rose, sweeping away from Gervase, who had tried to engage her in conversation again, and rushed after her husband.

He had made his way to the solar, and had gone up to their bedchamber. He stood there now, head bowed, staring at their bed.

'My love?' she asked hesitantly.

'Was it here, in my own bed?' he asked in a broken voice, and she felt her heart die and shrivel.

'My love, I . . .'

'Don't lie to me! I saw your expression in the room down there. I should have guessed before, but you've always made yourself appear so loving that no hint of betrayal ever occurred to me. But I should have known. Why should a woman so young, so . . .' he choked on the word. 'So lovely! Why should you look at a grizzled old captain like me? Anne, I know it's Gervase's baby, not mine. Just tell me truthfully: did you pollute my bed as well as your body when you *whored* for him?'

'I did not.' She set her features into a steady, calm expression and sat on the edge of their tester bed. 'I couldn't. That would have been disloyal.'

'*Disloyal!* Madam, how much less loyal could you have managed? By St Peter's bones, are you mad, or just taunting me? Are you a mere common stale, ready for any tarse in the castle? Have you fucked the guards as well as Gervase? Why stop there? Perhaps you sought the ostlers too – or the scavengers?'

'Husband, please, listen to me,' she said with a break in her voice.

She could feel her breast squeezing tighter and tighter as he spoke, spittle flying from his lips, pacing up and down the small chamber. He might harm himself, and it would all be her fault. It *was* all her fault. 'Husband, please . . .'

'I am no husband to you, woman. You are a whore, and the sooner you leave here, the better.'

'Please, Nicholas, don't do this to me,' she whispered feebly. She felt weak, panicked and full of tension. Her very scalp seemed to tighten.

'Think what you have done to me! You have betrayed me, betrayed any love we had for each other. Christ Jesus! I should draw steel and end your life now!'

He put his hand to his sword-hilt, and she closed her eyes, waiting for the blow to fall, but then she heard his grunt of contempt. 'Open your eyes, whore! What do you want of me? More pain? You can wait for that. I shall have my revenge on you and him.'

'What of *my* revenge?' she whispered.

'Yours?' he sneered, and then his face hardened like rock. 'You mean he raped you?'

'I was betrayed by a man,' she said. 'He said he loved me, and then he left me for months, and I had no idea what had become of him. I loved him, but he was gone without a message to tell me he was alive. What was I to do?'

'Remain chaste and honourable. That was what you were supposed to do,' he grated.

'My father left me, Husband. He never came back. And when we heard that he was dead, my mother died too, and I was an orphan. I was thrown from my vill, because there was not enough food to fill even one useless mouth. All I could do was walk, and I was taken in by a man – to live the most demeaning life I could imagine. I swore, when I left that place, that I would rather die than return. And then,' she stood, walking to him slowly, 'I found a man who loved me as much as I loved him. I loved, adored, worshipped him, and when I thought he might be dead, it was as though my father had died again, and I was forced to imagine life without him. I began to have dreams of returning to that hell-hole, where any man could buy me. Can you imagine what that made me feel? A whore. Yes, I was a whore. My honour gone, my shame permanent. Do you condemn me for trying to escape that?'

'You should have waited for news.'

'There was no news. You sent no message in months!'

'You should have kept faith, woman! You should have trusted me, trusted our master!'

'I suppose he would have taken the time to write to a woman who was merely the wife of a captain in his host,' she said with a sneer in her voice.

'And then, when I came home, you dragged me to your bed as though to prove your desire for me, when all you intended was to hide the fatherhood of your baby!'

'No! I swear that's not true! Husband, please believe me when I say that I love you, and I was so delighted that you returned, I was overwhelmed. I had to take you to my bed immediately.'

'To the bed where you lay with him.'

'No. Believe me, I—'

'*I can't believe you!*' he shouted. 'All you say is false!'

'I still love you. Please, for my sake, for our child's sake . . .'

'Damn you, and damn it!' he blurted, and as she put out a hand to him, he first knocked it aside, and then clenched his fist and swung it at her belly.

'Masters? I have a message for Father Adam. Do you know where I can find him?'

Simon was squatting and throwing stones at a twig when the fellow arrived.

The newcomer was a young man, short and slight of frame, with a sunbrowned, oval face, and Simon did not recognise him. Roger didn't either apparently, for he looked enquiringly at the fellow. 'You aren't from round this vill, then?'

'No, I come from Temple. Father John sent me.'

'Ah. Well, Father Adam's up there in the church,' Roger said.

The two watched as the youth made his way up the bank to the porch of the church, and then entered.

'Did you learn anything from Nicholas at the castle?' Roger asked.

Simon shook his head. 'Only that he is the father of Richer, and I see no reason why he should claim paternity unless it is true.'

Roger nodded, but just then the messenger came back from the church. As he passed them, Roger could see Adam peering out at them from the vantage point of the church's porch, and the clerk had the impression that Adam wanted to talk to him. He asked Simon to wait a short while and walked to the open door.

'Is that Bailiff outside still, Brother?' Adam hissed from the shadows.

'Yes,' Roger said, and then he gasped as he saw the flash of a knife. He tried to leap back, stumbled on the step and fell, shouting, 'Murder! Murder! He's killing me!'

'Not soon enough, you devil!' Adam screamed, and rushed forward, the dagger gripped under his fist, ready to plunge it down into Roger's breast.

Roger saw the silver-blue steel racing towards him and raised both hands to block it. As luck would have it, his wrists crossed, and the knife fell between his hands, caught in the scissor-like grip. Roger bleated, shoving his fists up over his head as Adam fell onto him, pushing the knife higher, the point scratching over his right eyebrow, and then Roger gripped his assailant's wrist in both of his own and tried to wrest the knife from him. Adam responded by pounding Roger's face and neck with his free hand, Roger shrieking at the top of his voice all the while. And then the clerk was sure that he must have fainted, because all became quiet, and the weight of Adam's body grew lighter and lighter, as though Roger's soul was passing away. He closed his eyes when he seemed to see Adam's face receding into the darkness, and then he heard a chuckle and opened his eyes fully to see Simon standing over him studying Adam's knife.

'Don't worry, clerk. He's no threat to you now,' he said off-handedly as he shoved the knife into his own belt and stood over the body of the priest.

'Is he dead?' Roger managed, climbing to his feet.

'Nope. Not yet,' Simon answered. 'But I'd like to know why he sprang on you like that. Have you any idea?'

'None,' Roger said, his hand on his forehead at the scratch. If it had been an inch lower, it would have spiked his eyeball, he thought, and suddenly felt quite sick, leaning his back against the doorway.

'Well, as soon as he comes round, we'll ask him,' Simon said.

'Yes,' Roger said, and then, quite elegantly, he fainted and sank slowly to the floor, a ridiculous smile fitted to his blanched face.

John finished the service and put away the vestments and sacramental vessels in his little ambry, then locked the door over the hole in the wall.

He was filled with a sense of looming disaster. There was little he could do to avoid it, bearing in mind Warin's close questioning, but it was no help to be aware of the fact.

It had all started many years ago, when John's grandfather had been a close ally of Sir Henry's. The two men had been companions in the crusade of the last century, both going to the southern reaches of Christendom to fight the heretics known as Albigensians, and since then the two families had been close. John had known Sir Henry all his life, and counted him as a friend, although Sir Henry was much older. It was entirely due to Sir Henry that he had been granted this little post in the backwater that was Temple.

He had been given this position in early 1315 at the height of the famine. Yes, there had been hints of disputes even then, but the vitriol that later came to characterise the relationship between Earl Thomas of Lancaster and his cousin the King were less apparent in those famine years.

John remembered those times so clearly. Even to journey here had been difficult, with food for his pony rocketing in price as the rains fell. Harsh, terrible weather, it was.

And then life changed dramatically. Earl Thomas's arguments with the King had grown more acrimonious, and the Earl himself had been captured and executed, along with his followers and supporters – many of them John's friends. He felt sick again, just thinking of all those good men – comrades of his father, some of them. At least his father had himself died many years ago, at Bannockburn, when the Scottish made King Edward II turn and flee.

His father had been a loyal supporter of the Crown, but John's uncle had gradually changed his allegiance. It was all to do with the situation on the Marches. When the Despensers began to increase in power and wealth, taking any pieces of land they wanted, one man to suffer was his uncle, and he resented it. As a result, seeing his holdings reduced to a few small farms, he took up his weapons and went to support the Earl of Lancaster. And he fought in the last Battle of Boroughbridge, dying at the side of the Earl of Hereford. The poor man had been stabbed in the vitals by a man under the bridge. The fellow thrust upwards with a lance, and the point found the gap between the Earl's buttocks, entering his backside and tearing him apart. While he screamed, John's uncle went to him, and as he reached out to comfort the man, a bolt slammed into his breast. He was dead in moments.

Afterwards, John had waited, certain that the family's disloyalty must have been noted. Perhaps the King would order that he was one of those who must be punished for association. Many were. Or Sir Henry might realise that the man he had installed in this chapel was related to a traitor, and seek to have him removed to show his own devotion. Yet nothing had happened so far. Only that visit from Warin, and the subsequent veiled threat from the Coroner's man, Roger. Damn him!

Here in the wilds of Cornwall he had thought himself as safe as a man could be, far from the centre of power, whether it resided in

London or York or one of the many cities dotted about the English countryside, but even here there was no security. John was grown accustomed to searching the faces of all visitors, always alert to the wrong expression. There were too many travellers who might be spies sent by the King. Or by one of his enemies.

Warin had appeared to be safe enough at first. He reminded John of their fathers' friendship, chatted happily about their pasts, and only later did he spring on John the reason for his visit. He was here to investigate the allegiances of all the men in the vills hereabouts. He wanted to know, should his father Sir Henry seek an alliance with an enemy of the King, would his people obey him.

Whatever John said could be reported and used against him. If he said that he was a devoted supporter of the King, and Sir Henry sought to turn to Mortimer, John would be in danger, but if Warin's father was testing him, and intended remaining loyal to King Edward II, John could be branded a traitor. No, there was no safety. His only security lay in praying for Bishop Stapeldon's support, were he to be arrested. The good Bishop was absolutely committed to the King, so he could be a useful ally, but not if he felt John was himself turning to treachery.

He'd thought Warin was joking at first, but then he'd realised that the squire was too well briefed. He knew all about John's uncle, and that meant John was in danger, as was Adam, because Warin had hinted at suspicions about the priest at Cardinham too. Not for treachery, but for that other sin which even the Bishop couldn't condone. Ah, Christ, what could a man do, when all these forces were ranged against him?

There was *nothing* he could do during the morning, because there was no one whom he could send to warn Adam, but when the men started coming back from the fields for their lunch, he quickly scribbled a note, gave it to one of them and asked him to ensure that it only went to Adam's own hand.

Yes, he had sent the message to warn his neighbour of the risks which he ran. And in the meantime, John had time to sit and contemplate the dangers. Not of his allegiance becoming more commonly known – since that was already a problem, if Warin was telling the truth – no, it was the hideous fact of becoming embroiled in the nation's politics. That didn't bear thinking about. Shivering, John wrapped his arms about him and he entered the church to kneel and pray, staring at the cross all the while.

That was what Warin had said, that Sir Henry sought to turn his allegiance from the King. There was no Lancastrian power with authority enough now, but others would soon appear, especially if Roger Mortimer was executed, as was rumoured. Then others would be bound to come forward and Sir Henry wanted the vill's people readied for the coming wars. It was John's duty to prepare the way, Warin told him.

He had seen the country at war; he knew what war was like. When the Lords Marcher had laid waste a wide swathe of the country, winding up at London, their armies drinking and whoring the nights away, John had been on pilgrimage to Canterbury. He had seen armies at close range, and had witnessed the depredations. Men argued and slaughtered each other, or threatened others with death if they were stopped in their drunken, thieving progress. He had come across a poor family standing sobbing in a road, because a man-at-arms had ridden down their youngest son – not by accident, but for fun. He galloped off, laughing. John had done what he could, but the boy was dead long before he arrived, and he could only give consolation to the family, not save the lad's soul. He said prayers for the child, and continued on his way, a sad, more fearful man.

If war was to come here, to Temple, he knew the result. Bodies lying in the roads and fields; homes burning; women raped and slaughtered. In the fields, cattle killed for sport. Not even dogs or cats would escape. His little church would be razed to the ground, the ambry broken open and the church's most prized possessions taken.

This was what Warin and his father threatened to unleash upon the vill.

They must be *mad*!

Chapter Twenty-Seven

Nicholas couldn't do it. As his fist approached her belly, her sweet eyes closed, tears trembling on the lower lids, he gave a loud bellow of rage and frustration, and sent his fist slamming into the mattress beside her instead.

Spinning around, he made for the stairs. He couldn't hurt her, but he wouldn't stay and listen to her. She was a whore, just some bitch who would spread her legs for the first man who came along. He would have nothing to do with her.

'Do you want me to go?'

Her voice, teetering on the brink of despair, halted him. He stood at the top of the stairs, staring down like a man contemplating jumping from a cliff. 'I don't know what I want. I want revenge. Someone to pay.'

'I thought you were dead. I was terrified. I thought I must again become what you detest. I thought I had lost my home, my love, everything. I was desperate, Nick.'

'What do you mean, you thought I was dead?'

He turned, and now her floodgates opened. She sat outwardly composed, apart from the streams running down either cheek, and he felt his breast sear with sympathy. 'What can I do? All I wanted was to love you, but you have betrayed me.'

'Nick, I grew convinced that you were lost to me. Gervase and I . . . it was consolation I sought, nothing more.'

'And the reward is another man's brat!'

'It could have been yours,' she said.

'No.'

'You are very definite.'

'I . . .' His throat felt as though it was closing. 'I had a disease sixteen years ago. It was mumps. I can't father a child. The only child I will ever have is Richer. I had thought – hoped – that God had been generous, had given me a miracle. But it was just the foolish dreams of an old man. I am barren.'

Alexander sat silently as Warin and Richer chatted to Sue. Iwan stood again, sipping at his ale, and as he finished his cup and was about to leave them all, the door slammed open and two more knights walked in: Baldwin and Jules.

Knights! Honourable, chivalric men! They all made Alexander want to puke. These two in particular: one a Coroner, one a Keeper of the King's Peace, and neither could find out the real killer of his brother or Athelina. Gormless fools!

'Wine! A jug for us here,' Baldwin roared as he entered. 'Now, Sir Jules, I wish to delay the inquest until we have had time to speak to a few more people . . .' He caught sight of the group sitting at the farther wall. 'Good! We have been looking for you. Master Richer, Squire Warin, may we join you?'

'By all means,' the squire said easily, and pushed himself away from the table, his bench scraping loudly on the rush-strewn packed-earth floor. He stood as the two knights approached, and moved the table for them, Richer swiftly getting to his feet and helping. When Baldwin and Sir Jules were seated, Richer and Warin returned to their own seats.

'You are commendably courteous,' Baldwin said when they were seated.

Sue arrived with wine and a pot of ale for Alexander, who sat glowering darkly as the others spoke.

'I have been long in my master's service,' Warin said.

'He is Sir Henry?'

'Of Cardinham, yes. I am his son. I am here to look over the castle with a view to making it secure. When I am done, it may defy any siege.'

'I did not appreciate you were Sir Henry's son,' Sir Jules said. 'I'd thought you were a mere squire.'

'Thank you,' Warin said, but there was no amusement in his voice or on his face.

'Nicholas did not tell me you were his master's son,' Jules said in a rather sulky tone. 'I'd have thought he could have introduced us.'

'He was ordered to keep my position secret,' Warin said. 'I'm here to assess the security of this place without great fanfare.'

'So the people at the castle did not recognise you?' Baldwin asked.

'I was sent to Sir Reginald of Goddestoun's household to learn my duties when I was seven years old,' Warin said. 'That was long before most of the men came to my father's manor.'

'You arrived a little before Athelina's death,' Baldwin noted.

'Yes. It is very sad,' Warin said with a notable lack of feeling. Richer bowed his head.

'You do not sound particularly regretful,' Baldwin said.

'Should I? I regret the loss of so many of my father's villeins. Some are valued, such as Alexander's brother, Serlo. To lose a good miller is a matter of concern. It will be difficult to replace him in a hurry, and we have grain to be milled.'

'I miss him because he was my brother,' Alexander burst out.

Iwan sniffed loudly, hawked and spat. 'Not everyone knew him so well as you, Alex.'

'Not many wanted to!'

'What sort of man was he?' Baldwin asked.

'A strong, powerful fellow. He had the muscles of a Goliath . . .'

'And the brain of a midge,' Iwan added.

Alexander stared at him. 'You insult the dead?'

'Alex, I insulted him alive – why change my habits?' Iwan asked.

'We've heard that he might have had enemies, Alexander. Can you think of any who would be bold enough to kill him?' Baldwin asked.

'Only one,' Alexander said.

'Speak!'

It was a relief. At last he could unburden himself of the story he had just worked out. 'The way he died. It's unnatural, to murder and then shove his head into a mill. I think that was a message. It was the killer showing that he killed justifiably, not murdering. This was retaliation.'

'For what?'

'Killing the apprentice.'

'We know all about that,' Sir Jules said. 'The apprentice slipped and fell into the machine.'

'But rumours persisted that the boy might have been pushed,' Alexander said.

'Why would Serlo do that to the lad?' Baldwin asked, adding sarcastically, 'To save the cost of a meal?'

It was Iwan who responded. 'No, Sir Knight, it was to get back at the man he thought was making his life difficult: the man whose taxes were striking so deeply into his pocket.'

Baldwin was interested now. 'Who do you mean?'

Iwan sighed. 'You asked me about the father of the lad. Well, perhaps you should be told. I can say so while Warin is here, because 'tis something his father should know. The dead apprentice? Most reckon he was son to Gervase, the castle's steward. Gervase's been here a long while, and he's had his fun with many of the women, so 'tis said.'

'Baldwin, did you hear that?' Sir Jules said. 'It was Gervase's boy, this apprentice Dan. Surely that means that Gervase had reason to want to see the instigator of his son's death die in just such a painful manner – and not only that, he also had good reason to want to punish Serlo for his behaviour in taking tolls. This *was* simply a means of getting revenge, after all.'

'Perhaps,' Baldwin mused, staring keenly at Iwan. 'But why did you not tell us this earlier when we asked you? All you said then was that the boy was the son of a rich man. Is Gervase rich?'

It was Warin who responded. 'Wealthy enough, Sir Knight. He controls much of the business of the manor, and that makes him rich beyond the wildest dreams of many villagers in Cornwall. He sleeps on a mattress on a bed each night, he has a fresh tunic and shirts and robe each year from my father. Yes, I'd say he was very well off.'

'What would you say, Iwan?' Baldwin pressed. His eyes hadn't left the smith's wrinkled face. The old man stared back at him without apparent fear, but there was something in those eyes, some wariness, like a dog who sees a haunch of fresh meat held out, but wonders whether there's a stick concealed nearby to thrash it, should it approach too close.

'I'd say that the father of that boy is responsible for Serlo's death.'

'It's obvious!' Alexander burst out. 'Look, my brother is dead, and Iwan's just confirmed who the killer must have been! Let's go and—'

'No!' Baldwin said, and although his voice wasn't raised, it cut Alexander short like a whip. 'There will be no more deaths here which are not sanctioned by the law. If a man is to be accused, he'll stand before you and declare his guilt or innocence, and he'll have his opportunity to call witnesses for his defence, just as you'll have a chance to call your own for the prosecution.'

Baldwin spoke firmly, but he tried to show compassion. It was no surprise that Alexander wanted his brother avenged: the two had been inseparable and now that his younger brother, the brother whom he had always sought to protect, was dead,

Alexander's life, Baldwin thought, was all but over. He couldn't keep still. Even as Baldwin watched, his fingers were twitching, as though they had minds of their own and wanted to grasp Gervase's throat and squeeze tightly. The man was twisted like a cable under tension, by his desire to see revenge wrought on his brother's killer.

'Come,' Baldwin added more gently. 'Better by far that we find the man responsible and make him pay the full penalty. You don't want the killer to escape, do you?'

'I want his head for what he did to Serlo.'

'We understand that,' Sir Jules said. 'We'll see to it.'

'I want to see him punished! If you don't take him now, he might escape! What then? The Hue and Cry rarely fetches back a man who escapes into Devon or beyond. What would you do, leave him to run free?'

Baldwin spoke firmly again. 'Alexander, trust us. We shall find your brother's killer and bring him to justice.'

'Justice? Whose justice will that be? Give him to me and let me shove *his* head into the machinery until *his* eyes pop. That would be *justice*! But you won't let me, will you? My kid brother is going to go unavenged. He's only a villein, isn't he? Not a rich servant to a knight,' Alexander sneered, and he stood and lurched from the room, more than a little drunk, and very peevish.

'I can understand his feelings,' Warin said. 'I have a younger brother. If someone were to harm him, I would let nothing stand in *my* way. I would personally punish the man and ensure that he felt that his end lasted a lifetime.'

'But that is not what will happen here while the good Coroner and I are investigating the murder,' Baldwin said with acid in his tone.

He was about to say more when Roger entered, panting slightly, his face flushed from the exertion of running. 'Coroner, I think you should come.'

Pausing, he took in the faces staring at him expectantly, and felt a small surge of pride to be the centre of attention for once. 'Master,' he continued with a certain hauteur, 'the priest has just tried to murder me.'

Gervase had left the room shortly after Anne, and he went down to the orchard which he knew she loved so much.

It had been changed so much by her presence. It was like the rest of the castle. Before she arrived, it had been a rough, uncultured place, just like any other outpost far from civilisation, but when Anne came and ensnared their hearts, she had an impact far beyond anything she could have imagined.

Gervase couldn't have imagined it either. He could not have conceived losing his best friend so swiftly.

Six years ago, before he laid his heart at her feet, Nicholas wouldn't have dreamed of putting a woman before his comrades. He was a man's man – hearty, rugged, but honourable. The kind of good companion whom others would follow into battle joyously.

Gervase didn't know what he could do now. Clearly he couldn't stay here. He had hoped that Anne would leave with him. Yes, it was a forlorn hope, but he'd imagined that he could persuade her. However, that look of near-loathing on her face as she rushed off after her husband, proved that he had not won her heart. No, she only wanted her man. Nicholas was hers; Gervase was merely an interlude. Or, as she had sneered, he was a source of protection in case Nicholas never returned. The hard bitch! Gervase had honestly believed that she loved him. Shit, he'd been prepared to give up everything for her.

Well, there was no point weeping over it. She was not Gervase's any more, and never would be. And a secret like theirs would be bound to come out, which would be . . . painful. Gervase had no doubts that Nick would seek to take his revenge.

He couldn't punish someone miles away, though. No, and if Gervase left the manor, he wouldn't have to endure the sight of Nick fondling and kissing the woman they both loved. It would be better that way.

Gervase sniffed and wiped at his eye. This was not how he had expected things to go. No, he'd thought that life was going to resume its even tenor. But now his life was altered for ever. He had certainly burned all his bridges. No Athelina now, no Julia, and certainly no Anne. His women tended not to last long, but he regretted the lack of a woman now. A woman who could soothe his anger and hurt.

Damn her! Her and him! Why hadn't Nick been killed in the war, like so many others? Then she'd have decided to love Gervase, and the two of them could have been happy. She was bound to love him, had she got to know him better. It was pure misfortune that Nick had won her.

Jealous, bitter and angry, Gervase walked slowly from the orchard to the stables, and called to the nearest hand.

Simon dragged the priest from his church as soon as Roger had gone to seek Baldwin and Coroner Jules, lifting Adam by his belt and depositing him in the yard. He used the priest's belt to bind him to a small sapling, and then sat back to watch his charge, chewing a blade of grass.

'Simon, are you all right?'

He looked up into Baldwin's dark, anxious eyes. 'Of course I am,' he said testily. 'Did you think that streak of piss could hurt me? Now, did you bring a skin of wine like I said?'

Baldwin smiled to himself as he passed over the skin. Made from a kid's entire skin, it had a leather strap sewn to it, which ran from one foreleg to the opposing hindleg. Clearly the possession of the lady of the tavern, Simon looked at it with a dubious eye. It was rather too new, in his opinion, and a skin that fresh would surely colour the wine's flavour.

He was right. The wine was harsh and strong, but there was a gamey tang to it from the poorly cured skin. Still, he reflected as he opened his mouth and poured in a decent amount, the flavour would probably grow on him.

'So this is the fool?' Sir Jules said, glaring at the unconscious priest. 'He dared attack my clerk?'

'Yes,' Roger said. 'Yet I have absolutely no idea why he should suddenly take it into his head to do so.'

'We shall ask him presently,' Baldwin said. 'Richer – is there a spring nearby, or a brook?'

Richer smiled in response and set off towards the mill. The stream was only a short way beyond Alexander's house, and he banged on Alexander's door as he passed.

'Letitia, I need some water. May I borrow a jug or bucket?'

'Um . . . yes, I suppose so,' she said, distractedly.

Over her shoulder he could see her husband sitting on a stool beside the dead fire, his hands covering his face. Two men from the vill stood at his side and stared back at Richer coldly.

'They refused,' Letitia said.

'Refused what?'

'Refused to storm the castle and pull out the steward for killing Serlo. None of the vill wants to offend your master.'

Glancing at her, Richer nodded understandingly, and gratefully took the proffered bucket. 'Thank you.'

'Just go!'

Later, as he walked past with the freshly filled bucket, he could hear laughing, as though a madman was shrieking with delight – or perhaps more like a demon laughing at the death and destruction all about Richer. That reflection made him hurry his steps towards the men around the priest.

* * *

Adam woke to the sting of freezing water, the annoying torrent running down his back, the swirl of moisture in his eyes. Trying to wipe it away, he realised his hands were bound, and he gave a whimper of fear.

His head hurt appallingly. If someone had possessed a poleaxe at that moment, Adam would have welcomed their use of it on him.

'So then, priest. What would make you decide to launch an unprovoked attack on my clerk?'

The whole scene reappeared gradually before his closed eyes. That messenger, telling him in hushed tones that he had a missive from John, and the feeling of delight mingled with trepidation with which he took the note from his love. Written notes were rare from John, ever since that afternoon when Adam had declared his love for him.

That afternoon would be printed on his memory for ever. They had been down at the river not far from the mill, searching for fish, but neither had anything to show for it. Then Adam had stumbled and tipped headlong into the slow-moving waters. Gasping and blowing, he came back upright, overwhelmed with delight. It was mad, but what a glorious madness! He'd thrown his hands over his scalp, wiped the water from eyes and ears, and then put his head back and roared his pleasure to the world!

'You, dear friend, are mad!' John had said from the bank, but he was smiling.

That smile! So calm, but bright with contentment. If he could have kept one picture in his mind for all time and gone blind, it would be that one: John at the side of the river, the sun glinting off the waters, the trees dappled with golden light, and that wonderful, life-enhancing smile on John's face.

It was then that Adam realised he adored his friend. More, he loved him – and not in a kindly manner, such as men usually would, but totally, unswervingly, with his whole heart. He loved John as another might love a woman.

John helped him from the river, and aided him in removing his clothing, shaking his head and murmuring his irritation, but all the time with that amused smile. And when he was tousling Adam's head to dry his hair with his tunic, Adam impulsively took hold of John's face and kissed him on the forehead, nose, and then the mouth.

That was the end of the idyll. John stiffened and pulled away. Nothing was said – there was nothing *to* say – but from that moment, their relationship altered. John kept away. A double punishment for Adam, who at a stroke lost his love and his friend.

He had chosen to keep his secret and protect John. It might be unrequited, but Adam's love for John was the most passionate affair of his life. Others might mock or ridicule him, but he didn't care. He was in love, and that was enough. Like a squire serving a lady who was impossibly out of his reach, so Adam paid compliments to John, no matter how often John rebuffed him. It didn't matter. Adam's only fear was that the rural dean might learn of his infatuation and remove him from this place, so that he could never again be near his love . . .

He tore the seal from the scrap of paper and eagerly read the hurried writing inside. Then, and only then, did his smile fade.

'Are you all right, Father?'

The messenger's voice had brought him to himself, and he'd given the lad a coin, sending him off with his thanks.

Then, outside, he saw the agent of his lover's destruction, and knew what he must do.

The man was only a clerk, when all was said and done. There was no possibility of Adam's overwhelming the Bailiff as well as Roger, but he fancied he was able to kill at least that one, provided he could get him on his own. Adam tried to recall what happened next. He had beckoned Roger, that was right, and Roger told the

Bailiff to wait. The clerk stepped in through the porch, and immediately Adam leaped on him. But his blade went wide, and after a few moments of struggling, all went black. It was peculiar, like falling into a well.

'Why am I bound like this?' he asked pathetically.

'Why did you try to stab this clerk?' Baldwin asked.

'I only . . . I don't know.'

'Really?' Baldwin said. 'Then we had best read out the note here, hadn't we?'

Eyes snapping wide, Adam stared at them. 'No, that's a secret note!'

'I am impressed that you can read,' Roger said scornfully. His head hurt like hell. 'Most shit-covered arse-for-brains like you can't scrawl your own names, let alone another man's.'

Adam was stung to defence. 'I was well taught; better than most fools whose only task is to record where wounds may lie on a body!'

'What does the note say?' Baldwin asked.

'So *you* can't read it?' Adam sneered. 'I won't tell you.'

'Was it from Father John?' Baldwin asked mildly. 'There is surely no one else with whom you communicate up there.'

'Just do your worst and be damned!' Adam snapped. They had the evidence in their hands of his offences. It was known by that little bastard clerk, and he must have told all the others.

'What made you attack me, though?' Roger asked plaintively. 'I still don't know why you jumped upon me!'

Baldwin had spread out the small fragment of paper. It was much creased and wrinkled, because Adam had balled it in his fist before throwing it to the ground, and it bore the stains and marks of many hands, especially the villein who had brought it.

'This says *Beware the clerk to the Coroner,*' Baldwin read out slowly. '*He knows about my uncle, and you and me.* What does that mean?'

'I won't say anything. You can do what you want to me, I'll not speak!'

'Then you'll be held in the castle until you see sense or the Bishop comes to collect you, Adam,' Baldwin said, glancing at the Coroner, who nodded.

It was baffling, though. Baldwin detested unexplained events of this nature, and he eyed the clerk with consternation, wondering if he was mad. Yet although the fellow's eyes were wild, he was sure that the way that the man held his gaze without shame was a proof of pride, and when he sat back, it was as though he was dismissing the company from him. He looked like a swain defending his woman's honour.

Warin was staring at the priest with a disapproving expression on his face, but without condemnation. 'I think I know what the note means. I should welcome an opportunity to speak with Adam alone.'

'You can do so when we have returned to the castle, then,' Sir Jules said. 'For my part, I should welcome a rest in front of a fire with a good pitcher of wine in my fist. This matter is finally resolving itself. Sir Baldwin, it's late today, but I shall hold my inquest tomorrow. Perhaps then I can return to Bodmin,' he added hopefully.

However, that hope was soon dashed. As they walked towards the castle, Ivo met them near Father Adam's house. 'Sir Baldwin?'

'What?' he grunted tiredly.

'I thought you ought to know that the steward has taken a horse and fled the place.'

Chapter Twenty-Eight

There was no doubt of the rage felt by Nicholas when he learned that Gervase had fled. His escape from what Nicholas saw as justice was humiliating. It was only after he had spoken to his wife at some length that he had tried to find the man, but by then there was little to be done. Gervase could be many leagues away.

'I'll find him,' Nicholas swore.

'I hope so,' Coroner Jules responded. 'You must raise the Hue and Cry after him. He is a suspect in these murders, after all.'

It was Baldwin who urged a little more calmness, saying they should wait until the following morning before attempting to follow him. 'He is not a practised horseman, and he will not travel far at night in any case. Better to save ourselves the risk of more broken bones by following him now, when we may take entirely the wrong path. Let us rest well tonight in a warm hall, and chase after him tomorrow, when he'll have spent a miserable, cold night on the ground, or better, have had no sleep at all.'

'I prefer to follow him now,' Nicholas said.

Warin glanced at Baldwin, and nodded. It was his agreement which carried the rest of the men, and all were commanded to be ready at first light. In the meantime Nicholas ordered their meals to be readied so that all would sleep well.

While he marched away to the kitchens, Warin smiled at Baldwin enigmatically.

'Sir Baldwin, would you speak with me?' Warin said in a low voice. 'I would like to consult you on a grave matter.'

They had eaten well, and the hall was growing quieter as men nodded drowsily, basking in the comfortable warmth that only hard work followed by a fire and filled belly can induce.

Beside him, Simon was already asleep, his head resting against the wall, arms crossed over his breast, mouth slack and drooping, making him look rather like a bewildered mastiff. Baldwin himself had not been able to relax. The thought of the murders was preying upon his mind, and he was concerned that the following day's inquest could well lead to bloodshed. Alexander's hatred of the men of the castle who might have caused his brother's death made him fear the worst. 'Please do so,' he said as the two left the hall and stood on the small platform at the top of the stairs.

In the open air, Warin seemed to take some time to collect his thoughts. Then he gave the knight a long, serious stare. 'Sir Baldwin, war is again going to rend our country. You have heard of Mortimer's escape?'

'Yes. The whole land is discussing it, either more or less openly,' Baldwin said suspiciously.

'A prudent lord will always listen to his people and see what they believe, where their loyalties lie. You would agree?'

'A prudent lord will ensure that his people are fully aware of his loyalty to the Crown above all else,' Baldwin said firmly.

His hackles were rising – or maybe it was alarm that stimulated the hairs at the back of his neck. He had a hatred of politics and politicians: he doubted their words, their honour and their integrity, and his purpose was to avoid becoming embroiled in political issues. It could lead to advancement and wealth, but more often it resulted in a swift descent and painful death. He had seen that during the destruction of the Templars, and again when Piers Gaveston, Earl Thomas of Lancaster, and others were executed. Recently the victims had been the Despensers, but now the tables had turned, and the King's enemies were the very men who had forced him to exile Hugh Despenser and his father. At such a time the only sensible course was discretion. No man could be blamed for loyalty to his liege-lord.

'I can't disagree with that,' Warin said. He was quiet for a short while, then, 'Sir Baldwin, I consider you a man of integrity so I shall explain. I have told you that the lord of this manor, my father, Sir Henry, is concerned about the loyalty of his folk. Where he lives at his other manor, in Kent, the people are very antagonistic to our King. There are tales of miracles at the grave of Earl Thomas of Lancaster – had you heard? – and these are giving rise to a feeling that he was wrongly executed. Rebellion is openly discussed in London.

'My lord is of course devoted to King Edward, but the people are less so. In London there have been many mutterings since 1321, when the King imposed his judicial enquiry. The City is angry because he curtailed their powers. Sir Henry is prudent: he can see troubles, he can hear murmurings of disquiet, and seeks to make sure that he is as well-informed as possible.'

Baldwin said nothing. A man might be determined to be well-advised either to make sure that he could properly support his master, or in order to know when to jump to *another*.

'That is why I am here,' Warin said. 'It is also why I went to speak to John at the Temple church, because John is related to Sir Henry's oldest friend. I sought to learn how the people are feeling down here.'

'This is very interesting, friend Warin, but . . .'

'I'm coming to the point. While I was here, I heard it suggested that John and Father Adam were close – very close. People have suggested that Adam might play the catamite to John. When I mentioned this, John was very alarmed. I need hardly say that he strenuously denied the accusation.'

'This is not necessarily of any interest to any man but them,' Baldwin said.

'I agree. I mention it only to show that the two are very close, as was proved by Adam's behaviour today.'

'What of it?'

'Only this: some seek to foment unrest against our King. John's family has always been loyal to the King, but his uncle died for Thomas of Lancaster at Boroughbridge.'

'I know. Roger, the Coroner's clerk, mentioned it.'

'Then you'll understand that if John's relationship to his uncle came to be bruited abroad, it could be embarrassing. A rebel in my father's manor would be sure to come to the ears of the King, which is why I ask that you keep this concealed.'

'You would have me hide a traitor?' Baldwin rumbled, alarmed. 'I will not! I am a loyal servant to the King. I shall have no part in concealing this man's crimes.'

'He has done nothing. What is his crime?' Warin asked reasonably, his hands held out palms uppermost. 'He is related to a rebel, that is all. He's not seeking to overrule the King.'

'I am not sure,' Baldwin said. This was a difficult matter. He needed to consider it carefully, and yet . . . It was awful to think of John being imprisoned, probably for many years until he was a mere broken shell, and all because of an act by his uncle which may well not have been condoned by him. It stank of the persecution of his Order, and he couldn't condone putting another innocent through such trials.

Warin saw his wavering. 'I went to see John and I mentioned that I knew his uncle. Perhaps I unwittingly upset him, and that's why he wrote to Adam warning him of me.'

'He didn't. He warned Adam about the Coroner's clerk. Because his secret support for Lancaster was out, he realised that other secrets might be unleashed too.'

'What Adam told me was, the note warned him to escape but when he saw the clerk, he was overcome with hatred. This clerk threatened the man he adored. In a sudden frenzy he decided to kill Roger, giving his friend John time to escape. He was offering himself up as a sacrifice to protect his . . . well, his lover.'

Baldwin shook his head. 'The damned fool! He'll be in a cell for years to come.'

Warin stared up at a wandering man-at-arms on the wall who was glancing down at them with interest. The whole castle was by now aware that the man who had lived among them was in fact the heir of the manor and this castle. More than one man-at-arms had blenched at the news, remembering some slight given in the confident knowledge that they were safe. The man on the walls was in no danger, though. He'd made no insulting comments that Warin could remember. And he would have remembered, had the fellow done so.

He said, 'In truth, Adam seems a good enough priest to me. I've heard nothing against him, apart from this foolishness with John from Temple. That being so, I was wondering whether there might be some means of protecting him from the full force of ecclesiastical law.'

'How could we do that?'

'We could persuade Roger that it was a genuine mistake.' Warin grinned. 'We could say that the attack was caused by a sudden brain fever, and that after a chance to cool off, Adam is better.'

'You would be well served to think of a better excuse, and a less lame story that would be acceptable to Roger,' Baldwin said unenthusiastically.

'I am sure we can think one up,' Warin said.

'Why would you do this for him?'

Warin smiled, his teeth gleaming in the dusky light. 'Sir Baldwin, this manor is my inheritance. Adam is younger than me; he'll likely outlive me. All the time I own this manor, I shall have a reliable spy. What would such a spy be worth, would you say, when the country is disturbed? The same holds true for John.

Both can keep me informed of malcontents before trouble has time to brew.'

'It may not be disturbed for long.'

'Aye, and the pigs in the sty may sprout wings!' Warin declared dryly. 'Mortimer has flown. There are men who would support him against the King's friends. Wouldn't you?'

'Why do you ask me to help you?' Baldwin asked, ignoring such a dangerous question.

'An ally would be useful, especially if I have to try to persuade the Coroner's clerk to withhold his charges.'

'And why should you expect me to help you?'

'You are keen to resolve the murders here, aren't you? Well, if you will help me, I can throw a sacrifice to you. I have heard that Gervase may have been out of the castle on the night that Athelina died. He was out last night when Serlo died, too.'

'So you are convinced he is guilty?' Baldwin asked.

'Who else? The man has fled. That at least is how the Coroner thinks – and apparently Nicholas too.' Warin chuckled, and then he grew serious. 'Gervase is disloyal. I detest men whom I cannot trust, and I do not trust him. From what I have seen and heard, he is a man whose brain is led solely by his tarse.'

At last, Baldwin thought, I am getting to the meat of this matter. He feigned disinterest. 'That scarcely sounds like justification for my aiding you to persuade Roger to forget Adam's attack on him.'

'You would help me do that? In that case, you shall have the facts: Athelina's boys were not Gervase's, but she *was* his lover after she became a widow. Adam's maid? The child is Gervase's. No matter where you look about the place, you see his colouring, his eyes, his mouth on the local children. He's taken advantage of his position too freely.'

'You said you could not trust him because of his disloyalty?'

Warin bared his teeth. 'Nicholas, the castellan here, had a row with his wife earlier. Their words were overheard. She was put in pup by Gervase. Nicholas is barren.'

Baldwin scoffed. 'He told me himself that he was Richer's father.'

'So he is, but then, some years after Richer's birth, he was very ill with a fever. You know the one: swollen cods, the lot.'

'Christ Jesus, the mumps?'

'Yes. And since then he's fathered no children. That's one element of the proof. The other is, think how Gervase behaved when Lady Anne entered a room. His eyes never left her – more truly, they never left her belly. And she detests him now, from all I've seen. Perhaps because his seed has risked her marriage and life.'

'You say that this means Gervase is the murderer?' Baldwin said. 'But that supposes he killed his lover, Athelina, and her boys. Are you *sure* neither was his?'

Warin smiled at him easily. 'Quite sure, but I don't accuse Gervase of these murders, Sir Baldwin! I accuse Nicholas.'

That, Baldwin felt, was the grossest irony. To have to watch your woman bloom and blossom into motherhood, and know that the child was not your own. Nicholas must surely be within his rights if he wished to kill the steward for this cruel treachery.

He remained in the bailey contemplating all he had learned for some while after Warin left him. The man on the wall found him of little interest now his master was gone, and returned to staring idly over the land about the castle.

Clouds raced by, although there appeared little wind in the bailey itself. Baldwin stared up at them, catching glimpses of stars every now and again, and wondering what to make of all the hints he had heard.

'You all right, Baldwin?'

'Simon! I thought you were asleep. There seemed little point in waking you.'

The Bailiff sniffed. 'So you could speak to Warin alone, you mean?'

'You saw us?' Baldwin grinned.

'I woke when he came back just now. So what's it all about? Why did he want to talk to you?'

Baldwin sighed and gazed up at the stars. 'I don't know whether to believe him or not. He's thrown us a dainty tidbit: Nicholas. Gervase is a womaniser and untrustworthy, as we know, but Warin alleges . . .' Baldwin hesitated. He disliked slandering a woman, but if she had taken part in an adulterous liaison, she had only herself to blame. 'He said Lady Anne bears not Nicholas's son, but Gervase's.'

Simon stared. 'Well, swyve me with a blunt bargepole! Are you sure? I mean, do you believe him?'

'He may be right. He's an astute fellow.'

Simon considered. 'It's not unknown, is it? I can think of a few widows who've gone for their steward as soon as the old man pops his clogs.'

'No, it is not unknown,' Baldwin said. 'But usually the woman has the decency to wait until her husband has died.'

'Is it so rare?'

The soft voice sounded almost sad, and as Simon turned to greet Lady Anne, any embarrassment he might feel at being discovered discussing her adultery was wiped away by his fascination with her.

Although Simon preferred his wife, Meg, to any woman he had ever met – and if were to state his preferences, he would choose a blue-eyed blonde like her – this Anne, with her blue-black hair, oval face and slanting green eyes, was a sorely beautiful temptress.

Drifting nearer on feet which were still light, for all that her belly was enormous and her back bent to balance her, she said quietly, 'Yes, I heard you both.'

'Did Squire Warin send you to me?' Baldwin asked.

'Yes. He said you'd want to speak to me, and I agreed. If not, he said he'd tell Nicholas to command me to come here.'

'Better now than at the inquest,' Baldwin said harshly.

'If I tell you all I can, would you swear to save me such a public humiliation?' she asked shyly.

'My lady, I would save you any embarrassment I can,' Baldwin said, but his tone was brittle, and he continued, 'but I cannot do so if there is any risk to an innocent, no matter how lowly. If by withholding anything tomorrow, I put the wrong man's neck in the noose, I shall speak.'

She paled as he spoke, and her hand went to her breast, then down to her belly. 'I suppose that is reasonable. But there is nothing I know which could put a man's life at risk. I can't believe that.'

'Tell us all you know, and we can judge it for you.'

She led them to a small stone seat near the gate, from where they could see the entire bailey. Sitting, she surveyed the whole of the area as though distrusting the very ground to hear her words.

'It is difficult to speak of this,' she said, putting her face in her hands. When she took them away, there were streaks down both cheeks. It made Simon feel guilty, but he knew that a small detail from one life could sometimes explain the most confusing murders.

'I was born near Fowey. During the famine I was orphaned, and must find a new home. My father died in Exeter, I believe, on his way to the Scottish wars. I was forced into a common house – a brothel. I remained there some weeks, but food was scarce, and so were customers, so I was told to go. I resolved to see my father's grave.

'On the way, I met with a group of travellers, one of whom was a friar, who tried to rape me. It was only the arrival of another man which saved me, and when we came here, I realised I was secure at last when I saw that I had won the heart of my husband.

'Nicholas is a good, kind man. I love him. He saved me from the rapist, he gave me his name, his honour, and he treated me like a lady. He thought me beautiful.'

She looked up then and met Baldwin's stern face unflinchingly. Simon immediately felt a tingle run up his spine. This was the practised acting of a woman who knew that her looks could win over any man. She was not to be believed, he thought, but surely Baldwin would be moved by her beauty. Baldwin was always easily swayed by a dark-haired woman.

Simon opened his mouth, but before he could speak, Baldwin said, 'Come, Lady Anne, you do not expect me to respond when you test your skills as a flirt. Tell your story and give us less of this coquetry.'

Her face hardened. 'Very well. I see that chivalry plays little part in your life, Sir Baldwin. Yet the point remains he thought me beautiful. He wanted me, and he persuaded me to give him my hand and my heart. He hoped that his love for me would produce an heir for him, and so did I. I was grateful to him, because he had saved me from that friar. I was glad to take his hand when he offered it to me, and I am pleased to give him an heir.'

'Except this heir is a cuckoo,' Simon said.

'You could say so.'

'He knows you carry another man's child, yet will allow that man to remain here?' Simon burst out in horror. 'Sweet Christ, I couldn't support my wife knowing she carried another man's bastard or—'

'This wasn't meant to happen!' she protested. 'I was desperate! Nicholas was away with the King's host, and I didn't know whether he was alive or dead. I thought he must be dead, because else why was there no message? I needed comfort!'

Dimly Baldwin comprehended. 'You thought he had deserted you, or died?'

'The only other man I have ever loved was my father,' she said with an air of pride, and then her voice grew cold and harsh. 'And he died and I never saw him again. I thought the same thing had happened, that I was again alone. I wanted him back, but if he was dead – and I had heard nothing for months, remember – then what was to become of me? This castle wasn't his, it was Sir Henry's, so I might lose position, wealth, my home, all in one swoop, if I was widowed. All I did was seek the protection of another man. What else was there for me? The brothel again?'

Simon looked away. It reminded him of his thoughts about Meg, were he to die. His reflections were not pleasant.

'What did you do last night?' Baldwin asked after a moment.

The change of topic startled her. 'Last night? I was here at the castle, of course.'

'Was your husband with you?'

'He slept with me.'

'Before that he was in his hall?'

'Why, yes. Except he went out for a while on his horse.'

'Do you know where he went?'

'He often rides for exercise. What of it?'

'He could have been in the vill; he could have murdered Serlo,' Baldwin said. 'What of Gervase?'

'I do not know.'

'And now he is a fugitive.'

'I know!' she sobbed suddenly. 'It's my fault! He wanted me to go with him, to find a new life – but how could I leave my husband?'

'You have lost your protection, Lady. If you depended upon Gervase, you erred.'

'I cannot believe he killed anyone. He's too gentle.'

'Athelina was Gervase's woman. It is possible that Gervase grew convinced that Serlo had murdered her and her sons; that enraged him, and he exacted retribution.'

'But why should he kill the miller in that terrible way?'

'Many say Gervase was father to the apprentice Dan who died in the mill at Serlo's hands. Gervase thought Serlo had killed his son as well as his lover.'

'No!'

'So, as I say, I think you should look to finding another protector, Lady Anne. Because there is good reason to doubt that Gervase will have that potential for much longer.'

'I am lucky that my husband is returned,' she said with a cool smile. 'He will protect me.'

'Even when you give birth to a bastard?' Baldwin asked, and her face shattered like a window struck by a stone.

Chapter Twenty-Nine

Simon was intrigued as they returned to the hall. He said, speaking low so that no one above could hear him, 'What do we do about this, then, Baldwin? Did Warin give convincing reasons for thinking Nicholas murdered these people?'

'He said that Nicholas probably guessed that he wasn't really the father of his wife's child, and deduced that his own friend Gervase, a known philanderer, had been disloyal. He was hurt and offended, and wanted to destroy Gervase's happy memories. That was why he killed Athelina, but also why he killed Serlo, producing "evidence" which would appear to show that Gervase killed Serlo in a fury because of the death of his own son.'

Baldwin fell silent, his face creased with concern, and Simon sucked his teeth. 'You think that makes sense?'

'Not really. If he wanted to avenge his son's death, Gervase would have done so sooner. The drive for revenge is less after a year. It could only be credible if there were another reason for him to kill.'

'I suppose a man could allow his desire to avenge his son's death to lie dormant until a suitable opportunity arose,' Simon suggested.

'Hardly likely, but possible,' Baldwin said grudgingly. 'Apart from that, the idea was sound. Nicholas kills Athelina and her children, presumably hoping that people will assume Gervase was trying to remove an irritation – this woman who kept demanding money from him. And then he kills Serlo because of the death of his son some months ago.'

'The alternative is, of course, that Gervase himself *was* guilty,' Simon said.

'Yes – which magnifies our existing reservations about Nicholas's guilt,' Baldwin grunted tiredly.

'We mustn't forget Richer. He believed that Athelina was murdered by Serlo, so it may well be he murdered Serlo in his turn.'

Baldwin nodded unwillingly. 'Except that Richer would never have had the imagination to thrust Serlo's head into the machine: that displays more thought than I would expect from a warrior like him. Ach, I don't know! Let us wait until morning, then pray that we find Gervase and learn a little more from him, because otherwise we'll end up with that fool of a Coroner coming to his own conclusions, and I doubt that the guilty man would then pay for his crimes!'

In Adam's house, Julia banked up the priest's fire, and then stood gazing about her at the room. Poor Adam, being held at the castle – but from what she'd heard, he'd tried to murder a man. It was hard to believe, although Julia knew well enough that any man was capable of violence if he got into his cups. Perhaps he'd been drinking a little too much of his wine in the church. She only hoped that he'd soon be released, because if he wasn't, her future looked uncertain. Where would she live if she was thrown from this place? It didn't bear thinking of.

Still, all was quiet for the night, and being a pragmatic woman, she put her fears from her. Taking a foul-smelling tallow candle from its spike in a beam and shielding its flame from the draughts, she walked from the hall into the parlour, and through that out to her little room beyond.

She set the candle on the spike and peered down at her baby. Ned lay quietly, snuffling a little in his sleep, but looked well enough, and she pulled up the old blanket a little, tucking it over his shoulder, before starting to untie her belt and make ready for bed herself.

It was a cold night, so she took off her overtunic, but left on her shirt and shift. With a shiver, she went to the door and dropped the wooden slat into its two slots, one on the door, one on the wall, which served her as a lock, and then went to her stool and ran her old bone comb through her hair a few times. It snagged and caught on the knots, but she persevered.

She was almost done when she heard something. There was a slight rattle, as though a stone had been kicked against her wall by an incautious foot. It was odd enough for her to pause, head tilted, listening intently, but she heard nothing more, so she shrugged to herself and pulled the comb through her hair again.

There was a stumble. She heard it distinctly, the slip of a leather sole on loose gravel, then a muttered curse. It made her leap up, ready to demand who was wandering about Adam's yard, but then a little caution came to her. Athelina's death had affected many in the vill, and suddenly Julia felt a faint expectation of danger. She caught her breath, thinking of Athelina's children, and threw a nervous look at her own sweet boy, before walking stealthily across the room to her clothes. On her belt there hung a little knife, not much protection, but better than nothing at all.

The door was moving. She could see the timbers shift, could hear the wood scraping on the packed earth of the threshold, the hinges protest. Gripping her knife firmly, she stepped forward, her brow tight with anticipation and fear. 'Who is that?'

There was no answer, but suddenly the door was struck a huge blow, and the planks rattled, the slat almost jumping out of the sockets. She screamed. Behind her, her baby moved, jerking awake, but she paid no attention. Her whole being was focused on the door, the door which leaped and bounced as blows were rained upon it.

And then, suddenly, there was silence, apart from the noise of her child sobbing with terror, and her breathing, ragged and fast. Her eyes moved about the room, but there was nothing; only the door gave access. That and the roof. Her eyes were drawn upwards, and even as she heard the first sounds of the thatch being attacked, she screamed again, a primeval shriek of a hunted animal.

There was a renewed pounding on her door, and she nearly died of fright, but then she heard Ivo's voice, and with a blessed burst of relief, pulled the slat aside to let him in.

Baldwin woke with a tearing pain in his flank, and he pulled a grimace as he rolled sideways off the bench.

'This is too much!' he groaned.

There had been a time when he would have been happy to roll off a bench in the early morning. When he had been a Knight Templar, he would have woken earlier, and fresher, even if there had been neither bench nor rug. He would have been able to spring awake, leaping from his mat on the floor with the excitement of the new dawn. Not now. He was grown lazy and fat, and the last few weeks of travel had tired his frame. Even his bones seemed to ache and complain.

This wrenching pain was a little different, though. It felt as though he had torn a muscle in his side and he felt the area gingerly as he sat on the bench. It wasn't serious, he thought, but it would slow him today.

It was still dark. From here, at the top of the steps, Baldwin could see the thin glimmering on the eastern horizon, but as yet the only light here came from the torches and braziers, their yellow and red hues flickering, throwing up occasional sparks. The castle was already awake. There was a shouting and the clattering of hooves from the stables, which showed that Nicholas's men had heeded his command that they should all be ready to leave at first light, and there was a swirling rasp of metal from the smithy, where some squires and others were whetting their blades with the great spinning circular stone.

There was a fine mist on the ground, and smoke from the fires in the hall was hanging in long threads and streamers overhead. It looked as though the world of men was bounded by fog above and below, and Baldwin felt the idea strangely apt. Mankind wandered in a perpetual fog, he sometimes thought, seeing clearly only what was right in front of them, unaware of all that happened outside their near-sighted scope.

His mind was drawn to the great events which were happening in the country. The King probably had little idea of how much his advisers were detested in the realm; he only heard what his Household told him, which blinkered him to all threats. In the same way any great lord must be blind to all but that which his servants told him, and the intelligent ones would see to it that they were better informed. Sir Henry de Cardinham was a good example: he lived elsewhere, only very rarely visited this far-flung manor, yet knew full well that he must send spies to his old home in order to learn what his people felt about their lives. True, most villagers wouldn't care what was happening in London or York, but there was an atmosphere in a kingdom that could affect even kings, and it was a fool who ignored brewing trouble just because it didn't seem spectacular enough yet to merit action. Better by far to take off the bud of rebellion before the plant grew fresh branches.

Men stalking about, wandering witlessly through a fog . . . It was not a pleasing reflection, but he was sure that it was valid. Trying to sift through the irrelevancies had absorbed all their efforts, and it was only now, with Gervase's hurried departure, that they had seen the truth of his offences.

'A good morning,' Simon grunted at his side. The Bailiff was dressed and had wrapped a thick fustian cloak about him against the chill of the morning. 'Christ's cods it's cold isn't it? Do you think there's going to be food before we set off?'

'No. We'll have to take something with us, I think,' Baldwin said.

'Do you reckon we'll find him?'

'Oh yes. He's only a steward when all is said and done, not a crafty villein used to covering his poaching or thefts.'

'He's bright enough to get away with murder, though,' Simon commented. 'Athelina would have been easy enough. She wouldn't have expected him to kill her.'

'No,' Baldwin mused. 'Although wouldn't she have been suspicious when he came calling, since he'd ignored her for so long and refused her demands for money?'

'We can ask him later,' Simon said and sniffed. 'Maybe it wasn't him killed her. Maybe it *was* Serlo, and Gervase took revenge on him for her and his son Danny.'

Baldwin nodded, but all he could see was the drifting tendrils of mist and smoke encircling the waiting men.

Simon went to the kitchens and fetched some bread and hunks of cheese, which he shared with Baldwin while their horses were saddled. It was almost full light by the time all the men were ready. Nicholas had ordered that all the men-at-arms of the castle should ride to seek the fleeing steward, and had commanded that the men in the vill should also contribute to the posse. One of his men had gone and rounded up as many peasants as he could find.

While Simon and Baldwin walked to their mounts and swung up, both still chewing, and the men all about them organised themselves into hunting packs, a familiar face appeared in the gateway.

'Where's *he* been?' Baldwin muttered darkly.

Simon followed the direction of his gaze and grinned to himself. 'I'd imagine he's been enjoying himself.'

'Ivo!' Baldwin shouted, and beckoned with a crooked finger. 'Where have you been?'

'Well, master, there didn't seem much to be done here last night, so I thought I'd betake myself off to a place I know.'

'Especially while Adam was languishing in a gaol here, I'll be bound,' Simon sniggered. 'You'll never miss an opportunity, then?'

Ivo smiled, but looked concerned. 'I did go to Julia, yes, but there is something I didn't understand. Julia was settling down before I arrived, when someone tried to break into her home. He attempted to bash down the door, then dig in through the thatch to get to her, and when I arrived, she threw herself into my arms, she was so petrified.'

'She must have been,' Baldwin commented sourly.

Ivo gave him a hurt look,

Simon shrugged. 'She's superstitious. You know how women are – they can be scared by the daftest things.'

Baldwin shot him an astonished glance. To his knowledge, Simon was one of the most superstitious people he had ever met. Certainly more so than a sensible peasant woman like Julia.

Ivo was shaking his head. 'Don't think so. The door had chunks cut from it when I looked this morning, as if someone had taken a hatchet to it. And there were great lumps of thatch taken out. Luckily, it was thick and took him time to get even most of the way through.'

Nicholas had mounted his horse, and now his great black rounsey pranced closer to them. He had overheard their conversation. 'He tried to get into her room, you say? The foul devil's trying to silence another woman, then! He has killed Athelina, now he tries to murder Julia too. He must be mad, quite mad. All those he has loved are to be destroyed. Next he would try to slaughter my wife, I expect.' The reflection brought a black look into his eyes, and hurt too, Baldwin saw, and his heart went to the man who had lost his friend and his trust in his wife in the same moment. Nicholas set his jaw and jerked his reins about. 'Well, we shall catch him today. If he was here in the town after nightfall yesterday, our ride today must be all the shorter.'

Baldwin watched him musingly as he trotted off through the press, shouting commands and ordering men to prepare. 'Ivo, tell me – what time did you go to her last night?'

'It was late. I had my meal here first, then went long after dark.'

'So if it was Gervase, then we know he cannot have travelled far as Nicholas said,' Baldwin mused. 'Look – there's no need for you to come with us. Perhaps you should go to Julia's house and stay with her until we return.'

Ivo needed no second prompting. As Nicholas raised an arm and led the way from the gate, the young ostler gave a broad smile. Baldwin nodded, and he and Simon set spurs to their mounts to follow the press riding carefully down the corridor to the main gates.

'What's this, Baldwin? Beginning to like the lad?' Simon asked with a grin.

Baldwin gave a half-smile. 'Perhaps I couldn't bear his company all day.'

'Ah, good. For one moment there, I thought you might be growing soft!'

'Perhaps I am,' Baldwin said. Then he turned to Simon. 'But if you were going to flee, would you hang around for two or three hours first, and try to attack a woman?'

'I'd ride for the hills,' Simon said, 'but then I'm not a murderer. Who can tell how irrational Gervase might be?'

'Who indeed?'

* * *

Nicholas had ordered that their parties should separate at the Holy Well. Some would ride from there along towards Bodmin, while the main group would ride north and east, themselves splitting up into further small parties to cover the territory, unless they found good signs of Gervase's direction.

There was nothing that they could find through the vill and up northwards but they were lucky as they neared Temple. There a shepherd swore he had seen a rider flying past before dark the previous day. From his description, they could recognise the steward, and Nicholas led the way after him, up the hill from Temple east and north.

'We'll be heading homewards, then,' Simon said broodingly, 'eastwards to Devon.'

'Yes, and we'll have to come all the way back again,' Baldwin muttered with bitterness.

Sir Jules was nearby, and he spurred his mount until he was alongside Baldwin. 'I know the feeling,' he said. 'But at least we'll soon have this fellow.'

'Yes,' Baldwin agreed, but when Simon glanced over at him, he could see that Baldwin's mind was on someone or something else.

Gervase could have wept for desperation. The bloody horse wouldn't *move*! It was all he could do not to kill the brute there and then, but the last thing he needed was to be without a mount.

He'd ridden all the way here before nightfall, certain that the castle would send a posse after him as soon as they realised he'd run, and he'd thrashed the beast all the way to the other side of the moors, galloping wildly, but now he could see his mistake. The horse was tiring before it had grown dark, and as soon as night fell, Gervase could feel him flagging. In the end, he kept it to an easy trot, but even that had used up its resources, and now, in the early morning, although he was several leagues from Cardinham, his horse appeared lame. He stood with a leg lifted dolefully, like a hound with a thorn in his paw, and wouldn't continue. When Gervase climbed down and inspected the hoof there was nothing in it, but the fetlock felt very warm, and he wondered if the brute had strained it during their wild gallop last night. There was one point where the horse had stumbled – the damn thing could have slipped on a rock.

'Shit! Shit! Shit!'

He kicked a stone and watched it skate over the grass, only to fall into a pool. This wasn't a place he'd travelled over before. He'd thought it wouldn't be too difficult to ride over, because it always looked grassy and easy, but he was learning that Bodmin was a miserable, wet landscape, with rocks and boulders strewn liberally about it. It was one of these damned rocks which must have twisted the horse's hoof.

All around him were rolling hills. There was no sign of habitation anywhere, no house, no cottage, not even a fence or field. In every direction there was just this grassland interspersed with grey moorstone and the occasional twinkle of water.

He sighed to himself and gazed eastwards again. There was nothing for it. He'd have to walk. With a curse, he yanked on the reins and started trudging onwards, peering every so often over his shoulder, wondering when he could expect to catch sight of metal glinting in the sunshine. He hoped he'd left Nicholas and his men far behind, but until he was quite certain that there was no risk of pursuers, he would keep moving straight on.

The moors opened out quite suddenly. Baldwin had never grown used to the way that the land gaped before him on Dartmoor, and here it appeared the same. They had been riding up a track between tall hedges, and then, after passing a pair of trees, the vegetation fell away. There were no more trees, no more hedges and bushes, only low, stunted things, ferns dying back after the summer, heathers, some twisted and gnarled furze, and grass. Everywhere there was good pasture.

Here a man could be on top of the world. There were no high hills before them as they cantered on at an easy pace. Nicholas was no guide, but Richer had learned tracking during his time in Wales, and his eyes were still good, so he led the way. He had picked up the tracks of Gervase's horse at Temple. There was an irregular pattern to the nails on one of the shoes on Gervase's horse, and Richer was now keeping his eye fixed to the ground, keeping that horseshoe's print in his sight all the way.

Every so often, he would call a halt, and now he did so again. Baldwin kicked his rounsey a little nearer, irritated by yet another delay. Richer was crouching at a rock. There was a vivid scrape on one side, a deep gouge in the grass below it.

'Well?' Nicholas demanded, his horse stamping at the ground, eager to be off again. He was a thoroughbred, that one.

'A horse has been here, and he stumbled in the dark, I'd guess. This colour, it's steel. The hoof slipped down this side and tore out this hole in the turf. It didn't break a leg, but I'd guess this mount is in pain now. You can see that the beast favours its hoof from here on. Look there, and there! You can see that the hoofprint is less distinct than before, less than other hooves. It's favouring that hoof, and that means he'll not have travelled far after this accident.'

'Good,' Nicholas said as Richer climbed back into the saddle. 'In that case, I'll go on ahead with some faster riders. Richer, do you follow on and keep an eye on the trail in case the bastard turns off. I'd guess that he continues in a straight line, though, over the moors to the east. With luck, we'll catch him if we simply hurry in this direction.'

'Sir, you'll need good men with you,' Warin said.

'I'll take you, then, and two more of my men,' Nicholas said.

'I'll come too, and my friend,' Baldwin said quickly.

'There is no need. Your horses are not so fast as ours,' Nicholas told him.

'You do not need to have a charge of murder laid about you,' Baldwin said.

'There is no murder of an adulterer,' Nicholas said, his horse wheeling.

'There is when it's committed in cold blood. I won't see that,' Baldwin said more sharply. 'Simon and I will be with you, Nicholas, and if you try to outpace us and kill your steward, I shall *personally* appeal you for murder.'

Nicholas fixed a fierce eye upon him as he steadied his mount. 'You'd protect the man who adulterously took my wife, Sir Baldwin?'

'No! But we're here to find and question Gervase about murder, and I won't see him killed before he has his opportunity to have his say.'

'Who else could have done the murders? He ran, that's proof of his guilt. If not him, who?'

'There are some who accuse *you*,' Baldwin said. 'You were out on your horse the night Serlo died. If you kill Gervase now, you'll leave many people wondering whether that was why you slew him, to distract people from your own guilt.'

Nicholas pursed his lips with fury. For one moment he looked as though he might launch himself at Baldwin but then he jerked his reins and bellowed a command. Baldwin set spurs to his mount as the castellan galloped away, Warin close behind him.

'Thanks, Baldwin. Just what I needed – a fast ride,' he heard Simon call out to him sarcastically, but then they were tearing off across the brightly-lit grasses after Nicholas and Warin.

Chapter Thirty

It was past noon now, and Gervase felt frozen to the core. His horse was limping, if anything worse than before, and he could feel the sweat starting to form ice all down his back. It was being chilled by the breeze which had started up. Over the moor here, at the eastern fringe, there were thin patches of ice, and the wind was flaying the flesh from his face. He pulled a flap of his cowl over his mouth, but it helped only a little. This weather was too foul for a man. Oh, for a fire and a jug of warmed ale! He could have killed for a cheery flame and bowl of pottage.

The ground felt oddly springy, and every so often it gave way, as though it was merely a façade, a thin fabric stretched over emptiness. He paused, staring about him at the little tussocks of stuff, not grass alone, which moved gently in the wind. When he took another step, he saw that the nearer ones shivered. There was a pool of water nearby, and that too rippled as he moved.

In an icy terror, he realised that he was on the fringe of a bog, one of those terrible places into which animals often strayed, never to escape. Standing stock still, he threw an anxious look over his shoulder. The land was unremarkable, just another flat expanse, as it was ahead. But he daren't go on forward, he must go back. He pulled at the reins, then dragged the mount's head around until it was facing the way they had come. The horse snorted and nodded his head a few times to show his displeasure, and then started to limp back with Gervase.

It was then, when he had gone only a short way, that Gervase saw the tiny figures breasting the hill.

* * *

'The bastard! There he is!' Nicholas shouted, waving his hand, and then he clapped his spurs to his horse and sped away.

Baldwin kicked his own beast, but he was exhausted. They had covered at least ten leagues without pause, mostly at a good pace, and Baldwin's and Simon's rounseys were feeling the distance. It would be fortunate indeed if they could make the return without suffering strains.

'Warin, keep with him, in God's name!' Baldwin bellowed at the top of his voice. 'Don't let him kill the man!'

Warin gave him a negligent wave of his hand, and then snapped his reins and set off after the castellan. Baldwin patted his horse's neck, and then tried to urge him on again. The horse was game, and after tossing his mane, he started at a loping pace down the long shallow incline towards the men at the bottom. Simon's horse trailed after them.

Baldwin could see that Gervase was in no better condition than them. He was sore-footed, from the look of him, and he stepped towards them with a gingerish manner, as though he was testing his feet. Baldwin couldn't make out what he was doing, until Simon pulled up alongside him and roared to Nicholas and Warin: 'He's on a bog! Beware the marshes!'

But Nicholas and Warin were too far away to hear. Baldwin feared that they might run headlong into the mire and be swallowed, but even as he and Simon thrashed at their mounts, Gervase suddenly slipped beneath the crust, his legs and belly sinking below the green thatch.

His horse panicked, and leaped back as he disappeared, and then, as the reeds and grasses wobbled about him, he tried to jump. His momentum carried him over one patch, and he gathered himself and flung himself into the air again. This time, his landing was in the midst of a pool, and he reared, his hindquarters already disappearing in the filth that sucked him down. He splashed with his forelegs, but it could avail him nothing. All he achieved was a more speedy destruction. As he flailed, the mire's grip grew more strong, and by the time Baldwin and Simon caught up with Warin and Nicholas, the horse was already so worn out that he could scarcely lift his forelegs. He looked at the men with eyes maddened with fear, and Baldwin could read the plea, but he had no bow to put him out of his misery.

'Help!'

Nicholas glanced at Gervase with a sardonic expression. 'It's a shame you brought that mount. He was worth something. A good horse is hard to find, and you've thrown him away.'

'Do you have a rope?' Baldwin asked.

'I wouldn't let you use it if I did,' Nicholas replied, his forearms crossed over his horse's withers as he watched Gervase slipping relentlessly under the surface.

Baldwin glanced back at Gervase. He was petrified. This was surely one of the most hideous of deaths: slow suffocation as the body was taken down into the mire. It made Baldwin shudder to think of it, and as he did so, he saw Gervase's horse rear one last time. The brave mount was fighting, but his efforts were doing him no good, and were even helping Gervase to die more swiftly. The ripples from his straining were lapping the mire ever higher on Gervase's breast now, and the waters were almost up to his armpits.

'Please!' he begged.

It was piteous. The horse's head alone was visible now, and the eyes, red with terror, stared at the men standing so still at the edge of the mire. He looked at them accusingly, as though they could do something to save him, and then his head disappeared quite suddenly. It burst upwards once, a black froth blowing from both nostrils, a jet of mud from his mouth, and then he sank down again, and the bog moved twice, thrice, and then was still.

'Please! Sir Baldwin – Squire! Won't you save me?'

'Die, you bastard!' Nicholas roared. 'Why should we save a murderer and adulterer? Die there, and take your time. I want to enjoy this.'

Baldwin was looking about him, but there was no hope of assistance. There were no buildings in sight, not even a small plume of smoke to betray a tin-miner's camp. Reluctantly he accepted that they must either watch the man die, or try at least to reach him somehow.

He dropped from his horse. They were more than fifty yards from Gervase here, and Baldwin had no idea where the mire began. Gervase had managed to cross from here, so it must be relatively safe. He pulled off his cloak and untied his belt. With luck, the two together would give him the reach to rescue the steward if he could get close enough. He looked up at Simon, and Simon nodded, pulling his own belt free and joining Baldwin.

'Simon, I'll go over there, and try to reach him with my cloak. It's five feet long, and if he catches it, I can perhaps haul him free.'

'You're too heavy. I'd best go,' Simon said shortly.

Baldwin was going to argue, but Simon was serious, and Baldwin had to agree that he had right on his side. He was lighter, and could go farther on the rippling thatch than Baldwin. The knight nodded. 'Be careful, Simon.'

'That has to rate as one of the most pointless comments you've ever made,' Simon said thinly.

This was the aspect of the moors which he found most frightening. There was something about mires which brought out dread in any man with sense. They shifted and moved every year, like animals seeking fresh prey, and even when they dried up in the summer's heat, they were dangerous. A patch of firm grass could become a lethal trap for the unwary as a man fell into a hole that could be yards deep, from which the water had drained.

But the water was not drained from this one. This was at its most lethal, full to the brim, and working with that strange ability of mires, pulling on a man's feet to suck him beneath the surface. Gervase's expression was waxen, corpse-like. His eyes, terrified, stared at Simon with the full knowledge of his doom, should Simon fail.

If there was one breed Simon hated, it was murderers who hurt women. This man, he knew, might have killed Athelina and cut her children's throats. But he might be innocent, and Simon was no judge. Swearing under his breath, he eyed the land between him and Gervase. He could walk a certain distance, and continued until he felt the telltale springiness underfoot and saw the tussocks of grass and rushes bouncing with each of his footsteps. Then he cautiously crouched down and inched his way forward.

It was painstaking work. The ground so close to his nose reeked of foul exhalations. Every movement reminded him of his own danger, as a shift of his knee made the carpet under his chest move. He swore under his breath and moved again, trying to unsettle the ground as little as possible. Then, when he was within a couple of yards of Gervase, there was a belch of gas from where the steward's horse had been swallowed, and Simon felt the ripples expand outwards, jigging him up and down. Gervase was more obviously affected. The tears streamed down his cheeks, both now at water-level. His expression was one of simple anguish. He was convinced of his impending death, certain that nothing Simon could do might save him.

'Take the fucking thing!' Simon swore.

Gervase looked at him and lunged at the belt that lay within his grasp. He overbalanced and then almost drowned. His face sank below the water, and it was only by a lucky chance that he caught the belt.

'God save us from sodding stewards,' Simon muttered to himself as he began to haul on the belt, moving backwards, then pulling, then moving back again. Gradually, the sodden figure of Gervase emerged from the bog, gasping for breath and sobbing in relief.

'So why did he come back to scare me?' Julia asked again.

Ivo shrugged comfortably. They were in Adam's hall, seated on rugs and skins by the fire, still naked after their pleasing love-making, and the youth didn't much care for the reasons. No wandering spectre of the night was going to spoil his day. 'I expect someone heard that the priest was stuck in the gaol, and reckoned to steal a little of the church's silver, that's all.'

'But why did he come to my room, then?' she asked again.

Ivo considered. 'Probably knew there was a gorgeous wench in here and wanted to have his wicked way with you.'

She thumped him, smiling, and he grabbed her, pulling her up and over him, then clasped her to him, both arms about her torso. She tilted her head back to peer down her nose at him, and then her expression changed. 'It wasn't you, was it? You wouldn't have scared me like that just to climb into my bed?'

'Sweetheart, no,' he said, genuinely shocked. 'I wouldn't do a thing like that. No. And I think I saw a man at the back of the place when I walked in, though I didn't reckon anything about it at the time. Wasn't until I heard you scream and you let me in that I realised there could be something odd going on. No, I didn't do it, I swear.'

She subsided against him, turning her head and resting her cheek on his chest. 'I don't know what he'd have done if he'd got in. I think he was going to kill me.'

Ivo stroked her head happily. He did me a favour, he thought to himself, scaring you into my arms. 'He'll be caught by now, anyway.'

There was a moment's consternation when he wondered whether the man at Julia's door had actually been Gervase, but then Julia began to distract him, and he gave up all thoughts of the stranger.

Gervase was sprawled spread-eagled, taking in great gulps of air, unsure that he was truly safe at last. 'My God! Thank you! Oh, thank you!'

'Don't be too glad yet,' Simon said shortly. 'You're still deep in the shit.'

Gervase ignored the coldness in his voice, ignored everything but the thrill of being alive. A shiver ran down his body, from the tip of his skull to his feet, a shudder of voluptuous refreshment. God! Alive!

There was the tramp of hooves, and a harness squeaked and jingled. Then he heard the voice of the man who had once been his best friend. 'Get up, Steward. You have a long, weary walk ahead of you. Best get started.'

Baldwin insisted on allowing the steward to share his mount. The poor fellow was stumbling and falling every few paces. It was plain that his near death had all but emasculated him, and he was as shaky and gangling as a child. With him in this state, they would be fortunate ever to reach Cardinham.

'I don't care if he dies here!' Nicholas rasped when Baldwin raised his concerns.

'Well, you should. If he dies through your negligence, people will wonder why you didn't save him. Perhaps because you were the murderer yourself?'

'Oh, for Heaven's sake! Why in God's name should *I* have killed Serlo or the widow?'

'Because, Nicholas, if you knew of Gervase's affair with your wife, might you not seek to punish him by setting him up as a murderer? Might you not kill his own past lovers so as to make them appear like his victims? Athelina, for example: you could have killed her because everyone in the vill knew she kept pestering Gervase about money. And then there was Serlo, killed because of the death of his apprentice, Dan. Everyone guessed Matty had her boy Dan by Gervase. Thus, a man wishing to make Gervase look guilty might kill him too.'

Gervase heard this and looked up. He was slumped on Sir Baldwin's horse while the knight walked at the rounsey's side. 'What do you mean, Matty and her boy?'

'Your son, Danny.'

Gervase's mouth dropped. 'He wasn't my son!'

Nicolas swung his fist and Gervase almost fell from his horse. 'Don't lie to us, man! You killed Serlo because he let your son die,' Nicholas sneered. 'The whole vill knew that. It was a miracle you didn't kill the murderous oaf beforehand. *I* would have done.'

'Urgh!' Gervase wiped his bleeding nose on his sleeve, snorted, then spat out a gobbet of blood. 'I didn't kill anyone. I wouldn't hurt a hair of Athelina's head, and I certainly didn't take revenge for Matty's son's death. Why should I? Dan wasn't mine.'

Nicholas slowed his mount, turned a little in his saddle, and swung again. This time Gervase was ready, and rolled out of the way. 'You can hit me as often as you like,' he shouted, 'but I swear on my mother's grave, he wasn't my son! Christ's blood, Matty spread her legs for any man when she'd had a jug of cider. She was the sort of wench for one of the castle's cooks, not me! I wouldn't have gone near her unless there was little other choice.'

'Then whose son was he?' Baldwin asked.

'Everyone in the castle swore he was Gervase's. He's raised bastards all over the place,' Nicholas snarled. 'This was just one more. He seeks to deny paternity because he doesn't want his revenge to be known.'

Gervase sniffed gingerly. 'You think so? Then tell me, wise man, why I'd wait so long to enjoy my revenge. Ballocks! I have never killed anyone in my life. The man who says I have is a liar!'

'Then who did? Who else could have fathered that boy?' Nicholas demanded.

Baldwin looked up at him, then at Gervase. 'Either of you, I suppose, but then there are other men in the vill.'

The thought tugged at his mind all the way back to the vill: who else could have fathered the apprentice? Through the last days there had been a momentum which had all but prevented rational consideration of the issues, first because of the rush to find a reason for Athelina's murder, and then the murder of Serlo himself. His connection to the death of his apprentice was so apparent, the paternity of the child was so plainly crucial to the discovery of the killer, that all else seemed irrelevant. Yet now, Baldwin wondered again whether the thrust of his and Simon's questionings should have been redirected.

Something Susan at the alehouse had said was lingering in his head. It had felt important at the time, but again, other issues drew his attention away. All she had questioned was the sequence of the deaths of Athelina and her children. There was something in that. Surely, if the two boys had been together, killing them would have been difficult. A man like Gervase appearing might frighten them a little, because the lads knew he was an official at the castle, but that wouldn't necessarily make them trust him enough to let him get so close he could cut both their throats. Did that mean Athelina arrived after her children, or before? Perhaps she was first to die, and the murderer sprang upon the boys as they arrived? If only he could think straight . . .

At Warin's insistence they stopped at a tavern he knew up on the road to Launceston, and there as well as wines and some food, the party were able to hire a horse to speed their return. While they sat and ate, Gervase standing soaked and wretched, staring longingly at the food, for Nicholas refused point blank to allow him to eat, Baldwin glanced up at him with a frown. 'Gervase, you can see that you are the obvious culprit in the murders. Can you think of anyone else who could have benefited from the deaths of Athelina and Serlo?'

'Richer, of course,' Gervase shivered. 'He would have won the revenge of the years, killing the man who had wiped out his whole family.'

'There was no one else?' Simon asked. 'Surely someone would have benefited from Serlo's death?'

'Everyone in the vill gained from his death,' Gervase scoffed, a little of his past arrogance returning to him.

'Except his brother,' Nicholas said.

'His brother can be excluded from this,' Simon agreed.

'Although it's odd. Alexander is the only man I saw on the night Serlo died. He was out near the tavern,' Nicholas said.

Baldwin glanced up at him. 'Why?'

'No idea.'

Simon was peering into the middle distance. He sat back on his stool, resting against the wall. 'We thought Serlo could have murdered Athelina. What if . . .'

'What?' Baldwin asked. He was thinking of Athelina again, and as he realised how relevant Susan's comments were about the killer being known to the children, Simon squinted.

'Well, if Serlo had a financial motive to do away with her, surely Alexander had the same one? He had a share in the cottage where Athelina lived. And Serlo had been taking gifts when it was Alexander's money that paid for the farm of tolls. That meant Serlo was defrauding *Alexander* too.'

Warin was listening, and now he scoffed. 'You're simply guessing! Why should Alexander kill Serlo?'

Baldwin took a deep breath. 'It was odd that Serlo should be killed just now – but what if Alexander wanted children, and had fathered Danny? Serlo had allowed his son to die, crushed in the machine. And then Serlo allowed his *own* son to die, once again through his own negligence. Would not any father be so appalled that his mind could be unbalanced?'

'By Christ's bones!' Simon whispered suddenly as his eye caught Baldwin's.

Chapter Thirty-One

They were back in the vill late that evening. On the way they met with one other party, which included Richer, and left Gervase with them while Simon, Baldwin, Warin and Nicholas continued on their way.

'What is your rush?' Warin demanded as they clattered into the vill.

'When there is something to be learned, there is always a need to hurry,' Simon said shortly. It was galling to be so out of breath; he wasn't as used to fast riding as he once had been. All he could think about now was a warm fire, the chance to throw off his clothes and commandeer a bench to sleep on or, failing that, a cosy hayloft, than confronting a murderer.

Baldwin looked entirely fresh again. He had the knack of absorbing any pain and weariness when he had mental activity to stimulate him, and now he was frowning at the road, deep in thought. Simon knew why. The idea that Serlo's murderer could be his own brother was so appalling, and yet so logical, *if* Danny was Alexander's son. That gave them the motive of revenge for Serlo's negligence, added to his theft of the tolls. With regard to the death of Athelina, Alexander might well have killed her to remove her from the cottage which he and his brother owned.

'There is another thing,' Baldwin murmured as he drew up outside Alexander's house. 'The killer tried to strike again last night – at Julia. I had a feeling that the attacker was not Gervase, which was why I told Ivo to return to his woman and protect her.'

'Why'd anyone attack *her*?' Warin asked.

'Perhaps to distract us and confuse our enquiries? Or perhaps he detests women who have children out of wedlock. A jealous man whose marriage is barren might well form an irrational hatred of women who breed without effort.'

'If the boy Danny wasn't his, what then?' Simon asked as they dismounted.

'He must have been,' Baldwin said with quiet certainty, and drew his sword before beating on the door with his pommel.

The door gave way when he tried the latch, and Baldwin entered warily, his sword at the ready. There was no sound from within, and he walked into the chilly room with the hackles rising on his neck. This felt like a dead house. It was a simple hall, with the hearth in the middle of the room, a pair of stools, a bench, and a table at one end. Tapestries hung from the walls and a thick layer of rushes covered part of the floor. A tripod with a big pot stood over the cold fire. At the far wall was a thickly rolled palliasse.

Baldwin had a dreadful premonition. As Simon and Warin walked in and stared about them, he strode to the palliasse and pushed it over. His worst fears weren't realised, thank God. It fell open, displaying rugs and blankets, but no body.

He went through the screens passage to the buttery and pantry. Empty. He turned back and marched past the other two men, through the hall to the door at the rear. There might be a solar block where the couple slept, he thought, but when he opened the door, he found only another storeroom, containing two big chests. Baldwin looked at them: both were padlocked. By one there lay a number of bags. This, he thought, was where the man kept his wealth. And then he saw a small stain, and his belly lurched.

'Simon! Bring a light.'

'What is it? Oh, Christ's bones!'

Baldwin was crouching at the long red trickle, and as Simon entered, he looked up, his face haggard. 'This is my fault, Simon. I should have realised this before! It's all my fault!'

He squatted, staring at the chest, while Simon fetched an axe. It didn't take him long, and when he came back, he gave it to the knight. Baldwin swung it twice. At the second blow the padlock flew off. Baldwin took a deep breath and raised the lid.

There inside, neatly folded to fit the space, and with a small cushion under her head as though to give her some comfort, lay Letitia. The small stream of blood came from the savage slash in her neck, which had emptied the blood from her veins to form a pool in the bottom of the chest.

'So it was Alexander,' Simon breathed.

'Yes,' Baldwin said sadly. 'He killed them all.'

Ivo had left Julia early, thinking that he'd be able to get back to the castle in time for Baldwin and Simon's return, because he was keen to see whether they'd had any luck in their search for the steward. On his way, he heard hoofbeats approaching.

The first rider was a man-at-arms from the castle, who spat in his direction when he called out, asking whether they'd been successful. Ivo bit his thumb at him when he was safely past. Then a man Ivo had been friendly enough with rode past, and he shouted out that yes, they'd caught the bastard. The castellan was bringing him back, and God save him when he was thrown into the castle gaol, after what he'd done.

Ivo realised there was little point now in heading back to the castle. The place would be empty for some while, he had the news he wanted, and although the food was better in the castle, it was a long walk away and there were undoubted attractions to remaining in Julia's bed. He wavered, but only for a moment or two, and then set off back towards the vill and Adam's house.

The hall was dark and empty-looking when he arrived, and he walked straight through to the back, where Julia's room was. Just as he rounded the corner, he heard a strange noise, a kind of loud report, like a wooden peg snapping. Then as he peered ahead he saw a line of bright light in the darkness from her open door, a figure standing in it with a large bar in his hand. He heard the man laugh, then a scream, and in that moment, he flung himself across the twenty feet or so of yard.

He caught the man squarely in the back, and hurled him into the room, narrowly missing Julia, who stood with her hands balled at her cheeks as she screamed. The sudden eruption of her lover caused her to fall silent for a moment, but then Ivo and his target fell onto her palliasse, almost crushing little Ned, and her cries were renewed.

Ivo felt a hand strike his temple, then nails raked along his cheek, but in the meantime he seemed incapable of finding his own target. The man squirmed and wriggled so much, Ivo could scarce guess where his head would be from one moment to the next, let alone hit it. There was a rasp, and then Ivo saw the knife. He reached for the hand that gripped it, but missed and caught the blade itself. He felt the shearing of his muscles and the grating of the knife against his bones, and was struck with horror as he realised his hand was ruined. If he could, this man would kill him, he sensed, and he grabbed for the nearest implement. It was the iron bar the man had used to break open the door. Ivo raised it, even as his left hand grew slick with his blood; then he brought the bar down upon the man's head, once, twice, and then a third time, until he stopped trying to pull his knife from Ivo's grasp.

At breakfast, Anne watched her husband cautiously. He still loved her, she was sure, but his discovery of her unfaithfulness had hurt him dreadfully, as it must. There weren't enough words for her to explain how the emptiness of loss had affected her when she convinced herself that he was dead, nor that she still loved him. It was too late for all that. All she could do was wait, and hope, that he would rediscover his love for her.

At their table was a special guest. Gervase, clad in clean tunic but looking pale and fraught, was at his side as usual, but today without a trencher in front of him. The food was all for other people. Again Gervase must endure hunger, knowing that the only offering for him would be the stale, leftover crusts.

Nicholas finished his meal, and then stared at Gervase blankly for a long time, his expression utterly unfathomable. Then, 'So, are you ready to answer the Coroner?'

'Of course I am. I'll tell him the truth.'

Gervase couldn't meet his eye. Anne felt a fleeting sympathy for him, trapped here, with no way out. His face was mottled and bruised from the blows Nicholas had aimed at him yesterday, although Warin had ensured that he was safe enough when he returned to the castle. Warin said he wanted Gervase alive at least until he could brief Warin on the papers and records of the manor. The steward was a pitiful creature now, and the Lady Anne shuddered to see him.

'In front of the vill?' Nicholas rasped. 'You'd shame her like that?'

Anne could feel her face flush. She put a hand on her belly, the other on the table to steady herself. Would Gervase really do that – confess his crime with her, her adultery, before the whole mass of peasants and farmers? She'd never be able to look the villeins in the eye again.

Gervase looked unhappy. 'I wish . . . I am so sorry, Nicholas. This shouldn't have happened. I didn't mean it to . . . It was just something that—'

'Will you shame her before the vill?'

'I don't want to, I hate the idea!' Gervase was staring at *her* now, a kind of desperation in his eyes, the eyes of a stag at bay before the hunters rode in with their lances.

'*Will you shame her, I asked!*' Nicholas rasped.

'I'll have to tell the truth. There have been enough lies.'

'I see,' Nicholas said, and there was a sudden calmness in his voice. His two fists were set upon the tabletop and he leaned back, studying the man beside him with loathing. Then he almost lazily slammed a fist into Gervase's already broken nose.

The steward was hurled from his stool, weeping as the blood flew from his nostrils. He gave a shrill cry, making the blood bubble, then rolled on to all fours and vomited.

Nicholas stood and walked about him, and then lifted a boot and kicked with all the full force of his malice. Anne winced as she saw the boot crashing into the man's belly, and had to cover her eyes. She couldn't bear to see any man suffer, nor could she bear to see the hatred in her own husband's face.

'Puke it up, churl! And get used to pain, because if I see you accuse my lady of adultery in front of the jury, I'll ensure you receive more suffering than you could ever imagine!'

Gervase toppled, choking, to his side.

'My wife means more to me than anything. I'll protect her with the full extent of my power, and if that means I have to kill you, I *will*!'

Suddenly, Nicholas was overcome with uncontrollable rage. He kicked Gervase again and again, and Anne had to cover her eyes and ears as best she could against the terrible cries of the steward as the heavy boot crashed into his belly and breast, but when she heard his armbone crack with a noise like a mace striking a shield, she fled from the room even as Warin and Richer stormed in and pulled the castellan away.

Simon and Baldwin were already at the vill's church house; they'd been there since a little after dawn. Simon was unhappy to be up at such an unpleasant hour for the second day running, but the urgency of their need to learn the truth bore them both up. They had returned to the castle to hear that Ivo had caught the murderer. He was waiting in the hall to explain what had happened.

The culprit was being held in the church house, and Baldwin had been all for going straight to him, but Ivo said that he'd knocked the man out with an iron bar, and Simon had persuaded Baldwin both to stop interrogating Ivo, who was as pale as a candle from loss of blood, and to forget the idea of questioning a man who had almost had his head crushed. Baldwin had reluctantly agreed to leave things until next morning. Alexander wasn't going to escape them, after all.

But now, hurrying to the church house, he experienced an overwhelming urge to learn what this murderer could tell him. The man had killed so many, including his own wife, and the motives for the crimes were, at best, nebulous.

They thundered on the door, and a slightly bloodshot eye peered out at them before the door opened. A scruffy peasant yawned widely to display only five gleaming teeth, shuffled to lock the door again, and then led them to the figure bound on the rushes.

Baldwin knelt. 'Alexander?'

'Why, Keeper! You thought to come and visit me? That was kind,' Alexander said. 'Please – will you tell this churl to release me at once! He doesn't seem to realise I'm the Constable here!'

'We'll arrange for your release as soon as we can,' Baldwin said. 'But you have to tell us what has happened.'

'It was the steward,' Alexander said quickly. 'I saw him. Last night, he was trying to kill Julia – obviously he wanted to kill all the women he had polluted and got in pup, to try to atone for his fornication. I saw him entering the priest's house, so I smashed down the door to arrest him, when some fool ran me down and broke my head . . .'

'He wasn't there, Alexander,' Baldwin said gently. 'The man trying to break in to hurt Julia was you. We know that. We have witnesses.'

'No, that's wrong.'

'Why did you kill your brother?'

'Serlo?' Alexander looked up at him and tears started. 'I loved him. Always had. Serlo was my little brother, my best friend. I didn't want to see him hurt in any way.'

'Why kill him then?'

'He . . . It was Richer, because Richer heard Serlo fired his parents' house. Richer killed him.'

'Richer didn't realise Serlo had done that,' Baldwin said, his voice level and calm.

Simon stood behind Baldwin. Alexander was by turns calm, then furious; he hardly seemed to know his own mind, and to Simon this was the most terrifying thing: the man had lost his reason.

Baldwin was continuing just as patiently. 'Why did Athelina die, Alexander? Was it because of the money?'

'Of course it was! Serlo was furious with her. Do you know what he said to her? He said that she should go and whore, if she couldn't find the cash. And do you know, she tried! The bitch even tried it with me – the Constable. It wasn't our fault, was it, if her man had left her high and dry? No. But she refused to clear off. Dug her heels in. We couldn't allow that. We needed the money. I mean, *Serlo* did.'

Even the doorman heard that, the way that the miller's name was added as an afterthought.

'Serlo needed money to pay his fines and bills, didn't he?' Baldwin said.

'Yes. I helped as far as I could, of course, because he was my kid brother, but there's only so much a man can . . . and he was proud, you see. Serlo didn't like taking charity. Last time I offered him money, he was upset. Very upset. He threw his plate across the room and said he didn't need my alms. I can see why, of course. Letty was hurt, though. Well, she can't understand what it's like, having a brother. She never was so close to her family.'

'Did you kill her because of that?' Baldwin asked.

'*Kill Letty?*' Alexander peered up at him in amazement. 'How could I do that? I love her. She's the only bright light in my life, now Serlo's dead. Poor Serlo.' He began to sob, then stopped abruptly.

'It must have been very difficult,' Baldwin observed.

'What?'

'Having a child by Matty, when Letty couldn't conceive.'

'My Danny was no trouble.'

Simon felt his heart thunder. This was the proof, at last!

Baldwin nodded understandingly. 'But you were terribly hurt by Serlo's callous attitude after Danny died so tragically.'

'It was a very bad time,' Alexander agreed. 'Serlo didn't understand why I was so upset.'

'So why did you kill Serlo?'

Alexander looked as though he was about to deny it, but then his head dropped slightly and he stared at the floor. There came a time, Simon had observed, when a man stopped bothering to deny what was so obviously true, and this appeared to be still more the case with Alexander. If his mind was twisted and corrupted with madness, how much more difficult was it for him to invent a new tale? The truth was easier.

'He proved that he didn't deserve to continue living. I was hurt when he made disparaging comments about my son, my only son; I was hurt again when I heard he'd been taking gifts from people to escape the tolls, because that was taking money from my pocket too; and then I saw that he couldn't even protect his own boy. He left Aumie and Ham alone, and cost one of them his life. A man who was so selfish and stupid didn't deserve to live. I killed him, and I'd do it again.'

'And you went on to try to kill Julia. What had she done to you?'

'That slut? I thought if she died, it would prove that Gervase was guilty. He deserved to suffer anyway, for his disloyalty. Adultery is a terrible thing.'

'*You* committed adultery. You fathered Danny on Matty,' Simon said.

'That was different. She was only a peasant – little better than a whore. Lady Anne is the wife to the castellan. Gervase deserved his punishment! So did Julia. She gave birth to that boy. She was no better than any other stale.'

'Men have said that they saw Serlo near Richer's house when it was burned,' Baldwin said slowly. 'I don't think he set fire to it, though.'

'Serlo? He couldn't have – he didn't have the guts. Me, I have always been able to fight back when someone tries to ruin me. That fool Richer made sure that Serlo and I were thrashed when he let our beast loose. The lord of the manor took it for himself, and my father beat us so furiously, I had thought he might kill us. At the harvest, when all were busy in the fields, I went to Richer's house and set it alight. Serlo was nearby, but when he saw it was ablaze, he ran to fetch help and put it out, the idiot! I loved him, you know, but he was so stupid! His negligence cost me my son, and then he allowed his own son to die. How could I let him live after that?'

'What about your wife?'

'You asked me that before! What of her? She would keep going on and on about things . . . I put her in a trunk to keep her quiet, that's all. I wouldn't hurt my Letty. It's she who kept me sane after Danny's death. I love her.'

'What did she go on about?'

'Oh, she knew I'd killed Serlo. There was blood on my coat, you see, and she realised when she heard that Serlo was dead, that I must have done it. She wanted me to confess to Adam, to do a penance, but like I said to her, I wasn't going to do that, not when the man was openly carrying on with that slut in his own house. Oh no, I wasn't going to confess anything to *him*. But she would keep going on and on at me about it. In the end, I was so angry, I shut her in the chest in my strongroom.'

'You killed her first. You cut her throat.'

'*No!*' Alexander looked at him with anger in his eyes. 'You're lying. She's fine, she's just resting. I couldn't hurt my Letty. I love her.'

Just as you loved your brother, Simon thought.

Epilogue

There were many people who declared that, since Alexander was so obviously insane, they should take pity on his soul. The Bishop of Exeter himself was petitioned to ensure mercy was granted to him, but then one morning Alexander was found dead, hanging in his cell by the thongs which had bound his hosen to his tunic. He had spent the evening carefully pulling them free, one by one, and tying them together to fashion a rough noose.

There was no one to grieve for him. Sir Jules certainly didn't when he went to view the body. To him, the Constable was just one more corpse. Already he had seen more than he wanted to, and at least this was less traumatic – a convicted murderer and madman was not the sort of victim Jules could lose sleep over. It was other deaths that stuck in his memory and returned in his dreams to haunt him. Already he had told his Sheriff that he didn't want to continue in his post, and so far as he was concerned, the sooner the Sheriff could find another fool to take on this thankless job, the better.

Roger didn't seem bothered to learn that his Coroner was going to resign. He merely shrugged. 'Oh well. I'll just have to break in another one, then.'

Gervase had been in the hall that day, and heard his words. Sir Jules had looked offended, drawing himself up to his full height before stalking away. Roger shook his head. 'At least there's a chance I'll get a man with some brains this time.'

'Sir Jules wasn't the brightest?'

'Not in my experience. He needs a war to blood him. There hasn't been a decent chance to fight since the King stopped tournaments. That's what Sir Jules needs – an opportunity to prove himself in the lists, so he could come to the job with an experience of death and the reasons why people kill.'

It was one thing Gervase had no need of: he already knew some of those reasons. However, the thought of pitting himself against another man clad all in mail, was revolting.

No, his fights required more subtlety.

He had been very lucky, he knew, to survive the beating meted out by Nicholas. And in the end, it had achieved Nicholas's twin objectives: Gervase was far too unwell to attend the inquest, and the castellan had some compensation for his pain and hurt. Yet there was mitigation for Gervase.

As he fell to the floor, he had looked up just once, and saw Anne's expression. It was love. *It had to be.* She was looking down at him with that light in her eyes that spoke of her feelings, and the sorrow in her face to see how her bastard husband kicked at him told Gervase that this woman knew at last which of them she truly adored. It was him.

That had decided him, and although the course of action took some planning, it was going to be worth it.

After Warin's intervention, pointing out that without the steward the manor would soon fail, Nicholas conceded that Gervase might continue in his duties, but only if he no longer slept in the castle or ate at Nicholas's table. Warin had agreed and now Gervase lived in a small house on the outskirts of the vill.

He had bought the poison from a pedlar, ostensibly to kill some rats in his yard. Then he arranged to have some of Nicholas's favourite treats delivered on a day when Warin and the castle's guard were out hunting. The timing couldn't have been more propitious. Nicholas was eating alone still, not with his wife, because of her faithlessness, and the Lady Anne ate a meagre and curious diet in her room, pale and wan as the birthing came closer. So it was that Nicholas enjoyed the poisoned pies on his own, and scoffed the lot.

He was fine for some little while, but then Gervase heard that one of the men-at-arms had fallen from his horse, and Warin sent to the castle for a cart to collect the injured man. Nicholas himself escorted the cart, saying he needed some exercise, and on the way, his face reddened, his lips became blue, he complained of a pain in his chest, and suddenly toppled from his horse. He was dead before he hit the ground.

And Gervase was now content. He could wait a little while, he thought, for the necessary period of mourning, and then he could enfold his beloved in an embrace, declare his love for her, and the two of them would be content for the rest of their lives.

Except it didn't happen that way. Warin, apparently, had no regard for the niceties of decent behaviour. While Gervase watched in horror, the squire laid siege to Anne's honour, and in the week before the baby was born, he won her hand in marriage.

Gervase was stunned. All he had wanted to do was help his lover to be free so that they could be together, and now she had declared her love for another. He couldn't have misread the love in her eyes though, surely? In despair, a week later he went to the priest's house to speak with Julia, seeking to renew his relationship with her, knowing that the only way to exorcise the grief of losing this woman was in the arms of another. Once there, however, he learned that Julia had left the vill. The young ostler from Bodmin had claimed her as his wife, and she and the baby had gone back there with him.

Father Adam seemed less than happy about the arrangement. 'Who will cook for me?' he demanded petulantly.

Adam was relieved that his attempted murder was forgotten so easily, until he learned what the cost would be of Warin's silence

The idea that he could be forced to spy on his congregation was appalling. As he said to the new master of the castle, he had a duty to a higher authority than Warin.

'That's fine, then. We'll see what the rural dean has to say about you,' Warin had grinned.

It was that grin that cowed Adam. He had no idea what Warin might know of him, but there was something deeply unsettling about the fellow. It was almost as though Warin knew of his love for John. He couldn't, of course. John wouldn't have told anyone about the strength of his passion, surely? John was his soul, his heart, his love. Even if John didn't reciprocate Adam's fervour, surely he wouldn't have sought to shame him by telling of his desires . . .

That smile was very worrying, yes. The rural dean was an evil-minded old bigot who would push a homosexual into a fire himself, without waiting for official sanction from the Bishop. Warin was a danger to him, it was true, but all he said he wanted was to prevent another war. Any man would want to do that. Perhaps it wouldn't be such a terrible thing, to let him know if trouble was brewing . . . if doing so meant staying here and being left alone. He wouldn't be far from his John, apart from anything else, and he could still see him every now and again.

Perhaps all would be for the best. Especially if he could find a new maid.

When he heard that Muriel was looking for a home, it seemed as though his prayers were answered.

John was particularly happy to hear that Adam had been able to find space for the miller's widow. From all he had heard, she was an excellent cook. She would be so much better off away from the home in which her child had died before her eyes, and from the mill where her man's body had been found.

For John there was no such comfort. He lived with the constant fear of the mad squire at Cardinham arriving at his door with a troop of King's men to arrest him for preaching against the King. After Boroughbridge and his uncle's death, John didn't care any more. To him, the only thing that mattered now was his pastoral care, and he would only preach the truth to his parishioners. If that meant upsetting the King, so be it.

It was late in the year when he received a message from Exeter. He was told that the Bishop would like to see him. There was a parish church in the city which had need of a strong-willed priest keen to do God's work among the poor and needy. John had been suggested to him, and the Bishop felt sure that God wished John to take up His mission.

This was a decision that needed little thought. In one move, freedom from Warin and Adam. John packed his meagre belongings that very night, and left for Exeter without a backwards glance.

Simon and Baldwin reached Simon's home at the end of September. They had travelled together all the way to Lydford, and when they reached his house, both were weary after two nights in the open air. There was a sense of anticlimax about this end of their pilgrimage.

Both felt it. It was an unsettling sensation, and for a moment neither could speak. They stood like strangers, hardly able to meet each other's eye.

'Baldwin, it's been a marvellous experience,' Simon said at last.

'I am only sorry that it is over,' his friend replied. 'We must return to our true lives now. I am not sure I am ready to. There is a curious urge in me to go on another pilgrimage.'

'Perhaps you are better suited to travel,' Simon said. 'Especially sea-travel!'

'Yes, well – I think that we have been unfortunate in our choice of vessels and ship-masters.'

Simon nodded, and glanced westwards. The sky was already darkening with twilight. 'You've been all over the world, Baldwin, whereas I have never been farther than Exeter until now. You've made me see places I wouldn't have dreamed of seeing. Compostela, Ennor – the world is so much larger than I had thought.'

'And now you shall go to Dartmouth and be the Master of the Port for our friend the Abbot,' Baldwin said. 'While I shall retire to Furnshill and occasionally visit Crediton when there is a matter requiring my attention. Perhaps you shall become the traveller instead of me?'

Simon heard a squeal of delight, and turned to see his wife at the doorway, his son in her arms.

With a smile, he shook his head. 'No, Baldwin. I don't want to travel. I want to stay at my home, and will do so for as long as God allows me.'

The Devil's Acolyte

Michael Jecks

Amidst the myth and folklore of Tavistock, one tale above all others strikes fear into the hearts of the town's inhabitants – that of the murders on the Abbot's Way – whereby a young acolyte paid the price for stealing his abbot's wine when the devil himself led him to his death on the treacherous Devon moors.

Now, in the autumn of 1322, it looks as though history may be repeating itself. Abbot Robert has found his wine barrel empty, and a body has been discovered on the moors. Bailiff Simon Puttock is called upon to investigate but it soon becomes apparent that it's not just wine that's gone missing from the abbey, and the body on the moor isn't the last. With the arrival of Sir Baldwin Furnshill, Keeper of the King's Peace, the townspeople hope the mystery will finally be solved – but do the terrors of the past provide the key to their present turmoil?

Don't miss Michael Jecks' previous medieval West Country mysteries:

'Tremendously successful' *Sunday Independent*

'Leaves the reader wanting more' *Yorkshire Post*

'A gem of historical storytelling' *Northern Echo*

0 7472 6725 1

headline

The Templar's Penance

Michael Jecks

It is the summer of 1323, and Baldwin Furnshill and Bailiff Simon Puttock have been granted leave to go on pilgrimage. Together they travel across Europe to Spain, but danger seems to follow them even this far afield, as they are among the first on the scene when a beautiful young girl is found brutally raped and murdered on the hillside of Santiago de Compostela.

Baldwin and Simon lend their investigative skills to the ensuing enquiry headed by the local *pesquisidore*, Munio. With so many keen minds on the case it can only be a matter of time before the culprit is found. But they are reckoning without the unexpected appearance of a face from Baldwin's past – a face which looks set to threaten both the investigation and, it seems increasingly likely, Baldwin's very future.

'Tremendously successful medieval mystery series' *Sunday Independent*

'Brisk medieval whodunnit' *Literary Review*

'[Jecks] writes . . . with such convincing charm that you expect to walk round a corner in Tavistock and meet some of the characters . . . Devon and Cornwall do not seem the same after reading his dramatic tales' *Oxford Times*

0 7553 0171 4

headline

The Mad Monk of Gidleigh

Michael Jecks

As the winter of 1323 descends on Dartmoor, life has never seemed so bleak to the young priest, Mark, in his isolated, windswept chapel. So who could blame him for accepting some longed-for companionship when it is offered by the local miller's daughter, Mary? But when Mary and the unborn child she carried are found brutally murdered, it is obvious where the villagers will point the finger of blame.

However, investigators Baldwin Furnshill, Keeper of the King's Peace, and Bailiff Simon Puttock soon begin to have their doubts. It becomes clear that Mary was far from the simple village girl she seemed. What exactly was her relationship with the Squire of Gidleigh, Sir Ralph? Could he be responsible for her death? Or perhaps it was Osbert, the mill-hand whose love she rejected time and again? In their search for the truth, Baldwin and Simon unwittingly put themselves in the greatest danger they have ever faced, and by the time the investigation is over, life for themselves and their families will never be the same again . . .

Don't miss Michael Jecks' thirteen previous medieval West Country mysteries:

'Tremendously successful' *Sunday Independent*

'Leaves the reader wanting more' *Yorkshire Post*

'Jecks writes with passion and historical accuracy. Devon and Cornwall do not seem the same after reading his dramatic tales' *Oxford Times*

0 7553 0169 2

headline